THE DOXXING OF CLEARWATER HIGH

The DOXXING of CLEARWATER HIGH

a novel

MICHAEL ROSSI

To request permissions, contact the publisher at michael_rossi@live.com

Paperback: 979-8-9866413-0-0

EPUB Edition: 979-8-9866413-1-7

Kindle Edition: 979-8-9866413-2-4

Library of Congress Number: 2022914762

First Paperback Edition: November 2022

Edited by: Dani Segelbaum

Cover and Layout by: Jordan Wannemacher

For my mother, who taught me that every story maters.

*"…When he [Noah] drank some of its wine, he became
drunk and lay uncovered inside his tent.
Ham, the father of Canaan, saw his father naked
and told his two brothers outside."*
—GENESIS 9:22-23

"You guys gotta see this."
—HAM, PROBABLY

PROLOGUE

Jennifer Watson could think of few things more humiliating than writing a math problem on the board. When she had been twelve, her math teacher summoned her to the front of the class, handed her a piece of chalk, and asked her to show her peers how she had calculated the volume of a traffic cone. She was painfully aware of their eyes watching her diagram integers, and the fact that she couldn't see their faces as she worked intensified her discomfort.

But now she was a math teacher herself, and she understood the power of public demonstrations. Every kid in her class took a turn at the board; it gave her a chance to check their thinking and impress upon them the methodology of algebra.

It also helped her relate to her students. Sometimes they required coaxing or encouragement. And sometimes they simply refused to comply. Like now: 16-year-old Simran had her head down and was ignoring Jenn's summons. The teacher knelt beside her student and brought her voice down to a whisper.

"Hey," said Jenn. "Do you need to take a walk?" Simran was silent. Jenn persisted. "Need to talk to someone?"

"Please go," said Simran. Her voice was like wet tissue.

Jenn shifted her legs. "I know it's scary," she said. "But you've got this, Simran. I wouldn't ask you do something you couldn't handle."

"Ms. Watson?" said another student. "Ms. Watson, I can write the problem. I don't mind."

Sometimes all a kid needed was a little breathing room. "That sounds good, Katie," said Jenn. "Maybe you show us #14." She stood, but she leaned down to whisper to Simran. "I'll come back to you in a few minutes," she said.

She heard a chirp from someone's backpack, then another and a third. "Hey, you all know the rules," said Jenn. "Phones on silent." But she could tell that several more students had received messages; they were surreptitiously checking their smart watches and little black screens. It was a like a breeze blowing through the classroom, ruffling everyone. "Come on," said Jenn. "Phones away."

There was a loud crack outside her classroom that made Jenn flinch. Even Simran jolted upright. A strange silence settled over the classroom, then an uncomfortable laughter. Jenn's forehead furrowed. "You three," she said, pointing to three kids in the first row of desks. "Put problems 14-16 on the board. I'll be right back."

Carlton Wemish was in the hallway, gathering pieces of a shattered laptop. His classroom was across the hall from her own. She was used to Carlton greeting her each morning with some inanity about Star Wars or his trivia team. Now, though, he was on his hands and knees, looking like a frightened animal.

"Carlton, what happened?"

"Oh," he said. "I tripped."

She knew him well enough to recognize that he was lying. "On what?" she asked.

"It's…" he began. "Look, Jenn—"

He froze; they heard shouting down the hall. The voices were muffled, but Jenn recognized a familiar registry. "Can you keep an eye on my class?" she asked Carlton. "I'll be right back." He seemed relieved by the distraction.

Around two corners and down the freshman hallway, Jenn spotted a throng of students. Their phones were out, and they were recording a confrontation. She was close enough now to identify the voice. "GIVE ME THE PHONE!" shouted Stanley DuPont, her department chair.

Stanley had backed a student up against a bank of lockers and was reaching aggressively for the student's hand. Her department chair gripped the kid—probably a junior—by the coat lapel. "Let go, man," the kid said. "I wasn't doing anything."

"GIVE ME THE PHONE!" Stanley repeated.

Jenn pushed through the students and inserted herself between her boss and the kid. "Stanley," she said with a quiet firmness. "Stanley, what's going on here?"

Like a broken spell, the older man suddenly returned to himself. He released the student and backed away. The color drained from his cheeks. "Jenn, I…" he began.

"He fucking hit me!" said the kid. "You all saw it!" He gestured to the array of phones. Jenn suddenly realized that she was being filmed. She forced herself to composure and raised both hands in a supplicating gesture. "Okay," she said. "All right. Let's all take a breath here. Why don't we go down to the dean's—"

"Fuck this," said the kid, red-faced and on the verge of tears. He pushed past the gawkers and disappeared around the corner.

Jenn turned to face Stanley. "What just happened?" she pleaded.

He didn't seem to hear her; he ran his hands through his shale-colored hair, his nostrils wide and flaring. Jenn wheeled on the crowd. "Phones away," she barked. "I want you to head to the dean's office.

Every one of you!" No one moved for a moment; she added an emphatic "NOW!" to rustle them towards Bryan Yulders' disciplinary office. When they had dispersed, she returned to Stanley, but the distance in his eyes had only grown.

"I need to call my wife," he said absently. He pushed past her and descended a stairwell.

What was happening? Carlton was odd and awkward, but basically a nebbish. Stanley DuPont, on the other hand, was as steady and reliable as a sequoia. Stanley was who people called when their marriage was failing, when a parent moved to hospice. She had seen him defuse student fights on more than one occasion, once without even getting up from the table where he was tutoring a student in calc.

She decided to go after him, hoping that Carlton could keep a handle on her students. But as she emerged from the stairwell into the wider corridors of the first floor, she recognized that the chaos was not confined to two math teachers.

Leila Bells, a young Physics teacher, rushed past, her makeup streaked with tears. Jenn called out to her, but Leila pressed on, past a gaggle of students who filmed her with their phones. "Hey!" said Jenn. "What are you doing?" The students quickly fled. Jenn pursued the middle one, heading towards the cafeteria. As she rounded a corner, she collided with another student, who dropped his phone. Jenn apologized and picked it up. The screen displayed a penis.

The kid's eyes goggled. "It's not mine!" he said.

"The phone or the picture?" Jenn asked.

"Uh," said the kid. "Both?"

Jenn rolled her eyes. "Come on," she said. "We're going to the dean's office. You'll have to take a number at this rate."

As she moved through the hallway, Jenn felt strangers eyeing her derisively. Once, when she had been a dancer, she'd performed several routines with her tampon string hanging out of the side of her leotard before one of the few nice girls took pity and alerted her. She felt the same sense of restrained mockery all around her now. One smirking student made eye contact with her. "Oh, Bill!" he said.

Bill? Who was he talking to? Was the dick pic kid named Bill? But there was too much going on to pursue the thought; walking past the Language Arts office, she glimpsed two teachers consoling a third. She passed Andy Waters' classroom, but the young English teacher was missing. "He just walked out," one of his students shrugged. "Didn't say nothing to no one."

She led her prisoner through the cafeteria, eyes following them. One student spotted her and burst into laughter. Another looked at her and moaned. "Oh, Bill!" said a third.

"What is going on here?" Jenn asked. She turned to the dick pic kid, who seemed paralyzed by her attention.

"You don't know?" he asked.

"Know what?" Jenn asked. "What don't I know?"

The kid seemed to be weighing life in prison versus capital punishment. He made a decision. "May I see my phone?" he asked.

"What?" she said. "I'm not giving you your—"

"I won't delete the pic," he said. "Wouldn't matter anyway. Just… just… you need to see something."

Slowly, Jenn handed him his phone. The kid tapped the screen a couple times, then handed Jenn a video image of her having sex with the father of one of her students.

"Bill," said video Jenn. "Oh, Bill…"

It had been a mistake to get drinks with Bill Pastard after parent/teacher conferences. It had been a mistake to let him drive her back to her apartment, to invite him up. It had been a mistake to record the episode on her iPad. A daisy-chain of errors that was detonating in the Clearwater cafeteria.

"*Oh, Bill!*" said video Jenn on another student's phone. Across the crowded room, she heard her own voice answer, again and again and again.

1
COLLEEN

KENNY: CM, my math teacher has a Grindr account. And he's married!

EILEEN: OMG these Mr. Waters emails!

PETER SM: Guess who's PE teacher is on Ashley Madison. Also, guess what Ashley Madison is!

EILEEN: lol they got Mrs. Weinke's period tracker data. no wonder she was such a bitch on the unit 2 test

- - - - - - - - - -

December 1st was Colleen McTaggort's 18th birthday. It was also the day that a local gossip website posted hundreds of documents harvested from 41 members of the faculty and staff of Clearwater Community High School. There were emails, phone records, search histories, text and direct messages, GPS tracking data, Reddit profiles, and Craigslist ads. Colleen's inbox was filled with memes and reaction GIFs. Not a single friend wished her a happy birthday.

It figures, she thought. All her life, Colleen had felt her big moments overshadowed. The day she was potty trained, her parents brought home a little sister. She earned her driver's license two hours before her uncle got engaged. Still, there was a triple-fudge sheet cake waiting for her in the freezer at home. *I'm eating that cake*, she thought. *I'm sure people still got married the weekend Kennedy was shot.*

If the doxxing of Clearwater High was not quite as momentous as a presidential assassination, it was still a moment without much precedent. During fourth period, Principal Darten took to the intercom to place the school under soft lockdown. Everyone was to freeze in place; teachers were to keep teaching until further instructions. But in practice the entire school ground to a full stop and everyone—students and teachers alike—took to the Internet to pour through the files.

MEGAN: omg Mrs. Zeiller had an abortion. We went over Roe v. Wade in her AP US History class

KENNY: CM, you gotta watch this video where Mr. Wurtz sword fights. So fucking funny.

Except Colleen. Though she was receiving minute-by-minute spoilers of the files from her friends, she kept her phone tucked away. Something about the spectacle mortified her. The week before, she had watched a freshman trip and fall off his bus. Everyone had laughed. But something about the freshman's humiliation hurt Colleen. "Everybody falls," she told the kid. "It's bullshit that we act like it only happens to someone else."

Of course, there was no video record of the freshman stumbling off his bus. This was something different, a humiliation in slow motion, an endlessly remixed disgrace. Many of the files were merely embarrassing—Casey Steinem, for instance, had Spotify playlists dedicated to a Korean boy band; Betsy Rilke subscribed to Fashion Doll Quarterly. Some contained highly sensitive files: tax returns, medical records, financial account passwords. Already, she could imagine the TikToks, the soundtracks, the freeze frames and filters. It was just getting started.

PAIGE: Yooooooooo Mr. Rodriguez is into nun porn. Check out his VOD playlist.

ADITYA: You're not going to believe how much Mr. Sanderson lost at Four Winds. What a degenerate!

Her calculus teacher, Mr. Cespids, had abandoned his lesson on derivatives and paced the front of the room, texting. The class bubbled with whispered conversations and the quiet padding of touchscreens. Kevin Prossman, a broad-shouldered linebacker, drummed his fingers on his desk while twirling a pencil with his other hand. He stared at Cespids. Finally, he spoke without raising his hand.

"Whadaya think is gonna happen, Mr. Cespids?"

Cespids glanced up briefly before returning his gaze to his phone. "I don't know, Kevin," he mumbled.

"Yeah," said Kevin. "But whadaya think?"

This time, Cespids set down the phone and leaned against the whiteboard, arms crossed. "I don't know," he said. He gestured extravagantly towards the door as though to punctuate a greater statement. But when he finally spoke again, it was a subdued refrain. "I don't know."

Kevin twirled the pencil. "If I sent a dick pic at Culver's," he said. "they'd fire me."

Cespids stared at the floor. "Yeah," he said.

"If I was hooking up in the supply closet," Kevin continued, "I'd be gone."

Cespids shrugged. "I don't know what you want me to say, Kevin."

Kevin nodded. "I'm just sayin'," he said. "If I sent a bunch of racist emails—"

"Shut up, Kevin," said Colleen. The sound of her voice was sharper and harsher than she expected. Everyone looked up from their phones. Colleen didn't care. "Who are you emailing at Culver's? Who?" Kevin smirked.

Fifteen minutes later, the principal returned to the intercom. "Attention students. Due to a school security breach, we are cancelling classes effective immediately. Buses will be rerouted; we have sent emails and text messages to your parents to inform them of this unscheduled closure. We will update you all tonight as to the nature of our situation, and we will inform you when the school is ready to reopen." He paused; for a moment, Colleen wondered if the intercom had failed. "Until then," he resumed, "be wary of what you read online. Remember that your school is made of people. Think about how you would feel."

Colleen met her sister in the parking lot. As soon as Colleen was behind the wheel, Eileen reached over and handed her a joint. "Happy birthday, Big Sis."

Colleen scoffed, hiding the joint in the glove box. "Are you crazy?" she said. "Tournaments have random drug tests."

Eileen laughed and took a hit from her vape pen. "It's as they say," she said, "youth is wasted on the young. And now that you're 18, you're officially unyoung."

Colleen started the car but just sat with her hands on the driving wheel. She looked at herself in the rearview mirror. Tall, thin, and plain-faced with straw-colored hair perpetually pulled back in a harsh ponytail, she bore little resemblance to her voluptuous sister. *Did she have to wear the low-cut top?* thought Colleen. *On my birthday?* But of course she did; Eileen lived for other people's eyes.

"Can you believe this shit?" coughed her sister. "So fucking unreal."

"It is," said Colleen. "I'm scared for the teachers."

"Pfff," snorted Eileen. "It's their own fault. Don't send pictures of your junk. That's in the Bible." She pulled out her phone. "Did you see the text exchange between Mr. Lenk and Ms. Bells? You gotta—"

"No," said Colleen.

"What about Mrs. Moreso? Did you know she was, like, I don't know… some skinhead rocker?"

"I didn't see."

"Did you see Mrs. Kooner's emails to her ex-husband?" Colleen shook her head; Eileen squinted at her older sister. "Are you telling me that you didn't read anything, watch anything? Nothing?"

Colleen shook her head. "I can't," she said. "There's something wrong about it."

"Yo, for real?" said Eileen. "Our teachers are fucked up pervs."

Colleen shifted the car into drive. "Would you stop vaping in my car?" she asked. "And cover up your boobs. It's December."

KENNY: Colleen, what's a craig's list missed connections? And why does Mr. McMurth have one?

KENNY: Babe, why aren't you texting me? What's up?

Colleen had volleyball practice for three hours. Her teammates—many of whom attended other schools—peppered her with questions. They, too, had seen the files. Did she know the teacher in the sex video? (*No.*) Had she seen the racist emails from the basketball coach? (*No.*) Did the AP Environmental Science teacher have a chronic condition that required so much fentanyl? (*I don't know her; can we talk about something else?*) She drove home in silence

KENNY: omg. omg. omg. Ms. Watson, tho.

Her mother was sitting at the table with a laptop when Colleen walked in. She was reading the emails of Eileen's English teacher, Mr. Waters. Colleen groaned. "Mom, not you, too!"

Her mother looked up at her with fierce owl eyes. "Sit down, Colleen," she said. "We should talk."

Colleen was bone-tired. She slumped in a chair, resting her weight on her forearms. Her mother regarded her with heavy lids for a moment before speaking. "Do you remember?" she asked, "when you were six and you told us that the basement smelled funny?"

Colleen sighed. "Yeah, it was a dead cat," she said. "What's that got to do with anything?"

"We didn't know what it was," said her mother. "Or where the smell was coming from. In the end, we had to tear out the drywall next to the crawlspace. The damn thing got caught in there, chasing a mouse or something. My point is, something was rotting, and you told us about it, and we had to get it out."

Colleen shook her head. "It's not the same," she said.

"You're right," said her mother. "You're not six anymore."

Ten years ago, her mother had bought her a triple-fudge sheet cake with cream cheese frosting. She liked it so much that it became a tradition. All day Colleen McTaggort had looked forward that cake. Now she felt foolish. Her mother smiled, sadly. "Maybe this time, the cat's still alive," she said. "Maybe we can help it. But we won't know…"

Colleen thought of Mr. Cespids grinding his teeth. "We won't know unless we look."

Her mother nodded; her mouth drooped in the corners. She rose and patted Colleen's arm. "You're a good girl, Leeny."

Colleen looked at her mother. They had the same pale blue eyes, but her mother's looked like a road made rough by years of traffic. *How does she know I'm good?* she thought. *I can't stand to look at street people. I hate half the people I go to school with. I have dirty thoughts about*

Kenny, what I want to do after prom. I have a joint in my glove box. Why didn't I throw it away? Why?

Colleen grabbed the laptop. She called up the Clearwater Confidential. They were just thoughts. Only actions had consequences. *Witnessing has consequences, too,* she thought grimly.

"Happy birthday, by the way," her mother said. "Do you feel any different?"

Colleen clicked the first link. "No," she lied.

The First Doxxing

DECEMBER 1ST

2

VINCE

Vincent Darten had been an educator for 35 years, beginning as a history teacher at Calumet High School in Gary. He taught for ten years before finishing an administrator's degree and serving six years as a dean, then another seven as a guidance counselor. He had been approached by Darren Broach, Assistant Superintendent of Schools for the Clearwater School District following a presentation. The two struck up a conversation, then an email correspondence. When an assistant principal position opened in his district, Broach encouraged Darten to apply. Six years later, he offered him the head job at Clearwater High School.

Though no one ever said it, Vince understood that he had been hired as an outsider. Very few of the teachers in his district were black, and none of the administrators. Clearwater, an old mill town slowly transformed into an Indianapolis suburb, was 82% white. Vince felt their eyes tracking him as he toured the high school for the first time;

he thought of the warring tribes of the Ohio Valley who had briefly unified to push back against white settlers in the early 19th century. *A common danger unites even the bitterest enemies,* counseled Chief Tecumseh, the wily Shawnee; Vince scribbled the quote in his planner the day he'd been hired.

Yet Vince had won the staff's trust by slow degrees. Over the course of a year and a half, he had lunch or dinner with every teacher in the building. He learned their backgrounds, their ambitions, their rivalries and grievances. He set reasonable goals for test scores and built time into the schedule for shared planning. He introduced an after-school program for struggling students and a mentorship program for new teachers. He reassigned recalcitrant educators or got them transferred to other buildings. He helped the counseling department transfer all records online and upgraded the building's moribund computer network, convincing the PTA to sponsor a Wi-Fi initiative. He was not shy about firing a teacher—the tail end of his second year was dominated by the removal of an athletic director who consistently shorted female sports. But he was regarded by his teachers as clear, fair, firm, and—above all—inquisitive.

On the day of the Clearwater Cloudburst, Vince Darten was scheduled to observe two teachers in the Science Department, meet with some representatives of the Black Student Alliance, confer with Department Chairs about changes to the Final Exam procedures, conference-call with several other principals about HB5 (the state's so-called transgender bathroom law), and reply to a dozen or so urgent emails. It was supposed to be a quiet day.

Instead, he found himself on a Zoom call with police detectives, district officials, and a small cadre of lawyers. The police had convinced the site moderator to take down the files, but not before they had been copied and disseminated throughout the community. News agencies were picking up the story; the district's Director of Communications, expected it to be the lead of the Indianapolis news affiliates that night. "I mean, where have you even ever heard of this?" he laughed. "Sex! Drugs! Teachers! It's got everything!" The lawyers counseled a unified media blackout; until the nature and source of the leak was determined, there was no way of understanding the scope of liability. "Can't we go after the woman who posted this?" someone asked.

"The hack is illegal," replied a tall, hook-nosed detective. "Posting the files is more of a legal gray area. What you need to be doing now is plugging your leak."

The district had already shut down the servers and was conducting a building inspection of every integrated device. "It could take weeks," said one administrator grimly before admitting that she didn't even know where to begin looking.

"Jesus Christ, Jesus Christ," muttered the Director of Building Operations. "Do we have any precedent for this?"

Superintendent Broach shrugged. "I spoke with the State Superintendent this morning. The only comparable case he could cite was a teacher gradebook that was hacked in Muncie last year. That's just Indiana. He said he'd heard of a data breach in Wyoming where three teachers were doxxed."

"How many teachers are we talking about here?"

"Best we can tell so far? More than 40."

Darten sat in silence as the various officials checked in, squabbling interdepartmental factions debating district priorities. He hated district meetings. He hated being away from his teachers, his students. He despised the impersonal, flattening nature of Zoom. Elizabeth, his wife, had been texting him summaries of the worst files; he felt a sense of fear, frustration, betrayal, and pity, as though all of his emotions were jockeying to pass through a small door simultaneously. *'Nothing'* she'd texted him when he asked her if there were any files on him. A cascade of relief washed down his spine; *I'm safe,* he thought. But for how long? The detectives suspected these files were an opening salvo.

"We just don't know how long your network was compromised," said Hook-nose. "There's no way to tell how much more information is out there."

When the conversation had spun around the screen a few revolutions, Superintendent Broach trained his soft gray eyes on Darten. "Vince," he said, spreading his hands in a supplicating gesture. "What do you need?"

At 10:35 A.M.—right at the end of 4th period—Vince Darten took to the school intercom to announce the dismissal of students. He then asked his staff to meet in the auditorium fifteen minutes after student dismissal.

He did not have enough answers. He didn't know who was responsible; he didn't know how the information was obtained. He didn't know how much material was out there or if another data dump was imminent. He didn't know why certain teachers were targeted while others were ignored. He didn't know how long it would take to secure the district servers or if their own devices were infected. "The situation is fluid," he said impotently. "As soon as I have more information, I will pass it along to you."

"How?" laughed Betsy Rilke. "Email?"

The school reopened two days later once officials had determined the source of the breach. One of their tech specialists—MaKinzie Garvey—discovered a small 15 GB flash drive plugged into an office computer. "Near as I can tell, it memorizes keystrokes and gets past our firewall by tricking the OS into thinking the stick isn't a stick—that it's an H.I.D."

"A what?" asked Darten.

"Human Interface Device. Thinks it's a keyboard."

Garvey believed the flash drive had been used as an entry point, but she couldn't fathom how the user had proceeded from there. "The message boards just don't think it could be done," she said. "The information in those files—it was pulled from phones, pads, laptops… all those systems… I mean, how?"

"I'm not following."

"Someone hacks our server, they can get in everyone's email. That's not hard, relatively speaking. But a teacher's phone doesn't run through our server. Their medical files aren't stored there. Whoever did this, they've figured out how to do something completely new."

"Can you stop it from happening again?"

Garvey shrugged. "I mean, we can tell teachers to make sure there aren't more of these sticks plugged into USB ports, start using incognito windows for searches. We'll wash out all the cookies. But it's like trying to protect a herd of cattle from a fighter plane. Worse, actually—at least you can see a plane. Is this some kind of worm? A virus? If it is, there's not a filter on the market that recognizes it."

Vince nodded. "I'll let everyone know. Scrub everything. Let me know what you think we need to throw out."

Garvey laughed. "Yeah, right," she said. "Like the district is going to pony up for new computers."

"MaKinzie," said Vince sharply. "It's an open question if we'll still have a district."

He was losing teachers. Three of his youngest staff members resigned; he sensed that more of his untenured staff would follow. There was talk of civil suits, but no one could agree on a defendant. The union was compromised—one file contained a long email chain authored by their building rep, identifying board members with racial and misogynistic epithets. Several teachers were calling in sick; two had filed for FMLA leave, and the rest of the staff was watching to see how the district reacted. Jennifer Watson simply stopped showing up to work.

His tenured staff suffered the most. The longer a teacher remains at a school, the less likely he or she is to leave the district. A teacher with fifteen years' experience is unlikely to find another school that will honor her years of service, which could mean a loss of tens of thousands in salary and benefits. It simply didn't make sense to hire a veteran teacher when two new teachers could be hired for the same cost, bringing with them a twenty-something's metabolism and freedom from familial obligations. And so old pros like Betsy Rilke (24 years), Charles Sanderson (two kids in college), and Miguel Rodriguez (alimony) were stuck in classrooms where 14-year-olds carried intimate knowledge of their medications, gambling debts, and pornography preferences.

The community reaction was apoplectic. Daily, he met with more students and parents than he did aggrieved teachers. Some demanded transfers or teacher removals; one student claimed he no longer felt safe in Orchestra and asked for the music program to be suspended or dissolved. He heard from members of the Booster club who pulled funding, vendors who canceled contracts, and distributors who wanted to reopen negotiations.

Parent phone calls were already the most stressful part of Vince's job; an affluent community like Clearwater viewed schools as a utility and themselves as consumers. In six years, he had slowly learned how to shape a conversation towards partnership and mutual accountability. But it was as though the Cloudburst had unleashed a sort of sublimated frustration in Clearwater. Most people, he understood, carried around faceless anger generated by the dozens of inequities and indignities of their daily lives, but those resentments remained inchoate and unspoken. Now, they had teachers who swore in emails and filmed sex tapes and made political donations to atheist organizations. An administration that had not anticipated this, did not have answers, could not guarantee the safety of its students. Now they had targets.

Vince had never slept more than five or six hours a night, but in the week following the Cloudburst, he was rarely at rest. At first, Elizabeth tried to shoo him from his laptop. But she gave up after a few days, recognizing that even when he lay beside her in bed, Vince was at work, shoveling desperately against the breaching levees.

He reviewed every file he could track down, responded to every email as best he could. He spent an hour on the phone with Erin Kooner, a Family and Consumer Science teacher distraught at a particularly nasty chain of text messages surrounding the month of her divorce ("I thought, Vince, I thought that this was behind me. Now I find it will always be a Google search away."). He assured Kent Guillard that having an account with Ashley Madison was not grounds for termination.

It was due diligence, of course, that drove Vince so hard, but he understood, too, that more than just fear and professional obligation was motivating him. Vince Darten had always been the quiet kid, standing outside the throng, watching. He recalled growing up in the Pulaski neighborhood, two blocks south of the old Norfolk Southern Railway. On Sundays, his uncle Kendall—an amateur tenor and popular raconteur—would take him on a tour of the neighborhood, past the Polish grocer with their sprouts and basement-grown mushrooms, through the barbershop where they played Billy Paul, Luther Ingram, and James Brown. His uncle knew every joke, every line from every movie, could speak with any man of any age or any color about every topic. Years before, Vince gathered, the neighborhood had celebrated Kendall, a three-sport athlete and scholarship recipient. Yet Kendall had never gone to college, never left the railyards, and the unspecified reason dimmed the luster of the halo his nephew hung above his head.

Vince remembered his uncle would pause under the fire escape of one tenement and call out "ELSA! ELSA!" until a pretty girl with a tall afro and dangling earrings would appear at the window. They would talk and flirt, and his uncle would sing to her until she rolled her eyes and shut them out. The older man would whoop all the way home—"You see that, Vince? You see that? You put that in your memory—that there is a *celestial!*"

And then one day, his uncle made their tour in silence, purchased a fifth of gin that he nursed for a half hour before pausing beneath the fire escape and hurling the bottle through Elsa's window. He never spoke of it or mentioned her again, and Vince spent the next decade of his life trying to understand what had gone through his uncle's mind in that moment of violence. When he finally got it—when he loved a girl, unrequited, to absolute despondency—he was surprised to discover that he felt no sympathy for the older man, but rather a sense of disappointment. It diminished Kendall in person and in memory, his ordinariness. Gone was the dauntless optimist whose shoes shined bright as onyx and who reduced a restaurant kitchen to breathless laughter with his Red Fox impersonations. Here instead was a man of crooked teeth and unredeemed pawn tickets.

Yet Vince could not help himself. What did he really know of his family, his co-workers, his subordinates and students? Who were they behind the smiles, the professional courtesies, the caffeinated small talk? When they went home, he wondered if their singing stopped, if their eyes went dead like his uncle's. He wondered what buried trauma the gin unearthed.

Digging through the files, Vince Darten began to understand his teachers. Little signals that had gone unexplained—why did Evie Peters always eat lunch at her desk; why did Andy Waters (an English teacher) spend so much time in the Math Department offices—suddenly clicked into place. There was a certain exhilaration for Vince, so long an amateur sleuth of hidden motives, to have so many mysteries resolved so conclusively. Yet these eureka moments were almost immediately followed by the embarrassment that accompanies stumbling upon someone unexpectedly stepping out of a shower. There is simply no restoring the original relations.

Then there was this note, from an email sent by Catherine Sawyer, the longest tenured teacher at Clearwater:

> Tommy,
>   I don't know if you still check this address.
> I don't know if you read these notes. I don't know if
> you're alive, still angry with me. I'm sorry.
> Please come home.
> Love,
> Mom

Catherine carried herself with the reserved grandeur of a monarch. She was in the twilight of a distinguished and exhausting career, overwhelmed by technology and hobbled by arthritis. Yet she still paced her classroom with imperial sovereignty. It pained him to think of her great dignity mocked to tatters, her private failures exhumed and paraded online. He thought of the old queens of France, accused of heresy and adultery, made to do penance in the streets for the common herd.

But there were more files attached to Catherine Sawyer, and Vince read on. And these files led him to websites, to comment sections, to anonymous postings that bore the shrapnel-sharp voice of the grand old dame of his Social Studies Department. Vince felt the color drain from his face as this ragged curriculum revealed the ominous contours of a new Catherine Sawyer, and the longer he read, the clearer his responsibility became. For the first time in ten days, Vince Darten shut his laptop.

Everything changes once we're seen, he thought. His uncle's great humiliation was that Vince had watched him throw the bottle, a moment of ordinary weakness turned to shame by a child's witness. He never sang in Vince's presence again.

———————————

By December 13th, Vince was ready to meet with Catherine. He arranged the meeting at the end of the day, following a series of conclaves with various parent groups. Clearwater's Black Student Alliance was demanding the dismissal of Evan McMasters, who had traded racially insensitive text messages with his brother during a Colts game. The Fellowship of Christian Athletes wanted the censure of Miguel Rodriguez, whose search history indicated a fondness for softcore pornography featuring nuns. A group of boosters were concerned about the presence of Stanley Dupont, Math Department Chair and basketball coach, whose decrypted Grindr profile might 'pose a locker room problem.'

Vince listened with patient indulgence, sharing their frustration while always being careful not to adopt their positions. "We're still sorting through the files," he would say. "We're not ready to make staffing decisions. There are laws that demand due process." He tried to imagine himself in their perspective, learning about the furtive deviance of his daughter's teachers, but what astonished him was how little people seemed to care that this information had only come to light through the violation of private files. They were angry at the teachers! At Vince! Where was the recognition of the true crime? But of course, his true fear was their radicalization, that they might run for school board on a platform of disclosure and transparency.

He made a show of taking notes before bringing each dance, as Elizabeth would say, to its *desplante*. He promised to learn more, to share his findings, to answer the phone, to work with the police. He ended each session with a handshake and exchange of holiday pleasantries. *She smiled at me,* Vince thought grimly as the last one left his office. She had no idea of his own secret. Like a plague survivor, he had been arbitrarily spared. What if his own hidden history had been uploaded? What would have been her demeanor then? Would he even still be in the room?

The notion haunted him as Catherine Sawyer entered his office. "How are you holding up, Vince?" she asked as she sat.

"I'm not sleeping much," he admitted.

She snorted. "No, I don't imagine you are. I saw you meeting with Wemish earlier. What'd the board say about him?"

He smiled. He had met with Carlton Wemish about videos the young Math teacher had anonymously posted. Wemish, it turned out, was the notorious *El Clavadista*, a luchador-like figure who wore a mask and GoPro camera while leaping off the balcony of motel court-yards into swimming pools. "The district does not condone the behavior of this El Clavadista, whoever he is," Vince had said. "For all our sakes, let us hope that he has retired to the mansions of infamy." Wemish was suitably abashed, and Vince regarded him privately with amusement. In a more sedate moment, he might have simply dismissed a third-year teacher with such foolish extracurricular tastes. *El Clavadista Espectacular*, it would seem, had been rescued by spectacular circumstances.

"They left it to me," said Vince.

"And?"

"The kid stays in the picture."

Catherine nodded. "Well, it's 'all hands on deck' these days, isn't it?"

"Indeed."

She leaned back, pulling herself to full height. Catherine Sawyer seemed to be all neck. "What did you need to see me about?"

He hesitated. Then, slowly, Vince pushed a file folder across the desk to her. "This."

She opened it, read through the print-outs inside. After the third page, she closed the folder and set it down. "This wasn't in that data dump," she said.

"No."

"So then what are we talking about?"

"It is you, though, isn't it?"

She armored up. Catherine Sawyer was formidable; Vince had watched her once reduce a suspected plagiarist to tearful confession with little more than a raised eyebrow. "Let's say it is. What business is it of yours?"

That question, he thought. *Dear God, but she cuts right to it.* "Your views are your own, Catherine…"

"That's right, Vince…"

"…but you cannot libel our students…"

"…it's only libel if it's untrue…"

"…and you CANNOT publish their pictures without their consent." The cold violence of his voice silenced her for a moment. "You are Patriotica56, are you not?"

"How could you possibly know that?"

"Your search history, Catherine; they published your search history. And I checked it out. Just like your students have. Just as everyone has."

She was red-faced now, but not embarrassed. He could see now that shame would not move this woman. He opened the folder again and pointed to the top page.

"This is a website that defames people—teenagers—*your* students. Calls them racist, sexist, bigoted."

She rolled her eyes. "Because they are racist and sexist and bigoted. It doesn't defame anyone. It discloses what they say in public to one another. It's a transcription."

"You're not a stenographer."

"And you're not a constitutional scholar," she shot back. "This is protected speech. Not that I'm admitting to anything."

"You didn't read the whole file," he said quietly.

She had recomposed herself, the long straight lines of her figure once again aligned with the vertical stirpes of her chair. She tilted her head, the wispy strands of hair that framed her face brushing her cheek. "Summarize it for me."

He tapped the folder three times before speaking. "You write Amazon reviews. As Patriotica56. Books that the school purchased per your request. So I know who you are. And so will they."

She shrugged; Vince pulled one of the print-outs from the folder and began to read. "*Our children are venal, entitled, arrogant narcissists*'" he said, adjusting his reading glasses. "*They have the intellectual curiosity of a virus and the empathy of a rock garden. They mistake their endless privilege for the bounty of hard work, and they regard their toxic consumption as the right of caste.*"

She was silent for a moment. Finally: "I'm not sure what you want me to say."

"I want you to explain to me why you think it's okay to go on this website and call our kids thieves and children of thieves. To post their pictures, their words..."

She started to laugh and stood to leave. Vince slammed his desk. "Sit down. Catherine."

She sat. Eyed him, then leaned forward. "You would tell people it was me?"

"I would."

"Out me."

"Yes."

"After all... this." She waved her hand around. "After what *they* did to us? You would turn around and do the exact same thing?"

He nodded. "These are complicated times. I can't claim to know what is right, what is legal, what is just. I'm trying to keep it simple." He met her gaze. "You did wrong, Catherine. You went too far."

She looked away. "It was one of them, you know," she said finally. "A student did this."

"No doubt."

"And you wouldn't know about me otherwise."

"True."

They said nothing for a moment. Vince became aware of the snow drifting lightly outside his window. His office looked out on the front entrance of the school, and it had pleased Vince for many years to see the comings and goings of Clearwater, greeting them as a captain met storms and tides. But he could not read the weather moving across Catherine's face. She moved her hands to her lap, looking up at last. "May I go?" she said.

"You'll make a full apology. Get out in front of this, Catherine. While you can."

She arched her eyebrows, stood, and made a gesture to smooth her slacks. "You know, a lot of us have long wondered how you'd handle an actual crisis. I have to say, Vince, this wasn't exactly the speech to the troops at Tilbury."

"I think I'd prefer the Spanish Armada," he said flatly. Catherine didn't smile.

"I noticed there weren't any disclosures about you on the website, Vince."

"Small comfort."

"I don't think so. By the time this is all over, everyone will see exactly what you are."

He said nothing to this, said nothing as she left, and sat in silence watching the snow dust the grass for ten minutes before his assistant stuck her head through the door. "Vince," she said. "It's the police. They want you to come outside."

— — — — — — — —

The detective had borrowed the key from the landlord before Vince arrived. He recognized the man from a vandalism incident two years before—a Polish name, perhaps—wearing, if Vince was not mistaken, the same seaweed-colored shirt and tie combination from that earlier interview. The officer nodded curtly, his strong lower jaw jutting out as he worked a piece of gum. "I'm Detective Smigi. Good to see you again, Principal Darten."

"I would like to say the same," said Vince. "But it seems you only bring me bad news."

"Maybe one of these days I'll find a lost cat for you," Smigi said. "Anyway, I appreciate you coming out here. I imagine it's tough to get away right now. But with Missing Persons, every second counts."

"It's no trouble," Vince said. "What am I about to see?"

"Nothing untoward," said the detective. "I've already given the place a sweep. But I wanted to know if you could see something I might have missed. Have you ever been here before?"

Vince shook his head. "I have not."

"What is your relationship with Ms. Watson?" Smigi asked. He had an iPad out and was tapping it softly with a stylus.

"I hired her three years ago," said Vince.

"When was the last time you saw her?"

"It's been maybe a week," said Vince.

"Can you be exact? Was she at school on the day of the breach?"

"I would assume so. I would have heard from her department chair otherwise."

"She hasn't been back to work? Haven't heard from her?"

"No," said Vince. "Ms. Watson has been incommunicado."

He unlocked the door and led Vince into the apartment. His eyes were immediately drawn to the couch. Of course, he had watched it, the video, or at least the first few seconds of it. But the sight of Jennifer Watson, a slender twig of a girl, undulating rhythmically upon the lap of some half-dressed paramour, their faces blanked by concentrated pleasure, had shamed Vince Darten. He felt that shame rise again, heard in his memory the slamming of his laptop, and suffered a fresh wave of panic that some digital record of the viewing remained somewhere on his computer, or that his own face had been recorded by the screen-mounted camera. Now he was there, close enough to touch the pillows she had pressed her sweat-slicked face against, like some tour group led through the studio where a sitcom was filmed.

His eyes flicked around the room before returning to the detective.

"What did you find?" he asked.

"Wallet. Phone. Credit cards. Cash. Laundry in the washer. She left in a hurry."

Vince nodded, uncertain of what he should say. There were pictures on a shelf. A group of girls dressed in violet gowns, posing by an aquarium at a sorority formal. There was Jenn, maybe ten years old, straddling a tractor with a man whose wide-set eyes suggested close relation. A stack of CDs—Liz Phair, Bikini Kill, Juliana Hatfield. Did she listen to these? A PBS tote bag, a flier from the Cincinnati Zoo, a ticket stub from something called The Erector Set. All things collected by the math teacher he'd hired to teach Sophomore Algebra, who wore a black puffy coat all the way until mid-May, who stared at the ground when he passed her in the halls to indicate a quiet desire to be left alone.

He was jealous of her. She had run. He was stuck behind.

"Any idea where she might have gone?" asked Smigi.

"No," said Vince.

"Never mentioned a relative, maybe? Or any friends?"

"No," he repeated. His voice sounded tired and wet.

Smigi worked the gum rhythmically. "I'll show you the bedroom," he said, moving through the anteroom towards the apartment's throat. "I wonder if you can think of anyone on your staff who really knew her well."

Jennifer Watson, who in five days had become the most famous woman in Clearwater, was missing. Yet Vince could feel her every-where, on every phone screen, behind the black slumber of an inactive

computer, behind the eyes of every teenager, parent, and member of
the community who passed through his school's gates. On the message boards, in chat rooms and digital hallways, they laughed at her,
screen-captured her, traded images of her like baseball cards. They
called her names: Skank. Slut. Whore. *Teacher*, thought Vince, following the detective, and then, grimly: *Celestial*.

3
GUS

KEVIN LENK: He's trying to kill us.

"What am I looking at?" Gus asked, scrolling down Carl's phone.

"Mr. Lenk and Ms. Bells' text messages," replied the taller boy. "You are not going to believe how good this is."

LEILA BELLS: Quiet. I'm trying to concentrate on this very interesting PowerPoint about formative assessments.

KEVIN LENK: Maybe not kill us. Maybe just lull us into a mass comma.

KEVIN LENK: Coma :)

"What are they talking about?" asked Priya.

"They're at, like, a faculty meeting or something," Carl explained.

"Yeah, but what are they talking about?" asked Priya.

"Just keep reading."

LEILA BELLS: You're not taking this as seriously as I am. Your students are going to be deeply confused and borderline illiterate.

KEVIN LENK: As soon as the last of us slips into unconsciousness, Darten's going to wheel in black market surgeons to harvest our organs. You're going to wake up in a tub of ice with one less kidney.

Gus grinned. "This is how teachers flirt, right?" he said. "They're flirting?"

Priya scoffed. "It's like a nature program where the male bird spreads his plumage for the female. But instead of feathers, it's jokes about organ harvesting."

LEILA BELLS: Good. All the European models only have one kidney. Those skinny bitches stay thin by only processing half the lemon drop shots they drink.

KEVIN LENK: I need to see you again. When can I?

"Wait, Ms. Bells and Mr. Lenk?" Gus laughed. "Are you serious?"

"I can see it," said Priya. "He's got that sort of European footballer thing going."

"Right?" said Carl.

"I mean, she's kind of a spud, but some people like that."

LEILA BELLS: You can see me right now. See? I'm looking over at you, raising my "Do-Not-Distract-Me-From-This-PowerPoint" eyebrow at you.

"She does have great eyebrows," nodded Priya. "Very even. Too bad she dresses like a hobo librarian."

KEVIN LENK: That eyebrow is the sexiest judgmental strip of hair I've ever seen. It's like being seduced by a militant Catholic school nun.

LEILA BELLS: lol. We're about three conversations away from me shooting down your Catholic school cos play fantasy.

KEVIN LENK: You're killing me, Bells. Need 2 CU.

LEILA BELLS: I'm going to the faculty bathroom on the 2nd floor. Wait two minutes and then come   find me.

KEVIN LENK: <3

LEILA BELLS: This is strictly to save our kidneys.

"Great Googly-Moogly," said Priya.

"I told you!" said Carl. "I fucking told you!"

"There's a fountain by that bathroom," she said. "I fill my water bottle in that fountain!"

"I would bleach it. A lot," said Carl.

Gus frowned. The timestamps shifted forward three weeks.

KEVIN LENK: What r u wearing?

LEILA BELLS: Um... a hazmat suit.

KEVIN LENK: Hot damn.

KEVIN LENK: Tell me more.

LEILA BELLS: It's made of a yellow insulated plastic... there's a plexiglass shield and a breathing apparatus...I'm surrounded by highly infectious diseases.

"This is just… weird," Gus said. "I feel like this is weird sexy talk."

"I'm picturing them rolling around in their hazmat suits," said Carl. "It's like sex without people. Only condoms."

KEVIN LENK: Ur steaming up my plexiglass.

KEVIN LENK: #Hot4MRSA

KEVIN LENK: Take it offfffff.

LEILA BELLS: No tnx. I'll die.

KEVIN LENK: You haven't seen my high school yearbook. I was voted most likely to die humping a plaque victim.

KEVIN LENK: plague :)

"See, I can't tell if she's into this," said Priya. "Look at the time-stamps. She takes a long time to text him back."

"That's an awful lot of blue," said Carl.

"I wonder what she's thinking," said Gus. He blushed when he realized how quietly he spoke.

"Do you think she's talking to other infectious disease specialists?" said Carl.

LEILA BELLS: Good night Kevin

"He's so needy," said Priya. "It's just too much."

"Well, that's what happens when you have sex with a guy in a public bathroom," said Carl. "If you give a mouse a cookie, he's going to want to do you on the bakery counter."

"He likes her," Gus said. "Look how much he likes her."

The timestamps jumped another three weeks.

KEVIN LENK: U up?

LEILA BELLS: No

KEVIN LENK: Can we talk about this afternoon?

Five minutes passed.

LEILA BELLS: I'm sorry

KEVIN LENK: I'm not mad

Five minutes passed.

LEILA BELLS: liar :(

"Ooooh. What do you think happened?" asked Priya.
"I'll bet she made fun of the dolphin tattoo on his ankle," said Carl.
"Oh, he would TOTALLY have an ankle dolphin."
The next text messages were timestamped October 3rd. They were all blue.

KEVIN LENK: I'm calling you

KEVIN LENK: Where r u?

KEVIN LENK: Call me when you get this.

KEVIN LENK: Are you watching this documentary on Discovery Channel? It's got me ready to quit my job to become a deep sea oil rig welder. Call me if you're interested in being me salt wench.

"This is too sad," said Gus. "I can't believe we're looking at this."

"No, you need to look at this," said Priya. "You're a shit texter, and you need to learn from this."

"Oh, here we go…"

"There are rules, Gus, and Mr. Lenk is breaking them. Don't text back right away…"

"You look like a sad ass-chimp who stares glumly at an un-ringing phone," said Carl.

"…Don't text again until you hear back from them," Priya continued. "Look at this! This man has total losey- face."

"He's the kid who wanted everyone to come over to his house and see the dye-cast Civil War figurines he painted," said Carl.

"Don't be the last texter! The person who sends the last text loses, Gus!"

"Do you want to be the kid who won't play outdoor basketball because he's afraid of catching germs? Because I promise you, he's a last texter, Gus."

The next messages were timestamped October 7th at 10:13 P.M.

KEVIN LENK: Leila?

KEVIN LENK: Why did you just call and not leave a message?

KEVIN LENK: I'm calling now. Pick up.

The next text message was timestamped three days later.

LEILA BELLS: I was out walking Peppers just now. We were in the park by Coolidge. I saw you   there. I was going to talk to you, but I didn't. I don't know what's wrong with me.

The next set of messages were timestamped October 15th.

KEVIN LENK: I talked to Carly, Leila. I know.

KEVIN LENK: Are you going to answer your phone?

KEVIN LENK: I know you're seeing these messages.

KEVIN LENK: Talk to me.

"Sweet Christmas, this just gets better and better," said Priya. "What now?"

"I bet she erased all of the unwatched episodes of *Real Housewives* from his DVR," said Carl.

"She left the lid off his jar of Vick's Vapor Rub," said Priya.

"You goddamn bitch! Now it's all crusty and won't open my sinuses!"

KEVIN LENK: Okay, I'll talk. We made a mistake. It happens. It happened. And you did what you always do—you quarantined the crime scene and tried to clean it up on your own.

KEVIN LENK: Maybe you don't trust me. Maybe when I laugh, you hear someone else. Maybe when I'm looking at you, you're looking three moves ahead. Idk.

KEVIN LENK: You fucked up, Leila. Goddamn it, why didn't you tell me?

KEVIN LENK: I think you do this on purpose. I think you try to make yourself unlovable to chase people away.

KEVIN LENK: What do you do if that doesn't work, Leila? What happens if you burn away all the good stuff, and I'm stuck here loving you without liking you anymore? What if I can't go away?

"Wow. He's doing a deep dive into his vault of Basic White Boy disses," said Priya.

"Look at the time stamps," said Carl. "I'll bet he texts her, then runs to his computer to look up old transcripts from *Grey's Anatomy.*"

"I'll bet he's got a spiral notebook full of Taylor Swift lyrics," said Priya.

"What do you think happened?" Gus asked.

Priya shrugged. "Same thing that always happens. She's just not interested in him."

They reached the bottom of the text exchange; Gus kept thumbing the phone to see if there was more. "Is that it?" he asked.

"That's all of the texts," said Carl, taking back the phone and fiddling with the screen. "But there's oooooonnnne more truth-bomb." He opened his iTunes app and played a voice recording; they leaned in and strained to hear.

At first, it was just breathing—wet, ragged breathing. Then Ms. Lenk's voice. A copy of her voice. The sound of someone exhausted beyond thought or performance. A transmission.

"I'm… sorry, Kevin. I'm so….. so…. sorry. Please… please don't call me." Then air. Then a click. Then nothing.

"That's it?" Gus said. "What does it mean?"

"It means," said Priya, "that Mr. Lenk is back on Tinder."

"I can't believe we can see this," Gus said. "I feel like I've entered a crime scene."

"A real whodunit," nodded Carl.

Gus took the phone from Carl and played the voice twice. He found the text chain and scrolled back to the beginning. Carl and Priya returned to their French fries.

Gus wasn't surprised Ms. Bells and Mr. Lenk's messages hadn't received more attention. There had been so much dirty laundry aired over the last week that the little thread of messages escaped broad notice. Even with the bathroom nookie, it was hard to compete with

Jennifer Watson's sex tape or footage of Carlton Wemish donning a wrester's mask and leaping off a third story balcony into a swimming pool. Nobody liked reading anymore.

But there was something in the little dialogue balloons that he found arresting. Mr. Lenk was his floor hockey teacher; Gus saw him every day. "Were I to diagram Lenk's emotions on a spectrum," Gus had once said, "they would begin with 'Ummmmmmmm….' and end with 'Gwah?'" Yet here—right under everyone's ignorant eyes—was a man of pain, love. What else was he hiding?

"Anyone know why they broke up?" Gus asked. Carl shook his head.

"Cary thinks STDs. He says Lenk's got the drips."

"Let's not rule out ankle dolphins," said Priya. She held a silver pouch of Carpi Sun in her left hand and her phone in her right, thumbing through another page. "Have you guys seen Mr. Rodriguez's nun porn?"

They were moving on. Gus looked around the cafeteria—banks of tables arranged like barracks, packed with teenagers sending and receiving messages on tiny screens. On, on, on. But Gus found himself stuck on Ms. Bells' last message. The pauses between her words, a sad lurching. *She left the phone on so he could hear her breathing. What was in that silence?* Gus closed his eyes and listened all over again.

— — — — — — — — —

Next period, Gus texted David.

GUS: U see the Lenk txt msgs?

DAVID: No. Watched the sex tape again.

DAVID: Gave me some good ideas :)

DAVID: Hang on.

DAVID: Wow. Who knew?

GUS: U had Wells for Bio, right? What's she like?

DAVID: idk. She's fine. Sarcastic. Kinda dull.

DAVID: She had a thing for ceramic cats.

DAVID: U know lenk?

GUS: Got him for PE. Think I might see him after school.

DAVID: My little detective. Let me know what you find out.

GUS: Facetime 2nyt?

DAVID: We'll see. Might have study group.

Gus called the huge grin on his face his "David look." It had been in his facial rotation for eleven months, often accompanied by Carl's "I-just-swallowed-dog-ear-medicine" face and Priya's "I-can't-believe-people-still-wear-Crocs" sigh. Gus dismissed the ridicule as routine jealousy. But beneath all that shade he understood was a genuine concern for his emotional well-being. The argument was simple:

1. You're in high school; David's in college; it will never last.
2. You're a virgin; David's not; it will never last.
3. You dote on him ceaselessly; he flakes on you constantly; it will never last.
4. 'Love' is a biochemical reaction produced by the release

of unsafe amounts of dopamine; on brain scans it resembles mental disorders usually classified as OCD; it will never last.

Gus acknowledged the validity of the claims. Distance sucked. He hated not being able to see David whenever he wanted. He grew paranoid and despondent at every stray comment of another guy. Furthermore, David DID flake with some regularity, which Gus expected given how different collegiate life was from 12th grade. Every high school relationship ends; one couldn't stroll through the cafeteria without stepping over the corpse of some September-May romance murdered by the move to a freshman dorm. Their arguments were valid. Gus simply didn't believe they applied to him.

"You have to understand how deep in the closet I was at the beginning of my junior year," Gus had explained. "My closet had closets." Yet David somehow saw him and initiated the slow, tenuous communique. Gus had always felt like a diver submerged in a scuba suit, unreachable. His friends had no idea what it was like to be buried alive, to take that first breath when excavated. He understood how naïve and foolish he sounded; he could hear the cliché in his mind nano-seconds before it passed his lips. But David made him feel like their story was the first of its kind, the only one he'd ever heard. *Yeah, I think we're special*, Gus thought. *Isn't that what love is? A shared sense of specialness?*

And yet Ms. Bell's voice message rattled him. He wondered what he was hearing in the pauses that Priya and Carl could not. All he had of David most days were characters on a screen, a disembodied placeholder where arms, fingers, heat belonged. Something was missing. It was what brought him to the gymnasium at the end of the day, when other students were fleeing the building as though there was a gas leak. He spotted Mr. Lenk, alone, dragging a trashcan of hockey sticks to a storage closet.

"Hi Mr. Lenk," Gus said.

"Hey Gus," he said. "What're you doing here?"

"Thought I might ask about joining the hockey team," Gus lied. "You're the coach, right?"

Mr. Lenk raised an eyebrow. "The hockey team?"

"Yes."

"Gus, you dive out of the way of the red rubber ball like it's a hand grenade. What were you screaming yesterday?"

"Not in the face. Not in the face."

"You want to join the hockey team?"

"No."

"No."

He let go of the trashcan, came over to Gus, and crossed his arms. "So what's up?"

Gus considered a different tactic. "I, um… I'm having relationship problems. I wanted some advice."

Lenk rolled his eyes and went back to dragging the trashcan. Gus came over to help him. The teacher wouldn't look at the student.

"This is about those text messages," Lenk said.

"No," Gus lied, before thinking better of it. "Yes."

"I don't want to talk about it."

"Okay." They pushed the sticks against the closet wall amidst shelves of soccer balls, badminton rackets, and orange cones. He walked out quickly to retrieve another trashcan; Gus followed.

"It's inappropriate for you to look at those. They were private."

"Right," Gus said. "I'm sorry about that. It's just…"

Lenk wheeled on Gus. "It's just what?" he asked sharply. "What could my private life possibly have to do with you?"

Mr. Lenk was the same height as Gus, but the 12th grader felt as though he'd poked a bear. *When will adults stop intimidating me?* Still, he had to know. "I'm… I'm losing someone I care about," he said. "How do I stop it?"

Lenk's shoulders dropped an inch. He looked at the floor, then back at Gus. "You're happy with this person?"

"I think so."

Lenk breathed through his nose for a few moments, rubbing his hand along his stubbly jawline. "All right, I'll give you some advice. On the condition that this is the last time we ever speak of this. You don't mention this to anyone else. I'm serious. All I want in the world is to be ignored again."

"Okay."

"You say you're happy. Good. Now imagine your friend says to you, 'I'm happy, too. I like you. I like being around you, with you, together. I think we've got a future.'" He paused, closed and opened his eyes and pointed at the storage closet. "Now imagine that person says, 'Just don't look in that closet.'"

"That, um, seems like an arbitrary condition."

He nodded. "Yeah. But how long before you're looking in the closet?"

Gus realized with a start that he felt sorry for his PE teacher. "The end of the day."

"The end of the conversation, Gus. It's like telling a person not to think of an elephant."

"So… so you're telling me not to look in the closet?"

He shook his head. "No, Gus. I'm telling you that once you've got an elephant in your head, it's all over."

When Gus got home, he found his grandfather at the kitchen table working on a children's puzzle.

"A little old for Sesame Street, aren't you?" Gus asked.

"Never too old for Sesame Street," the old man replied. "Saddest day of my life was when you told me you didn't want me to read you that monster book anymore."

Gus laughed. "*The Monster at the End of the Book*," he said. "Gosh, I haven't thought about that book in years."

"Well, it's all you thought about from ages three to four," his grandfather replied.

"Guess I finally got tired of the twist ending."

"Guess so."

Gus sat down to help him. He had been doing a puzzle a day for the past few weeks on the advice of his neurologist. It was an insatiable habit; Gus was not surprised the old man had started raiding Mooch's toy bin.

"Where's Mom?" Gus asked.

"Taking your brother to that piano teacher's house," he said, examining a patch of Oscar's fur.

"And Keith?"

He grunted. "At work, I suppose. Who knows with that one?"

Despite a generous offer to pay for the old man's home care, Gus's grandfather had never taken a shine to Gus's stepfather. He never missed an opportunity to bring up the younger man's gambling, and when Keith drove home in a new Tesla, one would have thought he'd just sold Anne Frank's location to the Nazis.

"How's that crazy school of yours?" the old man asked.

"Horrible," Gus said. "Everything is insane right now. Teachers yelling at students. Kids walking out of class. I don't know why they didn't just cancel school for the year and let us come back in January. Give people a chance to calm down."

Gus's grandpa nodded, looking at him over the ridge of his glasses. "I'll say it again," he said, voice sliding into the familiar tone and rhythms like the runners of a sled into a groove. "We never should have invented the Internet. That's why Al Gore was never president!"

"That's not why."

"Fifty years ago, a man humiliates himself, it stays in the past. No one else's business."

"Watergate was fifty years ago."

The old man laughed. "Clever kid," he said. "Hand me that red piece by your elbow."

Gus passed it to him. "You know, Grandpa... 50 years ago someone like me would have a hard time finding other people like myself."

The old man raised an eyebrow but kept his eyes on the puzzle. "People like you," he said. "They found each other just fine."

"Did they?"

He shrugged. "Look, I didn't know that world. We just didn't talk about it. But we all knew where they went."

Gus's social circle didn't include anyone over the age of 20, and he only had the one grandfather. But he'd always thought that the older generation was less careful in the words they chose to describe others. Sometimes, he acknowledged, that was a good thing; sometimes it was not. "Where... um... where did they go?"

The old man seemed to sense he'd offended his grandson; he reached across the table to put a hand on Gus's. "I didn't mean to sound like a *jamoke*," he said. "I just mean that the gays back then, they didn't have a lot of choices. Keeps things simple, don't you think?"

"Maybe," Gus shrugged. They worked in silence for a while, slowly filling in the yellow profile of Big Bird, the red slouch of Telly. Finally, the old man leaned back and rubbed his temples. "I need to take a break," he said. "All these primary colors, I'm liable to have a stroke."

"Don't joke about that, Grandpa."

He waved it away. "What, I can't tell a joke? Humor's the first thing that they take from you, August—remember that."

"Okay."

"Your grandmother and I didn't have a lot of rules. Laugh every day, that was one of them."

His voice was filling with fluid again. Gus got up from the table, massaged the old man's shoulders, then went to pour them both a glass of orange juice. Gus considered his grandfather a romantic role model. He had heard the story so often it was a mantra. *They met at a Halloween party in 1968. He dressed as Paul Newman, she as Anne Bancroft. He asked for her number; she gave him a fake one. He got in touch with the party host, tracked her down.* It turned out that she lived in his building, the roommate of a nurse on the fourth floor. A year later, they married. The next 45 years of his life, and all he had to do was walk up a flight of stairs.

And he loved her—loved her still. Never spoke ill of her, always observed her favorite holidays, always reminded the family of her favorite meals. He never talked about other women; as far as he was concerned, other than Gus's mother, there was only THE woman. Gus's grandfather worked a job he hated for a boss he didn't respect to protect her, his Anne Bancroft. Last year, Carl and Priya and Gus watched *The Graduate*; he told them his grandfather married Mrs. Robinson. "That's deeply fucked up," said Priya. "Like… Oedipal." But Gus believed they had missed the point, again. Oedipus was beautiful *because* it was a love story.

Gus brought the old man the juice; he patted his grandson's hand. "Shall we try again?" he asked.

"Yes," Gus said. He sat down to help his grandfather work a children's puzzle, to hang on to his memories so he wouldn't lose her a second time.

<hr>

"What do you think, boys? The open back? Or the strappy back?"

"What's that?"

Carl and Gus looked up; Priya was holding up two dresses the color of spilled red wine. "I need you queens to focus for me," she said. "My back is sexy as hell, and I need to know which of these dresses brings that to everyone's attention."

"Open back," said Carl, watching a man parsing through neckties across the store. "Strappy back looks like a tuna net. Like the climax of *Finding Nemo*."

"Maybe Dylan wants to get caught," said Priya, holding the open back dress against her tiny frame.

"I thought you flushed that turd," said Carl.

"Well… he's persistent," she said. "Plus, he's got a Jetta. I don't want to spring for an Uber."

"Wouldn't be a problem if Dominic Toretto over here would share his wheels," said Carl before dropping his voice into the Vin Diesel registry. "*Gus, don't the family mean nothing to you?*"

Gus bristled. "I told you both—I want the car for me and David. I'd like to have one date with him where I'm not also taking the kids to soccer practice."

Priya and Carl exchanged arched eyebrows. The gesture wore on Gus like a wet sock. "What?" he said. "Spit it out."

"David's coming?" said Carl.

"He's coming," Gus said. "I told you that."

"Are you sure?" asked Priya, drawing out the last syllable.

"Would you like it in writing?" said Gus.

"Okay, okay. Don't blow out your O-Ring," said Carl, puffing out his cheeks. "We just don't want you to get all worked up like you're going to see Billy Joel or something, and then some shitty cover band comes out with a Casio keyboard and half the words to 'Piano Man.'"

"I don't even know what that means."

"It means," said Priya. "That he stood you up at Homecoming. And we had to pick you up like some wet tangle of hair fished out of the drain."

"He. Was. Sick." Gus said.

She rolled her eyes. "Right, right. My B."

Gus stood and thrust the discarded dress at her. "Go with the strappy back," he said. "Anything that draws attention away from your chest. If either of you need me, I'll be waiting in my car."

— — — — — — — — —

As he wound through the mall, Gus texted David.

GUS: Ur coming to Winter Bash, aren't u?

It occurred to him that he had gone too far with Carl and Priya. They were looking out for him, like always. The dynamics of their friendship were complicated but mutually beneficial. Carl was socially bold but too queer for mainstream high school culture; Priya was a fringe member of the ruling caste, but secretly miserable in ways that only a formerly closeted kid could understand. They were linked together by a mutual cynicism and quick wit, which, like acid, would melt through them without a basically sincere kid like Gus to balance it out. For the past three years, they had reinforced one another like a tripod, pushing, yet joined by the lightest of touches at the vertex.

Yet sometimes Gus hated them so much that he wondered why they were even friends at all. There were no naturally occurring social phenomenon that would bring them together; only the forced incarceration of high school compelled such alliances. They were ugly, hurtful people at their core, and Gus often worried their toxicity was infecting him through proximity.

He paused in the food court to try and scrub the thought from his mind, waiting for a reply that was taking too long for his comfort. He was surrounded on all sides by communal behavior. Couples leaned into one another, chatting intimately; groups of teens sunned themselves on tables and benches like sealions, whooping and yelling. There was a mechanical bull in the center of the court, and people of all ages were lined up to ride, shouting as they slid from the saddle. *I am surrounded by Sbarro and Cinnabon and Orange Julius and laughter,* thought Gus, *and I can't feel any of it until fucking David looks at his phone.*

He saw a girl three tables over, alone and alert. She turned her head profile, and suddenly Gus recognized her—it was Ms. Bells. She was dressed nicely—cleaner than he'd ever seen her. She was wearing a blue and white striped blouse under a tight leather coat; lime green pants cuffed over black velvet heel boots. Her hair was swept back in a messy up-do, with little wisps framing her taut, elegant face. Stunned, Gus realized that Ms. Bells was beautiful.

Her phone was out in front of her, and she periodically reached out and pressed the home button to check the time. Otherwise, her hawk-like eyes restlessly swept the court. Who was she waiting for? Gus glanced around, wondering if Mr. Lenk was lurking in the crowd, watching her and deciding whether to approach. *Is this a date? Is she here for him? For someone else?* Her leg twitched beneath the table, and Gus could see her grip it, willing herself to stillness.

This is my chance, Gus thought. *Go talk to her. You can find out what happened.* But that was foolishness. What would he even say? Unlike Mr. Lenk, she didn't know Gus; plus, she was clearly waiting for someone else. Any distraction would prove an unspeakable irritant. That much he knew.

On the other hand, this woman was obviously in pain. She was lonely. He remembered the previous week, walking alone in the hallway on the way back from the bathroom when he passed a girl crying. He just kept walking. *Why hadn't I stopped?* Why hadn't he put his arm around that stranger, that comrade in suffering, and held her in solidarity? *Don't give up,* he wanted to say to her. *Fight for him. You can still fix this. You can be together.* More than anything in that minute, Gus wanted to be the one who took care of others, who restored their faith.

But he did nothing, and after ten minutes, she hurriedly gathered herself and padded away. Gus was left alone, wondering about why she was abandoned, where she was going, and how far in the future it would be before he knew.

4

ANDY

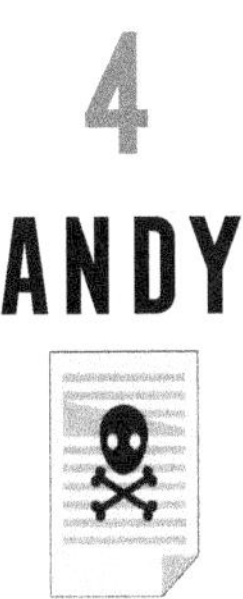

Andy Waters was sixteen years old when he first thought of teaching English. He was late to practice, and the entire team had already left for their six-mile run. Andy lingered on the loading dock, stretching leisurely against the dumpster, wondering whether he would actually run, or simply hide again in the supply closet. He heard a coughing behind a baler; peering behind the industrial machinery, he discovered his American Lit teacher, Mr. Jadarary.

"Andy," he said, flicking away a cigarette.

"Mr. Jadarary," Andy blushed. He was always blushing. The older man regarded him quizzically; he was wearing jeans, a bright collared shirt, and an argyle vest that matched his socks. His hair, graying at the temples, was swept back in the style of Johnny Depp, and his sideburns peeked out mischievously.

"You share my love of grease traps?" he asked the boy.

"I'm sorry?"

Mr. Jadarary gestured at the corrugated canister behind them, the repository for the cafeteria's waste. "Oh," said Andy lamely. "We all just stretch out here. Close to the locker room, you know."

"How unfortunate for you," said Mr. Jadarary. He leaned back in a metal folding chair and opened the book that had been resting on his thigh. Andy didn't recognize it.

"What book is that?" he asked.

"It's not for you," said Mr. Jadarary flatly.

Andy approached and tilted his head to read the cover. "*Naked Lunch*," he read aloud. "Any good?"

His teacher peered over the top of the book. "It's fantastic." He tossed the paperback to Andy, who caught it fumblingly. "Of course, I didn't think so when I was your age. And I found it pretentious and overwrought ten years later. But now," he said, lighting another cigarette, "now I find out it knows me better than I know myself."

"What's it about?"

"What do you think it's about?"

Andy hated when his teacher did this, answering a question with a question. He looked at the cover, battered cardstock the color of lettuce, a glowing hand superimposed on an enormous stag beetle. He flipped through the yellowed pages. "I dunno," he said. His eyes lighted from phrase to phrase, resting poignantly on the phrase '*mugwump jism*.' "I suppose the title's a metaphor?"

"Smart boy," his teacher smiled. "And what does the word naked mean to you?"

Well, thought Andy, *it means the stack of magazines my father hides in his closet, Cinemax Saturdays at 2 A.M., Lisa Anthony in Driver's Ed*. But he voiced none of those thoughts. Instead, he found the perfect word: "Exposed."

Mr. Jadarary exhaled a long stream of smoke, nodding. "That's right. 'The title means exactly what it says: the naked moment when everyone sees exactly what's on the end of the fork.' Jack Kerouac said that. Do you know who that is?"

Andy shook his head. "No."

Mr. Jadarary stood, crossed the concrete porch, and gently plucked his book from the boy's hands. "When you do, come find me," he said, resuming his repose in the chair. "We'll talk about what's on the end of the fork."

Andy went for his run, but he did not trace the path of his teammates. Instead, he repaired to the public library, where he found a dog-eared copy of *On the Road.* After an hour, he realized with a start that Mr. Jadarary was the coolest person he'd ever met.

— — — — — — — — —

A decade later, Andy Waters was the most popular teacher at Clearwater High. He greeted his students at the door with a high five or an occasional guitar serenade. He frequently inserted Chance, Migos, and (when he wanted a big laugh) Kanye lyrics into his lectures. The Venn Diagram of student cliques he connected with looked like the Olympic Rings—he talked to Paige Howard about Doctor Who and Manga, Mateo Himenez about Reggaeton, and Trevor Bulst about NASCAR. He hosted a "Paperback Fight Club" where students brought in their favorite books and passionately extolled their merits. He played music frequently, rarely gave homework, and wore bow ties every day, which he left casually untied on Fridays. He had a diamond stud earring in his right ear.

This is not to say that Andy was a good teacher. He rarely communicated learning targets, and even less frequently collected exit data. He could be digressive to the point of distraction, and he tended to favor extroverted learning styles. His content knowledge was spotty, and it had been thirteen months since he'd actually finished a book.

He massively curved his tests and rarely retaught concepts. He kept a sloppy desk, was delinquent in returning email or phone calls, and even struggled in rudimentary teaching skills like wait time and question framing. Yet in each of his summative reviews, Principal Darten praised Andy's ability to build community, to identify with student interests, to model a passion for learning and enthusiasm for literature.

His older colleagues regarded him with skepticism and incredulity. Leonard Fisk, English Department Chair, recommended remediation through the mentorship program in Andy's third year after a phone call from a parent revealed that the young teacher had not graded a set of essays in ten weeks. Laura Gouch walked away shaking her head after a conversation where Andy kept referring to George Eliot as a man (he later compounded the impression by claiming, "I was confusing her with her husband, Robert Browning."). Steve Carmichael couldn't stop laughing when recounting a story about a sophomore who earnestly claimed that he wanted to be "an English teacher just like Mr. Waters."

Yet Andy was already a legend among the younger staff, and he had assumed duties as the unofficial chairman of the Clearwater High School Social Committee. Through a quirk in the district payroll system, new hires did not receive a paycheck until completing their first month of teaching, which meant that it was well into September before a 22-year-old teacher was paid. Until that time, Andy opened a bar tab each Friday evening and paid for rookies' drinks. When he was 25, he bought a motorcycle and gave rides to and from the local taverns (Andy himself did not drink). He had a beautiful singing voice, a quick, improvisational wit, and could reasonably approximate 17 Springsteen songs on his acoustic guitar. He quietly dallied with some of the younger female teachers, most recently Jennifer Watson.

It was an imperfect, messy life, yet one that Andy regarded as a roaring success. He was 26, had his own apartment, a girlfriend, and a job that made him feel important. He played pickup basketball Friday mornings, lead guitar in a 90s-cover band on weekends, and Call of Duty on the PlayStation network most evenings. His Golden Retriever was named Whiskey Tango Foxtrot. "Most people I know would trade places with their high school selves in a heartbeat," Andy explained to his bandmates one night over beers. "But this thing I've got going here?" he gestured to his apartment. "The life of kings, fellas."

He thought of that conversation on December 1st, when several dozen hacked teacher files were uploaded to Clearwater Confidential. Andy's contribution was thousands of emails extracted from his "Sent" file, neatly assembled in a PDF. He got the news from several text messages, including an ex-girlfriend, his college roommate, and his mother. His face drained of color as he scrolled through the files on his phone. "Shit. Shitshitshitshitshit," he said.

Most of the emails were innocuous, the sort of bureaucratic minutia one would expect from a generic educator. A series of messages arranging and confirming a student make up exam. A registration for a district institute day. Several dozen conversations about grades, conferences, course selection, and assignment instructions. A tax form related to union dues. Some emails were merely unopened.

But mixed in with these trivialities were several revealing, unflattering messages.

WATERS, ANDREW

> To: Sarah Mays <sarah_mays@ghastcorp.com>
> Hey,
>
> I know it's been awhile, and you haven't been taking my calls. I wanted to let you know that I've been to the doctor, and I have some information that I think you need to know about. Not life-threatening, but we need to talk. Call me.
> —Andy

WATERS, ANDREW

>To: Bryan Yulders <bryan_yulders@csd.org>
>Bryan,
>   Heard you caught Ryan Westend with a katana blade in his locker. Doesn't surprise me. If I had to name one sick fuck on my roster most likely to bring a weapon to school, but would be Ryan. Let me know if you need anything.
>—Andy

There were emails where he complained about parents, disparaged the administration, made fun of colleagues, and gossiped about students. There were emails where he whined about district policies, including one with a reference to Superintendent Broach as a "Bitch-titted TwatWaffle." Several messages revealed Andy's fondness for the word 'cunt.'

Andy called his girlfriend Celia first. "Hey, hon," he said, smoothing over the ragged panic in his voice.

"Hey babe, what's up?" she said.

"Listen, I—" he started, before thinking better of it. "Have you checked the news yet?"

"No, I'm neck-deep in email. What's up?"

"Look, there's going to be some stories about Clearwater," he said, closing his eyes and trying to picture her face. "There's been a leak. Of… files."

"What kind of files?"

"Just… really embarrassing stuff," he said. "Listen, Celia… I need you to do me a favor."

"Sure."

"It's a biggie," he said. "This is one of those relationship-milestone moments."

"Oh boy!" she laughed. "All my coworkers laughed when I got that 'Relationship Milestone' coffee mug! But who's laughing now, bitches?"

"Celia, this… this is serious." He waited for a moment before speaking. "I need you not to read the files that have to do with me."

"Okay."

"I'll talk to you about everything. I promise. No secrets. But," he said, running his hand over his face. "But I really, really need you not to read those files. Okay?"

"Okay," she said.

The school district closed the school later that day, and Andy holed up in his apartment. He spent two days pouring through the files, answering emails, trying to distract himself with video games and the Chinese delivery menu. He blew off Celia; he felt like he wasn't ready to face her. He was afraid of her voice in his voicemail.

He called his mother, his brother, his sister-in-law, his bandmates, a few other friends and acquaintances. Some had heard; some had not. Some had already perused the files, including his mother. "Andy, I don't understand," she said tearfully. "Why would you write these things?"

"Ma!" he said, trying to calm her. "Ma, look, it's not that big a deal!"

"You're going to lose your job!"

"There's 40 other teachers on that site!" he shouted. "They can't fire all of us!"

When classes resumed two days later, he retreated to his classroom without even stopping by the office. He couldn't face his coworkers. He had mocked Chloe Fichte's Beanie Baby collection; he had derided Juliette Brocius's tedious PowerPoint on Ernest Hemingway. "I can't even look at Carmichael anymore," he had written to Jennifer Watson. "His face looks like it caught on fire and someone tried to put it out with a fork."

But there was no sanctuary to be found with his students. Every single one of them had their phones out on their desks; the minute he turned his back or wrote something on the board, they compulsively scrolled through their content. Unlike many of his colleagues, Andy had always welcomed phones in the classroom; he had tacitly encouraged his students to message during his lessons, and he knew that dozens of kids received daily Snapchat footage of his shenanigans. But now he saw their impassive faces through a filter of paranoia and felt none of his usual looseness or ease.

"Phones away," he said to a murmured response. "Come on. We've got work to do."

Alden Watts raised his hand. "Mr. Waters, did you see all the stuff that's been released online about the teachers?"

"Online? What is this 'online' you speak of?" said Andy lamely. "We're talking about Hawthorne right now. The man used an inkwell."

Kevin Prossman raised his hand. "Mr. Waters, do you think Hester Prynne had herpes?" he said as the class burst into laughter. "Is that what Hawthorne means by 'a halo of misfortune?'"

More laughter. On an ordinary day, Andy Waters would tease this conversation out, turn the students to the text to search for subtextual suggestions of STDs, to challenge them to support their ideas, however farcical, with the language of the book. Instead, he scowled. There was a hint of ridicule in Kevin Prossman's mouth that Andy had never noticed before in his classroom. He could feel his face turning the shade of Hester's infamous letter.

"No, Kevin. I don't think that's in the book," said Andy.

"I just think having herpes would be the worst," said Kevin with a shrug. "Don't you, Mr. Waters?"

He's read them, thought Andy grimly. *And now he's trolling me.* The only refuge was the lesson. "I think Hester's got it bad enough, Mr. Prossman," said Andy. "Could we take a look at chapter eight?"

— — — — — — — — —

It was a long, miserable day. Andy grew increasingly querulous throughout; by eighth period, he simply had his students sit down, take out their books, and read for fifty minutes. He spent his lunchbreak sequestered in his room, pouring over the files, texting the younger teachers (once he saw Jennifer Watson's video, he understood why she wasn't returning his calls).

He waited an hour after the final bell to allow the halls and parking lot to clear out; when he heard the vacuum of the janitor, he knew that he could walk out. Passing through the cafeteria, he spotted Vince Darten on his hands and knees in his dress pants, scraping a wad of gum off the bottom of a table. For a moment, Andy froze, wondering if he shouldn't take a more circumlocuitous route to avoid confrontation. But the principal looked up at his footsteps, and Andy knew they would have to speak.

"Hi Vince," he said. "Don't we have maintenance staff for that work?" He sat down on the bench next to Darten.

"Well, I should know better by now," said Vince, getting to his feet and shaking Andy's hand. "If I don't stop and look, I won't have to clean it up."

"Rough day?" asked Andy.

Vince sat down on a bench across from Andy and removed his glasses, which he polished with his tie. "The roughest," he said. "Andy, I don't mind telling you—I wish I was the janitor today."

Andy smiled. "I um… I need to talk to you."

Vince nodded. "Yes. We do need to speak."

"There are… there are some emails that came out that I'm, ah, embarrassed about." He tried to make eye contact, failed, and instead focused on his hands. "Some messages I wish I hadn't sent."

"You mean like a series of emails where you and Jennifer Watson imagine me leading a faculty meeting like I'm a character on *Good Times*?" said Vince.

"Uh, yes," said Andy hoarsely. "Yes, emails like that."

For an agonizing moment, Vince said nothing, and Andy debated whether he should fill the silence with protestations and apologies. But finally, the older man spoke.

"You were invisible. You didn't even know how transparent you were. I've never been invisible, Andy. When you're an outsider, everyone watches. When you're the principal, eyes are always on you. When you're black, you don't get to just blend. Sometimes you get to forget for a moment that people think of you differently. But you can't get too comfortable in that posture. It hurts too much to be reminded."

Andy squeezed his hands together. He felt as though he were about to cry. Suddenly, Vince clapped his hands, and Andy flinched.

"I need time to look everything over, to take an official position. We're going to talk in my office as soon as I know what a principal is supposed to say to all of this," said Vince. "But if we're just two educators, chewing the fat after hours, let me say that I wouldn't worry too much about the boss, Andrew."

"Oh," said Andy. He still couldn't look up. "I'm not those emails," he said after a moment. "You've got to believe me."

"Andy," said Vince. "Yes, you are. And so am I. It's just not *all* we are."

Darten got back down on the ground, grabbed his trowel, and began again to pick at the gum. "I hired you, Andy Waters. I've watched you teach for four years. Even if there's rot behind the walls, I still trust the edifice. I'll see you tomorrow."

Andy Waters thought about helping him, about getting down on the unclean floor to search for discarded waste. But the man's kindness had shamed him, and suddenly he felt a great revulsion for his principal. He said nothing else, leaving behind the man who scraped and forgave the gum everyone else just ignored and forgot.

5

JENN

This was the third time Jennifer Watson had run. The first was when she was ten and had set fire to her father's lawnmower. "'t'wasn't your fault, Jenny," her father growled as he drove her home from the gas station where an employee had noticed a small girl dragging a suitcase across a vacant lot. "Bit 'o grass caught in the muffler. Lawn'll be back, green as the Grouch." And sure enough, by summer's end, the burnt patch had scarred over, and a bright new stripe of Kentucky bluegrass had grown in.

The second time was her sophomore year in college. She had moved into a small apartment unit with three other friends from the McCutcheon dorm—Sandy from Idaho Falls, Marjorie from Crown Point, and Kesha from Savannah. The vision had been a sort of anti-sorority, an ironic send-up of the gilded houses that formed the spine of Purdue's traditional social scene. But the dream fell to ruin almost immediately when Jennifer, with characteristic impulsiveness, bedded

Marjorie's boyfriend. "Babe, it was nothing, less than nothing," Jenn heard the boy plead the next morning. "She's just some dumb trick!" Mortified by the scene, Jenn borrowed Kesha's car to go get some milk. She then drove to Pittsburgh.

This was different. Two weeks past her 26th birthday and three months into her third year as a math teacher at Clearwater High School, a sex tape featuring Jennifer Watson was released. Hers was not the only file leaked online; indeed, it was not even the only file featuring sexual content. But Jenn's tape was the one that gained the most infamy on social media. It was watched and rewatched ceaselessly by members of the student body, in privacy and in laughing clusters. It pinged around Instagram as though it were its own electron cloud. There was commentary online, screen captures of every expression and position. Her eyes, clouded by ecstasy; her breasts cupped by his hands. Long, sinewy legs wrapped around his waist like a mantis's pinchers.

It had become the topic of derision and moralizing and lewd solicitation in unbearable proportions. Changing her number had no effect; she deleted her accounts and shuttered her email, but the feedback still reached her in the mockery of strangers, the lingering eyes of men of all ages who suddenly went face blind and began to peer through her blouse. Part of the tongue-wagging was because of Jennifer herself, who, despite her wideset eyes and off-center mouth, was a healthy, lean, and attractive woman in the prime of her sexuality. But it was also due to her partner, a man nearly 20 years her senior.

Why had she done it? There wasn't enough music in the car or weed in her system to drown out the question, and it dogged her relentlessly as she drove west through the vast unlit stretches of Romain Road. It was the question that had kept her from taking her parents' calls, that chased her from her classroom, that seemed to confirm every hateful thing Sandy, Marjorie, and Kesha wrote about her for months after Purdue. Still, the case had to be unraveled. She reviewed the facts again.

1. Bill Patsurd had been her final conference of the night. "I'm here to follow up on something I read on Twitter," he said, shaking her hand. "Is this where the kids can get the good drugs?" As first lines went, it wasn't bad.
2. Bill wore a tailored suit made of some sort of expensive wool. He was dressed to sell—a buttoned waistcoat, a plaid pocket-square. Jenn had teased him about it. "What happens if I pull that out?" she asked. "Actually, it's tied to thirty or so colorful handkerchiefs, so please don't," he replied. She had laughed. Loud.
3. They went for drinks. He had expensive tastes. When he smoked, he looked like Jack Nicholson in *Chinatown*.
4. They went to her place. It embarrassed her for him to stagger through her squalor, but by that point he was so busy with her shirt and skirt that he didn't seem to notice the grease-slicked wok or the murky aquarium. Perched on her couch, he also didn't notice her iPad, which she set to record while he fumbled with her bra clasp.

Jenn was vain; she knew this about herself. As a teen working at her father's shop, she had used the convex security mirrors to watch herself flirt with the rough boys who came into buy cases of Natty Ice. This was the same thing, right?

But when she had viewed the video the next night, looking to arouse herself after a few glasses of Zinfandel, she found that her gaze did not linger on her face or torso or splaying legs. Instead, she stared at Bill's face, which now seemed to look less like young Nicholson and more like mid-90s Paul Sorvino. He was jowly and graying; his body jiggled, rimmed by cellulite and patchy skin discolorations; his mouth opened and closed like a large-mouth bass. He was an aging, unattractive man. How could she have missed it?

The real mistake, of course, had been keeping the file, but between how little she used the iPad (she preferred her Kindle) and the speed with which she moved on from Bill Patsurd, she had simply forgotten about its existence. But now, the recklessness and stupidity of her behavior was a sinkhole so inescapable in her psyche that it had swallowed up every positive thing Jennifer Watson may have ever thought about herself. *Before I am anything else,* Jenn thought, *I am an idiot.*

So she ran. A final, conclusive bout of idiocy. She left her phone, her credit cards, and the majority of her cash. She left her lights on, her dishwasher running, her wet clothes in the drum. She grabbed a bag of toiletries, a stack of ungraded papers, and her keys, and she started driving west. The plan—such as there was one—was to go someplace without the Internet, without Wi-Fi, without cell phone service. Passing over the Wabash River into Illinois, Jenn cursed the expansiveness of Verizon's coverage.

This was a stupid plan, and Jenn knew it. But she was committed to it now, and she simply didn't care about the morning's consequences. The truth was she had long nurtured a vague fantasy of junking it all and starting over. She remembered the flat, empty sound of her father's voice after Perdue. "This is the last time, Jenny," he'd told her. "You run again, and we won't be there to pull you back." She had been good now for five years, but like a prisoner forced to hold a live grenade, the posture was beginning to wear her down. Better to let go, better to explode it all, then to live clenched and ready to blow.

Teaching was hard, unforgiving work marked by long passages of tedium and soul-grating minutia. Four days before the data leak, she sat in a meeting with two special education instructors who fought like stray dogs about the font-size of a quiz modified for a kid with a learning disability. *I'm dying,* she thought to herself as they toggled back and forth between 12 and 14 point. *20 minutes closer to death.* She was a year from tenure, a deadline that felt more like a lodestone being fit around her neck. Her desk in the math office adjoined Betsy Rilke's, who was the same age as Bill Patsurd. Betsy Rilke lived for *Dancing with the Stars.* She spoke at length about making applesauce from scratch. She once called the Keurig 'a percolator.' Betsy Rilke was already dead.

The car died six miles past the Chauncey Marsh Nature Preserve. It was an old Nissan with a bad gaslight, and Jenn felt it shudder, then cough, and finally roll to a stop. She was alone, her vehicle awkwardly straddling the cracked winter pavement and the gravel easement of unincorporated county. There was no light but that of the moon, a silver coin peeking through the awning of naked boughs and twigs clattering with December breeze. Only minutes ago, she had sped by a row of modern farmhouses bedecked in red and green Christmas lights. Now the only signs of civilization were the telephone poles that stretched out into the darkness, standing sentinel for so long that they had lost their posture and now resembled teeth jutting from the land's ancient gums.

"Shit!" shouted Jennifer. "Shit, shit, shit, shit, shit!" She leaned on the horn, then switched off the radio. She cried and wailed in the darkness until she was too tired to care anymore, until the word *idiot* was nothing more than wet, unintelligible sound.

____

She awoke just before 6:30 A.M. to the pink light of morning. She wrapped her hands around her neck for warmth, then used an empty hash brown wrapper to wipe away the fog of her windows. Her breath came out white and sharp; there was none of the lazy vapors of Southern Indiana's moist winters. Illinois, it seemed, was more unforgiving.

She tried the engine another half dozen times, but it never so much as wheezed. She was cold and tired and hungry and pissed off, and so she opened the door, scraped "Gone West" into the windshield frost, and set off walking.

Jennifer wore boots whenever she could, and was glad of it this morning, her toes perhaps the only extremity not in bitter retreat from the wind and harsh air. After about a mile and a quarter of trudging, she began to pick up the faint presence of humanity—a thin trail of garbage and waste. Plastic wrappers, shell casings, a child's red mitten. Like trickles building to tributaries, the trash gathered intensity as it approached its source, a small cluster of trailers and vacant buildings radiating out from a central domicile. The house was a two-story farmhouse whose shingles were green and gray with lichen and whose paneling had been stripped of luster by wind and sunlight. There was a light coming from a first story window; the rest of the windows were as black and inscrutable as a beetle's eyes.

Jenn entered the trailer park calling out; there was no movement and no response. She ascended the house's front porch, admiring the intricate lattice, and knocked at the door. For a long time, she heard nothing, but eventually the sound of heavy feet came through. The door opened, and a man with gray-blue eyes and a shock of white hair appeared. His mouth was drawn back in an expression that reminded Jenn of when she was a child and her vet would examine their old dog's gums by pulling back its lips.

"Help you?" asked the man.

"I um… my car broke down 'bout a mile down the road," she said.

He nodded. "Come inside," he motioned.

She followed him into the foyer. *Christ, he's a hoarder,* she thought. The entryway was packed with artifacts, trinkets, appliances, and articles of clothing. Boxes of Ritz crackers, antlers, several tape decks, an old refrigerator, couch cushions, a stuffed pheasant, a stack of tires, fishing tackle, bike chains—the sight of it all overwhelmed her.

Peering into another room, she saw an elaborate table set with a model train, complete with a station, two little towns, a mountain with track winding around and through, dotted with miniature vehicles, stores, houses, and people. The old man rummaged through a stack of manila folders in an accordion file and produced a business card that he handed to Jenn.

"Now this here—Randy Faldow—he's the closest mechanic I can recommend."

"Thank you," she said, before adding, "I don't have any money."

"Well, that'll be a problem for Randy. He don't work for pretty smiles."

"I cut hair. Does Randy need a haircut?"

"Man's got a head like Yule Brenner. Actually, he may be dead. Haven't seen Randy in a season."

"Can I use your phone?"

"What, you got no phone?" the man eyed her suspiciously. "Thought all you kids had phones."

"Battery's dead," she said.

The old man was not charmed. "No money and no phone. What exactly is the plan here?"

That was a good question. The part of Jenn's brain that made adult decisions ordered her to call her father, call her sister, call Andy Waters, call her department chair. Hell, maybe call Bill Patsurd. Some-one—anyone—who might drive down here and rescue her, haul her home, lecture her on making better decisions, assure her that things would be all right, that the smoking crater of her life was nothing more than a kerfuffle that would pass like a Hollywood romance. Someone who would buy her a coffee, maybe take her to bed, let her smoke a joint and watch a few hours of Netflix on the couch.

But Jenn didn't want to be rescued. She wanted a deeper crater. More shrapnel.

"I need a place to stay," she said.

"This look like a flophouse to you?"

"No… I," she said. "I just need a few days. Please. You've got a bunch of trailers outside. Give me one of those."

"For free?"

She tossed him the keys. "You like junk. How's a busted Nissan sound?"

The old man—Cy Travis—showed her to a building at the edge of the property. "Trailer's're all full," he explained. "But this'll suit you I expect."

It was a three-room single level, the sort of home they used to build as starter units; now it seemed to have outlasted much of the surrounding hamlet. Rust-encrusted on the outside and mold-curdled on the inside. Two windows boarded up, and much of the drywall caved in by scavengers searching for pipe. A cut-stone fireplace jutted into the middle of a kitchenette; there was a cot in the corner and a few cupboards lining the wall.

"Bathroom?" asked Jenn.

"Out back," Cy gestured. "Help yourself to the wood afterwards," he said, pointing to the fireplace.

"Well, all right then," said Jenn, flicking a wall switch on and off; nothing lit up. "Don't suppose you've got a couple Yankee candles back there in your hoard."

"I'll bring some down to you," said Cy. "When I think of it."

"How fast do your trains go?" she asked. "Back in the house?"

"Trains ain't for racing."

"I'm gonna be back, old man," she smiled weakly. "We're gonna race trains."

Cy waved this off and shuffled out, shutting the door behind him. She was alone. "Home," she said.

She retrieved some firewood and got the hearth going (the flue had been shut; getting it open was a half-hour's work). She began investigating the shack for evidence of prior residency. Everything was distorted by thick layers of dust, soot, and soil, but as she excavated it, she realized the building was a former welcome center for Landes township. She found a brochure labeled "Crawford County Historical Center."

There were books. Jenn lay on the cot and flipped through a copy of *Watership Down*, reading for an hour before dozing off. Her dreams were dark and troubled. She awoke and started reading an edition from *The Babysitter's Club* called *Dawn's Big Move*. She remembered reading the entire series when she was ten. "Oh, Mary Anne," Jenn sighed. "You were always the best babysitter."

I'm safe, Jenn thought. *No one knows me. No one can find me. No more running. I can be alone here in my haunted Scooby Doo Historical Center. I can rest.*

She closed her eyes again. Her stomach growled.

— — — — — — — — —

She met Hobby at a bar a mile down the road a few days later, but it turned out that he lived in an adjoining trailer on Cy's property. He was handsome in a plain sort of way, his long black hair pulled back in a ponytail, his face unevenly groomed. She thought he looked like Danny Trejo without the facial scarring.

They fucked in his trailer for a good hour, and Jenn felt the old thrill of anonymity, of being anyone else in the embrace of a man. Afterwards, she lay against him, lightly running her fingers up and down his chest while he played with a child's electric keyboard, plinking out broken Billy Joel.

"What kind of name's Hobby?" she asked. "Thai? Cantonese?"

"Short for Hobson. Named after my old man's dog," Hobby said. "What kind of name is Mary Anne?"

"Same," she laughed.

He was Winnebago, or had been generations ago. "Mom was from Honduras; grandpa was from Estonia," he explained. "Blood's so thin it might as well be tap water. Dad never lived on the Res. Truth is, I'm only Indian once a year on my taxes."

"Anything else I should know?"

He tapped out the notes for "Ode to Joy." "Well, you probably don't recognize me without my mustache, but I was in Hall and Oates."

"Oh, this is going to be awkward," she laughed. "I already slept with Hall."

"Everybody does," he said. "Fucking man-whore."

She watched him key out the melody to "Private Eyes." "You're good," she murmured. "Where'd you learn to play?"

"Just sort of figured it out," he said. "Gonna give it to my daughter over in Vincennes. Wait—here's the best part." He pressed a button; a tinny, prerecorded beat played. "Drum solooooooooo!" Hobby fake yelled.

He worked in a grain elevator when there was work to be had; otherwise, he did odd jobs around town. He warned her about messing with Cy—"He's a spider, girl. He don't look like much, but just about everyone around here owes him something. House is full of other people's treasures. He figures out the one thing you can't do without, and then he makes sure he's the only one selling it."

For an hour, she felt at peace with him, and she playfully wrenched the keyboard away. "Let me show you what Hall taught me," she said. "A real man." But after mangling "Hot Cross Buns" while singing the lyrics to "Maneater," Hobby put his hands on hers and shaped her fingers. "Like this," he said, forming a chord. "Now like this." She let him move her. "Good," he said softly. "Now it sounds like you're just strangling the one cat."

She shut her eyes. "No fooling, you're good," she said, nibbling at his ear. "You ever think of teaching?"

"Only one thing I'm any good at," he said. "Let me show you."

— — — — — — — — —

She got a job at a diner two blocks from the bar. At first, the owner had her washing dishes, but once she ascertained Jenn's competency, she "put that pretty face to work waiting tables."

Her name was Ruth; she was 54 and very New York. "How'd you end up in Southern Illinois?" Jenn asked.

"A wandering tribe, I'm from," said Ruth. "Some of us wandered too far."

Jenn asked to be paid in cash; Ruth was happy to oblige. She had Cystic Fibrosis, which had lately manifest in swollen fingers and a whooping cough; it relieved her mightily to have a younger woman minding the floor. Jenn learned the menu quickly and proved a canny up-seller. She flirted with customers, talked everyone into dessert, and began racking up tips. She showed up early and stayed until close. She made friends with the cooks (Estevan and Juan) and started expo-ing the food for them. She scrubbed the counter, washed the dishes, mopped the floor, bleached the bathroom, and even cleaned the light fixtures. It felt good to busy herself, good to go somewhere, and good to have warm meals waiting for her at the beginning and end of each shift.

A week later, Ruth watched Jenn effortlessly tabulate a lengthy ticket, figuring out the tax in her head. "Where'd you learn math like that?" asked Ruth, coughing into a handkerchief.

"Ruth, I'll let you in a secret," said Jenn, tucking her pen behind her ear. "I am a witch. Very powerful."

"Well, I'm a beauty queen," said Ruth, wiping her nose. "I'd say both our talents are being wasted."

She asked Julio to mind the counter while she and Jenn went for a drive. "My grandfather, he came here with nothing, nothing," said Ruth while waiting for a train to pass. "He gets a neighbor to let him have a dead dog. Trades the dog meat to a pig farmer for a broken radio; fixes the radio and trades it to a factory foreman for an old stove. Turned that over to a restaurant owner for a wagon cart; goes back to the neighbor, sells that for $50, then buys a stake in the diner he ends up owning five years later. Everything's an opportunity, Mary Anne." She pulled into the gravel driveway of a small but freshly painted split level. Motioning for Jenn to follow, she entered through the front door. "Reuben!" she bellowed. "Reuben, are you proper?"

"Mom, how many times I gotta ask?" came a voice from down the hall. "Call me before you come home! A little warning!"

"I asked if you were proper," she said. "What do you want, a signal flare?"

Reuben was seated at a computer at the center of a nest of technology. Motherboards, hard drive casings, dissected monitors, knotted cords, and diagrams littered the room. He wore a green bathrobe and sweatpants. "Who's the tits?"

"Oh, he thinks he's so edgy," Ruth said, rolling her eyes. "Apologies, dear. This *shmendrik* is my son. Reuben, this is Mary Anne."

"Hello, Mary Anne!" said Reuben. "She's perfect. Just what I wanted. Thank you, Amazon!"

"So sorry, little Reuben," said Jenn. "I'm *shikse*."

This amused him. "Mother, I'm converting! Right now!"

"Enough, enough of this comedy," said Ruth. "Let the grownups talk." She turned to Jenn. "Mary Anne," she said. "I call that name in the diner, it takes you a minute to respond. I think, and it's none of my business, but you haven't been Mary Anne for very long."

"Ooh, a pseudonym!" laughed Reuben.

Jenn regarded her coolly. "You're right, it's none of your business."

"Not my business, no, but an opportunity, maybe. Reuben, show her your homework."

"Ma, who is this…?"

"Show her."

Reuben rummaged in a drawer and produced a black binder; opening it, he leafed through several plastic photo sleeves before handing it over to Jenn. It was three pages of Illinois drivers' licenses.

"What is this?" she asked.

Reuben patted his computer. "A DMV."

"Opportunity, opportunity," said Ruth. "Juan, Estevan—in America, they see a new life with good jobs. The IRS, they, too, see an opportunity—as long as they don't ask questions, they can tax the *hombres'* paychecks. So, everyone gets to be here, nice and quiet. As John and Steven. Life is about making sure everyone gets a taste."

Jenn eyed the woman warily. "What—ah—what's your take?"

Ruth smiled. "He's a smart boy, my Reuben. Figured all of this out. But the schools around here, they're failing him. The older he gets, the less they can offer." She sat on her son's bed and mopped her forehead. "My problem, as I see it, is I never learned my figures. You teach him your witchcraft, and you can be Mary Anne for as long as you like."

Jenn smiled, then looked at Reuben. "Looks like we're both converting."

━ ━ ━ ━ ━ ━ ━ ━ ━

Three weeks later, she banged on Cy's door. When the old man answered, she smiled and held up a model train—an Atlas Master Line locomotive.

"Ready to race?" she asked.

"That's N line," said Cy. "My trains're HO."

Jenn rolled her eyes and pushed past him into the foyer. "May I come in?" she asked.

"Seems you already have," he said sulkily. "What'll it be?"

She pointed. "The trailer at the edge of the lot. The one with the graffiti. It's empty."

"'Tis."

"Heat work?"

"What's it to you?"

She pulled a billfold from her coat pocket. "I'd like to fill it. *Pronto, pronto, cameriere!*"

He narrowed his eyes at her, his mouth working back and forth like a saw. "Where'd you get that?"

"I'm a woman of means."

"That so? Well, I'm afraid the unit is already spoken for."

Jenn nodded and pulled a second billfold from her coat. "By me?"

"Perhaps," he said, taking the money and counting. "Long as you're straight with me."

She mulled it over. "Diner over on Cemetery Blvd," she said.

"Ruth's place?" said Cy, the corners of his lips turning up. "What's she got you doing?"

"Waitressing. Some work as a life coach."

Cy chuckled, tucking the money in his back pocket. "Tell you what," he said. "I might have a vacancy coming up on trailer five by that old evergreen," he said, gesturing out the window. "Heat. Kitchenette. Top of the line."

"Sounds charming. Shall I have the bellhop bring my bags?"

"Well, I've got some questions about Ruth's place," said Cy. "You tell me what she's got on the menu, say, and I'll see about moving you on up."

He never raised his voice or corrected his stooped posture, but Cy seemed to grow darker in Jennifer's eyes. "No that's okay," she said. "I'll take the trailer at the edge of the property."

He sighed and grabbed a key from a peg by the wall. "Suit yourself," he said, handing her the key. "If it starts to feel tight in there, maybe you change your mind."

"I'm gonna leave this for you," said Jenn, setting down the train. "Since you and me are good friends now." She left hastily, but not before noticing a child's electric keyboard in a pile of junk by the door.

6
FINSTA

Like most kids her age, Colleen hated buses. Her lanky athletic frame no longer fit most middle school spaces, and though she possessed excellent powers of concentration, sitting still induced an anxiety that somewhere there was work she should be doing. She radiated a restless energy that served her well in volleyball, her coach observing that Colleen "had a knack for finding where the ball was about to be."

This particular trip seemed especially interminable. Twenty-nine AP Government students—and their sponsor, Mrs. Tenimen—were crawling down the farm-quilted corridor of I-65 towards Indianapolis, their trek slowed by wet, thick snowfall. The occasion was the Indiana High School Legislator Convention, a two-day collection of panels and simulated government exercises where students ran for office, drafted laws, and interviewed former state senators. The itinerary called for the group to check into the Crowne Plaza, change, then attend the opening ceremonies. But the weather rendered this agenda unlikely, and a twitchy frustration percolated all along the bus.

Colleen tried rehearsing her speech, but she found it hard to concentrate through the braying laughter of boys playing video games, and she cursed herself for leaving her air pods on her bedroom dresser. There was also the distraction of two girls sitting immediately behind her, scrolling through photos, offering commentary.

"Gross," laughed one. "Is that a dildo?"

Colleen was fairly certain they were looking at pictures of Mrs. Tenimen, among the 326 images released without commentary in the doxxing. Colleen had seen the picture in question—yes, it was a dildo—taken at a friend's bachelorette party. She had wondered if Mrs. Tenimen would address the issue when everyone boarded. But the teacher merely took attendance with her husky Wisconsin accent, not even looking up from her clipboard to make eye contact.

Colleen tried stretching her legs by leaning back the chair. "I wish they'd shut up," she muttered to Grace Chen, the girl seated next to her.

"Oh, just ignore them," said Grace, clicking a Snap notification. "Look at this from Vishant," she said, sharing the screen. "What do you think of him?"

There had been some question as to whether the trip, an annual affair, would be canceled in light of Mrs. Tenimen's humiliation. Colleen had always found the teacher funny, engaging, and winsome, her black corkscrew hair framing her face like curtains opened to a sunny day. Three years earlier, Mrs. Tenimen made a paper mache bust of Julius Caesar and invited her World History class to stab it with pencils. Last year, the teacher had commandeered the tour mic to lead the students in a spirited rendition of the *Mamma Mia!* soundtrack. Colleen had downloaded some songs from the sequel, but the longer the ride lasted, the less she expected a cabaret. She glanced at the enormous mirror the driver used to monitor passenger behavior. She could see Mrs. Tenimen, hood drooping over her eyes, lost in a podcast. The curtain had been drawn.

The girls behind her sounded like Daisy Duck and Minnie Mouse from *Mickey Mouse Clubhouse.* They were debating whether certain pictures required a filter or should be posted as is. "Whataya think?" asked Daisy.

"Oh, for sure," said Minnie. "Use the wacky mirror. Then it looks like she's peeing in the fridge."

"Ha ha ha!" laughed Daisy. "Oh my God, look at this one with the Euphoria filter! Ha ha ha!"

"Oh, she should totally post that one," said Minnie. "Makes her borderline fuckable."

The average length of a photo exposure was one-sixtieth of a second. That meant that less than five and a half seconds of Mrs. Tenimen's life had been included in the data dump. The girls talked about the pictures all the way to Indianapolis.

By the time they finally arrived, the opening ceremony was almost over. Mrs. Tenimen handed out room keys and instructed the kids to go straight to bed. She did not deliver her usual speech about the value of an engaged citizenry and the virtues of American democracy. She did not go over the rules. When 10:00 PM arrived, she did not perform a curfew check. That fact was noticed by several of the kids, who planned to meet in one of their rooms the following night and share a few handles of pilfered alcohol. "You should come," said Grace, penciling her eyebrows.

"No, I've got the speech," said Colleen.

The next morning, she was awakened at 4:30 by a text.

GRACE: lobby bathroom. bring my coat and jeans. pls hurry

Colleen found Grace huddled in a bathroom stall. She was missing her skirt and ponytail holder. There were black marks all over her forearms and thighs. Someone had written SLUT across her forehead in thick black marker. She was shaking but not crying.

"Did you bring your phone?" she asked.

"What happened?" asked Colleen.

Grace shook her head, digging absently at her scalp. "I don't know," she said. "I woke up on a luggage cart. Can you just… can you find out if there are pictures?"

It was a pointless request; they both already knew. "Let's get you cleaned up," Colleen said.

She found the discarded skirt and ran water over the vomit. She found a toothbrush and emptied the soap dispenser to work on the ink. The edges barely blurred. Someone had pressed hard.

"Oh my God," Grace said. "What if colleges see this?"

The soap wasn't working; they would need something stronger. "It's going to be okay," Colleen told her. "People forget."

7
BEAUMONT

Jono said, "There used to be more skaters at this park." It was mid-December, and the ground was now hard. He centered his feet on his board and rolled back and forth along the quarter-pipe, leaning and extending, building up enough speed until he crested the ridge and kick-turned. Beaumont snapped a few shots on his Minolta. The gray sky offered perfect lighting.

"Thing is," he continued, "They built this whole park in '96, maybe '97, as a sort of—what do you call a fancy cease fire?"

"Armistice," said Beaumont.

"Right, armistice," said Jono, attempting a drop from the top of the pipe. "I mean, you talk to the older guys, the 80s were like, the Wild West for the skate scene. The whole town was shred city. Every public stairwell. Every curb in town. They were a real menace."

One of the things Beaumont liked best about Jono was his appreciation of history. For his 16th birthday, they drove out to Winchester where the last Hollywood Video was closing and bought 12 VHS cassettes and a player for $10. Beaumont was fairly certain that he owned the Midwest's last copy of *Rad*, perhaps the greatest movie ever made about BMX racing. It did not exist on DVD or Netflix.

"Anyways, the city sunk maybe 30 grand into this park, set aside some money for maintenance. The deal was, the police stay out of Skate Town, and skaters keep clear of Clearwater. And for a while it worked out."

"What happened?"

He shrugged, tried a kickflip, and stumbled on the edge of his trucks. "Fuckin' X-Box, I guess," he said. "I mean, why take the skin off your knees if you can dark slide a triple kink while whackin' it in your basement? Tony Hawk, man. He saved skateboarding and ruined it."

Jono is indeed a dying breed, Beaumont thought. A few summers ago, a longboard fad seized the imaginations of Clearwater teens, and some stirring videos circulated of amateur combos. But appetites roamed elsewhere, and of late Jono would often find himself alone in the park, rolling back and forth for hours trying to master his craft.

Beaumont snapped a few more pictures of his warmups before turning the lens on the surrounding neighborhood. The open field and unincorporated road had been colonized by pre-fabbed homes and solar-powered streetlamps. The sidewalk was clean and the foliage well-groomed. Plenty of Wi-Fi access. In a few months, the park district would begin aerating the soccer field for youth league. It was safe out there. There were no rough edges for Jono to grind.

Clearwater High School was shaped like a shopping mall, with classrooms lining the interior and large auditoriums and athletic field houses balanced on the ends like department stores. Jono pulled his wood-panel station wagon into the senior lot, late as usual, and they filed silently through the art wing, joining the larger swell of bodies. It was Beaumont's favorite part of the commute—hurried as he was, he always slowed down to admire the student work showcased in the display cases.

That week, Mr. Lain had chosen 15 charcoal self-portraits from his Drawing 1 class. The technique was solid, but it was a largely uninspired lot. For the most part, it was a panel of pale faces—thin lips, straight hair, narrow noses, and toothy grins. There was nothing revelatory here; no suggestion of hidden depth or conflict. Just white folk, smiling.

They wound through the crowd, past the band rooms where a gaggle of White, Indian, and Asian kids were playing Coltrane, past the classroom where Ms. Ghents was prepping her marketing students for an upcoming DECA competition, past the editing bays where the tan girls with long, lean torsos were assembling their stories for Clearwater's weekly news program. Some of the freshmen were caught staring at Jono's mohawk, but two months in the shock had worn off, and by now he was just another studied pose. *Everybody's moving in this hallway*, thought Beaumont. *Everyone's got somewhere to be.*

As they made their way to the main rotunda, the principal's voice crackled over the intercom. "May I have your attention?" he said in a voice that hardly demanded it. "Please join us in the Commons for a spontaneous flash-mob performed by Clearwater's own Steppers Dance Team."

Jono's raised eyebrow elicited eye-rolling from his shorter friend. "We're late," Beaumont complained.

"We're always late," he said. They swim backwards through the crowds to the Commons.

The performance was already underway when they finally pushed through the throng. There were eleven members of the Steppers, a mixture of sophomores, juniors, and seniors under the supervision of

Mrs. Sathrypap, a guidance counselor. The Step Dance style is part cheer routine, part call and response, part tap dance, part hip hop. It is usually performed without music, with the dancers' hands and feet supplying the percussion. Against the hard tile of the Commons, even a crew as small as this could produce a stirring rhythm with a polished synchronicity.

"Ready!" shouted the captain, Jhanelle Boulley; her lieutenants answered with a stomp-stomp-clap, bringing their hands underneath their feet like an elaborate jump-rope routine. "Roll call!"

The crowd was impressively attentive, the circle several bodies deep, phones out and recording. Snap Stories were filling with content, and a few spectators were using Instagram or Facebook Live to expand the circle. Beaumont took a few frames with his Minolta before he ran out of film.

Stomp-stomp! Stomp-stomp-click! The lines moved back and forth, faces stoic in concentration. They began in unison, but as the routine unfolded, they layered different movements and rhythms on top of one another, a mosaic of syncopation and whip-smart movements. Beaumont had seen Step done with song, with exuberance, but this was a military operation executed with clinical precision. Still, the girls mixed in a hip thrust and suggestive hand gestures, and they grabbed hold of Jono's full attention.

"Mercy," he blinked. "Jhanelle is going to snap my dick off against my fly. You think she'd ever go for a handsome white man?"

"Maybe," said Beaumont. "You know any?"

Jono slapped the back of his friend's head playfully. They had started as comic book friends in sixth grade when Jono backed Beaumont's claim that Miles Morales was a worthy successor to Peter Parker as Spiderman. "Why don't you make yourself useful?" said Jono. "Hook up with that crew and introduce me."

Beaumont had already had a chance; Jhanelle approached him last year about joining. "I don't dance," he told her.

"You can learn," she said, smiling. "Anyway, it's not about the dancing. It's about taking pride in yourself. In *us*."

They're good, these kids, thought Beaumont, *certainly, better than they have any right to be*. Still, something felt off. A small crew of black students, stamping and sliding with mock defiance. A swarm of white bodies, ringing them like tourists, filling their phones with content they'd never appreciate or even consider. A pre-planned act of school-sanctioned spontaneity, as provocative and memorable as brushing one's teeth in the morning.

"Naw, man," Beaumont said. "Ain't my scene."

— — — — — — — — —

One month after the Cloudburst, and the chaos of discovery had settled into a tenuous truce of normalcy. Students and teachers remained on edge, and every day someone discovered a new nugget or detail that started a new fire—this week, for instance, there was talk of a student walkout of Ms. Okun's Orchestra class. There remained a great fear and expectation of further disclosures, whispers of a second batch of revelations, this time perhaps targeting students. But the suburbs are motivated, and any extended disruption of the great wheel of college acceptance threatened the very core of Clearwater, which meant that most families were warily acclimating to this strange new exposure. And the thing about TikTok feeds and Snap streaks is that they just keep *going*, churning through material, generating new images, different distractions, fresh memes. "You may sit in a class with a slammer like Ms. Watson," Jono had said, "just dreaming about seeing those perky little titties. But then the day comes where you can watch the video, get a few screencaps, and it's just sort of like, 'what else you got?'"

The teachers, Beaumont suspected, hadn't moved on quite so fast, and they had made themselves remote. When lunch came, they holed up in their classrooms or their offices or the lounge, and they shut the door. No more greeting kids in the hallways, no more showing up to student concerts or contests. Last week he had to email his math teacher about making up a test, and he got a four-word response, sans salutation or valediction. Just *"Meet me before class."*

That was why he hesitated outside Mrs. Moresoe's room after school. She was his freshman-year English teacher, a very chill presence in an otherwise manic season. Beaumont wouldn't have said he and Mrs. Moresoe were exactly close—he hadn't exerted much effort in class, and she wasn't the sort of buoyant extrovert that went out of her way to know her students. He intuitively understood that for Mrs. Moresoe—unlike chatty teachers like Mr. Waters—teaching was just a job. She clocked in at 7:10 A.M., clocked out at 4:30 P.M., and didn't think of Clearwater High School in the interim. He could respect that. *Hell*, thought Beaumont, *I envy that.*

But he had to do this. Senior year was a desperate flight from regret, and if he knew that if he didn't have this conversation, he would be forever looking back.

He knocked at her door and entered when he heard her summons. She was sitting behind her desk typing an email; when she recognized him, she shut her laptop. Mrs. Moresoe wore jeans and a denim top. She had pulled her cornflower-silk hair back into a pony tail to hide the flecks of gray. Her face was a bit puffy and lined about the mouth and eyes, though not, as he remembered, from expressiveness. Even though he hadn't spoken to her in three years, she betrayed neither shock nor pleasure at his entrance.

"Beaumont," she said. It did not surprise Beaumont that she remembered him; Clearwater's student body was less than 6% black.

"Mrs. Moresoe," he said.

"What can I do for you?" she asked. Her room was just as he remembered it: six rows of plastic desks, thirty in total. Plain white walls adorned with posters diagramming sentences, quoting Salinger, and tracing the Modernist movement. A poetry anthology was open on her desk, where she was grading a stack of essays.

"I…" and he paused, cursing himself for not anticipating such an obvious question. "I saw online that you used to be in a punk band."

She crossed her arms and leaned on them. Her posture suggested that she was armoring up, but her eyes betrayed no alarm. "That's true."

"The Mudskipperz."

"That was a long time ago."

"Yeah, but…" and he began to smile at the thought of this 45-year-old teacher thrashing across a stage. "They were kind of a big deal."

"We… we went on tour once with a bus," she said, her face not matching his smile. "I guess that's one way to measure 'big deals.' But we came home to Indiana in a rental van."

"No, I… I just had heard your last record from '97. Really good stuff."

"Thank you," she said, and the air thickened with awkward silence. "Is there something you wanted to ask me?" she finally said.

"Oh!" he said, and he unslung his backpack, rummaging in the rearmost pouch. He produced two cassette tapes, which he placed on the desk before her. She picked them up, then looked up at him warily.

"*Truth and Soul*," she said, sliding the Fishbone tape back to him. "*I Against I*," she continues, picking up the other cassette and reading the tracks. "I haven't… I haven't thought of these guys in years." She looked up at him, an eyebrow arching slightly. "You got a tape deck in that backpack of yours?"

He produced his father's Walkman; she plugged the adaptor into her laptop, and they listened to the title track, a dead-sprint power chord intro before the band downshifts tempo and Angelo Moore's vocals fall to a desperate, plaintive chanting of the chorus:

> *Oh let me tell you*
> *The same old story, no factual glory*

I against I against I against I
And I say I don't like it, and I know I don't want it
I against I against I against I
Almighty watching, almighty watching
I against I against I against I
And I say I don't like it, and I know I don't want it
I against I against I against I

She switched off the Walkman and examined him as though she were staring at a holy scripture in its original language. "Why did you bring me this?"

Here we go. "You were… you played lead guitar," he said.

"I did."

"I play a little, too," he said. "I would like you to teach me to play this. Please."

She leaned back, but to her credit she neither laughed nor condescended. "Don't they have YouTube videos for that?"

"There's a lot, but… it's not right," he said. "I don't know how to explain it. Something about punk that you can't paint-by-numbers."

"It's just three chords," she said. He stared at the floor sullenly; she filled the silence with a voice of sad detachment. "You always struck me as someone who was born too late, Beaumont," she said. "Like you showed up just as the band was packing up their equipment."

"They don't have to pack up," he said. "They could play one more song."

She drummed her fingers on the laptop cover. "You ever sit in your car waiting to turn left, watching the turn signals of the cars in front of you? Most of the time they're flashing out of sequence, askew. Every now and then, their blinking lines up. For just a few seconds, they're blinking in harmony."

"Oscillations," he said, recalling a lesson from Physics that used that example.

"So which is punk rock?" she asked. "The harmony? Or the askew?"

But he could already anticipate her argument. "I hear that all the time—Punk's not technical, punk's too sloppy. I don't agree. There are plenty of technical punks—Matt Freeman, Earl Hudson."

"No, no, you're right, Beaumont," she said. "But I wasn't talking about the music."

She's a damn tough read, he thought; he realized that her eyes reminded him of his cat's. "Are you… are you saying I'm not punk enough?"

Now she laughed. "No, Beaumont. *I'm* not punk enough. Look at me," she said, gesturing up and down her middle-aged frame. "That's all in the past. I'm blinking with everyone else now." She smiled at him, all lips, no teeth. "Where you going to school next year?"

"Purdue."

"What're you going to study?"

"Engineering."

She nodded. "A good choice. You'll do well," she said, handing him back the Walkman. "Engineers build bridges and roads. And punks?" she tapped the tape deck. "They burn them down."

— — — — — — — — —

Beaumont's mother had loved Shakespeare. Four years ago, his father surprised her with three tickets to *Julius Caesar* performed at the White River State Park. It was agony for the two of them, but she was thrilled, so they put on their best *"Mmm, this meatloaf sure is delicious!"* faces. Midway through the play, Antony incites a riot among the Romans, who turn murderous against the conspirators. The mob is depicted hunting down a senator named Cinna, instead cornering a minor poet who shares his name. "I'm Cinna the poet!" the unlucky man yells. It does not matter. They kill him.

"Cinna the poet!" said Beaumont's dad on the ride home.

"Motherfucking Cinna the poet!" He so rarely swore, and he remembered his mother putting her hand on her husband's leg to calm him.

"You remember that, boy," he said to his son, glaring through the rearview mirror. "When they come for you, they won't care that you're the poet. All they'll see is the simplest thing."

Beaumont knew that his father still thought about Cinna the poet. A month ago, Beaumont had made the mistake of telling him about a comment one of the white boys at lunch said to his back while he was waiting in line for Bosco Sticks. "Need to build a wall around Eastside!" hooted the white boy, referring to one of Indianapolis' poorest and most dangerous neighborhoods. "Am I right?"

What scared Beaumont's father was that a few years earlier, those boys would have kept those comments in their basement. But they were growing bolder, testing him like a pack that was slowly closing in on a buck. Beaumont had shrugged it off. His father, on the other hand, tightened the reigns.

"I'm picking you up from school from now on," he told him over dinner. "4:30 P.M. By the flagpole. No arguments."

So it was, every day. They mostly rode in silence. They did not agree on the radio. Beaumont did not share his father's enthusiasms for sports. The older man could not stand that his son had dyed his hair blue. After three weeks of this, all the father-son time is wearing on them both.

"You don't have to do this, Dad," said Beaumont. "Pick me up. I can get a ride with Jono."

"Ain't no trouble," he said.

"No trouble," Beaumont scoffed. "Don't you have work? Numbers to balance?"

"I meet with my team at lunch," he said. "Get the work done then."

Once, eight years ago, Pops wasted a half-hour doing nothing, Beaumont though wryly. *He still regrets it*. He decided to shift tactics. "Your team still the same?"

"Mmm-hmm."

"Mr. Carver? Mr. Wright? What's the name of the one that looks like a walrus?"

"Majors," he said.

"Right, right. Majors," said Beaumont. "And Ms. Evans? The one who looks like the sister from *Justified*?"

"Her, too," he said. Beaumont looked at his father's hands. They grip the steering wheel tightly.

"You have lunch with Ms. Evans *every day*?" he asked. "That's real nice of her. It is "Ms.", ain't it Pop?"

"Far as I know."

"You ever think she might like something more than lunch?" he asked. "Maybe dinner sometime?"

He pulled the car over to the side of the road. They were in a quiet subdivision a mile from home. His father watched a woman wrapped in a puffy Northface coat, walking her dog.

"You weren't there, so I'll forgive you forgetting," he said plainly. "But I remember. The words were, 'Til death do you part.'"

"Yeah, but Dad—"

"I look dead to you?" He held his son's gaze until the boy dropped eyes. Then he shifted the car back into drive and piloted them home.

His father still set a place at the table for her. He had a final voice message on his phone that he refused to listen to. He would not cancel the subscription to *People Magazine*. He accused Beaumont of being too in love with nostalgia, and Beaumont supposed he would know. He thought of Outkast, singing "Forever. *Forever*? Forever ever. *Forever ever*?" *But Andre 3000 was just clowning*, thought Beaumont. *My father doesn't joke.*

— — — — — — — — —

A few days later Dale Bautista handed Beaumont a flier in their journalism class.

"Where'd you get this?" Beaumont asked. It was an old-school black-and-white concert handbill featuring a skeleton in a toga performing some sort of sex act on a man who appeared to be the governor of Indiana.

Dale pointed to the band listing. "Never mind where I got it," he said. "Look who's opening." He kept his voice low and conspiratorial. They were supposed to be working on the layout for the sports page of the November edition of The Talon.

The headliner was some band called Atari Shitburger; the opening bands included Coke Bottle Contraceptive and Three-Ball Coin Purse. None of this meant anything to Beaumont. "I've never heard of any of these guys," he said.

Dale rolled his eyes. "That's because you haven't heard any music from the 21st Century," he explained. There was perhaps some truth to that; on the spectrum of hipsters, Beaumont drifted backwards in time, while Dale craved the novelty of the new and *avant garde*. "First of all, Atari Shitburger is pretty good if you like hip-hop fusion punk—"

"I don't," said Beaumont.

"—but the fossil find is this group," he continued, pointing to Three Ball Coin Purse. "Heard of them?"

"Can we skip ahead a few slides?" said Beaumont.

"It's the Mudskipperz," he said. "Or, what's left of them. I started seeing videos on Snapchat—they've been popping up in clubs around the Midwest. 'Course, it's not the original lineup, but it's Robert Nukem and Jean-Pierre Doppelgänger for sure. And maybe Mrs. Moresoe!"

"You're kidding," frowned Beaumont. She had not mentioned any sort of reunion.

"You want to check it out?"

Beaumont turned back to the computer screen and resized a picture of the Wrestling Team. "Hell yeah," he said.

Beaumont felt that convincing his father was like changing the weather's mind. "Absolutely not," he said. "This is not going to happen."

"Dad, come on!" said Beaumont. "You know I'll be careful!"

"Oh, well, if you're *careful*," he said. "Here I thought you were going to be freebasing coke off a cop's leg, but since you're going to be *careful* about it…"

Beaumont understood that his only hope was to play the trust card. "Dad," he said, "I'm going to be on my own in five months. How'm I s'pposed to be ready for that if I haven't practiced?"

"Watch a YouTube tutorial," he said stubbornly. "Ain't that what you kids do?"

"Us kids don't ask. We just do," Beaumont remind him. "But I'm asking, Pop. This time."

His father breathed through his nose for a few moments, considering his options. "Dale gonna be there?"

"And Jono," said Beaumont.

"That don't make me feel better," he said. "Any fool that takes a nail gun to his own face hasn't got the sense to keep his tongue out of a mousetrap."

But he relented, letting his son borrow the car for the evening. "Back in this garage at midnight, or else you're not going to college until you qualify for a senior discount," he said.

On the ride there, Dale played songs from the headliner off of a Spotify playlist. They were slippery, these Atari Shitburgers—just when Beaumont thought they were aping the Misfits, they slipped into Gaslight Anthem, and then all of a sudden, it's Op Ivy and The

Toasters. But that was just the music—the lyrics were mostly speed rapped, and sloppily.

"I… I don't know what I'm listening to," he said.

"It's like 80s punk and 90s ska and Busta Rhymes are having an orgy," said Jono. "But they're doing it wrong."

"You guys don't even know," said Dale. "This is the future of punk. Still DIY, just DIY-ier."

Beaumont joked that they had spent as much time getting ready as a girl on the night of her Quinceanera. Jono's mohawk was meticulously coiffed and fanned out like a peacock's tail, and Dale's denim Black Flag jacket was held together by safety pins. Beaumont wore a leather coat, a kilt, and the baddest M-Fer boots this side of D.H. Peligro. They wore rings, collars, and earrings; Jono, true to form, had a fresh nose stud.

The venue was an abandoned barn just outside of Cloverdale. Someone had run a ton of power to the space; there were floodlamps and space heaters set up, and they could hear the rumble of generators even over the whine of sound tests.

Punks were pouring in from all directions, like ants returning to the colony. They came in pick-up trucks and jalopies, old rust-eaten Buicks and discontinued Saturns. Despite the nip of January, their torsos were often sleeveless and shredded, white patches of skin checkering the holes of sweat stained black tees. They showed off tattoos that spiderwebbed over every fold and expanse of skin, snaking around their necks, up and down their biceps, into the underground passages beneath their waistline.

They were not the only teens in attendance, but Beaumont was certain he was the only black kid. While not unaware of the subtle ways his skin affects a public space, he was still a bit unnerved by how long their glances lingered on him as they made their way past the Greek column of a bouncer collecting cover at the mouth of the barn. Dale was a light-skinned Filipino, and Beaumont wondered if he felt it, too. But Dale's hair was straight, his pores smaller, and his nose fuller—with the right story about an autumn tan, he may have even enjoyed passing privilege.

A makeshift stage had been assembled from hay bales and shipping pallets, and the opening band was just finishing their sound check when the trio finally get a good look at them. "Jesus, look at those dinosaurs," laughed Jono. "That's gotta be the Mudskipperz, right?"

Beaumont squinted—there were three of them: a drummer, a bassist, and guitarist. All middle-aged men. No Mrs. Moresoe in sight.

"These guys, I saw 'em in Michigan City," said a squat little punk with a shaved head and ginger goatee. "They do a lot of Bad Religion; some Buzz Cock covers. They're a'ight. Six songs in, like, 20 minutes. But you gotta stick around for the finale."

"What happens then?" Beaumont asked.

"Oh, man—you've just gotta see it," he laughed, taking a hit from his vaporizer.

When the sound check was over, the band almost immediately took their positions. The drummer stripped off his hooded sweatshirt, the outline of his ribs pressed against pale, clammy skin. He twirled his sticks in twitchy anticipation as the bassist adjusted something with the foot pedal. The guitarist, a goblin with the physique of an oil drum and a shock of bottle-blonde spikes like Guy Fieri, sidled up the mic.

"S'up cunts," he said. "We're Three-Ball Coin Purse. Reports of our death are only mildly exaggerated. But we've got one round left in the old chamber, eh?" He turned to the bassist and nodded before swiveling back and shouting. "ONETWOTHREEFOURONETWO-THREEFOUR!"

And like that, they were off. They played "Henchmen" by Bad Religion, "I'm Not Interested" by Husker Du, and a few songs Beaumont couldn't recognize or decipher. The equipment quality was poor, and the acoustics of an open barn were not quite an ideal soundscape for a listening event. But it didn't matter. The drummer's arms blurred like a propeller, and the bassist picked up and down his fret as though he was cocking and discharging a shotgun. The singer's face was the color of a ripe beet, and he alternated between squeezing his eyes shut and bugging them like Henry Rollins. They were punk as fuck.

The audience responded accordingly—a scrum formed almost immediately in front of the stage. Bodies whipped around, churning and colliding. Jono whooped and disappeared when the tempos shifted and the singer barked "DON'T BE A HENCHMAN!" The mohawked teen emerged only occasionally, as a sperm whale might for air. Beaumont held back to capture the scene. He had left his Minolta in the car, but the aperture of memory was wide open. A bottle smashed against the wall, and he could feel something inside him break loose with joy.

But then the guitars slid from something by Vandal into the hooks from "Pay to Cum," and he could hold back no longer. He launched myself into the melee, dropping his shoulder and ramming a middle-aged punk, rebounding into another body, then another and another. His whole life was about restraint, about keeping his torso and demeanor in placid equilibrium even as his emotions roiled and the backbeat of his spirit thrashed against the confines of its cell. In this human grinder he felt as movement without thought, action without hesitation, motion without regret. Beaumont was finally free.

Something was off, however. The rhythm of random encounter sputtered, and he could feel rough hands shoving him from behind, pushing him towards the edges of the fray. Too late, he realized that he was being sought out and targeted. Something hard struck the back of his head, and he staggered.

There were boots suddenly—hard, sharp shots to his shins, and when he recoiled, he only moved into body blows that dragged him back to the center. There were indistinct faces, shapes, and furtive lunges. He called out for his friends, but the music and shouting drowned it out. *I have to stay on my feet,* he thought, *or I am done for.*

There was a crash, and the violent splinter of glass, and one of his assailers reached to the back of his head and pulled it back, red and liquid. The crowd of four or five goons suddenly grew distinct, only to evaporate like smoke. Beaumont felt his face, tender and throbbing, and suddenly realized that the music has stopped. A muscled figure stood before him, panting and holding the shattered hilt of a bottle. It was the lead singer of Three-Ball Coin Purse.

———————————

"Christ, kid," said Robert. "Maybe you were pretty before, but you're going to be a character actor from here on out."

"Punk for life," nodded Jean-Pierre, sipping his coffee.

They were at a Denny's just off of I-70. Beaumont held a Ziploc bag of ice against his face. Jono and Dale were eating their pancakes in huge, wolfish bites.

Robert Putnem was the guitarist and vocalist, a mound of doughy flesh and hair. In the harsh light of the diner, Beaumont judged his age at just under 50, but he was squat and tough like an armadillo. Jean-Pierre was the drummer, a lean and delicate physical contrast. He had ordered an egg-white omelet that he sent back to the kitchen to be remade. The bassist was Phillip Cush. He worked for Hewlett-Packard. "I'm just filling in for a few months," he said.

"So you're Linda's kids," said Robert, grinning. "Goes by Moresoe now, right? Can you believe this, Jean?"

"Unreal," said the drummer.

"How is the old slit?" asked Robert. "God, I miss her. What a pair of tits."

"A much better guitarist than we've got now," sipped Jean-Pierre.

"Fair enough, fair enough," nodded Robert. "But she had her chance, didn't' she? I tell you what she said when I ringed her up, didn't' I?"

"Soccer practice," said Jean-Pierre.

"Motherfucker can't work around her kid's soccer practice! Can you believe that? What's happened to us?"

"It's punk rock, Robby," said Jean-Pierre, snatching a cigarette out of Phillip's mouth before he could light up. "You either die or you buy the minivan."

"Fuck that, right?" laughed the singer. "Tell you what, kid, I'm sorry that you got your ass kicked like that, but I'm not sorry, not really. Been a long time since I been down in the scrum."

"You're welcome," said Beaumont.

"I can't believe I'm eating with the Mudskipperz," gushed Dale, and Jono nodded enthusiastically. "I mean… you guys are legends!"

Jean-Pierre raised a skeptical eyebrow at that. "Seeing shit and doing them are too different things, son. Those that lose track are old fools."

"Nah, we can own that, Jeanny!" laughed Robert. "We've lived like gods at the feast of mortals, boy! Mixed it up with Dexter Holland and the boys at Echoplex. Saw Brett Guerwitz kill a man with a guitar in Radio Flats!"

"Didn't kill him," Jean-Pierre corrected. "Broke his eye socket is all."

"Well, it was a legendary spot of violence, is what I'm saying," said Robert. "So what'd you boys think?" he asked, pointing a fork at the three of them, wedged in the booth.

It was a question Beaumont was not even sure how to answer. On the one hand, his whole body hurt, and he knew that it would be worse in the morning. He had been around casual racism his whole life, suspicion and condescension wrapped in every suburban greeting or helpful teacher. He had never seen it—felt it—unrestrained. Something rough had slipped the leash in those boys, and he had almost lost himself to it. On the other hand, it was strangely refreshing to see the thing between them naked and raw. And if he was being truly honest, it felt good to hit back. But there in this diner, Beaumont was once again the picture of restraint.

"Well, I didn't get to see very much of it," he said wearily. "But for 20 minutes, you guys thrashed."

"Best concert of my life," gushed Jono.

Jean-Pierre's face was bland and impassive, but Robert visibly swelled to the praise. "That's right, that's right," he said between rough bites of sausage. "What'd I tell you, Jeanny? Punk rock will never die!"

"Right, right," said Jean-Pierre wearily.

"It's not dead," said Dale. "Look, I know it's not like it was back in your day, but there're still punk scenes. The sound is evolving. The movement is transitioning."

Jean-Pierre finished his cup, then motioned to the waitress for a refill. "You seem like a nice enough kid, and certainly a foot smarter than I was when we were hustling for our first gig. But don't fucking lecture me on punk rock. You've been here for 15 minutes."

Dale physically jerked back at that; Jono looked away. But Beaumont stared straight ahead at the lanky, long-armed drummer as he mixed in his cream and sugar.

"Where'd you get that jacket?" asked Jean-Pierre, his voice tired and raspy. "Where'd you learn to style that mohawk? E-Bay? You-Tube? Thirty years ago, you dress like that, it scares people. Now it's just another brand at Hot Topic."

"I like my mohawk," said Jono. "What?" he said when Dale whacked his arm. "What? I just like it!"

"Don't mind Jeanny-boy here; he's just an old grouch," said Robert. "The cream in his nutsack curdled a few years back, and now it hurts him to whack off."

"Who're *you* to say what's punk?" Beaumont said evenly. He was surprised by the sharpness of his retort, but the pain in his face made him bold. "I thought punk was about questioning authority. I thought it was about *Never Mind the Bullocks* and all that shit."

That clearly amused Robert, who chuckled and slapped Jean-Pierre across the shoulder. The drummer eyed Beaumont with bemusement, perhaps unsure how to explain a black kid with blue hair and a kilt. "Those men who beat you tonight, they weren't standing up to authority. They saw a little black boy and an excuse to do their evil," he said. "All the energy, all the anger ginned up by the music. Against Reagan, Wall Street, fucking yuppies and paranoid neo-cons. It never went anywhere. Wasn't supposed to go anywhere, I suppose. Punk's a flat circle, boys. An ouroboros." He lit the cigarette he swiped from his bassist and breathed a long, thin stream. "The snake that swallowed its tail."

"Did you ever hear the story of when our van broke down between Chattanooga and Murfreesboro?" said Robert. "This is fucking famous. The middle of a driving rain storm, and so we have to push it to the side of the road. And we sleep under the van! Better that than get the equipment wet!"

"Robert," said Jean-Pierre. "Shut the fuck up."

The waitress came over to ask him to put out his cigarette. Jean-Pierre extinguished it in his cup of coffee.

— — — — — — — — —

Beaumont's father was up waiting for Beaumont when he pulled in. The old man was volcanic when he saw his son's face.

"Son," he said after the explanations. "I'm glad those white boys didn't kill you. That's the only pleasure I've got left."

"It just happened," Beaumont said, staring at the scuffed tiles of their kitchen floor. "Wasn't my fault."

His father shook his head. "You chose to go there, didn't you? Dressed like Nazi-bait? I don't want to hear it. We going finish this talk in the morning."

"Dad—"

"I'm too disappointed to punish you now," he said, and he climbed the stairs, muttering something about Cinna the poet.

His swollen face and bloodshot eye brought him looks in the hallway on Monday, and he marched proudly past a table swarming with lacrosse players in the lunchroom. *Let them look, get an eyeful of the beaten punk.* Beaumont was sullen all day, snapping at Crystal, the sweet cello player who was copy-editing his column on athletic trainers. Beaumont regretted the look on her face, but not the release of emotion.

A dean's assistant delivered a pass to him late in the day. It was from Mrs. Moresoe, summoning him to her classroom after school. He was in no mood for another lecture, but he was curious enough to honor the invitation.

She was again lodged behind her desk, a look of kindness and curiosity lining her face. "I heard you ran into some of my old friends," she said, motioning for him to sit.

"Yeah," he said, easing into the chair. His whole body was stiff and sore. "Yeah, they sort of saved my life."

"Tell me about it," she said, and Beaumont recounted the whole story. She asked a lot of questions about Robert and Jean-Pierre—what did they say, how did they look, what were they doing now? Her face was warmer and more open than Beaumont supposed he had ever seen.

"They haven't changed," she smiled, looking up at the line where the ceiling abutted the wall. "God, but they're still little boys playing Black Flag."

"They sounded more like Pennywise," he said.

"You know, I loved them both," she said. "Ronny, too," she said of the absent Mudskipperz bassist. "For a little while there, we were all in love with each other. It was such a heady time. They saved me, too."

"What happened?"

"Oh, the same thing that always happens," she said. "We got tired. I did, anyways. Punk rock feels great at first, rebelling against the president and the CEOs and your parents. But after a while, you realize it's also rebelling against everything. Piano lessons. Vaccinations. Savings accounts. I met a boy. He got a job. And that was that."

"Jean-Pierre said punk's dead."

She nodded. "Well, Jean-Pierre is a wounded idealist," she said. "Probably gave you the speech about how it's just recycling the same Rancid shtick. More nostalgia. More reboots. An unkillable brand, just like those wretched *Transformers* movies. That sound about right?"

He nodded.

"So the opinion that really matters in this room is yours, Beaumont," she smiled at him. "What do you think? Is punk dead?"

He took a long time before replying. "That depends," he said, meeting her eyes. "Will you teach me?"

8

SWORDS

Evan Remoras was the last file for the day. When he had been an English teacher, Bryan Yulders would sometimes place his best students' work on the bottom of the pile so he would grade them last. After fighting through the bramble of indifferent syntax and wrongheaded analysis, a simple, erudite essay on *The Great Gatsby* or Hemingway's short stories could do much to restore Yulders' faith in public education.

Now that he was dean of students, Bryan appreciated an easy case even more. Since the cloudburst, Bryan had struggled to navigate disciplinary challenges invited by the doxxing of the faculty. How do you hold a student accountable for plagiarism, for instance, when it's revealed that the baccalaureate speech delivered by his social studies teacher lifted entire sections from the 2007 Harvard faculty address? How can you punish five hockey players for drinking at a house party when the background on their iPhones is now a picture of their coach passed out in a wading pool?

But Evan Remoras was easy. He hit four kids. Broke one of their noses. This was not his first time in Yulders' office; the two had developed a grudging respect for one another. Hell, on some level, Bryan *liked* the kid. Evan was a thug and a loose cannon and a dangerous element. But he never lied about it.

He called Evan out of the waiting area; the big senior shambled in and slung himself into the chair across from Bryan. Yulders wordlessly offered him a stick of gum, which Evan wordlessly accepted. Bryan put on his reading glasses and examined the file.

"What'd you do this time, Evan?" he asked.

"What's it say?" said Evan.

"Says you started a fight in the cafeteria with two sophomores and two juniors."

Evan nodded. "That's right."

Bryan closed the folder. "Here's what I heard. I heard that you didn't even know these kids, had never talked to them before. I heard that they were just minding their business, and you walked up, knocked a phone out of one of their hands, and started swinging."

Evan tossed his head back and forth lazily as he considered this account. "More or less," he agreed.

"Evan," said Bryan. "You've been in that chair for vandalism, theft, and even arson. But you've always given me a reason."

Evan worked his gum, scratching his chin. "You want a reason?"

"Please."

Evan exhaled through his nose. "Okay," he said finally. "You know that video of Mr. Wurtz that's going around? The one where he's doing all the fights from *Game of Thrones* with a mop?"

Bryan nodded. "I've seen it," he said. Even amidst the bevy of humiliations, poor Sam Wurtz's had been particularly acute. The leak featured a three-minute video where he expertly mimics the sword choreography in exquisite detail. That video had since been reposted backed by a Hans Zimmer film score and viewed thousands more times.

"So they were watching it," said Evan. "And they were laughing. And they were doing the moves, too, you know, like, in a mocking way."

"And you decided you needed to stick up for Mr. Wurtz."

Evan smiled out of the corner of his mouth. "Naw, naw, it ain't like that." He looked around Bryan's office, then gestured at a lacrosse stick resting on top of a file cabinet. "May I?" he asked.

"Go ahead."

Evan held the stick in his right hand like a Louisville slugger, testing its weight with a few lazy one-handed swings. He then gripped the stick with two hands, bringing the pocket close to his face, obscuring his eyes with the shooting string.

"So they were doing the moves like this," he said, swinging the stick with long, broad motions. "And this. And this." He waved the stick like he might shake a scarecrow.

"So?"

"So it's like this," said Evan, bringing his hands up so they brushed his ears. His posture was suddenly straight as a lamppost, his body taut yet still. "And this." He stepped forward, bringing the stick down in a quick, powerful, and precise downswing. "And this." He stepped back, rotating his grip so that the stick swept up and across his body as though to block an assault. And just as suddenly, Evan relaxed his posture and tossed the stick to Bryan, who caught it midair with an old goaltender's reflexes.

"I mean, I don't know Mr. Wurtz," grinned Evan, plopping back into his chair. "But the man had the moves right. I mean, if you're going to do the moves, then fucking *do* 'em."

9

ELSIE

Six weeks earlier, a group of kids walked into the CVS where Elsie Raccione worked and stole $130 worth of cosmetics and cough syrup. The short one—maybe 13, wearing a Colts knit cap—peppered Elsie with questions at her cashier's station while his partners pocketed the merchandise. Elsie was vaguely aware a con was afoot, and she had little patience for middle schoolers. But her natural diffidence kept her from calling a manager, and afterwards she and the other employees were punished with training modules on shoplifting. "From now on, no unsupervised minors after 8," said Adam Gouth, her manager. "You can't trust kids anymore."

Elsie swallowed the hypocrisy. Roughly two-thirds of the pharmacy's workforce—herself included—were currently enrolled in high school. She was also aware of the statistics suggesting that most shoplifting was done by people over the age of 25 during daylight hours. But mostly, Elsie felt humiliated that she, the person tasked with policing this new law, weighed 95 pounds and believed her voice was closest in pitch to a kazoo.

"Where are your parents?" she asked a pair of twins whose age she cannot determine. They had faces like Shia LeBeouf—doughy Midwestern vacancies. They could have been anywhere between 13 and 25, staring at her, the one on the right chewing gum like a goat, his brother broadly smiling. "Your parents," Elsie repeated. "You can't be in here without them."

Elsie couldn't tell if they were fucking with her; she couldn't tell if they spoke English, were performance artists, or had bellybuttons. They just kept staring. She grabbed the walkie-talkie next to the register and radioed Gouth, currently ensconced in his office.

"Handle it yourself," he said. "I'm busy."

Elsie radioed again; this time, Cooper picked up.

"What?" she said.

Elsie closed her eyes. "I need a manager up front."

Cooper sighed; the radio dissolved into static. Elsie heard Cooper's black shoes clickclackclickclack against the store tiles as she snaked towards the front. "What's all this?" she asked. Cooper was five months older than Elsie, but she carried herself like she was born in a gunfighter's saloon. Long black hair teased up in a bun; thick mascara; a copper-colored nose ring threaded through her left nostril, which, Elsie noted, was against store policy. Her shirt was misbuttoned, a detail that had shifted since she clocked in earlier in the evening. She pointed a long purple nail at the twins. Elsie shrugged; "No parents," she said.

"Out!" she said. "Back to whatever Ouija Board conjured you!'

"We ain't doin' nothin'!" said the one on the left. Cooper whipped out her phone.

"You can do nothing in the parking lot or in the intersection just as well," she said, her eyes wide and unblinking. "I'm authorized to taze the both of you if you don't scurry back down your hole with the rest of the unformed rat babies."

"Yo, that's not a Taser; that's an iPhone!" said the one on the right.

Cooper pressed the home button; the phone crackled and flashed like the genuine article. "That sound like I'm downloading Lil' Yachty to you?"

The one on the right took a step back; she advanced on them and hit the button again. This time they turned and ran. Cooper looked at Elsie and tossed her the phone.

"Thought I told you to download the app for this," said Cooper, foisting herself on the counter and picking up the Sudoku puzzle Elsie had been working on.

"I did," said Elsie. "Doesn't mean I'm going to use it on customers."

"There's no crime in scaring up the stupid," Cooper said. "That's actually my campaign slogan."

They first met in grade school. Elsie had been a frizzy-haired hobbit with a too-big-for-the-bus art portfolio. Cooper wore a green plaid jumper and brown shoes, even though all the girls at that age wore tight jeans and black Lugs. And a white buttoned shirt; Cooper always wore a buttoned shirt. Like now, although Elsie's eye kept drifting to the pink skin peeking out of the misaligned plackets running down her torso.

"What're you and Gouth doing back there?" Elsie asked.

"What?" Cooper said, looking up from the puzzle.

"Back there. In the office."

Cooper looked back towards the rear of the store, then up to the security camera secure above the register. "Oh, you know," she said. "He was playing some song for me by that band he likes. The Wombats."

"What song?" Elsie asked.

"Um… 'Enemy Lines.'"

People always underestimated Elsie. Maybe it was because she was short; maybe because she was quiet. The world tends to reward the tall and flamboyant, particularly when they're armed with faux-Tasers. But being an introvert had its advantages—Elsie was always paying attention, and she retained information that others might let slip. She knew every song by The Wombats, and every song by the Pigeon Detectives, too, the band who actually sings the song "Enemy Lines." *So, either Amy Cooper doesn't know shit about the music she claims to rep,* thought Elsie, *or she really doesn't want to talk about why her shirt is misbuttoned.*

━ ━ ━ ━ ━ ━ ━ ━ ━

They closed at midnight, and the rest of the gang met them on their way out. They all piled in Elsie's little Honda—herself, Cooper, Denver, Yael, and Dale. Yael drove, which was fine with Elsie—she never liked driving at night, and it was Yael's father's lodge they were heading towards. Besides, it let Elsie sit in the back—wedged between Cooper and Dale—and when Yael hit the left turns, Elsie got to lean into Dale.

Tall Dale. He of broad shoulders, beautiful coffee skin and hair so black it almost glowed purple. He let Elsie share an earbud, listening to a new band, the Squirrel Knots. They sounded a lot like Dispatch Oasis, but he insisted that there's more going on.

"Listen," he said. "Are you hearing that?"

"Yeah," Elsie said. "Her vocals, they're amazing."

He shook his head. "No, not the vocals. Listen how long they hold off the drums. Much longer than you'd expect. They're very deliberate in their layering."

Elsie nodded; Cooper offered a half smile to go along with her *I cannot believe this fucking hipster* eyebrows. But Dale was right. There was no rhythm; just the sound of voices first, then a single guitar, then another. Elsie smiled. *Leave it to Dale to hear the silences that other people miss.*

It was a complicated group. Together for so many years, yet still waiting on one another. Dale was waiting on stringy, curly Yael, who only seemed to come alive when she was around Denver, whose huge hairy forearms and patchy teenage beard was the star of her erotic rap lyrics. Denver was waiting on Cooper, who he used to hook up with before she started messing around with Gouth. Elsie was waiting on Dale. They all know this about one another. It was like Pangea—they were held together by mutual pressure, and if anyone were to shift, the continents would fly apart.

When Elsie was 14, the only thing she wanted in the world was for a boy to kiss her. Any boy, really. To be wanted, pursued, held, desired—that was everything. She watched episodes of *Austin and Ally* until she could recite every line, talking herself into a romance with Dez since she would never have a shot with Austin. Elsie read One Direction fanfiction (and tried her hand at writing some); she would put on her headphones and play Moonface while dreaming of Bradley Steven Perry until sleep would take her and she would dissolve into his liquid embrace. She was so lonely; Elsie suspected that if she had Cooper's confidence and breasts, she would have gotten herself in a lot of trouble.

But she had neither. She had big eyes and a long, hollow face that made her look like "The Scream" if she got too emphatic. She had thick, nappy hair that she dyed first pink, then purple, now silver—that always looked like cotton candy. And she had her art, which, she realized, had saved her. No one came for her. No one picked her. So Elsie picked painting, and for the first time in fifteen years, there was something about herself she loved.

She felt different now with Dale because she was no longer a starving animal ready to fall upon any hunk of meat, however odious or spoiled. She didn't need him. But she wanted his off-center smile, and she was willing to wait for him. He was smart without needing an audience; he was kind without being a pushover. Elsie thought she could sense him gravitating towards her—*he could have had the front seat, Denver would have loved to sit back here with Cooper*. But he wanted to play Squirrel Knots for Elsie. And she wanted to listen.

Yael's father worked for an insurance company, which she said stressed him out. He bought a hunting lodge two years ago adjacent to Turkey Run State Park so that he could go off every couple of weeks to exorcise his murderous rage on the local waterfowl. It occurred to Elsie that all their parents had sordid outlets—Dale's dad owned three jet skis; Cooper's mom did more Yoga than a block of Hollywood starlets; and Elsie's father had affairs. None of them objected to the teenagers staying over at the lodge; its remoteness from civilization placated their concerns about the dangers of underage drinking. The only downside was that it offered lousy cell phone coverage and lacked Wi-Fi, which meant that Denver and Yael would be insufferable until the wine started to work.

"God, I hate Sprint," said Yael, tapping at her phone as though doing so would somehow resuscitate it. "I got no bars. I had to send out a whole bunch of pictures this afternoon just to keep my Snap-streaks alive."

"Oh yeah, thanks for the picture of your ceiling fan," said Denver. He moved through the cabin with his usual lack of concern for other people's space, his arms swinging like loose ropes. For some reason, his shirt was off. He had located Yael's father's gun safe (unlocked) and was loading one of the rifles. Elsie hated when he did that.

Dale had a playlist going—top 40 for the rest of the group—and was leaning against a window pane staring out into the darkness. Elsie loved how black it got in the woods. Even with some snow on the ground, the darkness was total, and she felt like the hunting lodge had been swallowed by some immeasurable giant, and the five of them were slowly drifting through his digestive track, waiting to dissolve into one another.

They talked about the data dump, about the lives of their teachers, about how humiliated they must be, and how well-deserved was that humiliation. Denver reserved particular animus for Mrs. Sawyer ("That goddamned bitch," he yelled. "I hope she never sees her son again!"); Dale couldn't believe that Mrs. Moresoe used to play guitar with The Mudskipperz ("I mean, I knew she played, or was into some scene or whatever, but DAMN! They opened for NOFX!"). Elsie wanted to bring up her art teacher—Mr. Lain, whose only data was a set of mysterious numbers (Example: 41.911284/-87.76099), but she never found a conversational on-ramp, and the moment passed.

After a while, the wine made her sleepy, and she watched from the couch while Cooper danced on the counter like she saw in an old movie and Denver shot off rounds into the darkness. "What are you aiming at?" Elsie asked.

"I'm not aiming," he said. "Just shooting."

Dale was talking to Yael, who had her head on his lap but was staring at the space heater, and Elsie could tell that Yael was about to cry for reasons that none of them understood. But Dale was oblivious, just happy to have all that shiny golden hair cascading off his lap. He smiled at Elsie, and she hoped that it was the last thing she saw before passing out so that the night wouldn't be a total disappointment.

She roused everyone and drove the group home in silence early the next morning. They all had work, and she didn't want to catch too much of a lecture from her father. But he was still asleep when she slipped in at 7:30 A.M. His girlfriend Vivian was up, however, and it seemed to Elsie that the mistress had taken every article of food out on the counter just to fry up some eggs.

"Hey," said Vivian as Elsie walked in and hung her keys on the hook by the door. "Want an omelet?"

Elsie first knew Vivian as Dr. Partking, her pediatrician; it was only recently that she'd begun sleeping over. It made Elsie's life very complicated, partly because she was complicit in the arrangement. For months, she'd wondered why her father cheated and why she allowed him to skate. As near as she could tell, her mother—a regional rep for an epoxy company—was completely oblivious. They had not slept in the same bed for three years. Her father started seeing Vivian a year and a half ago and promised to pay Elsie's car insurance until she was out of college. Elsie felt some guilt at accepting so paltry a bribe, and she might have acted on that feeling if her relationship with her mother was better.

The other problem with Vivian was her relentless charm offensive. Yet Elsie could see no way around her, so she sat at the counter and poured herself a glass of milk, leaving her sunglasses to shield her eyes.

"So, where you coming from?" Vivian asked while sprinkling some cheese.

"Um… Cooper's house," said Elsie.

"Not the lodge?" Vivian asked; Elsie shook her head. "That's good," said the doctor. "Because that lodge is about an hour away, right?"

"Depends on traffic."

"Right, right. And if you were drinking, say five or six hours ago, well, you'd probably still be drunk right now. Especially if you only weigh 98 pounds." She scooped the omelet out of the pan and placed it on a plate. It was still runny and undercooked. "Eat," she smiled.

Goddamn this bitch, thought Elsie. For a while, the only sound was the two of them chewing. Elsie couldn't stand the pediatrician's jawline, the sight of her working her food. She couldn't stand that she'd taken all of the cheese out of the fridge, even though she clearly only wanted the cheddar. Elsie hated that Vivian gave her a tetanus shot and now was shacking up with her father. She hated the presumption of the advice, and she hated the cheerful tone with which it was delivered.

"I'm not drunk," Elsie said.

"I didn't say you were."

"And I weigh more than 98 pounds."

"Fine," she nodded. "I'm sorry I brought it up. It's just…" she stopped for a moment, chewed, and stared at Elsie. Then she pulled her hair back and pointed to a long, jagged scar running from the top of her ear down the back of her neck. "See this?" she said; Elsie nodded. "I don't remember getting it. I don't remember the day it happened. I don't remember the other car, the windshield, the faces or names of the EMTs and doctors who saved me. There's a 36-hour gap in my memory, which, it turns out, was the most important day and a half of my life. I've spent the past 27 years trying to tell the story about something I don't even remember."

Elsie was unsure how to respond. "I have an airbag."

The doctor laughed. "Well, that's a blessing." She chewed the last bite of eggs. "You know what I do remember—there was a bible verse written on my hospital chart by one of the nurses. *"For I know the plans I have for you,"* declares the Lord, *"plans to prosper you and not to harm you, plans to give you hope and a future."* Jeremiah, I think. I had nothing to do for two weeks but read that sentence. And it made all the difference."

She meant that as inspiration. But to Elise it sounded like a threat.

School is not easy for introverts, what with the Common Core's focus on speaking and listening assignments. The next day Elsie's English class held a Socratic Seminar, an exercise where the desks are arranged in two concentric circles. The inner circle of six desks is supposed to discuss a literary question ("Is Estella's marriage to Bentley Drummle an act of hatred or love towards Pip?") while the outer circle listens in silence. The teacher had her laptop set up so that the outer circle could text follow-up questions via the projector, but the tech wasn't working properly, and she was completely distracted by the profanity that one student was anonymously posting. Meanwhile, Elsie was stranded in the inner circle, waiting for her turn to make a point, only to get steamrolled by more assertive girls hellbent on securing their participation points. It felt like being sealed in one of those promotional chambers outside of car dealerships where shoppers can step in and grab money cycloning around, except Elsie was in the chamber with five other bigger, stronger grabbers. After eight painful, inarticulate minutes, the teacher excused the inner circle and replaced them with six more gladiators. Zero points for Elsie.

She was so frustrated by the whole episode that it bled over to her drawing class, which was usually the calming koi pond of her day. But even art felt against her; she violently "X'd" out a sketch she'd been fruitlessly working on for the past two days. Mr. Lain, who moved around the class like a hollow bag in the wind, drifted over to her.

"What's the trouble, El?"

Mr. Lain was so quiet that Elsie had once pretended to be blind when he was talking in the hope that her sense of sound would heighten as compensation. He was a small, timid man with white hair, graceful hands, and a closet apparently filled exclusively with black turtlenecks. No one knew anything about him—whether he had a wife, kids, a home. Last year when Cooper found out that his first name was Edmund, Elsie almost didn't believe her. It seemed weird that there could be more to Mr. Lain than what he offered in class.

Today that included a sympathetic ear. "No trouble," Elsie said.

He looked at her abandoned sketch. "None?" he said gently.

"Well... okay, I'm having a lot of trouble with this assignment," said Elsie. "I mean, it's not that you're asking for much... I'm just supposed to draw my favorite space."

He nodded. "Are you having a hard time settling?"

Elsie shook her head. "No... no... I know exactly what I want to draw." The Elbo Room, a bar in Chicago that Cooper got them into last summer so they could see The Lionel Experiment play. *The lighting was... the sounds... the smell...* but it was too slippery in her mind. She couldn't make the pencils get it right. "I know the place," she explained. "I can see it in my head. I can... I can feel it." She could feel Dale's hips against her own, his frame draping over her as they crowded together towards the stage. "I have every detail on the back of my eyelids. But..."

"But you can't draw it right."

"I can't."

He sighed; it was a gentle sound, a sigh of commiseration. "Wait here," he said, and he shuffled into the supply closet before returning with two wooden cigar boxes. "Here," he said, handing her one. "This is for you. Go ahead and peek inside. That's your beetle."

She lifted the lid and checked. Inside was a purple flower, freshly cut. "It's a flower," she said, confused.

He smiled and shook his head slowly. "No, no. I'm sorry, I'm not explaining this right. It's an old philosopher's thought experiment." He held up his box. "I have a box. It's my box. Only I can look inside my box, and only you can look inside yours."

"Okay."

"And each of us has something in our box we call a beetle. It doesn't matter if it's an ACTUAL beetle. It could be a cockroach. Or a flower. Or nothing at all."

"Yeah, but then why are they calling it a beetle?"

"Because the thing in the box doesn't matter as much as the shared term we use when talking to one another. I've never seen your beetle;

you've never seen mine; we have no way of knowing if we mean the same thing when we use the word. But we can have a conversation about beetles without ever looking at the same thing. It's… it's the shared experience of talking about beetles that matters."

"I don't get it."

Elsie wasn't sure that he did, either. He stroked his chin for a long while, as though it were a great effort to get his words to slow down and configure themselves. "This is the problem of being an artist, Elsie," he said finally. "Your head is a closed box. It has so many beautiful things inside it. Wondrous secrets, and horrific images, too. Pain, excitement, anxiety."

"And beetles?"

"And yes, beetles." He chuckled. "You want so much to show me what's inside your head, to get it exactly right. When you paint happiness, you want it to be exactly the happiness I'll recognize. But you don't know about the happiness inside of me. You don't even know if I *have* happiness inside of me. All that you know is what's in *your* box."

She still didn't understand. "So… so, what? Art is futile? We're all just painting a bunch of gross bugs without hope of having people recognize them?"

He shook his head. "No, no. Well, yes, to an extent—you'll never know if I see what you see, feel what you feel. But what I'm trying to say is that it doesn't matter, Elsie. What matters is that your art makes me curious about your beetle. Makes me want to talk beetles with you, feel beetles with you."

"That sounds gross."

He ran his hands back over his hair, which stood up comically like an albino yard. "I'm saying good art—like yours, Elsie—doesn't have to draw it right. All it has to do is make me curious about boxes other than my own. To make me wonder, even if it's futile, what it might be like to see your beetle, too."

"It's YOUR beetle!" Elsie shouted.

"But it's not a fucking beetle!" Denver shouted back. He tipped over the box and dumped out the action figure. "Look, it's a GI Joe!"

"No! It's… it's, like, a metaphor! How many times do I have to explain this?"

"At least once more!" he shouted back.

But she was done trying. It was too dark in Denver's basement, they were too high, and it was too Monday night. "You know what? Just keep the box," she said, shoving the cigar box back into his arms.

"Fine," he said. "I'm going to cut a hole in it and put my dick inside. For Christmas."

"Small hole," said Cooper. Denver turned bright red despite himself.

"I don't get it, either," said Yael. "Sorry, El. Like, why can't we look in each other's boxes? Why can't we put a picture on Instagram? Then we'd know who was talking about beetles."

"Because…" said Elsie, trying to organize her thoughts. "Because you can't text what's in your head!"

"Um… sure I can," she said, tapping her phone. "Look, I just did!"

"No," said Elsie, looking plaintively at Dale, but he just shrugged and focused on his book.

"Peeking in your box. Looking at your beetle. That's code," said Cooper. "That man is grooming you."

"Ew," said Elsie, blushing. "Gross."

Cooper couldn't help herself, though. "I'm serious, El. Lain is weird as fuck. That man is straight outta pedo-central casting."

Denver nodded. "I heard from Reid Strough that she was explaining a still life last year, and she turned around to see him rubbing up against her chair."

"Chair predator," agreed Cooper. "No chair consent!"

Elsie shook her head. "Sorry, but Reid Strough claimed she hooked up with DJ Topspin at Warmfest. I wouldn't believe her even if she told me corn was yellow."

"Corn is yellow—"

"IT'S A FIGURE OF SPEECH, DENVER! Look, you guys don't know anything about him. Mr. Lain is a sweet old man. He's not a pervert. He's not grooming… anybody. He's just trying to help me draw."

Cooper's eyes flicked around the room before settling on Dale. "You don't know anything about him, either," she said quietly. "You should be more careful, El. Everyone has secrets."

Dale looked up from the book he was pretending to read. "Anything about Lain in the data dump?" he asked.

Elsie shrugged and pulled out her phone. "Just a bunch of numbers. I don't know what they are, what they mean."

Yael looked over Elsie's shoulder. "Those are GPS coordinates," she said. "Lain must have one of those anti-theft trackers on his car. It records everywhere he goes." Everyone stared at Yael, astonished that for once she possessed relevant, useful information. "What?" she said after a moment. "My parents put one on my car to track me."

Dale moved to look at Elsie's screen; despite the stench of skunkweed in the basement, he was so close that she could smell his deodorant. "Well, there you go," he said. "Put those into Google Maps, and you'll know all about Mr. Lain."

Elsie closed her eyes and imagined his mysterious routes. Did Mr. Lain have a house? An apartment? Where did he shop? Was he a churchgoer? But she couldn't see him going anywhere else, doing anything else, being anyone else. Just a slow, deliberate painter with a voice like the release of steam.

"You just wait," said Cooper, laying back and blowing out a long stream of smoke. "You're going to find out he's a custom dildo manufacturer, and he's got an irregularly shaped rubber dong he's named after you." Her eyes were shut, and the shadows made it look like they could peer straight through her sockets into her skull.

——— ——— ——— ——— ——— ——— ——— ——— ———

According to the data dump, these were the places that Mr. Lain liked to go:

1.   His home (an apartment on Delaware Street).
2.   The Kroeger on Hickory Street.
3.   The Clearwater Public Library.
4.   Two different Starbucks in town.
5.   The Kerasotes Showplace 8 Movie Theater.
6.   Chile's.
7.   Rasmuss and Williams' Mortuary.
8.   Space Ranger's Comic Book and Card Store.
9.   Luger Art Supplies (in Shelbyville).
10. Cyprus Club (in Chicago).
11. The CVS Pharmacy on Bradley Street. *Holy shit!* Elsie thought, *My CVS!*

She'd never seen him in the pharmacy, but she only worked 20 hours a week. *He couldn't know that I work there;* she thought *I've never mentioned it; I barely ever talk at school.* But what if he knew, the way that teachers sometimes knew personal things about students without ever even making eye contact? Yael loved to tell a story about how Mrs. Kraft once excused her to go use the bathroom without Yael even asking because she could tell that Yael was about to get her period, a power she dubbed ESPMS.

It was the rare Wednesday afternoon where Elsie didn't have any-where to go or anything to do, so she decided to drive around town and trace Mr. Lain's route. She cruised by the movie theater. It was the middle of winter—the Cineplex was filled with cartoon animal movies, a holiday rom-com, a film set in the Holocaust featuring Emma Stone acting very sad. Which of these would Mr. Lain choose? She watched people walking through the parking lot, huddled and hustling to reach the warmth of the lobby. *Does he like popcorn? Candy? Or did he just want to go someplace dark and loud where he could be among people without having to be of them?*

She wandered around Kroeger, wishing there was a GPS tracker for his shopping cart. *What does he shop for? Is he vegetarian? Kosher? Does he like candles or fabric softener? Does he buy cleaning supplies to bleach his kitchen until every microbe is extinguished?*

The mortuary was a funeral home, an old brick building with meticulous landscaping. According to the GPS data, he visited twice. Was he friends with a mortician? Or did he lose a friend? Family? It occurred to Elsie that she'd been there before—when she was a freshman, one of the Cross-Country runners at school drowned, and they all trudged through to pay respect. She didn't know the kid, but she went anyway. Did Mr. Lain lose two students? Or did he simply stop by to look at death?

She drove by Chile's, the Comic Book store, the library. She kept expecting to see him, and she realized with a shudder that was hoping to see him, to run into him in the real world. *What would I even say to him?* she wondered. *Oh, Mr. Lain! You collect Magic: The Gathering cards too? That's wild! Let's play a hand!* Suddenly, she was embarrassed by her curiosity. She drove slowly past his apartment; there was a silver Accord parked outside with a Clearwater parking tag. *A light is on upstairs.*

She remembered Cooper was scheduled to work, so she pulled into CVS. Maybe she had seen Lain in there before; Elsie wondered if that was why Cooper didn't trust him. But when she entered the store, it was Gouth at the counter, reading the latest issue of Cosmopolitan.

He looked up at the automatic door chime but then relaxed when he recognized Elsie.

"Oh, it's you," he said, his disgustingly wide mouth working on a Dum-Dum. "What do you want?"

God, I hate him, Elsie thought. "Where's Cooper?"

He snorted. "I need to talk to you about that," he said. "Did you know she was stealing?"

Yes. "What?" Elsie said. "What do you mean?"

He eyed Elsie suspiciously, his fat lips wet with candy resin, then reached behind the counter and pulled out a fifth of vodka. "Caught her in the act," he said. "She goes back to restock the Absolut, then switches out a bottle with water for the vodka. Found three bottles like this one, seals broken, refilled with H2O." He pointed at her with the lollipop. "You know anything about this?"

Yes. "This is the first I've heard of it," Elsie said. "So what'd you do?"

He returned to his Cosmopolitan. "I fired the bitch."

"You *what?*"

"Got to, El. She's a goddamned thief," he sniffed. "You actually just missed it."

"You…" Elsie started to say, but then thought better of it. Adam Gouth was a 26-year-old community college dropout who regularly ate store property, hooked up with minors in the office, and sold weed out of his car in the parking lot. If he was unaware of the blinding hypocrisy of his management practices, then it was doubtful a tiny screaming girl with silver hair would bring it to his attention.

She left the store without asking about Lain, then heard a faint crackling from above. It sounded like a bug zapper, and suddenly she knew where Cooper went. Elsie ran around back, hopped up on the dumpster, and climbed the step ladder leaning against the wall. On the roof, she found the girl in the white button down, sitting in a lawn chair smoking a cigarette. Her free hand dangled at her side;

she was triggering her Taser app, making her iPhone crackle and pop.

"Christ, Cooper, it's freezing up here," said Elsie, pulling her coat around tight. "Come on down. Let's go get something to eat."

Cooper didn't look at her; she was staring at the traffic patterns at the intersection. Lights changed, cars moved, and a couple of kids on bikes stopped and waited. "I'm not hungry," she said.

Elsie sat down beside the chair, pulled her knees to her chest, and breathed into the arms of her coat. "Gouth is an asshole," she said.

"They're all assholes," Cooper said. "That's all we get, from cradle to grave. A buffet of assholes. Hell, I'm an asshole, too."

"You're not an asshole, Cooper."

She looked over at Elsie, flashing the shrewd, unblinking look that she used to cut boys down to toothpicks. "How do you know that?"

"'Cause I know you," Elsie said. "I've known you. All my life."

She nodded. "That's true. God help me, after all this time, and you're the only one I've got left." Suddenly, she looked away. Elsie had never seen her do that before. "You don't know the things I've done, El," she said.

"Like what?"

"Like…" she started, but then stopped and flicked away her cigarette, stuffing both her hands in her pockets. "Oh, Elsie," she said, and it took the smaller girl long time to realize that Amy Cooper was crying, that there were tears leaking from her eyes and the noises she was making were sobs. "Elsie…" she said. "Elsie, I wish I could be you. I wish I could be you so badly."

Elsie laughed. "No one has ever, ever thought that, Coop. Look at me! Look at *you*! I'm… I'm just another face in line at the DMV. You're the girl that cuts the line, fucks the driving instructor, and then steals his car. Why would anyone ever choose me over you?"

"Because!" she said. "Because you can love things! People! And you do! Like, all the time."

It's true, Elsie realized. Despite everything—her sad little body, her disappointing parents, her weakness and timidity, she was overfilled with love. For Cooper. For Dale. For her art and the kindness of Mr. Lain. For the beauty of the boring suburban intersection. But as usual, she didn't know what to say in the moment, so I stood and pulled Cooper into her and held on as she sobbed, the breath coming from them both white and wispy, the traffic circulating ceaselessly below.

10
ANDY

One of the things he most liked about dating Celia was that because his apartment wasn't handicap accessible, she couldn't just drop by. Instead, he was the one who decided the relationship's moments of availability. After another miserable day of humiliating stares and whispers, Andy hoped to lose himself in the consolation of her smile, her freckles, her bed. He drove to her split-level, fantasizing about pulling her wordlessly from her chair until she straddled him, unclasping and unbuttoning manically until they released one another in the middle of her floor.

She took her time buzzing him up, which wasn't unusual if she had been on the couch or at the table. But when he let himself in her foyer, the garbage bag filled with his clothes told him that her lassitude was intentional.

"You want to talk about this?" he asked.

"I did," she said. "You wouldn't pick up."

He crossed his arms and clenched his jaw. "You promised."

She nodded. "I did."

"But you read them anyways."

"I did."

He looked at the bag. It must have been physically difficult for her—she would have had to remove the drawer, load the bag, and then place it on her lap to wheel it into the foyer. It infuriated him. He grabbed it by the elastic band and dumped it out onto the floor. T-shirts, razorblades, a comb. A book of matches from The Lizard Lounge. A ticket stub from *Mike and Dave Need Wedding Dates*. Paperback copies of Krakauer's *Into the Wild*, Vonnegut's *Breakfast of Champions*, and Bukowski's *Women*. A snow globe from Mammoth Caves.

"This is my life!" he shouted at her. "This is what has happened to me the past month! All I asked you to do was to not look at the mess, but you couldn't even do that!" He picked up the snow globe and threw it at the wall; a framed program from *Guys and Dolls* came crashing down.

She rolled over to the picture frame, picked it up, then handed it Andy. "Would you mind?" she said. Flustered, he walked over and replaced it on the wall. He leaned against the closet door, then collapsed. "I'm sorry," he said.

"I'm sorry, too," she said.

"What… what was it?" he asked. "The email. The one that you're mad about."

"Is this a question you want answered?"

Was it? He realized that he was afraid for her to read his own words to him. Yet he couldn't leave this place until he knew which message had soaked the tissue of their relationship to dissolution. "Yes," he said finally. "Please."

She pulled out her phone, tapped the screen, scrolled until she found the offending document. "Hey Jen," she read, and he closed his eyes in defeat. "Heard you were planning a vay-cay over break. I wanted to share with you my top 10 questions to ask when booking a trip. #10: 'What's the urine-to-chlorine ratio in your swimming pools?'"

"Okay…"

"Note: Any ratio over 50:50 is probably unacceptable, depending on the Groupon…"

"Okay! *Okay!*" he said, jumping to his feet and grabbing the phone. He read over the message. "I don't say anything bad here," he said petulantly. "It's just some jokes."

Her shoulders fell. "You really don't remember, do you?"

"Remember what?"

She rolled forward and plucked back her phone. "Those are the same jokes you sent to me last March," she said sadly. "Word for word."

"So I reuse material…"

"It's not material, you jackass! Those were *our* jokes! *Our* story! The problem isn't that you stuck your dick in the mouth of some rando, although—lest I bury the lede—fuck you. The problem is that you cut and paste an email you sent to *me*. Laughter you sent to *me*."

She began to fold his t-shirts, stuffing them back in the plastic bag. "This t-shirt, for Coachella? You never went there. These books, you haven't read them. Everything is just a prop for your insatiable desire to be *liked*. Including me, the handicapped girlfriend. God, I feel like such a fool."

He took a step towards her. "You're not a prop," he said, placing a hand on her freckled cheek. She brushed it away.

"Why would I believe you?" she said, handing him the bag. "I read somewhere that in the end, every relationship is a power struggle, and the person who is in power is whoever likes the other person less. I am sorry your life got upended. I really am. But you know what? Maybe it's worth it for you to finally feel what it's like not to be in control."

— — — — — — — — —

Over the next weeks, Andy did everything he could to reassert control. He reactivated his gym membership and deactivated his Facebook and Twitter accounts. He stopped answering calls from his mother and cleaned his desk. He was polite and professional around colleagues, firm and humorless around students, and deferential at band practice. Rather than roaming the lunch room or LMC during lunch to josh with students, he drove home to walk his dog. He started to read *Into the Wild*.

Andy handwrote a four-page, front-and-back apology letter to Celia. He accepted responsibility for his betrayal, admitted the validity of her critique, and lamented that she might have felt anything less than a strong, beautiful woman in his presence. He also observed the extraordinary nature of their circumstance, how they had been granted a rare and powerful window into one another's deepest vault, and that perhaps they could grow from this. He ended with a lengthy explanation of Hester Prynne's decency in the face of public scorn. The next day, he found the note stuffed in an envelope tucked under his driver's side wiper blade. She had marked up his spelling and punctuation errors with a red pen. "Terrible. F. Zero Stars." she wrote on the final page.

The student body had settled into an unspoken pact of *omerta* in the week leading up to final exams. There were fights and demonstrations, and a group of kids had refused to enter the band room, but the students on Andy's roster seemed eager to resume regular business, and Andy was happy to oblige. Yet even in their cordiality, Andy could feel mockery behind their eyes. He heard laughter in the hallway and assumed that he was the subject, saw memes drift past as kids scrolled through their feeds and presumed himself the target. He had lost his aura of lightness, affability, being in on the joke. He was just another teacher.

On the day of his 5th period final exam, he watched them file into the classroom. He was seated behind his desk, drumming his fingers on the stack of tests. He did not greet them when the bell rang, instead standing wordlessly, passing out scantrons and exams and reading packets. Students began work immediately, reading and bubbling in silence. One student had left in his earbuds, a soft rhythm barely audible from his ear canal. Andy popped them out with a quick flick of his finger and resumed distribution.

He came to Mateo Himenez, a junior Andy privately considered one of his greatest successes. Mateo was a hard, taciturn presence; other teachers shook their heads when describing his disengagement, his sullenness, his head-down-on-the-desk-ness. He had been in and out of trouble with Dean Yulders throughout the past year and a half, and although he would probably qualify for the school's ELL program, his parents had been adamant about leaving Mateo in the general student population. Yet Andy had cracked his exterior, first by showing him a YouTube video of MMA fighter Cain Velasquez. The next day, he received an email with links to fights by Dominick Cruz and Nick Diaz. Once Andy learned that Mateo had seen Fetty Wap in concert, they were practically coffee buddies. Mateo didn't say much in class, and his grades had not improved markedly. But he greeted Andy with consistent eye contact and the occasional handshake at the door.

Now, however, Mateo stared at Andy with a narrow, unflinching gaze. Andy paused to try and read it. There was something simmering behind his eyes, something hot and wrathful just barely restrained by the young man's eyes, the color of dark stained wood. His hands rested in the center of his desk; when Andy tossed the testing packet down, Mateo swept it onto the floor.

Andy froze for a moment. Mateo looked away. Some students had noticed; others were already lost in their exams. The only sounds Andy could detect were the scratching of scantron bubbles and the deep, rhythmic breathing of this brooding kid. He bent down to pick up the test but was checked by Mateo's hostile whispering.

"Don't even."

Andy drew himself up to full height. Ordinarily, he would seek some method of de-escalation. He might let the student simmer for a moment, maybe send him out into the hallway to calm down until they could have a conversation. Andy was good in these situations. But in Mateo's hostility he saw Celia's judgment and Vince's paternalism. It enraged him. *Good* he thought. *Something to fight.*

"Excuse me?" he said. Every head in class snapped to attention.

"I said," growled Mateo, matching Andy's registry, "Bitch, don't *even.*" He leapt to his feet and shoved Andy into another student, then stomped past them out of class, slamming the door behind him.

No control, thought Andy, panicking. *No control. No control. No control.* He looked around; every student was staring. Some had their phones out; they were recording, transmitting. He had to act.

He walked over to the intercom and pressed the button; Yasmine answered. "Main office," she said in her songbird's voice.

"Yasmine, I need Dean Yulders and some assistants in room C115," he said and hung up. The class remained frozen. "What are you looking at?" he barked. "You've got a final exam. Eric, give me that phone."

When Bryan Yulders arrived with two dean's assistants, Andy met them in the hallway to explain the situation. Bryan nodded and then checked in on his walkie talkie to investigate whether Mateo was still in the building. Andy peered through the plexiglass windows that rimmed C115's doorway. "His backpack's still there," he said. "His phone. He won't leave without that."

Andy asked one of the dean's assistants to monitor his class, and he and Bryan split up to search for Mateo. Yulders thought Mateo might head for the parking lot, but Andy suspected otherwise. He retraced a conversation they had had about school water fountains and repaired to the bathroom outside the wrestling gym.

Andy could see a pair of legs in the second stall, and the sound of his footsteps caused the legs to stand. There was a flushing sound. "Mateo?" called Andy. The door swung open, and the junior swaggered out. His face remained impassive and hostile. Despite his hooded sweatshirt, Andy could make out the imposing physique of a wrestler, taut and ready to spring.

Andy met his eyes. "You want to tell me what that was about?"

Mateo scoffed. "I got nothing to say to you."

"You mind if I say something then?"

Mateo began to wash his hands. Andy took a few steps towards him. "This has been my month. I wake up, go to work, and find out I've pissed off someone I care about. My mother thinks I'm a fuckup. My girlfriend dumped me. My coworkers think I'm a fraud. My students think I'm a loser."

Mateo began to dry his hands. "That ain't nothin' to me."

"Oh, it's not? Because you're acting like a little bitch right now, and I'm thinking you're lying."

Mateo's eyes flashed at him. "I'm a liar?"

"You know that word?" said Andy. "I can say it in Spanish, too: *embustero.*"

Mateo snapped. He swung with his right hand, punching the trashcan next to him, sending it sliding across the room. The lid flew off; paper towels, soda cans, and other refuse scattered. Andy held his gaze.

"*Cabrón,*" said Mateo. "You can't talk without getting shit wrong! You called me Carlos for two weeks in September. *Idiota.* Everything you say is a lie!"

"I lied to you."

"*Sí.*"

Andy pulled out his own phone and handed it to Mateo. "When?"

Mateo stared at him for a long moment before taking the phone, tapping the screen, and scrolling for a long, silent minute. They were both breathing heavily. Finally, he found the file and handed back the phone.

Andy stared at it, confused. "It's an email you sent me."

"That's right."

"I don't understand."

"I sent you a song," said Mateo, looking away angrily. "Verses. You didn't even open it."

Andy looked again. He was right. There was a blue bar next to the message indicating it was unread.

"You remember now, asshole?'

Andy closed his eyes. "I told you I liked it."

"You're a liar, Mr. Waters. The word is *mentiroso*."

Andy's legs gave out. His back crashed into the tiled wall, and he slid to the floor. He began to laugh.

"All right, all right. I give up. I am a liar." He buried his hands in his hair, ran them back to his neck. He felt the stud of the earring; he unfastened it and flung it against the wall. Mateo regarded him with vague skepticism; Andy raised his head to meet his eyes.

"I am sorry, Mateo. Truly. I could say that I was tired, that I had a million emails, that I had papers to grade, that I forgot. Maybe all of that is true. But what's more true was that I just didn't care. And you did. So I'm sorry."

He hauled himself to his feet, and went to lean against the sink, staring at himself in the mirror. "My boss thinks I'm not so bad. Says I can't fake being a good teacher. I'm not so sure. I help people. I make them write better, maybe love a book or two. I listen to them, share their excitement. But maybe I only do that so I can tell a story to other people that I'm a good person. Which is," he turned to face Mateo, "another lie."

Mateo regarded him for a long moment, then walked across the bathroom, bent down, and picked up the earring. He handed it to Andy.

"Dropped your rock," he said.

Andy smiled. "Thanks," he said, refastening it.

Mateo picked the phone up off the floor. "You got Soundcloud on this?" he asked; when he found the icon, he keyed in an address and pushed the touchscreen. A beat began to play—simple, regular. A piano and a snare—rat-tat-tatta-tatta rat-rat-rat-rat-rat-rat-tatta-tatta. Mateo began to sway, then to bounce slightly as he found the rhythm. "Yeah," he said. "Yeah…." And then he began.

Y'all know me, from the I-N-D
Hotter than the oven fi'hundre' degee
I was playin' when we started, 'til the shit got real
Never know it's all over 'til they bring yo' las meal
But I'm a man now, Ma; you should see your l'il boy
Been a few years now since I finished wi' them toys.
Got a crew, got a life, got the hustle and flow
Got my whole plan set like a line of domino
And there's some things I shouldna said back when I was a pup
But you can't get water back once you knock o'er the cup
Want to tell you that we cool now and I wish you was here
All that shit is gettin' smaller in the rear-view mirror
Wish that I could call you up 'cause too much is unsaid
We could go get all them pancakes shaped like Mickey Mouse's head.
Pero te vas a ir porque eres tan terco
Y no iré a buscarte porque tu hijo es un cerdo.
Ambos seguimos corriendo como un par de conejos
Culpando al otro en vez de mirarse en el espejo.
La madre empuja a su bebé en el carriola
Cuando lo deja en la calle es como entregarle una pistola
Depende de mí, mamá; Soy el capitán de mi nave.
La ira me puso en esta jaula, pero el amor me dio la llave.

The beat kept running for a more hooks, but Mateo was done. He turned to face Andy. The recognition of the older man's presence suddenly reminded Mateo of his own vulnerability, and a curtain of defensiveness once again descended over his features.

"Well?" he said, looking away. "Mr. Teacher man? What you think?'

Andy stared, agog, at the young man who only moments ago had throttled a trash can. Mateo Jimenez, who sat with his hood drawn in math class, who was written up without defending himself. Mateo who bused tables at Whataburger, who wore the same Massimo sweatshirt to school every day. Whose backpack straps were held together with duct tape. Who he called the wrong name for the first three weeks of school.

"Mateo, I…" he said, shaking his head. "That was amazing."

The young man cocked his head, seemingly offended by the simplicity of his response. "That's all?" he said. "The last essay I got back, it had more red on it than a drive-by."

Andy laughed, then caught himself staring at his reflection in the mirror. He heard Vince imploring him to be the good teacher; Celia branding him a fraud; Mr. Jadarary drawing his focus to the thing on the end of the fork. *None of it matters*, he thought to himself. *Forget the reflection.*

"Well, all right," said Andy Waters, taking back his phone. "I've got some ideas. Let's hear it again."

11
CONNOR

<u>meme</u>

(noun)

1: an idea, belief or belief system, or pattern of behavior that spreads throughout a culture either vertically by cultural inheritance (as by parents to children) or horizontally by cultural acquisition (as by peers, information media, and entertainment media)

2: a pervasive thought or thought pattern that replicates itself via cultural means; a parasitic code, a virus of the mind especially contagious to children and the impressionable

On January 29th, exactly 50 days after the initial doxxing of Clearwater High, a second set of files was uploaded, this time to a community blog curated by Anne-Marie Slodder, a local homemaker. Once again, 41 teachers and administrators were targeted. This time, however, the files were organized and labeled. The difference in impact was striking. Whereas the first data dump had suffused through the community like sewage slowly leaking into a water table, the easily parsed and digested files of the second dump was more like an environmental cataclysm, something like the fire on Deepwater Horizon.

It took minutes for the community to fully search the data dumped on Ryan Cespids, an AP Calculus teacher with nearly two decades of service to Clearwater. Cespids' file contained a list of unfiltered code that belonged to a search engine. One student—Jason Alcindor—figured out how to decrypt the information, which he reposted. It contained 427 terms from Cespids' Internet search history.

Cespids had exhaustively researched players for his fantasy football team. He had looked up theater show times, weather patterns, the cast list of the movie *Sneakers*, the pound/dollar exchange rate, how to jumpstart a Prius, and tour dates for Pearl Jam. He had also looked up the age of sexual consent in Indiana and information on organizations friendly to pedophilia.

Ryan met with Vince Darten to discuss the revelation. He assured his principal that much of the information was not true, that it was fabricated. Some of the items in his search history were accurate—he could remember dates and times for looking up the football players. Some of the information he simply could not recall (had he really looked up whether or not penguins have knees?). "But Vince—this pedo stuff? It's not me." He turned over his phone and computer to the police.

Vince Darten believed him. So did the police. On February 5th, Vince released a brief statement on the school website:

> *I have met with the staff and students identified by the leaked files. Working with the police department, I have investigated all disclosures. At this time, it is our determination that no teacher or administrator has broken the law or is unfit to resume*

his or her responsibilities. While some disciplinary action has taken place, I do not believe there is any risk to our students.

Our community has suffered tremendously through these episodes. I want to assure our parents and students that even amidst this disruption, we are committed to delivering the same high-quality education that has been our hallmark these past thirty years, to honoring the values of our district and state. We will work hard to re-establish professional boundaries and rebuild whatever trust we may have lost. We ask for your patience and consideration, and we thank you for your unfailing consolation and support in this trying time.

Vince received several dozen emails of encouragement and reassurance from parents and members of the community. He also received a petition from 28 students asking to be removed Ryan Cespids' class.

By Wednesday, the petition had swollen to 83 names, which was more than half the students on his roster. Vince was receiving calls from parents calling for Cespids' dismissal. They filed a FOIA to receive information from the police investigation. They demanded access to his phone records and hard drive. Vince patiently explained the law, the procedures he was required to followed, the findings of the district and police department. There was no evidence to confirm the information released in the data dump.

On February 8th, 34 students refused to enter Cespids' class. They simply stayed in the cafeteria. "Should I just let them be?" asked Bryan Yulders, the dean of students. "No," replied Vince. "Write them up. If we let students start deciding when they want to go to class, we've lost the school year."

Detentions began to accumulate. Suspensions were issued. Parents began calling their children out for one period in protest. Finally, on February 12th, Ryan Cespids called in sick. It fell to a substitute to prepare his students for their mid-quarter exams.

An emergency school board meeting convened on February 17th. Vince offered the use of the school auditorium, but even with a seating capacity of 752 there were several hundred onlookers confined to the lobby.

Fifty-four parents took turns speaking into a wireless microphone. Some had arrived to show their support for Clearwater teachers and for Vince Darten. Others were less charitable—"What I'd like to know is what sort of background checks are in place that we are hiring teachers with such sordid patterns of behavior?" asked one parent to robust applause. Superintendent Darren Broach responded to many such queries; Gail Nifrone, Director of Building Operations, explained the steps being taken to secure the school in the new year. Vince Darten spoke on behalf of his teachers, who "have had their lives ripped to shreds," he explained.

But the galvanizing comment of the night came from Carrie Anne Marder, a parent of a student in Cespids' 7th Hour AP Calc class. "Principal Darten, I can respect how hard this must be and how much work you've put in," she said. "But I'm sorry—I cannot let my son sit in Mr. Cespids' class. Knowing what we now know, I don't think it's fair to ask any parent to send their child into that man's presence."

Vince had to wait for applause to die down before responding. "I want every parent here to know that safety is my number one concern as principal. No learning can take place in an unsafe environment." He paused. "However, we have no reason to believe the allegations made against Ryan Cespids, who I have personally worked with for many years. I am a parent, too—I recognize the gravity of these accusations. But there is simply no evidence. I would ask everyone in this audience tonight who has come to demand Mr. Cespids' removal to consider his innocence, as I have, and to share my disappointment in the monstrous harm done to his reputation by this slander. He has served this town faithfully for 18 years. He is a husband and a father. He is a good man. And right now he needs our support."

———————————

On the ride home, Carrie Anne was seething. "That principal, that fucking principal," she said to Tanner, her husband. "He has always been so goddamned condescending. Didn't I tell you what Martha Winczak said about him? He spoke to her like she was a small child!"

"What do you expect?" said Tanner. "He's from Gary, right? Probably an affirmative action case. Another entitled mediocrity."

"I'll tell you one thing, that superintendent just guaranteed his own removal," she continued. "As soon as there's another school board election, he is out."

Their son, Connor, sat in the back seat, listening. He had a good relationship with Mr. Cespids, who had given him a homework extension in October after a soccer game had stretched into overtime. He had offered on more than one occasion to meet Connor after school, to help him with the finer points of partial derivatives. Now Connor viewed those offers with gathering suspicion. Why exactly was his teacher so keen to meet with him in private? From the passenger seat, his mother railed against Cespids, who she could tell from parent-teacher conferences was some sort of deviant. "He's shifty, like an eel. Cold hands. That man is not right."

———————————

Connor Marder frequented Clearwater Confidential, a repository for local gossip and the website that had initially posted all the files released by the first Cloudburst. He had been an active member of the chatroom for years, posting comments under the moniker Every-None04. He monitored the ongoing debate about Cespids without weighing in, lurking in the background while the various constituencies raged.

CONVERSATIONS

LARRY DUH CABLE GUY

I had Mr. Cespids two years ago. I don't think I'd have passed the AP Exam without him, let alone got a 5. He's a good teacher and a good man. People need to STFU.

YAKKOWAKKODOT

Hey, dummy. A guy can be a good teacher and a dick-smoking pedophile. Wake the fuck up.

CASHMEOUTSIDE

People are going to believe what they want to believe. Like I believe that Yakko's a mouth-breathing wank monkey who wandered out of the psych ward and is making the most of his reinstated Internet privileges smh.

"Wank monkey." Like a buried ship dredged from the silt of a deep river, the words pulled from Connor a memory. He remembered a P.E. class nine years earlier, when, as a third grader, he had carefully contrived to assemble the best dodgeball team Hamlin Elementary had ever seen. Connor understood his teacher was counting the team off by eights, and he arranged his friends—Billy Puncer, Anders Haines, Nathan Wylestone, and Robby Rinnse—to stand in line at intervals of exactly eight. They were large, rough boys whose manic

energies were barely restrained by the staid rituals of the classroom, and when turned loose on the blacktop or gymnasium, marked them as alphas. Connor masterminded the super team, dubbed them the 'Dodge Apes,' and established himself as its silverback.

For three days, the Dodge Apes ran roughshod over the competition, whipping the red rubber balls at such high velocity as to imprint the ridged patterns into the cheeks of his classmates. There were whispered complaints and suggestions of unethicality, but Connor dismissed them as the jealous bleating of the weak and guileless. "Hey," they could have stacked the teams, too," he told Robby. "It's not our fault they're dumb." In the end, it wasn't another team that unseated the Dodge Apes—it was a single girl: Karen Singh.

Karen had approached the PE teacher, Ms. Leahy, to ask for a reshuffling of teams. "It's not fair that one team is all boys," she pointed out. "It's better when boys and girls are mixed." Connor surmised her strategy almost immediately, and argued against it so shrilly that Leahy could not redo the rosters without delegitimizing the entire unit. Her compromise, however, made everything worse: Karen Singh was added to the Dodge Apes.

"Let's get her," said Billy, whose first recourse was always to violence. The plan, such as it was, involved shoving Karen into a pile of woodchips at recess. But Connor—who even then was a shrewd judge of character—understood that a girl who was unafraid to appeal to a teacher for equality would be similarly undaunted in seeking justice. "No," said Connor. "It's better if we make her quit."

The first move was to give her a suitable nickname. Each of the boys had adopted an ape moniker—Billy was 'gorilla,' Connor was 'chimp'—and so Karen would be 'Drool Monkey.' When Karen complained, Connor quickly pointed out that all of their names were derogatory and unflattering. They next isolated her on defense: rather than fling their balls as soon as they were gathered, the boys began using them as shields, thus drawing all fire towards Karen. They loudly and publicly chided her for missing a target, then even more publicly criticized her for her subsequent hesitation. Connor would also surreptitiously move her water bottle to different locations—careful never to drink from it—but always attempting to keep her unbalanced and insecure. These tactics had a gradual effect, and Karen began holding herself out of PE, claiming first allergies and then stomach cramps as cause for abstention.

Over the years as the boys grew larger and more extroverted, Connor found himself following a more subtle development. Where they favored action films, Connor was drawn to military history; when they discovered fantasy sports, Conner poured himself into Nietzsche and Rand. His one traditionally masculine indulgence was first person shooters, yet while he enjoyed playing classmates and strangers on X-Box, he eschewed a headset, preferring to stalk his prey in silence.

Connor began to recognize that his personal discipline set him apart from others. He saw his peers as creatures of passion, led by their animal appetites away from their potential excellence. At age fourteen, he discovered internet pornography; his greatest achievement was to forswear it six months later. All around him, he saw men controlled by lust and irrationality, irresolution and fecklessness. It was most despairing in the adults—on Christmas Eve one year, he saw his father's eyes glaze over, the blood vessels in his nose grow as red as his sweater. He laughed oafishly at his brother-in-law's racist jokes, and he leered at his niece's checkered lace sheath dress. It was their weakness as men that diminished them, that emboldened feminist critiques of the patriarchy or the media fictions of white privilege. His was a tribe that had forgotten its strength, apologized for its birthright, and hollowed itself with addiction and insecurity.

If the allegations against Mr. Cespids were correct—and Connor had no reason to doubt them—then he was yet another undesirable, thinning the bloodline of Achilles and Alexander. He was a corrupt man employed by a corrupt organization—like the Catholic Church, with a vested interest in disguising its own malignancy. His mother was right. It was clear to Connor that criminal justice was impotent in this situation, and the administration would willingly obscure the truth to conceal their malpractice. What was needed now was the unblinking eye of public shame.

━ ━ ━ ━ ━ ━ ━ ━ ━

Every day, the teachers Sheila Broth, Eliza Monk, Dylan Paters, and James Hapsten met for lunch in the faculty cafeteria, which was really more of a repurposed storage space adjacent to the student food court. Though they were from different departments and had been hired in different years, they were united by a certain spirit of youth and vibrancy that issues from teachers with a natural enthusiasm for the craft.

The day after the emergency meeting, however, their enthusiasm had dimmed to a sad torpor, Sheila unwrapping her egg salad sandwich without her customary yolk puns.

"He's got to fire him," said Dylan grimly. "He has no choice."

James shook his head. "No way," he said. "He's got to hold the line. If he gives in here, they won't stop until we're all gone."

Dylan rolled his eyes. James had become especially defensive of Vince since the second doxxing had revealed that he had been driving on a suspended license. "You believe Cespids?"

"Sure," said James. "Ryan's all right."

"How do you know that?" asked Eliza. "I mean, I've worked next to Kevin Lenk for five years. I never knew he was hooking up with Leila in the bathroom."

"Or that Robin liked those mascot sex videos," said Dylan, referencing the teacher whose classroom adjoined his own.

James shook his head. "It doesn't matter. He's one of us. We've got to stick together."

Eliza made a face like she had discovered rotting fish in her applesauce. "It matters if he's a pedophile, James. I'd say that matters quite a bit."

Sheila Broth listened to them argue, saying nothing. She looked around the room, her eyes resting on the kitchenette by the Pepsi vending machine. The sink was stacked high with unwashed dishes, flatware caked and grease-smeared, coffee mugs unclaimed and ringed with stains. "Whose dishes are those?" she asked quietly.

"I don't know. Everybody's," said Dylan. "People just leave them."

"He's got to go," said Eliza. "How're we supposed to look him in the face?"

Later that day, after everyone had gone home, Sheila Broth came back to the cafeteria. She washed every dish, placed each plate on the drying rack, and stacked the coffee mugs on a shelf by the microwave. *Somebody has to do something*, she thought.

▪ ▪ ▪ ▪ ▪ ▪ ▪ ▪ ▪

EVAN: Hey Connor have you seen these Cespid memes?

Connor smiled. Not only had he seen them, but he had created the first five. But that was two days ago—the images were everywhere now. There were dozens pinging around Snapchat every hour, and the public appetite showed no signs of satiation. The creation of memes had grown competitive, and students were jockeying to fill one another's inboxes with repackaged images featuring devastating takedowns in blocky Impact font.

Satisfied by his progress, Connor permitted himself his one indulgence. Quietly locking his door, he peeled back the Paul George poster that had hung by his bed since his twelfth birthday. Behind the glossy print, he located the small groove in the drywall. Licking his finger, he dug with his nail into the soft plaster, scratching loose the powder, cleaning the dust with a wet Kleenex as he went.

He would only allow a few scratches tonight. It was immensely satisfying work. The idea had come to him the last time he'd watched *The Shawshank Reception* on cable. Andy Dufresne, the towering pillar of patience and restraint, had tunneled through a solid wall of rock over several decades. Andy Dufresne, who escaped prison and destroyed his enemies through nothing more than his supreme intellect and self-control.

He replaced the poster, lay back, and closed his eyes. Those people in the chatrooms were weak. They would change nobody's mind with their emotional ejaculations. Only memes moved people. The ability for everyone to participate, to join in the revelry, to bring the whole fervor to climax with a single well-timed burn—that was what mattered. Connor felt himself grow hard, but he would not touch himself. This, too, would pass.

The Second Doxxing

JANUARY 29TH

12
VINCE

Every year, on the first Friday of February, Clearwater High School held a winter assembly. The purpose was to celebrate student achievement, to deepen the sense of community, to announce the court for the Winter Dance, and to implore the kids to exercise maturity, probity, and restraint over the weekend.

Everyone hated it. The students, while grateful for the momentary release from class, resented being herded into a gymnasium with poor circulation, squeezed onto painful, backless bleachers, and forced to watch the over-praised elite students lauded yet again as National Merit semifinalists or allowed to perform acapella renditions of Beyoncé hits. The teachers were reduced to standing sentry, silencing catcalls and side-conversations, and endlessly chasing kids off their phones.

Vince saw these ceremonies as a sad confirmation of the worst suspicions people had of teenagers—that they were cruel, selfish, braying smirks, that they were incapable of sincerity or respect, that they would mature into the same divisive, entitled township that had spawned them. "It's just like Thanksgiving," Harry Buchanan had once said. "You get all excited to get the family together, and then as soon as you're sitting together at the table, you remember why you hate each other." Vince had nodded, but said nothing. Since marrying, neither he nor Elizabeth had ever been invited home for Thanksgiving.

But as he stepped onto the stage, brandishing a wireless microphone, Vince felt more than weary disappointment. He was angry. There were nearly 2,000 people in this gymnasium, and one, he felt certain, had just released 208 illegally obtained files of 41 of his teachers. Fifty days after the first doxxing, after hundreds of phone calls and interviews and haranguings had slowly constrained Clearwater's forest fire, an accelerant had undone it all. Vince placed his hand over his brow to control the glare of the spotlight, to try and make out the individual faces of his students and staff. But they were indistinguishable, a faceless form directing its prisoner attention at the principal onstage.

"This is usually the point where I ask you all to make good decisions this weekend, to show yourselves and one another respect and care," he began. "So: make good decisions. Show yourselves and one another respect and care. We live with the memories we make for ourselves in this place," he said, pausing to take in the nattering chatter, underscoring his own impotence and irrelevance. They were not listening. He couldn't blame them; he had said nothing they could hear. He continued.

"But I also want to talk about what happened last week, what's happened this year. My first job as principal—before I can do anything else—is to make everyone safe. The students. The teachers. The staff. We cannot do the work of learning if none of us are safe."

"And I think it is pretty clear that I have not been able to do that," he said, pausing again. Now they were listening. "82 teachers were hacked. Had the contents of their private lives spread all over the interstate for people to gawk at. Think about that for a moment. The part of you most desperately want to hide, paraded in front of everyone."

"And you have questions about what you've learned. How do we go back into the classroom and pretend we didn't see what we saw? Well, we don't. We shouldn't. What is needed now is the constant acknowledgment that teachers are human, and humans need kindness and patience, compassion and grace."

"I can't promise you that this will end without pain, that we won't have to make some difficult choices. But I can tell you that based on what I've seen, my previous conviction remains unchanged. These are good people, these teachers. I have known them, worked with them, watched them toil for you. They care about you. And now they need you to care about them."

They were silent for a moment, before a voice in the back-right corner of the gymnasium shouted out, *"I care about them titties!"* The students showed enough restraint not to burst into laughter, but the aggressive murmuring that filled the chamber told Vince that his moment had been eclipsed. This was what they'd remember, what they'd talk about, what they'd Tweet and Snap and caption endlessly. He had made a rookie administrator's mistake, to address them *en masse* in full sincerity. On his way offstage, he grabbed Bryan Yulders by the arm. "Find me that kid," he said over the school orchestra's rendition of Clearwater's alma mater. "I want his head on a pike."

Part of the job now was simple numbers. There were 125 staff and faculty members at Clearwater, depending on how you classified support staff. Eighty-two had been doxxed. That left a third batch untouched, including Vince. He felt certain that another release was coming.

The Clearwater student body numbered 1,678. The federal investigation had successfully eliminated nearly a third of those students, and Vince had gathered enough information from his teachers to confidently rule out another 200 or so. The federal agents assigned to his case had been in semi-regular contact, but were often maddeningly cryptic about their investigation.

They believed the suspect to be male, between the ages of 16 and 18. He may be a child of divorce or abuse, but not necessarily. Paranoid, narcissistic, sexually frustrated. A regular user of Shodan (a search engine that allows users to locate linked devices), and probably a fairly well-known presence on the best-known spear phishing websites. "Honestly, our best bet is that he'll get careless," said Glen Davis, one of the two special agents brought in from Indianapolis. "We monitor a lot of small groups where an attack like this would create quite a stir. Someone almost always takes credit."

But Vince was in no mood for patience. For a second time, his school was on fire, and given the recent staff attrition, he had even fewer resources with which to extinguish the flames.

Cespids swore of his innocence, and Vince wanted to believe him. The police had identified two visits to websites tracking in pedophilia, one during the school day, and a second after hours. Cespids offered alibis for both timestamps—he had been teaching during the first— but could not account for his laptop's security. "The fact is, I could have been helping a kid during class and totally missed someone screwing around with it," he admitted sheepishly. "I mean, I dunno, Vince… sometimes I leave it open to take attendance, and then I get distracted. I've got 32 kids asking me for things every period." Agent Davis also suspected that the computer could have been activated remotely, that it could have been used as a bot, running programs or accessing files in the background without Cespids' permission. They were conducting interviews of every student on his roster, cross-checking them with the list Vince had compiled of especially computer-literate kids. But if there was one intersection point of the complex Venn Diagram of high school student groups, it was mistrust of authority. No one was saying anything.

His staff was exhibiting signs of trauma. The second doxxing had put many others in challenging positions. Those who had enjoyed a certain rueful pride in being exempted from the first dump now found themselves painfully compromised. Marshall Heitz, his automotive teacher, had been outed as an online gamer; Vince had had to ask him to delete his account. Dennis Agay, the Swim coach, had donated money to The New Dawn, a political action group with ties to white supremacists. His entire Varsity had quit in protest. Clearwater now knew that Nelson Kriegs had denied his ex-wife child support, that Irene Teniman had had two abortions, and that Michael Faders' girlfriend had left a five-minute voice mail where she compared his penis to "a pathetic little mouse that frequently got lost and had to stop to ask for directions."

Vince met with each of them, heard them out, tried to reassure them. But what could he say at this point? The toothpaste was out of the tube and had been screen-capped, GIFed, and retweeted *ad infinitum*. He could barely make eye contact with Lana Collins, whose released medical records revealed she had undergone genital reconstruction surgery to address body dysmorphic disorder. Lana had borne his promises with taut stoicism. "May I go?" she asked flatly at the earliest opportunity. "Yes," he told her. He did not mention that later in the day he would be meeting with a parent demanding Lana's dismissal.

There were scathing voicemails, excoriating emails, and nasty letters. Vince replied to each as timely and professionally as he could. Worse were the anonymous messages, which dropped the dog-whistle suggestions of his mediocrity for unrestrained racial invectives.

Lockers were spray-painted, cars were keyed, and fights had grown so frequent during lunch periods that Bryan Yulders had instituted a week of silence in the cafeteria. The Friday before the dance, a bag of microwave popcorn unexpectedly set off the fire alarm, which triggered a nervous breakdown in Allison Wadrese, one of his English teachers. "I don't know what happened; I sort of remember waking up screaming," she explained from the back of an ambulance, taking puffs from an oxygen mask.

He met with Darren Broach, his superintendent, at least three times a week, sometimes twice in one day. At the end of one session spent discussing transfer options, Broach had asked him about his own files. "Two doxxes, and nothing from the principal's computer," he noted. "Seems strange."

"I agree," said Vince.

"And when—*if*—there's a third release," Broach said slowly, "What do you think we'll find?"

"We're going to catch him," said Vince.

"Right," said the superintendent. "But if we're not in time—*if*, Vince—is there anything I need to know?"

This was, of course, the question that had hung over every session with every teacher. *Why haven't you been doxed?* they thought at him. It had thickened the barrier that naturally exists between teachers and administrators. *Among us, but not one of us,* his exclusion seemed to say. And now his boss was asking him about his own secrets. The Grand Inquisitor, begging confession with the threat of rack.

"No, sir," said Vince.

— — — — — — — —

"…as far as I'm concerned, the dog owes us a written apology, and I won't accept it unless it's on that papyrus stationary that I like so much," said Elizabeth between bites of her wedge salad. "I've had it with that little vomit spigot. She's one hiccup away from having every hole sealed with window caulk."

"Mmmm," said Vince absently. Elizabeth cocked her head; she'd begun the evening with conversational forays into culture, then talk of their daughter, then musings about the Oscars and the Superbowl. Now she was just saying whatever inflammatory thing came to mind. Her husband, however, was absorbed in a text message. Ken William Hastings, district attorney. An update about a class action suit. She continued.

"While you've been nursing that little black slab of yours, I've been casing the joint," she said, gesturing with her fork. "I think there's a safe in the backroom. If you can get the manager in a chokehold, I'm certain we can be in Gatlinburg before anyone else is the wiser."

Vince tapped out a response. He looked up at her warily. "Forget that idea," he said.

"You and I need to have a talk," she said. It was their first date in weeks; she had done up her straw-colored hair in an intricate nest of pins and bands. Her ivory earrings—the ones he'd brought back from New Orleans—dangled against her jaw as it worked on the pine nuts. "I'm only half-kidding about running away."

"I know," he said.

"Are you ready to clean out the fridge?" she asked. It was an expression they'd developed in their marriage that acted as prelude for difficult conversations.

"Not yet," he said.

She chewed her salad, watching him. The flesh around them had grown puffy, but those were the same blue eyes that had penetrated him three decades earlier. That had seen him as a man when everyone else saw a shirt and tie. She was looking for that man again. Finally, she shrugged. "Let's play the game," she said, tilting her head in the direction of a couple directly to their left.

"I don't enjoy the game as much," he said.

"Oh, come on now, Vincent, be a sport," she said. "For old time's sake."

Vince looked over at the couple. They were young—in their mid-twenties, perhaps—with clear skin save for a coyote tattoo on the woman's right bicep. She was thick in the middle but long of torso and round of face, brown ringlets of hair cascading down her wide shoulders and back. She wore glasses so thick they seemed to wrap around her face like sports goggles. The man had a head like an Easter Island moai, with a heavy brow, long, flat nose, and thick slug-like lips. His suit fit him poorly, and the color of his socks did not match his belt. She leaned into the table; he leaned back, as though his massive head might upend his chair were he to tilt it too far in her direction.

"First date. He's her optometrist," said Vince.

"How can you tell?"

"He carries himself like a doctor, but he's too young to be in residency. He's dressed expensively, but without taste."

"Classic optometrist," said Elizabeth into her wine glass. "They know everything about the eye but how to use them."

"And she keeps touching her glasses, trying to draw attention to them."

"They're hideous," Elizabeth noted. "They make her look like a panda about to operate heavy machinery."

"He sold them to her," said Vince quietly. "She wore them for him."

"Oh, very good, Vince. You've done it again," said Elizabeth wryly. Vince said nothing to this. It occurred to him that his ravioli had gotten cold. He noticed another couple staring at him two tables over. Had they heard him? Perhaps they were discussing the optics of a black man dining out with his white wife. But a third truth seemed most likely—they had recognized him as the principal of Clearwater High. As an administrator, he had always possessed a certain public visibility. But only recently had that visibility drawn stares.

His phone buzzed again, and Vince mumbled a lame apology as he scrolled through the message. It was from Leonard Fisk, the English Department Chair. Vince set down his fork.

"I'm sorry," he said absently. "We have to go." He stood and staggered towards the door; it seemed as though his feet no longer obeyed his commands.

"Vincent!" said Elizabeth. "The bill?"

"Oh," he said. He sat; they summoned the waiter. Ten minutes later, he tried to recall the sequence of events that got him to the passenger seat of the car, but he could not. As they rode together, the light of streetlamps flashing across them in regular intervals, Vince wondered how the whole scene must have looked.

Leonard Fisk was a wide man with big hands and thick forearms. He had begun losing his hair early in his adulthood, and in act of unpretentiousness that well-suited him, he had promptly shaved his head. He looked like a missile walking upright, and he had a habit of speaking with big gestures that required broad rooms to accommodate. He was a bass in his church choir, a fan of Cormac McCarthy, and deployed a laugh that rolled through the office like an avalanche. Vince very rarely saw him sitting.

Leonard rose when they entered the room and gave Elizabeth a hug. Everyone looks washed out under hospital lighting, but Leonard seemed especially bleached. Vince looked at the woman in the bed, three wires attached to her, her eyes swollen and bugging even as she slept. He must have been staring because Leonard spoke as a way of apologizing.

"I'm sorry that you have to see her like this," he said. "She's just… not allowed to be alone."

"How is she?" asked Elisabeth.

"Stable," he said. "They pumped her stomach. She may wake up in a few hours."

There was only one chair in the room, so Vince left to pull in two more from the hallway. He returned to find Elizabeth standing over the woman, lightly touching her hair. She looked up at Vince. Her eyes dipped at the corners. He knew that look from when Moira, their daughter, had been hospitalized with pneumonia. Powerless.

Vince dragged the chair next to Leonard and sat. "Did you find her?" Leonard nodded. Vince pressed on, gently. "How long?"

He took a moment before responding. "They think maybe a few minutes? I didn't… I didn't hear a thing. I was watching *Criminal Minds.*"

He looked over at Vince now, and the older man could see a thought coalescing across his face. He had been summoned to hear this.

"I never thought this could happen," he said slowly. "She had been… off, I guess, for a while now. But I just thought it was the post-partum."

Elizabeth stroked Carol Fisk's hair. Vince was grateful for his wife's poise. Though she said nothing, her very presence seemed to warm the room, as though her body generated a noiseless field that somehow dampened the sharpness of blame, desperation, and fear. For a moment, he thought that this might be the way of women, to draw the pain of helplessness out of a space like a magnet. *No,* he concluded, *it's just Elizabeth.*

"What will happen next?" Leonard asked. "The nurse told me, but I wasn't listening."

"When she wakes up, the police will come," said Vince. "They'll give her a choice. She can go with them willingly, or… they can take her." He looked over at the big man. He was leaning forward, his elbows resting on his knees, his round chin held up by those massive hands.

"How long?"

"A few days, probably. When she comes back to you, it will be different. But this is just getting started. You need to know that."

He nodded. "I know," he whispered. "I know." He turned to look at Vince. "Don't tell anyone, okay? Just… make something up."

"I will."

"They'll be worried about me. Tell them not to worry."

"Okay."

He returned to his stooped over posture. "I don't want that little bastard to have the satisfaction of this. Of any of this."

As a principal, Vince Darten had sat in hospital rooms with parents and kids. He had learned to hold his tongue, to let the silence invite the wound's slow reveal, to hand them bandages if needed but otherwise stand to the side. That is what it is to witness.

Leonard spoke slowly. "I'm glad the police will be here," he said, running his hands over his quads to remove the sweat. "I thought about Googling whether it was a separate crime to, you know, remotely activate a person's webcam while he's, ah, looking at certain sites…"

Vince and Elizabeth exchanged a quick glance. They had both seen the video of Leonard in the second data dump. Everyone had.

"The hacking, that's one thing, but to turn a person's camera on… that just feels like something else. Anyway, I thought about Googling it. But then I thought that that would look bad in my search history. And maybe he's watching my search history. So I'm glad that the police are coming. I can ask them."

There wasn't anything else to say, so Elizabeth pulled the chair beside the bed and held Carol's hand. They turned on the television and watched reruns of *The Golden Girls* for several hours, until it was morning, and it was time to go.

Two days later, he got a call from Bryan Yulders over the walkie talkie. "Bryan to Vince," he said. "Come to my office. We may have something."

The kid's name was Peter Hinchly. Fifteen years old. He had been spotted following another kid into a bathroom stall; a witness claimed he could smell drugs and alerted a dean's assistant, who brought Bryan. The other kid had vanished, and they were still trying to ID him on the hallway video feed. In Peter's backpack, however, they had found a small black flash drive just like the 15 MaKinzie Garvey had found after the original doxxing. The sticks that unlocked firewalls.

"Where is he?" Vince asked when he came into Bryan's office. Matt Reynolds, the school resource officer, was already there.

"I've got him in an empty science classroom down the hall with Scott," said Bryan, referring to the dean's assistant who had initially been flagged down.

"What's he saying?" Vince continued. He was suddenly breathless.

Bryan shrugged. "Says he found it in the cafeteria. Thought it was just another memory stick."

"And his phone?"

Bryan broke eye contact. "Everything's deleted."

Vince slammed the air with his fists. "Goddamn it, Bryan! How many times is this? Get the phone *immediately*."

Bryan Yulders, former lineman, took on the posture and expression of a chastened dog. Detective Reynolds gestured to the kid's backpack on his desk. "There's THC in that vape cartridge of his," he said. "So we have that."

Vince nodded. "Call his parents. Get them in here. I'm going to have a word with Peter."

He found him sitting with his head down on the onyx slab of a lab station. Peter Hinchly had black curly hair, a V-shaped face, long neck, and limbs that seemed to have grown past their owner's ability to comfortably arrange them. His face was speckled with acne, and he blinked painfully when Vince entered the room. *He's been sleeping,* Vince thought.

"Mr. Tetch, I need a word with Peter. Will you wait in the hall?" said Vince, excusing the dean's assistant. He stared at the sophomore for a moment. Was this him? Was this the person—the child—who had blown up his life? He looked almost exactly as Vince had expected him to: white, awkward, and untroubled.

"What were you doing today, Peter?" he asked.

"Nothing," said the boy.

"Nothing. In the bathroom stall, with another boy."

Peter looked away. He was blushing. "He was just showing me something."

"Oh? Can I see what he was showing you?"

A flicker of panic washed across Peter's face; his arms tensed momentarily before all the rigidity leaked out of them and he resumed his posture of slouched indifference. "It's private."

Private, thought Vince. That word. That horrible word. *How dare he use it in my presence?*

"Listen to me, Peter. In this school, you have no privacy. We are going to find your friend. We are going to take his phone. We are going to retrieve the files you deleted. We are going to know everything."

He took three steps towards Peter. Though the boy was perhaps three inches taller than him, Vince loomed, and Peter's posture shrank. *He's afraid,* thought Vince. The boy's legs dangled from the lab stool. One leg was bouncing.

"You brought drugs into Clearwater, Peter. That's above school discipline. That's a criminal matter. The police are coming. Fortunately for you, your principal got here first. So you have just a few minutes to help me decide what I tell them."

Peter shifted, still avoiding eye contact. "What do you want me to say?" He said flatly. Vince took a moment to compose his words.

"We have the memory stick, Peter. We know."

"What?"

"In your backpack. We have the stick you used."

"I've never used it. I found it."

Vince shook his head. *Goddamn it*, he thought, *why do they keep playing after the game is up?* But he had his man; he was sure of it. "You're going to lie to me? At this moment? You're going to lie to me, Peter?"

"I'm not lying! I dunno, check the cameras or whatever! I found it in the cafeteria."

Peter didn't seem rattled by the accusation. And he was right—the video feed could show him picking up the device in the lunchroom. But it might also show who left it. And Vince was convinced that Peter knew who it was.

"Who left the stick?"

"I don't know."

"Tell me, Peter!"

"I don't know!"

When he had taken over for Dave Winde 20 years ago as Dean of students at Crawfordsville High School, Vince had sat with the old man for a drink. "Best liars in the world, high schoolers," said the retiring Winde, sipping his Johnnie Walker. "They will tell you to be gentle with them, that they're just kids. But when you've got them, you can't step around the pressure points. You've got to step *on* them."

"Peter," he said slowly. "I've got witnesses. I know what was happening in that bathroom. And so will your parents if you don't tell me what I want to know."

For a moment, Vince expected Peter to crack, to spill. But instead, the boy's eyebrows made an elaborate dance, and defeat cascaded down his face, into his shoulders, his torso, and his dangling legs. "Please…. Don't…" he whispered, wiping his eyes. "They don't know about Jake."

"He's the one who left the stick?"

"No," Peter sniffed. "He's my… boyfriend."

The boy was shaking. Vince handed him a Kleenex box, which Peter accepted, blowing his nose. *He knows nothing*, thought Vince bitterly. This was no hacker; there was no conspiracy. It was so much more ordinary. A kid, getting high in the bathroom with his boyfriend. Another person at this school, just trying to hold on to his secrets.

———————————

He was at a bar ten miles outside of Clearwater. Vince had ordered a second gin when she finally arrived. "Thanks for coming," he said.

"Well, I simply had to see this for myself," said Catherine Sawyer, the disgraced History teacher. She slid into the booth across from him and smiled coldly.

"How have you been?" he asked, but he knew the answer. Catherine had taken a leave of absence in her final semester before retirement. She had saved so many sick days over her career that he doubted she'd ever return to Clearwater.

"I've been shoveling shit for two months, Vince, if you want to know," she said, signaling the waitress standing by the bar. "But by the look of you, I should be grateful that I at least had a shovel."

Vince laughed mirthlessly, like a valve shooting off an over pressured pipe. "Elizabeth says I need to try smearing some Preparation-H under my eyes so they look less puffy."

"Might work," said Catherine. "Does Preparation-H come in gallon jugs?"

The waitress took her order—scotch and soda—and they didn't say anything to one another until the drink came. "Where is Elizabeth?" asked Catherine, stirring the ice. "Why aren't you sitting across from her right now?"

"There are some stories of the sea that only captains will understand," he smiled, staring at his hands, his ring.

"That's true. So what happened?"

He looked up at her. "I went too far."

Catherine lit a cigarette; the waitress came to tell her to put it out, but the old teacher shot her a withering look honed on thousands of slackers and recalcitrants over the years. The waitress evaporated. "I suppose it was only a matter of time," she said ruefully. "You are, after all, only human, Vince. Despite what you try to tell the rest of us."

"That is the worst part of getting old," said Vince. "Figuring out, too late, that you were never anything more than that."

She nodded, blowing a stream of smoke from the corner of her mouth. "But they want us to be more, don't they? Teachers are mentors, caretakers, moralists, priests, first responders. Saints. And you know how they make saints, don't you? They martyr you."

He laughed again; she continued. "I don't know when it happened," she said quietly. "When I started to hate them. Maybe… maybe one day one of them asked to use my stapler when he should have stapled his work at home. Maybe one of them interrupted a great conversation to ask to use the bathroom. Maybe there was a certain number of lies I could absorb, and they finally exceeded my limit. But when I look at them now…" she trailed off, then looked up at him. "When did you decide to quit teaching?" she asked finally.

"I didn't quit teaching," he said. "I became an administrator."

She waved that away. "Semantics," she said. "Why did you get out?"

He took a few breaths through his nose. "I was always fascinated by them," he said. "Who they were. Where they came from. I'd see them through a tiny window—45 minutes a day—and then they'd vanish. I doubt they thought much about me."

"They never do," she said ruefully. "They just imagine that we stay in those rooms overnight. That we only exist when they're looking at us."

"But I could never stop thinking about them. I wanted to know what made them special. Different. Unique."

"And what did you find?"

"They weren't special. They were ordinary. It was, in a way, sadder than any abuse. They grow up to be people."

She nodded, exhaling a long stream of smoke. "Oh, yes. Yes, they do."

"I read a book about Houdini last summer," he said, one old history teacher to another. "You know, as great a magician as he was, he was an even more gifted debunker. He could go to any other magician's show, watch him perform, and then explain exactly how he did the trick. A fan once asked him, 'Aren't you proud? That you've never been fooled?'"

"What'd he say?"

"He said it was awful. He said he'd give anything to meet someone who could make him believe in magic."

She stubbed out her cigarette. "That's why you quit?"

"It is."

"Is that the truth?"

Vince smiled at Catherine. "A version of it."

She smiled, too. And then Catherine Sawyer laughed.

13
GUS

Gus's step-brother was named Morris, but they all called him Mooch because he preferred to eat his dinner off of other peoples' plates. His grandfather was making a big show of slipping the kid tator tots, both because he adored Mooch and because he knew it drove Keith insane.

Gus had lost his appetite, and he was listlessly poking his potpie as though he were digging through the junk drawer for change. The second doxxing had made everything worse. Every one of his teachers had been exposed, stripped bare, and no one knew how to deal with it all. He had logged on and watched an English teacher masturbate. He knew he shouldn't click, but he did so anyway, only to feel something inside irretrievably slip away. They were all different now.

Should he pity the teachers? But they were liars and frauds and (possibly) deviants. Should he be mad at himself for gawking at their humiliation? But what was he supposed to do? Uninvent Snapchat?

Keith regarded Gus suspiciously, chewing slowly with his fingers folded in front of his mouth. Gus could sense him searching for a target.

"How're those college apps, Gus?" he asked. Gus could sense his mother cringing, as she has updated him hourly on Gus's progress since July.

"Um… they were all due last month," said Gus. "Got 'em all."

"U Penn?" he asked; I nodded. "Miami of Ohio? Ann Arbor?"

"Yup," said Gus. "All of 'em."

"You know, I went to college with one of the admissions officers at Dayton," he said, jabbing a fork in Gus's direction. "Wouldn't be any trouble for me to put in a call."

"Really? Dayton? You never mentioned that," said Grandpa sarcastically; he dipped his eyes to avoid his daughter's withering look.

"I'm not saying you have to go there," said Keith. "It's a good school, though."

"I'm thinking about I State," said Gus quietly. Keith exchanged a look with his wife.

"That David's school?" he asked. Gus didn't need to confirm it; Keith already knew. He shrugged. "Well, I State's okay, I suppose. The main thing is to give yourself as many options as possible. The more choices, the better."

"Grandpa says too many choices is a bad thing," said Gus. "He says it was easier back in the day."

"Oh no, don't drag me into this," said the old man.

Keith was a big, confident man, but he read most rooms poorly. "Well, it's been a long time since your grandfather was entering the workforce. It's brutal out there—kids your age aren't just competing against their next-door neighbor. Did I tell you that last week I had a teleconference with a team of twenty-somethings in Argentina? Perfect English, those kids."

"Did'ja hear that, Mooch?" said Gus's grandfather. "The Argentines are coming for us! Better eat these tots before they get 'em!" He winked at the six-year-old, who winked back.

"Laugh it up, Charles, but I'm trying to give the kid some advice," said Keith. "Everything I've got now, everything I've earned—this house that you live in—but I could have had so much more if I had just *focused* when I was eighteen on giving myself options, on keeping myself open to better opportunities."

"That why you got divorced when you were 41?" said Gus, poking at his potpie.

"August—" said his mother, but Keith cut her off with a raised hand.

"It's all right, Maggie," he said. "It's all right." He stared at Gus with his chipped-ice blue eyes. At the end of most days, the gel in his hair wore out, and his concrete-colored bouffant fell across his enormous forehead. Gus returned his look impassively. Poke, poke, poke.

"I got divorced because I got married too young," he said finally. "I can admit that now, be a man about it. That's what it is to be a man, Gus. Taking responsibility."

Gus looked at his mother; she had her arms folded and was staring at her wine glass. *She won't defend me,* Gus thought. *So I can either submit or escalate.*

"I would have thought taking responsibility would mean not having an affair. Keith."

His mother slammed her fork, stood, and grabbed Mooch right out of his chair. She walked off carrying him, working to strangle her older son with her eyes. Gus's grandfather whistled, long and low.

"Clear eyes, right Gus? You see so much," said Keith, wiping his mouth and shaking his head. "So did I when I was your age. Do you know what I missed?"

"Something about choices?"

Keith smiled. All teeth. "Once you've burned something down, you can't put it back together from ashes. Fire only works one way."

He stood, tossed his napkin, and pointed at his step-son. "Remember that." He stormed off after his wife. Gus looked at his grandfather, who shrugged. He ate some tator tots off of Mooch's plate.

He found his mother in her car, parked in the driveway. She was drinking wine from a thermos. Her breath came out white and wispy in the winter air.

Gus slid into the passenger seat next to her. She was listening to Madonna; he lowered the volume and looked at her for a long while. Finally, he spoke. "Mom, I'm sorry."

"Oh, you're sorry," she said. "Well, that's terrific. You know, just once I would love if one of you apes would remember to be sorry before you decide to start tossing dynamite around the table."

Her indifference cut deep. He wondered if he was finally old enough that she just didn't yell anymore. It made him want to change places with Mooch. He reached for her hand; she pulled away and drank from the thermos.

"You didn't have to pick that fight," she said finally. "I don't know what's with you lately. Are you… are you feeling depressed again?"

She hadn't spoken that word in over a year. There was a time towards the end of sophomore year when Gus broke up three times with a girl named Sasha Koenig. He kissed her and felt nothing; he was awake—finally—to what he was. Yet he was so ashamed, so afraid of letting her down, so certain that he would never be touched, that he let himself sink into the tar pit of codependency. He was terrified that Sasha was his last stop. And she was, because that was when he met David.

"I don't know," he said. "Things are weird at school, weird with David."

She nodded. "I warned you," she said. "I told you what distance does. It's not a heartbreak. A pinprick and then a slow leaking."

"I just got to try harder," said Gus. "I've got to fight for us."

She laughed. "That's what you think, isn't it? That I didn't fight for my marriage?"

She picked up a hook from "Like a Prayer" and delicately hummed along. Even in the borrowed light of streetlamps and ambient suburbia, she looked old. Gus spoke. "Did you? Fight?"

She looked over at him, eyes dry but bleary. "Oh, I fought. But for what? With whom? All those trips he took, all those miles on the road. You fall in love, marry someone. And then day by day you both become someone else until there's nothing left. Two strangers hating one another in a bed."

She was drunk. How long had he left her in this car? "It doesn't have to be like that," he said. "It wasn't that way for Grandpa and Grandma."

She started to say something, then thought better of it, bringing the thermos to her lips. Gus pulled back her hand. "What?" he said. "What is it you were going to say?"

She cocked her head and stared at his hand, then replaced the cap on the thermos and placed it in the drink holder. "When I was Mooch's age—maybe older—I got home from school and went to find my mother. She was always in her chair, folding laundry and watching her stories. And this one day, I went to find her, and the TV was off, and there was a basket full of clothes. I went to the window, looked for her car. I waited there all night until my father came home. Never moved once."

"What happened?"

"She left. No note. No phone call. She just drove off one afternoon without warning."

"But… but I met her."

His mother smiled in the rear-view mirror. "Oh, she came back all right. Eight months she was gone. Comes home tan, hair cut short. I don't know where she went, what she did—that was the deal, Gus—we didn't get to ask. But something was broken in her after that. I folded the laundry. I made the dinner."

Gus couldn't square this. The woman his grandfather spoke of—the PTA stalwart, the neighborhood crossing guard—she never moved. All those pictures on the nightstand—his birth, Mom's graduation, her first bath. Was she lying in all of them? The wedding in '69—did she know even then? *Mrs. Robinson isn't the one who runs,* Gus thought. *It's Eileen.*

"Grandpa never told me that," he said finally. "I never knew."

She nodded. "That's because Grandpa married a girl and never acknowledged the women who came after her. But we," she said, gesturing to the rearview mirror, "didn't have the luxury of such fantasies. Nor do we now." She looked at her son sternly. "You'll apologize to Keith. Make it right."

"Yes."

"No more scenes. Never—not *ever*—in front of Morris. I don't care that you're my son. Do you understand?"

"Yes."

She looked at him a long time, then nodded. "You look just like him, more and more," she said quietly. "I need to be alone right now. I'll be in in a little bit."

There was more he wanted to say, but he nodded and conceded the moment to silence. He closed the door softly, then let the ground spin beneath his feet. His mother was behind him, seated in a car with the engine quiet. It occurred to him that she knew more about her mother's flight, understood it in the language of blood. Some great and terrible curse bound her to the family, kept her from throwing the car in reverse and driving until she ran out of road and regret. He wanted nothing to do with it. Gus realized with a shudder that his mother had shown him the adult face of love.

— — — — — — — — —

GUS: Where r u? We're at the dance.

"Oh wow. They're really going hard with dub step tonight, aren't they?" asked Priya, referencing the music coming from the gymnasium. "It sounds like a Michael Bay film fucking a smaller Michael Bay film."

"It sounds like a vacuum cleaner motorboating a subwoofer," said Carl.

"I was going to make a dubstep joke, but I'll DROP it!" said Kip Cato, Carl's date. *Shut him the fuck up,* said Priya's eyebrow to Carl.

GUS: I've been calling. Why won't you pick up?

"So, yeah. I told Akarsh that we're not going to fool around too much tonight," said Priya over the music. "Ashra told me he's obsessed with Watson's sex tape, and he's dying to try reverse cowgirl."

GUS: Don't do this to me, David. Please, just call me.

"Can you believe how drunk those two are?" shouted Carl, gesturing at Keenan Wurtz and Stacy Goebels packed tight and writhing on the dance floor. His groin was thrusting aggressively and unrhythmically against the back of her dress; her arm was wrapped around his neck for support. "I mean, come on. What is this, a very special episode of *Degrassi*? Act like you've been to war, soldier."

"She's not drunk; they're high," shouted Priya in his ear. "I saw her in the bathroom."

"What? For reals?" shouted Carl. "Bitch better hook me up!"

GUS: This isn't how it's supposed to end. Call me.

"All right, we need to have an intervention," said Carl, ripping the phone from Gus's hands. Carl and Priya locked elbows with Gus's and led him to the cafeteria, where tables had been decorated with inflatable beach balls and sea life cutouts commemorating Clearwater High's "Rock Lobster Winter Ball." A few dozen sweaty couples sat recuperating, suit jackets off, dress slits widened. Carl shooed away a freshman who had taken a necktie and wrapped it around her head like a bandana. They sat at the table. Gus couldn't look at them.

"You know that you are being the least fun Holocaust victim at the party, don't you?" asked Carl. "I can say that because I'm Jewish."

"David is an idiot," said Priya. "He's been an idiot for months now."

"This is true," nodded Carl. Gus shook his head.

"There's an explanation," he said. "He's stranded somewhere. His phone's out of juice. He forgot what day it is—"

"FUCK, WOULD YOU FUCKING LISTEN TO YOURSELF?" shouted Carl. The soft murmur of other groups dipped as others turned to stare. "What the fuck happened to you, Gus? You were my smart friend. The one who could explain, like, *Interstellar* to me or some shit. Now you're too fucking sad for even a Sarah McLachlan pet adoption commercial."

"You wouldn't understand," said Gus.

"Oh? Is this a subtitled film? Kindly translate, professor."

"You…. You both are *incapable* of loving someone else. Everything is a goddamn joke to you! You see everyone as their worst detail, their ugliest thought! It's all just one long urinal for the two of you to piss on!"

Carl laughed; Priya looked away listlessly. "Wow," said Carl. "I didn't realize until this moment how far up your own ass you are. What d'your tonsils look like from the backside, Gus?"

"Carl—"

"Let me start with 'fuck you,' and then I'll elaborate with 'you goddamned arrogant, entitled, *doucholio.'* You think that you're the only one who feels things, the only one that hurts. What a sad gay stereotype you are. Like the worst thing anyone could do to you is stand you up. Like the only legitimate pain is hurt feelings."

He leaned in to his smaller friend; Gus smelled the Jaeger on his breath. "I'd love to tell you about real pain, Gus. What it feels like to be held down until you black out. But I don't think *you'd* understand. So let me tell you something I *do* think you'd get. I hope right now David has a huge cock in his—"

Gus hit him. Not hard, but enough to stagger Carl. He faced Gus, shocked. Then his eyes turned to slits and he lunged. They tumbled backwards and sent a folding chair clattering. Carl was pressing down on Gus; he could hear shouting, see the waving of phones…

"ALL RIGHT, ALL RIGHT! THAT'S ENOUGH!" shouted Mr. Lenk. He grabbed Carl roughly by the lapel of his coat and yanked him off of Gus. Carl stumbled, then wiped his face, looking for blood. Kip and Priya flanked him.

"Who started this?" asked Lenk. The crowd of students, so vocal only moments ago, evaporated.

"I did," said Gus, pulling himself to his feet. A brief spasm of incredulity flashed across Lenk's face. He gestured to Dean Yulders, who was approaching from behind with a walkie-talkie.

"Carl, you go with Dean Yulders. Elliot, I'm gonna have a word with Conor McGregor here before I send him down to you." He spun on the crowd. "Everyone, scatter. I see even one frame of this online, I'll track you down and make sure we have words." Then he pointed at Gus. "You. Classroom. Now."

He led Gus to a special ed classroom that he opened with a key from his lanyard. It was weird for Gus to see Mr. Lenk in a suit and tie; as a PE teacher, he rarely appeared in anything other than track suits and sweat pants. He cleaned up very well. Gus sat in one of the desks while Lenk leaned on a dry erase board and crossed his arms.

"All right, tough guy. What's going on with you?" he said.

Gus wiped my eyes. *Christ, I'm crying,* he thought. *Just when I think I can't fit anymore humiliation into the evening, I discover a sliver of dignity I haven't given away.* "Look… Mr. Lenk, I don't want to be disrespectful. But can you just punish me and send me home? I… don't think I can stand another lecture on what a fuck-up I am."

Lenk's face didn't change, but Gus could see something shift in the teacher's eyes. "Hey now, hey now," he growled. "What happened?"

Where to start? "I don't know, Mr. Lenk. Nothing happened. It's like… everything's so shitty. Teachers are shit, students are shit. And I'm just…. so disappointed in myself. Nothing is the way I thought it is." Lenk didn't say anything; he just scratched the side of his face with a thumbnail. Gus kept talking.

"Did you… did you ever read that Sesame Street book 'The Monster at the End of the Book?' I don't know why I'm thinking of it now. It's about how Grover hears there's a monster at the end of the book, and he freaks out. Does everything he can to keep the reader from getting to the end. But he can't stop it. And then when you do get to the end, you realize Grover was the monster all along. Turns out it wasn't so bad." The tears were coming hot and steady now. "It's always a monster at the end. Isn't it, Mr. Lenk?"

Lenk sighed and sat in a desk next to Gus. They both stared ahead in silence for a moment. "I don't know, kid. I don't know about endings. I mean, that's the reason we do anything, isn't it? To see how it ends?" He looked over at his student. "This have to do with that friend you were telling me about?" Gus nodded. Lenk tossed his head back and forth. "Well, most of these things end badly. I guess you can't blame us for trying. I mean, when you're 16 and you say you want a girlfriend, what do you even know about that? Nothing. Everything we do is for things we don't know anything about."

Gus had no response. For a long while, they were both silent; finally, Lenk spoke. "Tell you what, Gus. Just this once, I'll let you ask me what you want to know. Just this once."

Gus looked at him. Lenk was biting his lips. *He seems genuinely nervous.* "What… what happened with you and Ms. Wells?"

He shook his head. "I don't know. We were doing well. I was farther along than I'd ever been. I felt… well, I felt happy. But then, she started to pull back. It got messy. Hard." He stood, walked back to the dry erase board, leaned against it on his right side. "You read all the text messages. I know you did. Well, here's what I didn't write to her. I was glad that it was ending. I was glad that I wasn't stuck with her. I didn't have what it takes to… to support a difficult person. That's my monster."

"So… so what are you supposed to do with that?"

He shrugged. "Not be surprised next time? Be more careful? Know that I'm not really a good guy when things get tough? I don't know, kid… I really wish I could tell you. But if I had it to do all over again, I wouldn't'a made her end it. I would'a done it myself. Been a man. Seems to me that was my cruelest mistake."

He's just a PE teacher, Gus thought. *He takes out the hockey sticks and sets up the nets each day. Most of the time, we don't even notice he's there.* But in this moment, he filled the whole room.

"Go see Dean Yulders," he said, sliding his hands into his coat pockets. "You're kicked out. You got yourself a Saturday school. Go make nice with Carl."

Gus nodded and gathered himself. "Thank you, Mr. Lenk."

"Gus?"

"Yeah?"

"You gotta believe in monsters. Gotta believe we can get it right."

———————————

Indiana State was an hour and a half away, but he made the trip in 75 minutes. He was ready. He was ready for an ending.

Saturday night in the dorm, and there were coeds everywhere. Some were drinking, some were vaping, some are listening to music and dancing. He looked out of place in his charcoal suit and cornflower tie. Yet most of the students in the hall paid him no heed. He wound his way through the corridor to David's room.

Gus knocked; neither David nor Edward (his roommate) were in. But their door was open, as it always was. He poked his head in and looked around. It was unchanged from his last visit—the lofted beds, the desks with their laptops closed. The room smelled like sweaty workout clothes with a hint of cut grass. He sat on David's bed and waited for him to return.

There was a picture of them taped to David's mini-fridge from one of their first dates. A petting zoo. They were holding ducks. Gus was looking straight into the lens; David's eyes were off to the side. *I never noticed that before.*

There was a knock at the door, and he sat up, ready to launch into his speech. But it was a stranger, a tall, rugged boy with brown-black hair that mismatched his eyes, just like Jared Leto. He was smoking a cigarette, which he removed as soon as he saw Gus.

"Oh… hey," he said, smiling. "I was looking for Eddie. You seen him?"

"Can't say I have," Gus said. "Eddie's the one with the facial tattoo and the prehensile tail, right?"

The boy laughed. "Yeah, yeah, that's Eddie, all right."

Gus nodded. "Well, if I see him, I'll tell him you said 'hey,' Mr.….?"

He put the cigarette back in his mouth to shake Gus's hand. "Taz," he said. "Tell him Taz stopped by."

"Okay, Taz. Good talk." But the boy just stood there, staring at Gus with big blue eyes, smoking his cigarette. "Anything else you want me to tell him?"

"Sorry," Taz said, laughing nervously. "Why're you so dressed up?"

Gus laughed. "What, this? Well, Taz, I work at a funeral home, and I heard that Eddie here has been stealing flowers."

Taz laughed. "Well, shit. Old flower-stealing Eddie."

"We take it very seriously."

"I'll bet you do," said Taz. He sat down next to Gus, who was trying like hell not to think of an elephant.

14
JENN

January became February, and the new year inspired Jenn to remake herself. She let her roots grow out before cutting her hair short. Every Friday she borrowed Ruth's car to swing by a Goodwill in Sumner. She bought new clothes, cutlery, and an old blow drier.

Though she appreciated the heat in her trailer, the diner was home. She got on so well with everyone that Ruth gave her a key after a while and trusted her to lock up on her own. She learned customer names and preferences; she could spot them as they walked through the door and could have their coffee poured before they even sat down. One day while walking to work, a regular passed by in an Oldsmobile. He offered her a lift, but Jenn declined. It unnerved her, being recognized.

The days when she didn't work were busy, too; Jenn set about cleansing and upgrading her trailer. She borrowed cleaning solutions and scrubbed every inch of her domicile. New sheets, a new table, and abundant air fresheners. She read, listened to music, and watched soap operas. Anything to stay moving, to keep her engine running.

She dropped a circumspect postcard assuring her parents of her health and safety. She didn't miss her old life. It felt good not to have a phone or email, not to constantly receive the bad news of others. She did not miss her parents or her siblings; intellectually it saddened her to find how little they meant to her, but a long lifetime of condescension made her revel in her remoteness.

She missed her students, surprisingly, and she returned over and over again to the ungraded papers she had brought with her. By now, they were all thoroughly graded, and she had gone back in many times to fix their errors, to diagnose their errant thinking. She wrote them notes of suggestion and encouragement; later, she flipped over each worksheet and wrote long letters to each student, telling them what she admired about them and where she saw them moving in life. It felt good to think of each kid at an intersection and herself as a figure who had been down the wrong road and could now speak with quiet humility about the benefits of better living.

One thing she couldn't adjust to was the darkness of the countryside. There were no streetlamps, and Cy shut the generators down around 10, so when night settled on the trailer park it fell like an inky curtain. Jenn wrestled with sleep, unable to quiet her mind, unsettled by the stillness of winter and the isolation of Landes. Many nights, she would creep out into the darkness, let herself into Hobby's trailer and slip into his bed. At first, it was exciting and they would burn together wordlessly. But after a while, he wouldn't even rouse, just throwing an arm around her roughly, and she would cling to him like driftwood. Some nights he simply wasn't there, and Jenn would ball herself in his tobacco-stained sheets that she was sure he never changed.

Reuben proved a bright and ready pupil, though also stubborn and slow to accept coaching. She had him order a textbook online, and three nights a week they met in his room to discuss its concepts, to check his work, to work backwards and assess his progress.

She liked him; he was smart, brash, cute, and quick-witted. But there was more to him than she surmised in the first meeting. Reuben rarely left his house; as near as she could tell, he had no flesh-and-blood friends. When he talked about his mother, the conversation always seemed to come around to her age, her health, how tired she seemed at the end of the day. He never spoke of college or future employment. Like Jenn, he seemed committed to digging a burrow for himself and a deep hibernation.

"Tell me the truth, Mary Anne, and be honest," he said one evening as she checked one of his worksheets. "Have I got any chance with you?"

"What are you doing here, Reuben? This is sloppy," she said, ignoring him. "You can't divide by zero; we've talked about this. It's undefined."

"I don't recall that conversation."

"Five minutes ago. I literally explained this to you—again—five minutes ago."

"Ah, well. Who can concentrate? I'm a man, Mary Anne. Do you have any idea how hard it is being a man like me—"

"Goddamnit, Reuben—"

"—looking at a woman like you?"

"Look, can I give you some advice?"

"Anything. Teach me."

"You've got to lay off these cheesy lines. Girls don't go for it; I don't care what you've read online. Just be yourself."

"Be myself. This, from a girl I made a fake ID for."

She laughed. "All right, that's fair. But let's do some algebra, shall we? You're a basic smartass white kid. Start with, say, five points.

You're not a big guy; your physique resembles a wet paper doll. Minus two points. Live with your mother, a little obsessed; minus three points."

"Zero? I have zero points for living at home? I'm sixteen!"

"Thanks for reminding me. Minus another three points."

"You're killing me, Mary Anne."

"You could add a point or two with a decent haircut and some clean clothes, but your current look suggests background extra on *The Walking Dead*. You're smart, and you've got a sense of humor, so hey— four points. But humor's weightless with most girls; nobody thinks about a joke again after she's heard it. If you're not real with someone, they're never going to look at you like you're a man."

"Is that so?" he said, balancing his pencil between his thumb and index finger. "All right, let's get real. Ask me something."

"Like what?"

"I don't know; this is your thought experiment. What will make me real to you?"

Jenn thought for a moment; Reuben, for once, was silent and attentive. "You know, I've always thought that everyone has two secrets," she said finally, "that they protect with all their strength, their dying breath. Even under threat of torture, they keep these secrets."

"What are they?" asked Reuben.

"The first is what they're most afraid of," she said. "The second is what they want most in this world." She let him think about it for a moment before asking, "What are you most afraid of, Reuben?"

He set down the pencil and leaned back with his hands in his lap. Reuben looked away; when he spoke, his voice had hollowed out. "Staying here," he said. "With her coughing. Dying in my bed."

"What do you want most? The real thing, Reuben," she said, cutting off another glib remark.

"I want… I don't know how to answer this…"

"Just say what comes to mind."

"A full tank of gas. A country road. Freedom from a sick mother."

Jenn laughed. "I know exactly what you mean," she said. "*Exactly.*"

Reuben cocked his head and raised an eyebrow. "Well? Real enough for you?"

She smiled and patted his forearm. "You have no idea how relieved I am that both responses weren't gross sex things."

He smiled. "What about you?"

"Do you have a more specific question?"

"Who are you? Really?"

She kept her smile fixed. "My name is Mallory Pike; I'm from Stoneybrook, Connecticut…"

"Stop, stop!" he interrupted, waving his hands. "More Babysitter's Club? Come on now, *shiksa*. Your two secrets. What are you most afraid of?"

She looked at him. He was sixteen years old. The contours of broad shoulders and a rugged jaw were coming into focus, but she had to squint to see them. Not yet a man, but soon enough. What would it be like if they met when she was 36 and he 26? 46 and 36? With each decade, the gap between them grew smaller. But it was a chasm now, and she didn't trust him to cross it. Still…

"Being caught, found out," she said. "Being seen."

"What do you hope for most?"

She thought for a moment. "To be found," she said. "To be seen."

He looked away; she felt embarrassed for them both. "I make a lot of IDs for my mom. Some people are looking for a home. Some are running. Women who are scared of husbands or exes, they're usually up front about it. That's not what this is, though, is it?" He stopped and looked at her earnestly. "I know I'm a kid to you. I know. But if I wasn't… if things were different… I'd find you. I'd… I'd see you. And you wouldn't need to run."

— — — — — — — — —

One Saturday afternoon, Hobby asked if she wanted to go with him to Vincennes.

"What're we gonna see there?" she asked. "Clambake? A jiggery-poke?"

He laughed. "My daughter's birthday," he said. "Thought you'd like to meet her."

She smiled, nodded. "I would. Should I bring her something? Kids like knives, right?"

It was a half hour to Vincennes, and she let the radio fill the cab of Hobby's truck. She glanced at him, uncertain what to say, unsure what he'd want to hear. Hobby seemed preoccupied; there were dark rings around his eyes, which were puffier than normal. Despite the cold, he was sweating, and every few minutes one of his limbs would unexpectedly spasm. When songs gave way to commercials, she turned it down to talk.

"So what's her name?"

"Evie."

"Another dog name?"

He shook his head. "Evelyn Tanner. After her great-grandmother. On her mother's side," he added.

Jenn fiddled with the drawstring on her hoodie. "You get along with Evie's mom?"

Hobby looked at her askance, then put his eyes back on the road. "Well, it's like this. Two kids meet at a barbecue, and the guy tells the girl the biggest lie he can think of. A real whopper. And the girl, she believes it, maybe because she's young, maybe because she's dumb. Who's to say… it was a million years ago."

"What was the lie?"

He waited a moment. "That I was going places. That I had a plan."

"Nothing wrong with standing still," she said.

He nodded. "True enough. 'Course, if you're both standing still, then you're just looking at each other."

"And?"

"And you might not like what you see."

Evie's mother—Amber—lived on a well-lit street at an address that nearly brought Jenn to tears. "246 *Kickapoo*?" she laughed. "Is that for real?"

"This here used to be Kickapoo land," Hobby grinned at her. "Try to be a little more mature than my six-year-old daughter." Jenn responded by blowing raspberries in the palms of her hands.

Evie was a whooping, galloping girl who wrapped her arms around her father as soon as he stepped out of his truck. "DAADDDYYY!" she yelled, scrambling up his leg like a lemur. "Look what I can do!" She produced a jump rope and skipped around the driveway.

"Oh my gosh," said Jenn. "Did I really just see that? Your dad didn't tell me that you were a tiny Chinese acrobat."

Evie laughed and kept skipping rope. "I'm not Chinese!" she said. "I'm WinneBAGo!" she sang. Hobby shrugged and led them inside, where Amber was setting up a crockpot filled with Italian beef.

The afternoon passed pleasantly enough; there were other family members gathered, and Jenn made polite small talk about the Superbowl, the Oscars, the state of the nation.

"Didja hear about that high school up north where all the teachers had their private shit published online?" asked Willis, an uncle whose enormous belt buckle drew unflattering attention to his midsection.

"Um, no," said Jenn. Suddenly she was sweating. Willis pulled out his phone and scrolled through something.

"Oh yeah, man, it's messed up. Buddy of mine is a vendor up there, said the school is falling apart. Said some teacher tried to kill himself at a hotel in French Lick."

"All right, that's enough, Willis," said Amber, swatting at his phone. "We all heard about that school. This is a kid's party."

"Hey, she's gonna be a taxpayer before you know it, Sis," he said. "Kid deserves to know what she's paying for!"

Jenn fled the family room for the garage, where she nursed a beer and tried to calm her nerves. She had managed to avoid thinking about Clearwater for a few days; had even allowed herself to think of herself as Mary Anne for the afternoon. Her world had shrunk so small these past few weeks that she had forgotten how easily it all could collapse on her. *Stupid, stupid* she thought to herself. *Why did I think I could leave my hole?*

The door from the laundry room opened, and Amber came out, wrapped in a North Face coat. She smiled at Jenn.

"See you had the same idea I did," she said, lighting a cigarette. "Quick trip to flavor country."

"Miller time for me," said Jenn, holding up her bottle.

Amber smoked in silence for a minute. "I'm sorry if this is weird for you," she said, ashing into the Styrofoam cooler holding the beers. "Hobby didn't tell me you were coming with him."

"Hobby didn't really tell me much about it, either," said Jenn. Amber nodded wearily.

"Figures. Not a forward thinker, that one."

"Oh, I don't know," said Jenn. "He bought a water filter."

Amber laughed. "You're here because you're a nice girl. A clean girl. And he wants me to see that he can be clean, too."

"Honestly, I'm just here for the giardiniera."

Amber shook her head apologetically. "Sorry, that came out wrong. I can be nice, too. It's just… he's been asking for more time with Evie."

"He talks about her a lot."

Amber nodded. "I'm sure. But she's six now. And she'll remember the next time he sells all her toys to get his fix." She eyed Jenn knowingly. "So I gotta ask—one nice girl to another—what's he into these days?"

The truth was, Jennifer Watson knew very little about Hobson

Tsosie. Some mornings when she left, his truck was still at the park; some nights when she came home he was elsewhere. His hours were his own; his comings and goings went unexplained. He didn't work; that much she surmised, yet he was sometimes curiously flush with cash. He drank often and sometimes stank of urine. She couldn't tell this woman anything for sure. But in the pit of her stomach where she felt hard truths, Jenn recognized a man in shameful retreat from his failures.

"Not much, near as I can tell. Wakes up, goes to work, comes home."

Amber nodded and stubbed out the cigarette. "When we met, he had a good job, a place to go. After he got laid off, he sort of drifted. Moved into that trailer, went dark for a long time. I'm glad he's working again; he needs that. A man's got to have a purpose, right? Otherwise, he's lost."

Jenn drank deep. "Right," she agreed.

On the ride home, Jenn was quiet. She stared out the window at the gray and oyster-colored fields, the crooked groves and copses, the frozen ponds cracked and thawing. Finally, she looked over at Hobby.

"What'd you bring her?"

"What?"

"Evie. For her gift."

"Oh," he paused. "A gift card. Target. You know, let her pick something out."

"Yeah, nice," said Jenn. "What, ah, happened to the keyboard?"

"The keyboard?"

"Yeah, you know. The keyboard that you had when I first met you. You were going to give it to her?"

"Ah. That." He said. "Well, I guess I lost it somewhere along the way."

Jenn couldn't help herself. "Lost it..." she said, teasing out the words. "Sold it..."

"Something on your mind, Mary Anne?"

Let's be real together, thought Jenn. "Where do you go during the day?" she asked.

"Work."

"Uh huh... and those night's you're not in your trailer, where are you?"

"Out."

She had a choice now—retreat or press. "Look, I... I know that I'm just the girl in the trailer park you sometimes fuck, and I'm not invited to have an opinion on things like your daughter. But you've been sweating all day, and it's thirty degrees out..."

He said nothing.

"Anyways... it was nice to meet her today," said Jenn. "She's a beautiful girl."

Hobby turned on the radio. "Reckon this was a bad idea," he said. "Not what I had in mind."

He dropped her off at her trailer, but rather than heading back to his own, he drove off. She watched the taillights of his truck grow dim until the night swallowed them. For a long time, she peered out the window, waiting for him to return, at once ardent in her remorse and furious at its presence. *This is what it's like to be run from*, she thought as the lights shut down at 10:00. *Remember.*

15
CONNOR AND COLLEEN

COLLEEN: U there?

olleen checked her phone again. It had been two hours. It wasn't like Alice to take this long. Finally, she heard the chime and hit the home button.

ALICE: Sorry. It's been a long day. Haven't been myself. :(

COLLEEN: U want 2 talk?

ALICE: You've seen all the shit online?

COLLEEN: >:(

COLLEEN: It IS bullshit.

Colleen McTaggort had met Alice Cespids through travel volleyball. The two had shared a hotel room several times at tournaments, and even though Alice was now halfway across the country at Iowa State, the two still spoke with some regularity. Colleen was the rare sort of friend who seemed capable of absorbing the pain and sadness around her without allowing the corrosive emotions to corrupt her bloodstream. She was the first to reach out to a teammate who missed a block, the first to bring up self-forgiveness, the first to show up with ice cream and a Hallmark Channel DVD featuring two impossibly beautiful, conflicted, and chaste professionals drawn together in some Thomas Kinkaid coastal town.

She dialed Alice's number and listened as her friend recounted the online horror of the past two weeks. "Even out here, in the corn fields, I'm hearing about it," said Alice. "These girls asked me not to stop by the sorority house this weekend. 'Daughter of a *pedophile*! What might the pledges think?'"

"I'll tell them what to think," said Colleen. "Mind your b'ness, bitches!"

Alice laughed. "No, no. I can't fight it, 'Leen. You respond, you just feed the trolls. They take it online, and they make it worse. I've got to just ride this out until something else comes along. I can't believe I'm saying this, but it would be great if there was a rash of teen pregnancies in the Bible Belt or something."

Colleen and Alice spoke for another 20 minutes before the older girl thanked her for listening and went to meet a study group. For a long time, she thought about Alice's absence at the sorority function. When she was thirteen, Colleen had gone to the shopping mall with her mother to buy her sister clothes. She had waited at the front of a Gap while the older McTaggorts tried on jeans in a changing room. A small child—not more than three or four—was crying in the food court across the way. No one stopped to help, no one even seemed to register his noises. Finally, Colleen left her post and walked to the child.

"What's wrong?" she asked. "Did you lose your mother?" The child nodded. So Colleen McTaggort helped him. She had been the only one to hear him crying.

She opened her laptop. The blinking cursor led the way.

"…We can turn to humor when we're happy or when we're sad. We can laugh at ourselves when we're too proud or excited, and we can laugh at others when they willingly make fools of themselves.

But allegations of pedophilia are not funny. The ruination of an innocent man's life is not a topic for comic strips. And when we read these comments or add to them, we do ourselves harm, too. Something is lost when we accept with laughter that everything is for sport and nothing is serious."

Vince Darten furrowed his brow. "A kid wrote that?" he asked.

"One of our kids," said Harry Buchanan, setting down his iPad. "Colleen McTaggort. Posted it on Clearwater Confidential."

Vince laughed. "That's the first positive posting on that rag in years. I wonder if they'll shut down the site now."

"She's going to get creamed," said Harry. "Absolutely destroyed."

Vince shrugged. "Well, we'll see," he said. "It was a disappointed crowd that watched Daniel walk into the lion's den. Sometimes it just takes a little faith."

Connor couldn't believe his good fortune. The McTaggort editorial read like some sort of parody of a Jezebel blog post. Yet it was sincere, absolutely free of irony. It was a target-rich environment. For God's sake—*she signed her own name!*

If there was one thing that Connor hated more than secret pedophiles, it was the encroaching fascism of Social Justice Warriors. There was a certain type he had come to loathe—the jack-booted Fem-thugs who scanned the Internet for the latest micro-trigger to whip up a faux-outrage at the imagined heresies against LGBTQ doctrine. They were extremists disguised as the moral majority, intolerant misanthropes accusing everyone else of intolerance. They were humorless, suppressive, unthinking, hateful, and—above all—hypocrites, basic white girls who screamed privilege without once reflecting on the entitled hegemony of their own upbringing. In their Puritanical zeal, they threatened everything democratic and empowering about the Internet, and here was one living right down the street from him, decrying meme culture, the most democratic form of art ever created.

But Connor knew that he would have to proceed with caution. For although Social Justice Warriors were zombie-like in their predictability, they were astute about attracting attention, and, when provoked, absolutely devastating in their recklessness. Connor recalled the Rolling Stone article that dragged a fraternity reputation through the mud because the author—a renowned SJW—refused to fact-check the false accusations of a co-ed, foolishly believing that we must never question "rape" victims, that to do so is 'victim-blaming' and could potentially 'retraumatize the sufferer.'

So a stealth campaign would be necessary. He logged onto The Breen, a subreddit he frequented with several likeminded dissidents. "Guys," he wrote, "what do you know about Colleen McTaggort?"

— — — — — — — — —

Colleen McTaggort was under attack by bots. They were suddenly all over her feed—anonymous accounts that began appearing with greater regularity throughout the day.

RODNEY LAYEL @MAXIMAN247: @LeenTag kill yourself; you are a hateful cunt that no one would mourn.

ELECTRICA @XANADUME12: @LeenTag I'd tell you to choke on a cock, but I respect cock too much.

There were more imaginative warnings in her DMs, graphic descriptions of rape and violence. But they were careful to avoid specific threats—there were no dates, times, locations, or names listed. She believed that they were purposefully hyperbolic to hide behind the fig leaf of satire should she ever secure a name on whom to pin charges.

Worse still, however, were the parody accounts set up in her name.

THE REALCOLLEEN @REALCOLLEENTAG: Really stoked to label some white people racist this weekend then deny that white people can suffer due to institutional racism!

She contacted site administrators to report abuse and harassment; sometimes the accounts were taken down, but more often than not she received a response informing her that the content she reported did not fit the company definition of harassment.

She tried to stay offline, but the knowledge that these accounts were proliferating dogged her. She received screenshots from her friends via text messaging. People in the halls seemed to leer at her as she moved among them.

The SnapChat harassment was worse—a picture of her changing in the locker room began circulating, attached to embarrassing filters and animal noises. Because of the ubiquity of Snapchat among her friends, it was only a matter of time before Colleen felt that the entire school had seen her in her least-flattering sports bra.

A website appeared in late February specifically designed to draw attention to certain links and search phrases. It was a crude technique known as a Google bomb, and Alice learned about it when she typed Colleen's name into the search engine to discover that the first searchable term associated with her was "judgmental bitch."

Colleen's body began to betray her. She caught a nasty cold that she could not seem to shake. She developed eczema in the pits of her elbows and scratched herself until she bled. She felt dazed and sluggish. Betsy Rilke noticed her put her head down in class one Thursday. "What's going on, Colleen?" she asked after the bell rang.

"Nothing, Mrs. Rilke," said Colleen. "I'm fine."

———————————

On February 27th, Colleen posted a second editorial on Clearwater Confidential. She included all the screen shots of the most offensive Tweets and all the captures her friends had sent. "*I stand by everything I wrote in my last post,*" she wrote. "*Every word. I am willing to meet and debate these people in public, face to face. What I find most cowardly is their insistence on hiding behind fake accounts and bogus names. If you believe in something, you should sign your name.*"

The last sentence was almost too perfect for Connor. He immediately whipped up a set of memes to immortalize it.

He couldn't believe how bad she was at this. Everything she wrote only reinforced his point. Every post she made only drew more attention to his cause and brought more supporters to the fight. There would be more accounts, more memes, more humiliations. His friends had figured out Colleen's brother's gaming tag; already, they were ganging up on him in Overwatch. He knew she was suffering, and he didn't relish the secrecy. He had a private fantasy of meeting her in the courtyard at school and humiliating her with her own illogical arguments. But she would only use such an encounter to exaggerate her own victimhood, to profit from its false posture. They had to make a public example of her from the shadows. He had to show what happened to the proto-fascists of high school before they metastasized into adults.

His own parents' efforts to remove Mr. Cespids had been stymied.

A group of concerned parents had met with some lawyers and representatives of the police department. They had been told the case was weak, circumstantial, incongruent from past behavior or character witness. "Without further evidence," the lawyer explained, "I'm afraid there just isn't grounds for an injunction."

"This is unacceptable. Unacceptable!" Connor heard his mother say when she arrived home. "There are hundreds of parents who want this man gone. Doesn't that count for anything?"

Late that night, Connor awoke to find his father sitting on the foot of his bed, staring out the window. It was a cold, clear night, the moon burning like a great white coin. "An awful sin, pedophilia," he heard his father say. "It is a stain. An abomination." Connor lay perfectly still, pretended to sleep. His father stared for many minutes before rising and gliding out silently. Connor sat up in bed and permitted himself seven scrapes of the wall.

————————————

"I wanted to meet with you, Colleen," said Vince. "To lend you my support. To put the full weight of this office behind your efforts."

"Thank you, Mr. Darten," she said.

"Cyber bullying is very hard to police, very difficult to address," he continued. "This is our school resource officer, Detective Reynolds. This is Ms. Burkle, a social worker. And you already know Dean Yulders and Mrs. Haymond, your guidance counselor," he said, gesturing to the other adults in his office.

"Hello," said Colleen.

"Colleen, we need to know," said Detective Reynolds, "Do you have any knowledge of who might be doing this?"

"No," said Colleen.

"Do you know if they are using school computers or school technology?" asked Dean Yulders.

"No."

"No, they aren't? Or no, you don't know?"

"I don't know."

Vince laced his fingers and rested his chin on his pointers. She was a smart, accomplished girl, clearly undeterred by the harsh judgment of her peers. But he could tell she was not sleeping, was not eating. Her skin looked yellow, and she was breaking out.

"Colleen," he said quietly. "I can't imagine how hard this must be for you. But I've seen this many times, even before we had cameras on our phones. Often, the victims are afraid to speak up. They think it will make things worse, that the adults won't do anything or take it seriously. Does it look as though we don't take this seriously?"

"No, sir."

"I need to ask again, Colleen. Do you have any idea who is behind this?"

Goddamn him, she thought. *The school has been on fire for three months. What has he been doing? He brings four adults into this room. Four adults who can't do shit.* She peered through the glass wall separating the principal's office from the main rotunda. It was teeming with students. They had seen her go in; they would see her leave. It didn't matter what she said; simply being here was making it much, much worse.

She looked Vince Darten straight in the eyes, unblinking. "I don't know anything," she said evenly. "May I go back to class?"

— — — — — — — — —

She sat down across from him at the lunch table quite suddenly and without introducing herself.

"Hello," said Connor, taken aback. Although his face betrayed neither shock nor disapprobation, he felt as though his body temperature raised ten degrees in less than a second.

"Hey," said Colleen. "Sorry. Do you mind if I sit here for a second?"

"It's a free lunchroom," he said. *What is she doing?* he thought, the panic producing a metallic taste in his mouth. He chewed some sunflower seeds to try and settle his nerves.

"Thanks," she said, unwrapping a sandwich and taking huge, wolfish bites. She was restless and not making eye contact; he could tell by the tension in her posture that she was using this otherwise empty table as a vantage point for the rest of the lunch room. Connor relaxed his fingers just a bit.

"Do I know you?" he forced himself to ask.

"Oh, yeah," she said, and his heart fell into his stomach before she added, "I'm Internet famous. Or notorious. I don't know; I've stopped blushing about it. That's the difference between nice girls and whores, right? The blushing?" She giggled absentmindedly before realizing what she had just said and looking at him in panic. "I'm sorry. I don't usually talk about whores. I don't think I know how to talk to people anymore."

"I've got to admit, it beats my usual conversations about sub-prime mortgages and nuclear proliferation."

She laughed, and a wet shiver ran down his spinal column. "I'm Colleen," she said.

"I'm Connor."

"Can we," she stammered, brushing her hair behind her ear, "Can we start over?"

"About whores?"

She laughed again. Connor found himself smiling. *Jesus,* he thought. *It really is a coincidence.* Maybe she sat across from him because her friends had abandoned her, and she was alone. Maybe she hoped that because his phone was away, he might not own one. Maybe he just looked nice. *She has no idea who I am,* he thought. *She has no idea what I've done. What I'm doing.* And then, with a pang of guilt: *What I will do.*

They talked pleasantly for fifteen minutes about classes, their teachers, the dance. *She's a beautiful, winsome girl*, Connor thought. *If I'd only met her a year ago…*

"Can I ask you something?" he said towards the end of the period.

"Sure," she smiled.

"Why did you come sit here?"

A look of confusion flashed across her features. "Um," she began. "I'm going through something with my friends. I don't really know how to explain it." She stared at her hands for a moment. Connor could see that her cuticles had been pulled back until they bled. "Like, when I was three, I was at church, and I was walking next to this set of legs. I thought they were my mother's legs. But when I looked up, it was a stranger." She ran her left thumb gently along the contours of her wrist. "It's like that, but with my friends."

The bell rang. "You know," said Connor, gathering his backpack, "you can sit here tomorrow. If you want. We don't have to talk about sex workers…"

She looked as though she might cry, but just as suddenly the clear sky of gratitude gave way to the gray clouds of mistrust. "Um, we'll see," she mumbled, before adding, "It was nice talking to you!"

"You, too," said Connor. He watched her walk away, a pathetic, wounded creature. *She's a girl, just a sad little girl,* he thought, *slowly losing her friends.* A spasm of pity washed over him; he chased it away by reminding himself that she was a pedophile apologist, a cultural totalitarian, a condescending moralist, and a base hypocrite. Six months ago, she would never have deigned to sit with him, before she had been justly humbled. He couldn't allow himself to be charmed by the slenderness of her shoulders or the melody of her laugh. They were at war, and Connor Marder knew exactly what he needed to do.

16
READING CAMUS IN FRENCH

Lana Collins began every day at 6:15 A.M. with 25 pushups and 25 crunches. She dressed, then brushed her teeth with an electric toothbrush for two minutes, during which time she made her bed and fed her dog. She ate a toasted English muffin with strawberry preserve. She drank 12 ounces of water. Then she got in her car at 6:45 A.M., drove five miles to work, and taught four periods in a row of French II to sophomores.

It was exhausting, relentless work. Each class contained between 28 and 32 students, packed into a windowless classroom adorned with laminated posters of dated celebrities and pictures of Nice. The term *sophomore* means 'wise fool,' which Lana always thought fit them well. Fifteen is an age where experience begins to ferment into cynicism, which Lana believed to be the bedrock of wisdom. Yet they were still mostly in the grips of the sort of reckless optimism that led to forearm tattoos and campus socialism. They could also be staggeringly stupid. Lana Collins was at an age where she had grown allergic to staggering stupidity.

For this reason, her fifth period lunch was often the highlight of her day, a time to close the door, play some Boney James, sip a kale smoothie, meditate, and read. She did not grade during these 50 minutes; she did not make copies or run scantrons. Fifth period was for Lana Collins to shut out the world.

To be sure, this had grown more difficult in the decade she had worked at Clearwater High School. Counselors had grown bold about scheduling IEP and 504 meetings during 5th hour, and her email inbox seemed inexhaustible in its appetite for parental and administrative requests. But from her first days, Lana had recognized the importance of a lunch period, how her entire integrity of a person depended on its preservation, and so she politely but firmly defended its solitude.

Ironically, the solitude offered by teaching was one of the things that most attracted Lana. Despite being surrounded by hundreds of teenagers for eight hours a day, Lana had minimal contact with other adults, which suited her more than her previous life as a paralegal. Teaching had also offered generous health benefits. Nine years ago, Lana—who had been born Laurence—had taken advantage of a loophole (since closed) in the district insurance plan to receive genital reconstruction surgery. To the Clearwater community, Lana appeared no different in September than when she had left for summer vacation in June, but the ten weeks that made up that break represented a consummation she had desired her entire life. She had, both before and after the surgery, regularly worn transdermal patches of estradiol and spironolactone. All of this information was released in a series of medical files included in the second Cloudburst.

Unlike many of her fellow educators, Lana greeted the release of her files with a sense of grim resignation rather than shock or betrayal. Her whole life, she reflected, constituted unwanted, forced exposure.

She had from her childhood felt an oppressive sense of nakedness, and although the past decade had allowed her a modicum of dignity and self-control, she was, and always would be, at the mercy of external forces. She could not dispel her Adam's apple, nor could she completely abolish (or even control) the growth and coarseness of her hair. Her voice was so low that people constantly thought she had a cold. There were two patches of fat that had stubbornly resisted years of side planks and smoothies. Her shoulders remained broad and ox-like, and her pores, despite an expensive and rotating regiment of nighttime moisturizers, resembled in her eyes the surface of an asteroid. She suspected her colleagues whispered about her, and it had brought her a certain rueful pleasure when all of their secrets had come tumbling out in December. The second dump, she reflected, was a deserved humbling, a reminder that her secrets were never in her control. Only in the classroom could she enjoy such dominion.

Not that these revelations were without their sting, of course. During second period, Lana had collected a set of worksheets that she had set to mark up and hand back while the class worked in small groups on translating modern pop hits into French. One worksheet, submitted anonymously had the phrase "Dieu ne veut pas de toi" typed over and over again. *God does not want you.* The words had instantaneously hooked onto a memory from her childhood, a Christmas nativity play where Laurence was asked to play Melchior, bringing frankincense to the infant messiah. Melchior had been issued a beard made of brown felt. Laurence had been yelled at for appearing in dress rehearsal without it. As an adult, Lana had laughed at the clumsiness of the metaphor, but now the shame rushed to her enormous pores, and she reached absently to feel for the fabric again.

She had scanned the classroom, where students laughed and shouted mangled Drake lyrics at one another. *Which one of them?* she thought angrily. But there was nothing—not a name, not a distinctive cursive loop—by which she could reveal the emboldened coward.

Lana taught the next two periods absently, returning again and again in sensation and memory to the shameful nativity scene, to her cul-de-sac of rage at the faceless tormenter. All this progressivism, all these lessons on the dignity of the Civil Rights Movement, the heroism of Laverne Cox, the embrace of Lady Gaga. None of it mattered. Nothing had changed.

She was sitting at her desk, staring at the worksheet when there came a knock at her door. *Go away*, she thought, but instead turned towards the latticed plexiglass panel and motioned for the student to enter. It was Whin-shen ("Winnie") Huang, from her third period. She was a small and slender girl with long black hair pulled into a pony tail that reached down between her shoulder blades. She wore a powder blue Foo Fighters t-shirt over a white long-sleeved turtleneck, a black skirt and black leggings. Winnie Huang was smiling.

"Winnie."

"Ms. Collins!"

She was strangely silent, her mouth hanging open as though she had begun to speak and then been interrupted by a distant noise. Finally, Lana filled the vacuum. "What do you need?"

"Are you busy?"

"This is my lunch period."

"Oh! Oh, I don't need anything, Ms. Collins. It's just…"

And again, a silence. "It's just what?"

"I need some place to read."

"We have a library."

"Yes, but, it's so noisy in there, and there's just this sort of maddening busyness, right? Like all these bees have taken human form, and instead of making honeycombs they're printing SparkNotes and copying math homework…"

"Winnie," said Lana slowly so as not to be driven to strangulation. "Winnie, this is not a space for students. This is the only time of day that I have to myself."

The sophomore nodded vigorously, but then scrunched up her face plaintively. "Yes, yes, I totally understand, Ms. Collins, I get it. Only, only… please? Pretty please?"

Despite its infrequency, Lana knew this wasn't an uncommon request; there were many teachers who shared their lunch space with students (Andy Waters being one of them). Lana Collins was not unfriendly to her students, but her professional remoteness had never seemed particularly inviting to them, and her lack of humor made the idea of spending extra periods in her presence unappealing to the average sophomore. In truth, this entreaty was a first in Lana's career.

So despite significant reservations, she established the following conditions: "You are not to speak to me or ask me for anything. You are not to make any noise. If I need to leave the room, even to use the bathroom, you will have to leave. I will not help you with your homework. I will not share my food with you. Can you abide by this?"

"Yes! Yes! Thank you, Ms. Collins, thank you! You won't even know I am here!"

Lana was highly skeptical of this, but Winnie proved true to her word. She pulled out a copy of *The Catcher in the Rye*, which she had been assigned in Honors English, and spent the period annotating in the margins. The next day she returned, and Lana made the same speech, and Winnie again obeyed her decrees. The third day followed the same pattern, and by Friday, Lana simply left the door open for Winnie Huang.

She made quick work of *Catcher*, and two weeks later Winnie showed up, sat in her desk, and simply folded her hands. She said nothing and did not make eye contact, but the presence of an unbusy student quickly unnerved Lana. "Winnie?" she said after a few minutes. "Winnie, where is your book?"

"Oh! Oh, I finished it, Ms. Collins."

"Well, then," said Lana. "What are you doing here?"

"Um… do you have anything for me to read?"

"Once again, Winnie. We have an entire library at this school. Straight down the hall. Fifth door on your right."

"Yes, yes, that is true. Right you are, Ms. Collins. But… but do *you* have something for me to read?"

"Why me?"

"I just… you know, you just seem very interesting, Ms. Collins. I thought maybe you might have something for me to read."

*I work very hard to be uninteresting, you jabbering twi*t, Lana thought to herself. But the girl's face was open and earnest. And the request was so benign that Lana found herself moving almost without thought to a supply cabinet in the corner of the room. She rummaged inside until she found the box she sought: a class set of *L'etranger* by Albert Camus left over from when she had taught AP French. She tossed Winnie a dog-eared copy. "Here."

Winnie flipped through the slender novella. "It's… it's French…" she said.

"I'm a French teacher."

"But… I don't speak French. I mean, I know I can say SOME things in French, like *boeuf* and *Vendredi* and *vignt-huit*, but, you know, I'm not NOVEL good…"

Lana tossed her a brick-sized pocket dictionary. "Also in French," she said. "Everything in life is an act of translation, Winnie. I think you'll find it worth the effort."

Winnie's mouth hung open, and for a moment Lana's stomach clenched in anticipation of staggering stupidity. But once again, Winnie surprised her. She put down her head and began to read.

— — — — — — — —

"So this guy, Meursault…"

"Shhh! No talking, Winnie."

"Just… just help me with this part… this guy, Meursault…"

"Meur*SAULT*."

"…Meur*SAULT*. His mother's dead. Did he kill his mother?"

"Keep reading."

"I just feel like he did it. Listen to this, "*Madame Meursault n'avait pas de moyens…*"

"Meur*SAULT*."

"That's what I said!"

"Please don't speak to me."

"*MeurSAULT.*"

"Keep practicing."

— — — — — — — — —

"Raymond wants to sleep with this girl and spit in her face?"

"Yes."

"Because she cheated?"

"Because he *thinks* she cheated."

"And Meursault is okay with this?"

"What does the book say?"

"I don't know. It's all in French."

"Find the page. Read it to me."

"Where?"

"Here."

"Je ne me souciais pas d'un…"

"That's it. That's it. '*Je ne me souciais pas d'un côté ou de l'autre, mais il semblait tellement fixé sur lui, j'ai hoché la tête et dit, "Oui."'*—'I didn't care one way or the other, but he seemed so set on it, I nodded and said, "Yes."'"

"He doesn't… he doesn't care?"

"No."

"About this girl. About his mother."

"He says he feels nothing."

The girl covered her eyes. There was suddenly a great quiet about her. She shook—first in the shoulders, then in her chest.

"Winnie? Are you all right?"

"I'd care." Silence. And then: "That's all I do."

———————————

"He shot him!"

"I know."

"He just… he just *shot* him!"

"Right."

"Four times! Five times, actually!"

"Correct."

"This book is nuts! The French are *fucked* up!"

"Winnie!"

"Sorry, Ms. Collins! Sorry!"

"Meursault is Algerian."

———————————

It took Winnie Huang more than six weeks to finish the book. She left the text in the classroom each day and promised not to Google it in between sessions. Some days she made great progress, others she was trapped by a particularly thorny idiom or intricate phrasing. But as they worked together, she gradually became more intuitive and fluent. Indeed, as the book approached its conclusion, she could feel Winnie slowing the pace, savoring the language.

Winnie hated Meursault. Hated his indifference, his strange bouts of heatstroke ("Basically, this whole book is over if he just chugs some Gatorade."). She hated how he divorces any feelings for Marie from the compulsion to sleep with her ("I know I'm not supposed to say this, Ms. Collins, but Meursault is a fuckboy. Let's make him take a

Buzzfeed quiz!") She hated the long descriptions of items he owned in his apartment. More than anything, she hated his passivity and endless desire for sleep.

"The only thing he cares about is yelling at this chaplain!"

"That's not true."

"Oh. Okay. Also, killing Arabs. Racist."

"You're missing the point."

"Isn't Meursault missing the point? Basically all he has to do—besides not shoot Arabs—is just lie and say he misses his mother. Or that he's sorry. Or that it was an accident, or heatstroke, or, like, a defective gun. Literally any defense would have saved his life."

"Yes, but for what?"

"For living!"

Winnie was growing surprisingly frustrated, angrily retying her pony tail; it intrigued Lana. "Here," she said, pointing at the last page. "It's all here." She began to translate into English:

"No one, no one in the world had the right to weep for my mother. And I, too, felt ready to start life all over again. It was as if that great rush of anger had washed me clean, emptied me of hope, and, gazing up at the dark sky full of stars, for the first time, the first, I laid my heart open to the benign indifference of the universe. To feel it so like myself, indeed, like a brother, made me realize that I'd been happy, and that I was happy still. For all to be accomplished, for me to feel less lonely, all that remained to hope was that on my day of my execution there should be a huge crowd of spectators and that they should greet me with cries of hate."

Winnie considered this. "So he wants to die."

"I don't think he wants anything. He simply accepts that he will die. We all will."

"Very few of us by guillotine."

"It doesn't matter how, Winnie. No one gets out alive."

She read over the last paragraph again. "Why does he want to be hated?"

"I…" Lana hesitated. "Well, it's been a while since I've had to teach this."

"What do you think?"

"I think he doesn't want to hope. That hope is just a torment. Being hated makes it easier. And he would die knowing that he is right."

Winnie shook her head. "I hate this book so much. It is the worst book."

"I'm sorry you feel that way."

"Why? Do *you* like it?"

"I—" Lana started before thinking for a moment. "I respect it."

"You agree with Meursault?"

"I didn't say that…"

"But you have no problem being hated."

Lana flinched and Winnie instantly realized what she had said. "I'm sorry! I'm sorry, Ms. Collins!"

"It's all right, Winnie…"

"Dad says I'm a blurter!"

"It's all right."

"I've been working on it."

Lana nodded. They were silent for a moment. Lana stood, walked over to the dry erase board, began to erase it. Winnie stared at her hands.

"I don't hate you."

Lana kept erasing. Then she picked up a marker and began to write the lesson objectives for her next class.

"I don't. I'm not just saying that, Ms. Collins."

"Okay."

"Can I ask you something?"

"Obviously, I can't stop you."

"What's it like?"

She wheeled to face the girl. Was this what it was all about? Was this why she had come to her? To ask this question? Lana had been asked this a few times over the years by the occasional student. Lost. Confused. Searching. Some were tourists. Experience-seekers. Some were trapped. But Lana had not been interested in mentoring anyone. After all, no one had mentored her. What could one person possibly say to another about anything?

Winnie stared at her. She was wearing baggy jeans, a thick, hooded sweatshirt. How long had the leggings been gone? Why hadn't Lana noticed?

"What are you asking me?"

She said it softly, but sharply. Winnie didn't flinch.

"You were one way. Now you're another. I wanted to… to know."

Lana leaned against her desk. She tried to remember being fifteen. It was too hard; despite her constant immersion amongst these wise fools, she could not recall the story that had led her from there to here. Those were Laurence's memories, and Lana wanted nothing to do with them.

Yet there was one day in gym class. Laurence had hated P.E., hated the gendered exercises, felt the constant exposure of his body and the loathing of the male figure. But one day his teacher told them that their cardio exercise was simply to run laps. Maybe the teacher had been lazy; maybe there was simply an extra day to fill in the unit. For whatever reason, for one period, Laurence and his classmates were tasked with running laps around a fieldhouse.

She remembered hating it at first. Sweating. Hurting. Breathing. But after six or seven minutes those functions faded to the background like crowd noise. She could think. She could feel the muscles of her legs, control them. She jogged, then moved a little faster. She passed a student, then another. They were talking, socializing, passing the time with one another. Lana, though, was moving through them. She moved faster. She ran.

Lana picked up *L'etranger*. She flipped through its pages. "What was it like when you started reading this?" she asked.

"Hard."

Lana nodded. "And what's it like when you're speaking English?"

"Easy."

"Why?"

"I… I think in English."

She handed the book to Winnie. "All my life, I had to speak French. It was hard. Now, I speak how I think."

Winnie smiled. Lana didn't. The next day, Winnie showed up in third period, beaming. She had chopped off all her hair.

━━━━━━━━━

Over the next week, Winnie didn't intrude during 5th period. Many times, on the first day, Lana jumped up when she heard a noise in the hallway—a noisy student passing by, a janitor pushing a cart of fluorescent lightbulbs—but no one was coming to see her. It didn't' surprise her that she found herself missing Winnie's visits, but it did irritate her. She had forgotten the inconstancy of teenagers; how myopic and thoughtless they could be. Over the years, she had written many letters of recommendation for students, a painstaking and exhaustive process. The kids rarely made eye contact when accepting the envelope—shouting 'KayThanksBye!' as they bounded off in pursuit of their next task. They never remembered to tell her which college accepted them.

Lana resumed her lunchtime regimen, but found it difficult to immerse herself. She tried Sudoku, then a crossword. She brought a yoga mat and did some light stretching. She played her James albums louder, then switched to Mingus. She paced more and thought about strolling down to the library, just to stick her head in. But who knew what conversations that might initiate? A closed door kept things simple.

A few days later, she called on Winnie during an oral exercise to read a paragraph from the textbook. Winnie had not raised her hand, but Lana suspected she was drifting in attention. Winnie cleared her throat and began to mangle a few sentences from a travel brochure on Marseille.

"'Les voyageurs visitent la ville portuaire de Marseille… la troisième plus grande ville de France… pour la renconter…' "

"RenconTRE," Lana corrected. "It means 'the meeting.'"

"…du style et de l'histoire... "Winnie resumed.

Something was wrong. Several students around the classroom were shifting in their seats, staring at Winnie. Two girls in the corner were whispering to one another. One was smiling. Smirking? What were they reacting to?"

"'La baie, flanquée par le fort Saint-Nicolas, et le fort Saint-Jean abrite le château…'"

Winnie's pronunciations were abysmal, but no more so than the average swollen-tongued suburban teen. It was something else. Her voice. Winnie was dropping her voice an octave as she read.

"She sounds like Batman," whispered Jon Palmer. He, too, was smirking.

Another high school memory pierced Lana's carapace. They were sitting around the living room at Thanksgiving. Laurence's father had phoned his own father, then in the care of a home nurse in Minnesota. The family passed the phone around the room, each sibling taking a few minutes to wish Grandpa Collins happy holidays, to hear about the stuffing he had made with 'with apples!' When his father was about to hand the phone to Laurence, he hesitated, then gave him a stern look.

"Don't do the voice," he had said.

'The voice' was the sound of the man who spoke French on the Pimsleur Language Course cassettes Laurence had checked out of the library. He had lay on his bed in the darkness, listening to the soft and smoky voice of the man—"*Je m'appelle Jean-Luc. Je m'appelle Jean-Luc.*" Mouthing the words over and over again. The shape of his mouth, the faint suggestion of the consonants. Learning to speak.

And here was Winnie, stomping around the words like some clumsy giant in a Fabergé egg obstacle course. "Thank you, Winnie. That will suffice. Caitlyn, will you pick up where she left off?"

A look of mockery pinged around the class, wordless, knowing exchanges between kids too dumb to understand their own bodies but shrewd enough to intuit the Chinese girl with the short hair and man voice for what she was becoming. Lana risked a glance at Winnie; she seemed blithely ignorant, her eyes fixed on Caitlyn. She caught Lana's gaze and smiled. *Idiot*, Lana thought.

— — — — — — — — —

A few days later there was a knock at Lana's door during fifth period. It was Winnie, but she was accompanied by two older students—a taller, meaty boy with hair grown long and swept over his brow, his temples buzzed close to the scalp; and a shorter girl wearing a heavy black duster.

"Ms. Collins!" smiled Winnie. "Are you busy?"

She was surprised to find herself hurt by the intrusion. Who were these two interlopers?

"Um… I have a little time, Winnie. What's up?"

The three students swept past her without invitation; they sat in desks as Lana closed the door.

"Ms. Collins, I have so much to tell you!"

"Okay."

"This is Shane," she said, gesturing to the tall one, "and this is Desiree."

"Hello," said Lana.

"Heard a lot about you, ma'am," said Shane in a flat but sincere voice. "Winn here talks about you nonstop."

Lana felt a jolt of panic bounce up and down her spine. "That's nice," she lied.

"Yeah, it's true, Ms. Collins," said Winnie excitedly. "A lot has happened. A lot!"

"Okay."

Winnie smiled at Lana's reticence. The sophomore seemed prepared to launch into a breathless monologue, but instead she shifted in her chair and placed her palms calmly on the desk. "How are you, Ms. Collins. I haven't talked to you in forever."

"Um…" said Lana, dumbly. This was different. *She's changing her approach*, Lana realized. *The blurter is actually showing some tact, some consideration.* It made Lana deeply uncomfortable.

Shane broke the silence. "We wanted to talk to you about starting a club, Ms. Collins."

"A club?"

"Did you know," said Desiree, "that Clearwater has never had a GSA?"

"A what?"

"Gay-Straight Alliance," explained Shane. "Actually, it's now more of an LGBTQS Alliance, but, you know, that doesn't fit as well on a t-shirt."

"Alphabet soup," joked Desiree.

"Well," said Lana. "What is it?"

"It's a safe space," said Winnie. "You know, for kids."

Shane nodded. "We need a place to talk about sexual orientation, gender identity, gender expression…"

"There's a lot of phobia in this school," added Desiree. "We need to set the record straight." She laughed at that last part, before adding "So to speak."

"Winn thought maybe you could help us," said Shane.

"Really."

Desiree nodded. "Like you helped him."

Lana leaned against the doorframe, then opened the door. "Shane, Desiree… would you mind if I talked to Winn for a couple of minutes?"

The two seniors exchanged glances but calmly acquiesced. Lana closed the door and turned to face Winnie. "Would you like me to call you Winn now?"

She smiled. "Yes, thank you. I'm also going to start asking my teachers to start using different pronouns. I know it seems like a lot, but you'll get used to it. We all will."

"And the GSA will help?"

"It will! It will! You have no idea, Ms. Collins, how much it's already helping me. I'm learning to express myself, Ms. Collins. How I dress teaches others how I think about myself…"

"Why are you using that voice?"

"I mean…" Winnie trailed off. "I mean, it's all part of expression."

Lana shook her head. "I don't know if I can help you with this."

"No, Ms. Collins! You can! I know this seems like it's happening so fast, but you have to remember that things are different for my generation."

"Are they?"

Winnie nodded. "Everything is coming out in the open now. I was so lucky to find Shane, Desiree. I was so lucky to find *you.*"

Lana stared at this strangely indefatigable girl. It was true that there was a generational divide between the two of them, but there was more. Winnie was different than Laurence; Winn was different than Lana. Bolder. More open. Still untrampled. *How much is the age and how much is the heart?* Lana wondered. *How wise is this fool?* "What do your parents say?" she asked finally.

Winnie reached for her absent pony tail, then thought better of it and wiped her hands on her jeans. "They… they just need some time," she said. "I don't want you to think it's because they're Chinese. My father is maybe the bravest man I've ever met. Came here without any English, all by himself. But he's never met anyone like me before. Or maybe he didn't know. Anyways… I'm on my own on this."

You always will be, thought Lana reflexively, but Winnie's simplicity pained her. This girl… boy… *person*… he was so raw and vulnerable. A naked civilian caught in a partisan forever-war.

"Winn," said Lana sadly. "I think you know some things, but you don't understand. You said that I'm hated. That's correct, and I always have been. But after the data dump it is so much worse. The whispers, the property damage… I'm convinced they spit in my food. Every day for a week, someone slipped a letter into my mailbox. Sometimes the letter called me a faggot. Sometimes an abomination. Once I sat outside in my car for an entire day and waited to see who dropped it off. I never caught him."

"So what did you do?"

"I cancelled my mail service."

"But… but how do you get your magazines?"

Lana rolled her eyes. "My point is that I'm radioactive. You can't be around me, Winn. It will cost you too much."

He looked away, then leveled a fierce gaze back at her. It surprised Lana, the heat of those black-brown eyes.

"You think I don't understand hatred? You work in a high school! Hatred is, like, the *lingua franca* of every conversation! So yeah, it's been hard since I've been seeing you. Everyone thinks you're grooming me. And it's been *hard* since I cut my hair. It's been *hard* since I've been hanging out with Shane and Desiree. Ms. Collins, It's been hard every day of my life! What you said, about being caught between

French and English, that was hard! But try having Chinese in your head, too!"

He moved to the door and stared up into Lana's eyes. It was the teacher that looked away first. Winn's posture slacked and his voice returned to its normal chirp.

"Please think about it, Ms. Collins," said Winn. "I know this will be good for us."

"I will," said Lana. "Close the door on your way out."

On the treadmill, Lana did think about it. She thought about Winnie's undented smile, of her frustration with Camus's men. She thought about her father, arriving as a young man in a place indifferent to his courage, where no one could possibly understand the color of the streets where he'd come from or the melancholy he carried within him. She thought of a safe space for people like the Huangs, who were in every classroom, every table in the cafeteria, every lonely seat on the bus.

She increased both the pace of the belt and its inclination. What if there had been a GSA twenty years ago? Where was her Shane, her Desiree? What if she had had a different conversation with her father, had better words for the great unspoken thing inside her? What if she had trusted the bravado of her college RA when she had invited her to that poetry recital, that basement concert, that road trip to New Orleans? What if she had known when she was 20 that there would come a day when no one asked her to do such things anymore?

Faster. She thought of being in the darkness with Mark, of his hands, slowly undressing her. Unlocking her. Touching. She thought of what she had seen in his eyes, what she had *thought* she'd seen in his eyes. She thought of the defensiveness of her hands when she realized they were the same size as his.

The timer sounded and the treadmill rolled to a stop. Lana struggled to gather her breath, leaning forward and resting her weight on her knees. She saw two patches of fat, same as always. Stupid to think otherwise. Five-and-a-quarter miles in 35 minutes, and she hadn't moved forward an inch.

They will destroy him, thought Lana bitterly. Already, the kids were lining up against him, the elastic judgment of high school calcifying into something hard, loadbearing, elemental. They will not care that Winn chose how to express himself. They will not applaud his courage; they will hate him for it. Every operation brings us further from the truth; every Obama is immediately followed by a Trump; every modest effort towards integration will be smashed to splinters by some laughing cockroach with a keyboard. She knew what she had to do.

They don't need a teacher, she thought grimly. *They need a lesson.*

— — — — — — — — —

The next morning in third period, she called on Winn to read. "Winnie, will you please read aloud from the italicized passage on page 52?"

Winn looked up, a brief look of confusion flashing across his face. He began to read: "'Lorsque vous visitez une boulangerie française…'"

"In your own voice, please."

Winn stopped abruptly. "What?"

"I want you to read the passage in your own voice," said Lana without looking up from the textbook. "From the beginning."

Winn was silent for a moment before restarting. "'Lorsque vous visitez une boulangerie française…' "

"Your real voice, Winn-shen. Not the voice you're affecting. Come on now. Start again."

"I'll read, Ms. Collins!" said Caitlyn gently. "I don't mind."

"Yeah, I can read this," said Meredith. "I think I actually understand it."

"That's all right, girls," said Lana calmly. "I'd like to hear from Winnie."

"Um…" said Winn. "I don't know how to read it any other way."

"That's not true."

Winn's face creased around his brow. He dropped his gaze and shut his eyes. The class was silent. Lana asked again: "Winnie. I asked you to read."

"Just… can you please leave him alone?" asked Jon Palmer. "He doesn't want to read." The class seemed to be nodding, although no one so much as twitched. Lana swept about the room with her eyes.

"That's the problem, isn't it," she said softly. "You all think you have a choice."

"Excuse me?" said Lisette defiantly.

"You give up, all of you, at the slightest discomfort. You back away from everything difficult, everything painful. You want people to accept a fake voice or a dye job or a new name, but the minute the world pushes back, you curdle. You're weak, and you're naïve, and you're entitled. The world doesn't care that you're uncomfortable. It can't care. It's a rock. It will feel nothing when you break."

When they're most battered, every teacher fanaticizes about a moment like this, when they can speak aloud the hurtful private thoughts with which they nurse their grievances. But looking at Winn, Lana felt no joy, no catharsis. Only a great and terrible fear. Would they hear her? Would they learn?

Slowly, trembling, Winn got up and strode wounded from the room. She slammed the door behind her. No one spoke. Then Caitlyn Pund stood and followed her out. Then Jasmine Nafriti. Then two more girls. Then a boy and three more girls. Lana watched through the glass panels. They went to Winn, enveloped him. He dissolved in their protective ring. They held him.

Alone at lunch, Lana unpacked her motives. Yes, it bothered her how much she had come to look forward to Winn's visits, come to rely on them. Yes, it was painful to be seen, recognized, to be summoned from her own safe space for some sort of LGBTQ mentorship program. Was she a hypocrite? Was she self-sabotaging? Was she caving in the mineshaft to keep the rescuers from reaching her? Was she just another 'self-hating trannie' as her brother had labeled her so many years ago?

Perhaps she was jealous of Winn. Maybe she resented the ease with which the child was making this transition. "Become a pariah? Court mockery and derision? Lose my friends and family? No problem, Ms. Collins, no problem!" Perhaps she was a mean and spiteful person who ripped up gardens so she wouldn't have to look on chrysanthemums. Perhaps… perhaps there was no reason.

There was a knock from outside, and Lana could see through the glass that a small group had assembled. She opened the door; it was Winn with a group of seven or eight other students. Shane and Desiree flanked her. Winn was silent at first, but he met Lana's gaze.

"What do you want?" asked Lana.

"The books," said Shane.

"What books?"

Winn pushed past her, walked over to the storage cabinet, opened it and rummaged around. He found the plastic milk crate packed with 32 copies of *L'etranger*. He wrested it from the cabinet, hoisted it from the bottom, and moved to leave.

"What are you doing?" asked Lana.

"Borrowing," said Winn.

"Borrowing? What is this?"

"DON'T talk to him!" said Desiree sharply. But Winn set down the crate and turned to face Lana.

"What do you want them for?"

"GSA," said Winn. The trembling girl was gone.

"They're all in French," Lana protested.

"I'll teach them," Winn replied.

His father's son, thought Lana proudly. "I thought you hated the book," she said lamely.

"I don't. I love it. It taught me what I hate."

He picked up the crate again and left the room. His friends followed. The room was quiet, but through the door, Lana could hear laughter.

— — — — — — — — —

She began the next day with 25 pushups and 25 crunches. *I saved him* she thought as she raised and lowered her body. *They'll all talk about what I did to him in class, how I humiliated him.* Up, down. Up, down. Up down. *And they'll tell the story about how he came to my room, defied me, took my books.* She brushed her teeth, made her bed, fed her dog. *In one day he went from a freak to a hero.* She applied her mascara, buttoned her blouse, draped a scarf over her throat.

He has friends now. In every classroom, in every clique, they'll know about Winn Huang. Dragon slayer. Monster killer. He'll be accepted because now they know true ugliness. She drove in silence, switched on the windshield wipers to clear away a light rain.

And I, she thought, *I will face a hostile mob in every class I teach. They will never relax around me. They will never invite me into their confidence, seduce me with their charms.* She could feel their eyes track her as she moved through the parking lot, into the lunchroom, past the library, down her hallway. She was finally free, finally alone. For the first time in months, Lana smiled.

The bell rang; her first period sat. "Okay," said Lana clearly. "I'm ready to teach."

17

THE RISE AND FALL OF EL CLAVADISTA

The video begins with a long, slow approach to the Greencastle Motel Palacio, a first-person perspective winding through the parking lot. The soundtrack is "American Jesus" by Bad Religion; the footage recorded from a forehead-mounted GoPro Hero 5, at least as near as Carlton could tell. Rather than enter through the front reception area, as Carlton might, the figure scales a drainpipe, hops between balconies, and then climbs atop the roof. The trespasser, whose limbs were occasionally visible in frame, is clad entirely in a wetsuit; gender is indeterminate. He—or she— paces slowly along the lip of the three-story motel, peering down at the sapphire pool, the jewel of the courtyard, glowing brilliantly amidst the somber twilight shadows. The guitars cut like chainsaws, the lyrics barked like orders:

There are things that seem to pull us under
And there are things that drag us down

But there's a power and a vital presence
That's lurking all around

The figure suddenly shouts above it all: "I AM EL CLAVADISTA! THE WORLD IS ME KIDDIE POOL!" With a lunge, he/she flips off the ledge, tumbling so that the entire courtyard spins like a gimble, before righting him/herself and submerging in a flood of blue-green bubbles.

Darten clicked the mouse. The image froze. The timestamp read January, this year. "Well?" he said expectantly.

Carlton Wemish could feel the line of sweat percolating across his wide and creased forehead. "It's not me," he said.

"I should hope not," said his principal. "Because it was not more than two months ago, that we discussed El Clavadista's retirement."

"It can't be me," said Carlton. "The voice is British."

Darten raised a skeptical eyebrow. "Is *El Clavadista* an old Scottish name?" he asked dryly.

"I'm Dutch-Irish," replied Carlton, dropping his eyes.

Carlton Wemish left the office with his anxiety at high tide. This was the second meeting he'd had with Vince Darten in three months. It was highly unusual, not because Carlton was a particularly good teacher, but because he was simply a person whose presence was rarely required outside of class. In the great bell curve of distinctiveness at Clearwater High, Carlton sat right in the middle. He was 5'10" with an inexpressive face and an American Eagle wardrobe. His ratio of Twitter follows to followers was roughly 3:2. His favorite book was *Tuesdays With Morrie*. He liked bagels, Seth McFarlane cartoons, and March Madness brackets. He never missed a Marvel movie.

Among his students, Carlton did not engender any strong emotions. After five years of teaching, he had only three comments on RateMy-Teacher.com, one that confused him with James Hapsten, a science teacher. His colleagues described him as 'punctual,' 'polite,' and 'a team player.' Subs praised his lesson plans as orderly and easy to follow. But it nagged at Carlton that others found his presence so ephemeral. "Hey, I'm Carlton," he had said to Sheila Broth, a young German teacher, at a faculty Cinco de Mayo party. He'd bought her a Corona, listened to a story about her trip to Coachella. A month later, he held his tongue as she reintroduced herself and told the exact same story.

But there was one thing that was memorable about Carlton. Over the summer, he had donned a metallic blue Lucha Libre mask, a tomato-red cape, and green Umbros as the star of "El Clavadista Motel Drops," a series of six videos he'd posted pseudonymously on YouTube. He had conceived the idea during a curriculum writing session with Suzanne Friedan, a Physics teacher who shared his love of backyard wrestling videos. "Could we not," she asked, "find some sort of cross-curricular application in professional wrestling?" They had laughed at the notion, but it stuck with Carlton, who carefully measured the arc of a two-story jump during a stay at a Motel 6 in Toledo. He considered it all summer, forcefully resisting the notion, until he found himself purchasing a GoPro camera at Walmart. The mask had been an act of exhibitionism. Carlton Wemish was afraid of heights. But *El Clavadista Espectacular*? He was born in mid-flight.

The first video attracted little attention, but Carlton had thrilled so completely in its production that he rapidly began planning a sequel. He spent a Wednesday scouting locations in the tri-county area. He discovered that Motel Palacios, with their interior courtyards and individual balconies, were ideal for his purposes as they offered a variety of precipices from which to leap. The videos though plain and unpolished, became a creative outlet; he punctuated each with a jaunty *corrido* he found online. Though Carlton spoke no Spanish, the rich guitars, bold trumpets, and polka rhythm seemed to suit El Clavadista's aesthetic, and he received many compliments online. The videos began to accumulate views, and Carlton had already begun to plan a spring break series when the first data dump outed his identity and imperiled his character in the eyes of Vince Darten. He had spent the past month keeping his head down, teaching his classes, and trying to forget that he had ever been a faux-Mexican daredevil. The second data dump—which contained this new footage—had upended his play for anonymity.

As he sat in his study hall supervision, drumming his fingers on the attendance binder, the footage of the new video tugged at him. A copycat had replaced him online. Stolen his idea, his character! Who was this mysterious interloper, and why did he think he could steal this character, as though it were some common meme?

The indignity of it gnawed at Carlton throughout his teaching day, extending into his evening activities. Carlton was a member of Les Quizerables, a pub trivia team comprised of his college roommate Shelton, Shelton's co-worker, Tony, and Tony's ex, Connie. Every Thursday they gathered at area bars to drink, unwind, and compete in trivia tournaments. Carlton's preoccupation proved costly. He second-guessed himself and could draw little of use from his memory well. He totally forgot the capital of Croatia as Sofia and missed an obvious musical cue for The Carpenters.

"All right, Carl. Time to cue up another training montage," said Tony afterwards, licking the rim of his margarita. "We're going to hit those Eastern European flashcards so hard you'll be dreaming of Warsaw."

"Dreaming of Warsaw!" said Shelton. "That's going to be the name of my Prog Rock band."

"Sorry, guys," said Carlton. "I don't know what happened back there." He peeled messy strips off the label of his Killian's, arranging them neatly on his coaster.

Connie raised an eyebrow and leaned in, trying to make eye contact. "What's wrong, Dummy?" she said gently. "You're so depressed, you've barely touched your depressant."

He loved Connie. There wasn't much that Carlton knew in this life, but of that he was certain. He had met her when she and Tony had dated two years ago. Since then, he had committed to memory every angle of her neck, every luminous tooth in her smile. He had initially demurred when Tony had asked him to join Les Quizerables, but when Shelton mentioned that Tony's ex was in, he drove straight to the library and checked out a 20-disc Great Courses set on literature so that he could ingratiate himself to the team.

Carlton allowed himself to look into Connie's fathomless brown eyes, but only for a moment lest he lose himself. "When I was living with the Delts, I moved into a room that was basically a biohazard," he said. "I know that's what people think of every room in a frat, but this one was a true palace of crotch-rot. Urine stains. Roach infestation. Something fecal petrifying in the corner."

"Fit for neither man nor beast!" nodded Shelton.

"Well, I fixed it up. Cleaned, scrubbed. Learned to spackle. Replaced the outlets, the trim. Found some remnants and taught myself how to lay carpet. Sanded, primed, painted. Everything. It was the nicest room in the house. It was… the only nice room in the house."

He looked around the bar. There were people laughing, tossing darts. He felt like a robot, studying human behavior to pass the Turing test.

"And… I went back two years ago. Felt nostalgic. When I found my old room, the door had been snapped off its frame. The carpet was peeled back. There was some dumbfuck in a wading pool. He'd soiled himself. 'Oh, hey!' he said to me when he saw me standing there. And I just walked away. I drove all the way back home, pissed at myself."

"Well, I get that," said Tony. "It was YOUR room."

"No, it wasn't my room anymore," said Carlton. "I'd graduated, moved on. But all I thought about for a week was driving back to that house, pulling that drip out of his wading pool, and tossing him into the street."

They were all looking at him, listening. It was the most alive Carlton had felt all day. "Here's my question," he said, straightening up. "What should I have done?"

Connie was the first to speak. "Well, I won't pretend to understand the Neanderthal brain," she smiled. "But it seems to me that the world's in short supply of beauty, Carlton Wemish. And if this drooling shitburger profaned something you held dear, well sir, it would be your responsibility to cave his shitty head in with a tire iron." She finished her beer. "If you want my professional opinion."

Carlton smiled. She made him feel like a Heisman-winning running back. "Tony," he said, signaling the bartender for another round. "The capital of Croatia is Zagrab."

El Clavadista posted another video two days later from the Motel Palacio in Spencer. *He's moving down 231*, thought Carlton. *But why?* He watched the video several times. The imposter again scaled the front of the lobby, shimmied up a metal casing, and then prowled the edge of the roof like a mountain lion. The leap was again a flip. It was showy, theatrical. Carlton sipped his coffee, clicking the tracking pad of his laptop over and over again.

Why hadn't anyone stopped him? Carlton's El Clavadista was quick, surgical—in and out before anyone knew what he was doing. But this person was prancing around the roof like he/she was Mick Jagger performing "Brown Sugar." Surely that would attract the attention of the motel's omniscient video surveillance.

It was that thought that drew Carlton to freeze the video on the 0:14 mark. The GoPro was pointed at the lobby; he could make out the figure of the desk clerk conferring with a guest. But the frame also revealed one of the motel's ubiquitous security cameras. It was dangling from its mounting. Had he/she disabled them? No, there were too many. Someone had spiked the cameras ahead of time. Carlton thought. He Googled. And called. And then he knew where El Clavadista would strike next.

On Saturday, he drove an hour East on Route 70 to Greensboro. He wanted to get there early. He wore his Canada Goose Expedition Parka, his insulated hiking pants, his alpaca wool socks. He knew he might be outdoors for a long time.

As he suspected, the cameras were already incapacitated, in a state of maintenance and repair. He walked right through the lobby, followed the signs to the courtyard, slipped in and stationed himself in a deckchair to wait. It was 40 degrees out. He balled his fists and slipped them in his pockets.

At 11:14, Carlton saw him/her peering over the edge of the roof. He moved stealthily to a position under a balcony that would be out of El Clavadista's sightline. He waited. "I AM EL CLAVADISTA!" yelled the diver. "BREAKER OF WORLDS! AN' I FEAR NO WINTER!"

He/she dived, and Carlton moved. When the figure surfaced, Carlton ripped the camera off his/her head and tossed it in the shrubs. The diver pulled back his mask; he was young, black, and male.

"Who the fuck are you?" he said.

"I'm El Clavadista," said Carlton. "We need to talk."

His name was Virgil; he was from Fort Wayne. They walked across the street to an Applebee's. The teenage hostess sat them at a table with impressive indifference, as though dripping men in wetsuits were Greensboro's most common guest.

"Do you want to dry off?" asked Carlton.

"Nah, mate," said Virgil. "I like being wet."

Carlton ordered a coffee; Virgil a beer. They sat in silence for a moment.

"Gotta say, brotha," said Virgil. "I thought you'd look different."

"Likewise," said Carlton.

"Still," said Virgil, mopping his brow with a paper napkin, "Big fan of your work."

Carlton said nothing, stirring in a cream and two sugars, without taking his eyes off Virgil. The diver smirked.

"What, you're not a fan o'mine?" he grinned. "You got to admit, I've got great taste in music."

"The music's a nice touch," agreed Carlton.

"I was gonna use Iggy for this one."

"No you're not," said Carlton. "You're done. El Clavadista's not yours."

"Ah, you're thinkin' about this all wrong," said Virgil, drinking his beer. "El Clavadista's a franchise."

"You're a thief."

"Nah, I'm one of those crabs that sees an empty shell and moves in. I'm a recycler, that's what I am!"

Carlton had nothing to say to that. Virgil's cheekiness was infuriating; he had hoped to intimidate him. Instead, he seemed to be a source of amusement.

"How'd you know where I was gonna be?" asked Virgil.

"At first, I thought you were moving down 231," said Carlton. "Then I realized you were using the motels that were having their cameras serviced. I called until I figured out which company handled Motel Palacio."

"And then you got the schedule, right, right," nodded Virgil. "That's some A1 detective work, that is."

"Stop talking in that accent," said Carlton. "I know you're not British."

Virgil smirked. "God, you are one salty sea bitch," he said, slipping into a husky Midwestern voice. "And I suppose you some Mexican?

You cultural appropriating mother-fucker… lecture me on cultural appropriation."

"I'm not lecturing," said Carlton. "I'm just saying—El Clavadista isn't British!'

Virgil laughed, clapped his hands. "Oh, I forgot we was dealing with the Royal Shakespeare company here," he giggled. "Who would have thought a man who leaps off of motel roofs would have such a stick up his ass?"

"You have to stop," said Carlton. "I could lose my job."

"You haven't lost your job yet?" said Virgil. "Well now. Don't we live in two Americas? My ass'd be out of work the second this shit got out. Hell, we'd probably be having this conversation through plexiglass."

Carlton's eyes wandered around the Applebee's. He'd long found it the tackiest of the Crazy-Crap-on-the-walls family stops, yet it was ubiquitous in Indiana. The lunch rush was just picking up; the faces were white, middle-aged, and heavy around the jowls. He imagined their eyes on him. What would they see first? The dripping wetsuit? Or the black face? Would they even see Carlton Wemish?

"Why do you do it, then?" asked Carlton, lowering his voice. "Why take the risk?"

Virgil rubbed his hands together, then stared out the window. He was thick around the middle, with a wide face smashed between apple-cheeks. He looked like the sort of figure you might run into at a rental car company. But his hair was wild, bushy, and coppery, unkempt in the fashion of a more dangerous time. "I work at an insurance company. Big one. Well, for Indiana it's big. I research claims, make calculations, recommendations. Math stuff, don't really require a lot of people skills."

"I'm a math teacher," said Carlton; Virgil's incredulous expression made him drop his eyes.

"Anyways," continued Virgil. "One day about a year ago, I made it through the entire day without talking to a single person. I thought to myself, 'Huh. Wonder if I could do that again.' Turns out, I could—I made it four straight days before I actually had to talk to someone. On the phone!"

"Sounds pretty sweet," said Carlton.

"That's what I thought at first," said Virgil. "Then I got to thinking, 'What if they ain't talking to me 'cause I'm lucky? What if they ain't talkin' to me 'cause I'm invisible? Not some Ralph Ellison invisible—ain't no secret brotherhoods or electric wrestling pits in my life. I mean, like, I work in a cubicle. Surrounded by other cubicles. I watch Netflix most nights. Get my groceries delivered to my door."

He finished his beer. "A coworker emailed me your video. You know how many times the last one was viewed."

"I don't know," Carlton said.

"Yes, you do."

"Three hundred and twenty-six thousand times," he admitted.

Virgil nodded. "Three hundred thousand motherfucking times," he nodded. "Could we have an appetizer sampler and another beer?" he asked the waitress, his voice suddenly raising an octave and enunciating his consonants. "Thank you very much!" He returned his smoldering eyes to Carlton, dropped his smile, and spoke in a low growl. "You look like the type of smoked-out-bitch that skimmed a philosophy textbook in college. Let me ask you something—what makes a man? Is it what he thinks of himself? Or what other people think of him?"

"Neither. Both," said Carlton. "I don't know. What's this got to do with anything?"

"Damn, Carlton, pass the ball back when I toss it to you!" said Virgil. "I got to explain everything? An invisible man ain't shit if he's got a boring-ass private life like me. Like you."

"My life isn't boring," said Carlton.

"It is now," laughed Virgil. "You took the one thing that was interesting about your ass, and you threw it away. You so basic, the Starbucks barista knows you're order before you even speak. You so basic, you point at a J Crew mannequin and say, "I'll have what he's having." The waitress brought Virgil his beer. "Thank you, Becky!" he said in his faux-voice; he watched her saunter away before speaking again.

"Yeah, I took your shit. Made it better. One week, I've got near half a million views," he said. "And I'm gonna keep going. Got big plans for El Clavadista."

"You're going to stop," said Carlton. "I'll call the police."

Virgil grinned. "We got there quick, didn't we? Sure. Call the police. I'll get a fine, maybe some community service. You'll be a little bitch the rest of your life. In your sad little basic bitch apartment, tugging on your sad little basic bitch dick."

Carlton looked at his hands. They protruded from a coat he'd bought at an outlet mall, where he'd also bought his pants, his socks, his boots. For hiking. Like everyone else. Virgil sipped his beer and softened. The hard corners went out of his eyes.

"Look, I don't mean to come down hard on you," he said. "I respect what you built. But I'm not going to fade away. *Ecce homo!* You know what that means? 'Behold, the man!' That's what I want on my tombstone, even if I'm under it next week."

They split the check and left separately; Virgil said he wanted to thank the waitress in private. *What a fraud,* he thought as he drove home in silence. *Acting like he's some brave iconoclast. Like he's Huey Newton or something.* He brooded all along the long interstate corridor. Farmland, corn fields, wire fences. Old barns and old families, blown past by traffic every hour of every day. *He wears a mask,* he thought. *Uses a fake accent. Didn't even think up his own shtick.* Then he thought of Virgil, flirting with that waitress, unashamed of his ludicrous wetsuit. Her laughing mouth, wide and uninhibited. He thought of Connie. Carlton squeezed the steering wheel.

The Greensboro El Clavadista video was posted early the next week. Virgil had improved the aesthetic considerably, adding a second, hand-held GoPro that he used to intersperse footage. The video included slow motion and color-saturation replays. It was brasher, bolder, more compelling. Carlton caught two students watching it fifth period. He confiscated their phones, reamed out the class, and ordered students to work on their workbooks in silence. The class kept looking up at him with obvious expectation.

"What?" said Carlton after three minutes of their staring.

"That's you, isn't it Mr. Wemish?" asked Lisa Boags. "El Clavadista?"

"No, it's not," he said.

"Okay, but… it IS you, right?" asked Jon Palmer. "I mean, we seen it online."

Carlton could feel hungry teenage eyes; it wasn't the usual bovine bleariness that greeted him. They were waiting on his response before taking their next breath.

"El Clavadista, whoever he is, is a man of danger," said Carlton. "I would stay far, far away from him, children."

Lisa Boags smiled, and blushed.

The video was circulating among the faculty as well. "Stud video, man," said Kevin Lenk as Carlton passed him on the way to the parking lot. "Wasn't me," replied Carlton lamely.

"Carlton! Come sit with us!" said Sheila Broth in the faculty cafeteria. Sheila ran around with Andy Waters' crowd. She was sitting with Eliza Monk, Dylan Paters, and James Hapsten. *None of these people have ever paid less than $50 for a haircut,* Carlton thought. They had never acknowledged him before. Still, if he carried his tray all the way back to the Math office (as was his habit), his chili would get cold. So Carlton pulled up a chair.

"I just saw that video!" said Sheila. "I actually stayed at that motel two summers ago. How wild is that?"

"It's a small world," said Carlton.

"Yours is the smallest there is," nodded James. "Where'd you get the idea for El Clavadista?"

"Um, it just came to me," said Carlton.

"Oh," said Eliza, running her hand along her throat.

"…when I was in Brazil. Studying with cliff divers."

"Right!" said Eliza. "I saw a documentary on them during the Olympics. Carlton smiled and let her explain Poco do Diablo, Orlando Duque, and the dark waters of Chapada Diamantina. Eliza ran marathons; she had a lean, limber frame but also full and lovely lips. Carlton watched them move while she spoke and ate her carrot sticks.

"So what's next for the diver?" asked Dylan.

"Oh, well, he's a man of mystery," Carlton fumbled. "Guess I'll find out when you do."

"Right," said Sheila laughing. "I heard Darten shit a pineapple about your last video. Heard he told you the next video was your last at Clearwater."

"Who told you that?" Carlton could feel his temperature spike. What were people saying about him? What fresh hell was he to catch from his weary principal? But the young teachers seemed to share none of his apprehension. These were people who got tattoos as impulse buys.

"I don't know; I just heard it," laughed Sheila. She had not stopped making eye contact since he'd sat down.

"Oh," said Carlton. "Well, I care about what Vince thinks of me. But *El Clavadista*? He doesn't give a *mierda*."

Burmer Insurance in Fort Wayne was a two-hour drive from Clearwater. Carlton called in sick and sent in his sub plans at 5:00 A.M., then watched the documentary on Orlando Duque for a few hours to let the morning traffic thin. He spent the drive practicing his speech, but as soon as Virgil caught sight of him winding through the maze of office partitions, Carlton forgot all but the central pitch.

"What are you doing here?" Virgil hissed, grabbing him by the bicep and dragging him past several closed office doors and fake potted ferns. "Thought you was a teacher!"

"School's out," said Carlton.

Virgil switched on a light in a conference room and roughly shoved Carlton inside, shutting the door softly behind them. The room was little more than a rectangular mahogany table rimmed by twelve chairs. Virgil motioned for him to sit; Carlton hesitated for a moment before obliging. Virgil was a new man; he had traded his wetsuit for a shirt the color of faded mustard and an orange-and-red patterned tie. He wore navy slacks and black shoes that glinted in the fluorescent lights.

"How'd you even find me?" he asked.

"A1 detective, remember?" said Carlton. "Not a lot of Virgil's in the white pages. Fewer still in the insurance game."

"All right, Veronica Mars. I'm gonna get us some coffees. You have until I get back to explain to me why I shouldn't throttle you and file a claim for losing my foot in your ass." He left and returned a moment later with two paper cups. "Cream and two sugars, right?" he said before handing Carlton the coffee black.

"Man, you really are a salty sea bitch," said Carlton. "Who woulda thought *El Clavadista* would have such a stick up his—"

"Oh, you funny now?" said Virgil, cutting him off. "Drove all this way to play the dozens?"

"And for this," said Carlton, pulling out his phone and sliding it across the table to Virgil.

"What am I looking at?" said Virgil, squinting. It amused Carlton to think that this man needed reading glasses.

"It's an Imperial Suites in French Lick," he replied. "It's different from their usual design—six stories instead of twelve, pool centrally located in the courtyard. They built it for some sports car convention. Anyway, I did the math—" he produced a densely scribbled sheet of folded graph paper from his coat pocket. "—and I think a jump from the fifth story is possible."

Virgil studied the graph paper. Carlton could see him doing the figures in his head. *Shit, he's good*, he thought. Virgil looked back at the phone, then at Carlton.

"Ain't no way," he said. "It's too far."

"It's not."

"We'd have to clear at least six feet. And those are rounded banisters. What if we slip?"

"So don't slip."

Virgil laughed. "Oh, I ain't worried about me. It's your white ass I'm picturing in a chalk outline on the tile below."

"I can handle it."

"Then let me be blunt with you, Carlton," he said, gesturing to the adhesive nametag the front desk had printed for his visit. "I work alone."

"I'm El Clavadista."

Virgil nodded. "You were. And now you ain't. Go find something else, bitch."

"I don't want something else. This is my thing, *bitch*."

Virgil slammed the table and leapt to his feet. Carlton flinched and stayed seated. For a moment, Virgil breathed deeply through his nostrils, then, slowly, he readjusted his tie, tucked in his shirt, and sat back down. He took a sip of coffee, staring at Carlton, who warily returned his gaze.

"The hell has gotten into you?" said Virgil. "A week ago, you were afraid of *the idea* of your shadow. Now you a 'bad mothafucka?'" he gestured comically. "What happened during commercials?"

Carlton shifted in his seat. What had gotten into him? He had been restless at night, going for long drives through strange neighborhoods. He stared at people at the supermarket, held them long in his gaze until they broke away and dropped their eyes. He was snapping at students and reveling in their submission. "You were right about me," he said after a moment. "I'm tired of being invisible."

Virgil nodded.

He held out his hand; Carlton took it. They shook. "*Ecce homo*?" said Carlton.

Virgil smiled. "That's right." He walked to the door, opened it, then turned to face Carlton again. "Showed me something today," he said, pointing. "Go do something worth watching. Fortune favors the bold."

Carlton found this advice inspired. He focused all week on bold public displays.

He started online, wandering into chatrooms and excoriating ideas or comments he found asinine. He ripped into a former student on Facebook for the overuse of #adulting ("It's just called being an adult," wrote Carlton. "The sooner you recognize that, the less you'll annoy the rest of us."). He mocked the wedding entrance dances in a video posted by an old colleague ("The sprinkler? The shopping cart? Is this a montage in an off-brand John Hughes movie?"). He reserved special venom for a comment on Clearwater Confidential that "Everything happens for a reason" ("That's factually true," he wrote. "And sometimes that reason is a dipshit teenage hacker decides to upend the lives of his teachers because he's bored and out of spank material."). He tracked the responses and 'likes,' and discovered that the more vulgar or 'straight savage' he was, the more frequent and intense the replies.

He brought this analysis to his in-person conversations. Carlton, so long a figure of reserve and restraint, began to loudly declare his most acerbic thoughts. He chewed out (to applause!) a cashier who wiped her nose with her hand before handing him change. He unleashed a two-minute monologue on the fallacy of "microaggressions" and "triggers" to a student who asked if she could take a quiz in the hallway ("I saw you wreck that girl on Snapchat!" one of his students congratulated him later in the day.). He rolled his eyes and mocked Eliza's use of the word 'mouthfeel' at lunch. It dissolved the group into laughter.

While it was undoubtedly cathartic to so freely speak his mind, a small part of Carlton throbbed with remorse at each castigation. Yet paradoxically, such behavior seemed to win him greater attention and approval. He had never been so famous at school, never been approached or congratulated by strangers in the halls, at the supermarket, or at Pub Trivia Night. It fed his confidence and crept into his posture, his facial expressions, and his wardrobe choices. One Thursday after school, Carlton treated himself to an expensive haircut.

That night was the area semi-finals, and Carlton had never been sharper. He knew the location of Kodiak Island ("Alaska!"), the popular name for 'granadilla' ("Passion-fruit!"), the eldest Marx Brother ("Chico!"). He was on such a roll that midway through the second round, Tony simply handed him the pencil and answer sheet. "All yours, pal," he said, patting Carlton on the back. "Take us home."

They won. It was the first time they'd defeated Tequila Mockingbird or You're a Quizzard, Harry. "Hell," laughed Shelton, "we've NEVER gotten more music cues than Frank Petrosvych and his crew. This is the greatest night of my life. Of anyone's life, really."

"What was your secret tonight?" asked Connie. "Was it drugs? Because I'll do the drugs."

Carlton shook his head. "I don't know," he said. "I just felt 'on' tonight. Actually, I've felt 'on' all week."

The bar was exploding with activity. The semi-finals had drawn a larger crowd than usual, and they had all remained to drink and carouse. A Pacers game played on several televisions, tables of men and women downed shots with a shout, waitresses circulated like busy white blood cells fighting off a disease. Phones out for pictures, for scores, for texting and the settling of debates. It electrified Carlton to have such an audience, and when the song turned to "One Boy, One Girl" by Collin Raye, he grabbed Connie by the hand.

"Dance with me," he said.

He had never been so close to her, never had his hand on the small of her back. She wore a checkered flannel and jeans, but beneath the thick fabric, he could feel the thin impress of a tank top wrapping her frame. A strip of elastic, a clasp. Long auburn tangles of bright curly hair. She smelled like grapefruits.

For a long time, they said nothing to one another. He couldn't tell if she was enjoying the moment or just enduring it, but when he peeled back to look at her, he could sense she had been leaning into him.

"How long have we known each other?" he asked.

She smiled and scrunched up her forehead. "Um… I don't know," she said. "I guess about two years."

"What did you think of me when you first met me?"

She laughed uncomfortably. "What are we doing here?" she asked.

"I'm just asking a question," he said. "Isn't that what happens at Pub Trivia?"

She leaned her face into his shoulder. "I, uh, I thought you were handsome," she said quietly. "But that was before you spoke."

"Oh," he said. "Well, I have that effect on women."

"No!" she laughed slapping playfully at his chest. "No, listen." She leaned into him again. He felt light, dizzy. A protective layer of silence extended around the two of them, drowning out the clamor of the bar.

"Tony and I were together, remember?" she asked.

"Yes."

"And he and Shelton, they introduced you to me, made fun of you for a bit. You were a good sport about it, just sort of sat there and smiled. And then Shelton asked if you'd been seeing anyone lately. Do you remember what you said?"

"No."

"You said, 'No, but lately I've started walking slowly on the sidewalk and pretending I'm dating the people who try to get around me.' You said, 'This week, I dated two joggers, a small dog, and a woman who I believe was Betty White.'"

"I said that?"

"You did. I thought it was very funny. I thought about it long after you left. Still think about it from time to time."

"It wasn't *that* funny."

"No," she said, running her hand up his bicep. "No, but it wasn't the joke. You were just creative. Are creative. You have an imagination, Carlton; you really do. And," she said, hesitating for a moment. "I just don't know many people like that."

Carlton pulled back from her, ran straight into her brown eyes. "I'm in love with you," he said. "Since that day, two years ago. The way you think, move. Your laugh. I live for the ten seconds right before I'm about to see you."

She stared at him, then looked away. "Carlton, I—" He could feel her body disengage, a space opening up between them like slivering ice. *I'm losing,* he thought. *Fortune favors the bold.*

"And I want to fuck you," he blurted. "Right here. In front of all these people. You are just… an insanely sexy woman."

She slapped him. He wasn't sure of how long it took her, or the sequence of events immediately following. Once, when he had been sick with the flu, he had fainted at the pharmacy. When he came to, it was like the rebooting a of computer—first he had to learn which direction was up, then he had to understand the configuration of human faces standing over him, then account for the missing gap in his memory. So it was now—he understood that she had hit him, was moving away, that people were staring, that Tony and Shelton were pursuing her, confused, into the parking lot. That there was music, laughter, shouting, commentary, pictures, images, words, sound.

He blinked. What had he done? What had he said? How could those words have come from him? Connie, Connie, Connie. Receding into the distance.

They were looking at him. All of them. The bar was his for this moment. "Fuck off!" he said to everyone. The messiness resumed.

There was a girl at the bar, stuffed in a green tank-top and leather jacket. She was staring at him, sipping a brown beverage through a stir straw. He stared back. Long, long they looked at one another, until she turned to say something to a barback. There was an empty stool beside her. Carlton moved.

— — — — — — — — —

On Monday, the faculty gathered in the auditorium for a faculty meeting. It was the first such all-school gathering since Vince had met with them following the second data dump. Most faculty meetings are exercises in endurance—teachers are independent, dismissive, and difficult to supervise in large groups. They are collectively the worst classroom imaginable.

But Carlton was more restless than usual. Every syllable spoken from the stage pained him. The presence of other people was an irritant—Erin Kooner's incessant coughing, the sight of the corpulent Bryan Yulders shifting in his too-tight pants, the sound of Chloe Fichte's knitting needles clacking behind him. Each PowerPoint slide screamed of incompetence, mismanagement, and waste. An administration so far removed from the day-to-day experience of its faculty that it might as well have been supervising by drone. It was like a military command radioing during a firefight for data on soldiers' socks.

Vince was finishing an update on the data dump. "The police seem to think they have a few new leads," he said. "I know you've heard rumors, but I'm not at liberty to comment." He paused for a moment to mop his brow with a handkerchief. Vince Darten was a brilliant principal in many regards, but as a public speaker he lacked an awareness of the moment. "I am just as in the dark as you are, actually," he continued. "But I'm proud of how you've handled this. You are inspiring professionals."

"Oh, fuck professional behavior," Carlton heard himself say.

Vince scrunched his forehead, raising a hand to shield his vision from the auditorium lights. "What was that?" he asked.

"I said, 'Fuck professional behavior,'" said Carlton. "Look, I'm sorry, Vince. I know you're doing your best. I know the police are doing their best. Everyone's doing their best." He paused. All heads had swiveled to look at him. The entire school. Was he doing this?

Yes. "When is someone going to admit that this isn't normal? That no one should be expected to work under these conditions? This is absurd! We've had our lives paraded through the community. Every kid with a phone has read our email, seen our text messages, Tweeted our private thoughts. In what other industry would this be tolerated? But noooo, we're teachers! Public servants! We're just supposed to "Keep calm, and teach on!"

They were murmuring all around him, stirring uncomfortably. "He's right," nodded Irene Jenkins.

"Are we going to talk about what's happening to Cespids?" asked Betsy Rilke.

"All right, all right," said Vince. "You're right. We've been through a trauma. This isn't normal. This isn't just another emergency." The audience calmed, but the tension of mutiny remained just beneath the surface. "I want to remind you that the district has made available grief counselors for you to work with—"

"I don't want a counselor, I want action!" shouted Carlton. "Catch this kid! Parade *him* through the halls! He's in one of our classes, laughing! Do something! Do something! *Listen to us!*"

Carlton was only aware towards the end how emphatically he was gesturing, bringing his arms up and down in a swinging motion. The auditorium was silent. Vince stared at him, blank-faced. Finally, he brought the handheld microphone back to his face.

"Let's take a ten-minute break," he said. "Teachers who need to leave for activities or child pick-up, you are dismissed. Everyone else, let's be back at 3:40."

Vince found Carlton in the auditorium lobby, and led him into an empty band classroom.

"Carlton, what you did back there was totally inappropriate," he said, his voice full of cold fury. "Not every decision I make will make sense to you, and God knows these are extraordinary circumstances. But I am your boss, and you will respect my voice."

Carlton said nothing. He stood by the door, arms crossed, breathing through his nostrils.

"Don't look at me that way, young man," said Vince. "You wanted to speak your mind? Well, here's your audience."

"You're losing the school," said Carlton. "You have done nothing—*nothing*—to protect us. You've left us to twist in the storm."

Vince laughed. "You know, I wish you could feel that storm without me to shield you. You do realize that I saved your job, don't you?"

"You never stop reminding me."

"Only because you seem to keep forgetting," said Vince. "I see there's an El Clavadista website now. A countdown clock. A Snapchat address."

This was the first Carlton had heard of this. He squirmed. "It's not me," he said. "I don't know anything about that."

"Right," said Vince. "I should hope not." Vince put his hands on his hips, bit his lip, stared at the ground. His suit jacket was unpressed, and his tie looked crooked. The staff had long debated the principal's age, but in this light and this moment, Carlton thought he looked very old.

"You'll finish out the year, assuming you can," said Vince after a moment. "In April, I suggest you get your resume out there. Until then, Mr. Wemish, I'll remind you that every subject's duty is the king's; but every subject's soul is his own."

He walked past Carlton imperiously, leaving the younger man alone. Carlton shouted at the empty classroom for a full minute and a half. He knocked over a music stand, and stormed out.

———————————

Darten was right; the website was nothing more than a vague logo, a countdown clock, and a Snapchat address. Carlton sent a friend request, but received no reply. *He must screen people somehow,* he thought. *He's setting up a secret network.* But for what? Carlton thought about Virgil, about his dream. Then he had an idea. He Googled and called to confirm.

The countdown clock showed four days remaining. "Friday at 8:oo P.M.," said Vince. He went to dig for his cape.

———————————

The Imperial Suites in French Lick was an opulent hotel, a cavernous six-story rectangular building built like a layer cake. Each floor was ringed by rooms that opened to a walkway and bannister overlooking the central courtyard that included a restaurant, viewing area, and enormous 72,ooo-gallon swimming pool. Normally, it was a favorite of families, but as Carlton walked through the lobby, he saw no children on any level. Even the pool—a magnet for the under-10-set, was emptied of the young.

He checked in and received a card-key to his fifth story room. He spotted a security camera in the corner of the lobby, removed from its plastic casing, wires exposed.

"I think your camera's busted," said Carlton, pointing.

"Oh," said the desk clerk. "No, they're fine. Just a routine servicing."

"Perfect setting for a casino heist!" joked Carlton.

He went to his room and set down his suitcase on the bed. There were just a few articles inside. A red cape. Green umbros. A camera. A mask. He looked over at the digital clock. 7:28 P.M. 32 minutes.

He dressed and sat in a green armchair by the door, which he left slightly ajar. The lights were off; he was completely motionless. He tried to breath shallowly. He wanted to miss nothing, to give away nothing. All would depend on the moment of surprise.

He could see through his window that people were stirring outside. The rooms adjoining his own emptied of people. They, too, were costumed—one Spiderman, one Furiosa. A Thor. Three Batmen. Bender from Futurama. A Rick and a Morty. They were everywhere on the fifth floor. *There must be 30 of them, all cos-playing* he thought in awe. Glancing down, he realized that it was the same on the other four levels. *Holy shit*, he realized. Virgil had called a convention.

At exactly 8:00, he saw a door across the court space open. Room 612. A man in a black wetsuit emerged, a lucha libre mask pulled over his face. A spontaneous applause broke out on every level as the cos-players rushed to their bannisters to see their king. Virgil held up his hands and silenced them.

"PEOPLE OF INDIANA!" he bellowed in his British accent. "I AM EL CLAVADISTA! LORD OF ALL THAT I BEHOLD!" He held the silence for a moment. "I HAVE SUMMONED—"

"STOP!" shouted Carlton, pushing past a Motoko lookalike. "HE IS AN IMPOSTER! I AM THE *REAL* EL CLAVADISTA!"

The heads swiveled to him. No one said a word. "USURPER!"

shouted Carlton, gesturing angrily at Virgil. "STAND AND FACE ME! LIKE A MAN!"

For a moment, Virgil said nothing. Carlton imagined the amount of time he must have spent setting this up, how many times he must have imagined this moment, sans a second diver. *Well,* thought Carlton, *we're together at last.*

"ECCE HOMO!" he shouted, and ran along the walkway, bending around the courtyard as he charged at Virgil. "*ECCE HOMO!*" shouted Virgil, snapping out of his spell. They met in a collision by room 633, Virgil lumbering in his wetsuit, Carlton streaming in bare-chested, his cape flapping behind. He clotheslined Virgil, catching him just below the neck, knocking him over so that his whole torso snapped to the floor.

"OW!" shouted Virgil. "Motherfucker, that hurt— "

But Carlton was already on top of him, straddling him in his umbros, slapping him open-palmed across the face. "SUBMIT, HOMBRE!" he shouted. He was suddenly aware of the cheering of the spectators, the pumping of fists, the catcalls and blaring of an airhorn.

"Ow!" snapped Virgil, slapping at him before grabbing at Carlton's chin. "Have you lost your fucking mind?"

"SURRENDER, IMPOS—" shouted Carlton before Virgil popped him square in the nose. He reeled back, his eyes clouded with brown spots as Virgil rolled on top of him. "Ah, ah, ah, ah! Uncle! Uncle!" yelled Carlton, shielding his face.

"Motherfucker, for sure I'm gonna beat you like you my nephew," growled Virgil.

"No," said Carlton, touching his nose for blood. "No, we've got to jump now."

"We?"

"I'm in this now," said Carlton. "Come on. We've got seconds before hotel security stops us."

Even over the tumult, they both heard the ding of the elevator. Two large men in sports coats emerged, pushing past the spectators.

"Behold the mans?" said Carlton.

Virgil shook his head, climbed off of Carlton, and helped him to his feet. "Behold the motherfuckers," he said. They climbed atop the curved bannister.

The fall of El Clavadista was discussed and debated for many months afterwards. It led to legislation, stiffer penalties, a nationwide change in security practices, higher insurance rates, several dozen think-pieces on Medium about public space and Internet notoriety. The actual Go-Pro footage from their battle and leap never aired. Afterwards, Carlton only remembered a few scattered images. A woman, dressed as She-Hulk, cheering lustily. Bubbles. The rough hands of a waiter, hauling him out of the pool. The bone, protruding from his shin. The impassive face of Vince Darten. The biggest moment of his life, and it was lost to him. It didn't matter. One hundred and forty-seven phones recorded it. Millions watched. Carlton Wemish was soon forgotten. But El Clavadista would never stop leaping.

18
BEAUMONT

The first of March. Jono was late. Beaumont sat on the curb and snapped a few shots of some geese wandering aimlessly across a field, disinterested in flight but bereft of feeding pond. Finally, he heard the rumble of his trucks on the sidewalk, and Jono rolled in looking miserable.

"Jesus," said Beaumont. "What happened to you?"

His head was shorn clean, the magenta strands of his glorious coxcomb now erased. One would never know a strip of pink once cleft his scalp. He had shaved it clear to the roots.

"I don't want to talk about it," said Jono, pushing off and gathering a head of speed to enter the quarter pipe. Beaumont watched him in silence for a few minutes until Jono was ready to speak.

"I guess my mom's sort of right," he said. "I've got that scholarship interview on Wednesday. If I don't get it, I… I don't even know." He rolled back and forth on the pipe, up and down wearily. "And it… it's just a pain to get ready in the morning, you know? I mean, what's the point of being a guy if you've got to spend girl-amounts of time on your hair?"

He attempted a kick-flip, but again caught the edge of his board and tripped. "Fuck me," Jono said.

"No, no," said Mrs. Moresoe. "E-minor, E-minor. Where're your fingers? Why does every black guitarist want to play A?"

"I dunno," said Beaumont. "Probably the same reason a bunch of white punks insist that skanking is dancing."

She laughed. "All right, all right. Let's try it again. Show me G-Major. Good. Now E-Minor. *Good!*"

"Now can we shred?"

"That is shredding. What did you think shredding is?"

They were in her classroom after school. He had an Epiphone Les Paul Standard electric guitar on loan from her son across my lap. It was unplugged for now; they were mostly working on fingering and strumming these days. He could play a few songs already on the acoustic, and he was excited to move on to some classics, but for now they were going slow.

"Who taught you?" Beaumont asked.

"Um," she said, fiddling with her tuning keys. "My brother showed me the basics. But I learned punk on my own."

"How?"

She looked up at him shrewdly. "That's what you really want to know, isn't it?" she said. "The music's just the vehicle. You want the lifestyle."

Beaumont pointed to his eye, which had healed up nicely. "I

mean, I already lived it, so I might as well get the membership card, right?"

She grinned. "Getting your ass stomped doesn't make you a punk," she said. "Mostly, it just makes you hamburger."

Christ, but she just keeps dancing around it, he thought. "Let me ask you something," said Beaumont. "Why do you make this so hard for me? I read somewhere that if you want to be a Jew, you have to get turned down three times by a rabbi. But I'm not tryin' to be the chosen people. Whatever happened to 'Here are three chords. Now go start a band?'"

"I'll answer your question with my own," she said, executing the infernal teacher jujitsu. "Why's a nice kid like you want to hang around a mosh pit?"

He ran through the fingers while pondering this. G-Major. E-Minor. C-Major. G-Major. E-Minor. C-Major. *Why are you mad at the world, Beaumont?* He heard them asking. *You got it good. A father who works. A strong education. A future. How many brothers are born and die in the streets without ever getting a taste of what's on your table every night? How many lose their lives to police, prison, drugs, or despair?* G-Major. E-Minor. C-Major.

"I read about this village in India, Jatinga I think it's called," he said finally. "It's near a rain forest. Nothing special, as far as villages go; probably hundreds just like it all over the continent. But every year around September, just after the monsoon ends, these huge flocks of birds get all dizzy or something. Happens at a particular time of day with a particular kind of weather. Every year, without fail. And these birds, they dive *en masse* into torches, buildings, vehicles. They just wipe themselves out."

"Why?"

He shrugged. "No one knows. They sent this bird expert—what do you call them? Ornithologist?—down to watch it a few years ago.

Could be pollution, wind, fog, magnetism… it's a mystery." He sped up his fingerings and start strumming. He was playing "Blitzkrieg Bop." "But I think it's because they're angry. Angry birds," he smiled at the joke. "That's how I feel. Like them. All the time."

"Are you depressed?"

He shook his head. He knew what depression looked like. "No."

"Traumatized?" she asked. "Lose a job? A family member?"

"My mother died two years ago," he said. "But I'm at peace about it. And I felt this way when she was alive, too."

She nodded. "I lost a parent, too. My father was an alcoholic. One day, he just stopped… just stopped being my father. I could find him if I needed him. But I told myself I didn't."

Beaumont set down the guitar. She was playing now; moving up and down the neck, her fingers dancing the way bees do when they're teaching the way to pollen. "My mother didn't take it well. Slept around. Got into heroin. Not a good home. Anyway, this ex-Green Beret started coming around. Real tough guy. Took care of my mom, cleaned the house, made dinner. But a hard-ass, and violent. My brother and I hated him."

"So I needed to get out of the house. About the time I was your age, I started following my brother to concerts. And that's where I learned about punk rock. How you feel about Bad Brains, that's how I felt about The Vandals. Like they were the only ones that were mad like I was mad. I couldn't play, but I could dress the part, and I started hanging out backstage, met a few bands, learned my way around a couple sets."

She was playing something he don't recognize now, but it was tight and complicated and dizzyingly fast. He felt like he was watching years melt off of her. She was 19 now, thick eye-liner, shredded jeans, and a tight tube-top. Her hair was green and shaved on the sides. Her eyes burned like charcoal. "And that's when you became a punk?"

"No," she smiled, setting down her guitar. "It's when I headbutted that son-of-a-bitch step-father. Broke his nose. He broke my jaw. I found Robert and Jean-Pierre. And I never went home again."

She moved to her desk and leafed through the poetry anthology. "Everyone thinks punk started with the Ramones, the Sex Pistols, maybe the Wailers or the Stooges. Maybe you think it was Death," she said, referencing a Detroit trio he'd found on cassette. "But punk is an anger, a despair at being beaten before you even got a chance. It's saying 'screw the old guard, screw the elites and pretty people. I'm here, I'm ugly, and I want my shot.' And it's much, much older than CBGB."

She found what she was looking for and handed him the anthology. "Imagine my surprise to find punk in the days of whalebone corsets," she said. "Percy Shelley was Sid Vicious; Lord Byron was Johnny Rotten. And this—" she gestured at the poem she found, "—this is my 'London Calling.'"

"Dylan Thomas," said Beaumont. And he read:

> *Do not go gentle into that good night,*
> *Old age should burn and rave at close of day;*
> *Rage, rage against the dying of the light.*

> *Though wise men at their end know dark is right,*
> *Because their words had forked no lightning they*
> *Do not go gentle into that good night.*

"Jesus," he said.

"I know," she said.

"That why you're not punk anymore?" said Beaumont. "Stopped raging?"

She smiled. "Oh, I'm still plenty mad. Sometimes I'll be waiting behind someone in line or I'll be listening to the news or I'll be watching my daughter practice her violin. And it will well up in me, just as hot and red and explosive as when I broke that asshole's face with my head. But being married changed me. Being a mother changed me. Being a teacher… being a teacher made me a different kind of punk. How's that Morrissey lyric go? 'It's easy to laugh/It's easy to hate/It takes guts to be gentle and kind.'"

"I don't…" he started, then paused to gather his words. "I don't know how to do that."

"You want to be your own kind of punk rocker, but you don't know what to push against," she said, tapping the Dylan Thomas poem. "Start here. Add power chords. I'll show you."

A three day weekend in early March provided Beaumont and his father time to explore Purdue's campus in greater detail, and he arranged for Beaumont to spend time with the nephew of one of his co-workers. Things had remained tense between father and son for a month, and the drive up I-65 was mostly spent staring out the window at pinstriped fields whose crop lines looked like the frets of his guitar. Neither of them disrespected the other by putting on headphones, but that was about the extent of their civility.

They pulled onto State Street and cruised past the green playing fields and parklands dotted with co-eds lounging, jogging, or playing Frisbee golf. Beaumont's father needed a few hours to meet with financial aid representatives; he let his son out at Harrison Hall to spend a few hours touring the campus. Beaumont made his way through the entrance hall (a few students are toying around with a grand piano) and trudged up the stairs to a third-floor Resident Advisor dorm. The door was open.

A spindly 21-year-old was spread out on a couch, a laptop perched on his knobby knees, watching a Migos video. He looked up as Beaumont stood awkwardly in the doorway. The co-ed was unwrapping a hot pocket.

"Well ain't that always the way," he said. "I get the fine china out, and some ass-out bitch shows up wantin' to share my Philly." An orange tabby suddenly leapt off his loft and padded along the back of the couch to lick at the food.

"There's a cat," said Beaumont.

"No, there ain't," said the co-ed, abandoning the food to the animal so he could stand to greet his guest. "No cats allowed in Harrison." He moved towards Beaumont, a strange swaying motion in his shoulders. "You must be Melville's boy. Well, come on now. Let's have a look at you." He moved his head back and forth, as though we were a pediatrician examining a reluctant child. "Mmm-hmm. You a shady-looking nugget. Probably try to sneak cats into Harrison. What's your name?"

"Beaumont," he replied. "You Lever?"

"LeVAR," he corrected. "Like Geordi Laforge. Like the host of *Reading Rainbow*." Levar correctly read Beaumont's silence as confusion. "Don't know *Reading Rainbow*?" He clicks his tongue. "This nugget don't know how to read."

He spent the next 45 minutes showing Beaumont around the immediate campus. "That creepy-ass abandoned power plant over there is the HPN," he said. "At least one brother goes missing in there every semester. The smoke stacks form the middle finger, pointing south towards IU."

He showed Beaumont a bell tower with a time capsule buried at its base ("All the unreleased Tupac tracks are in it."). He narrated the bizarre history of campus architecture ("John Purdue loved University Hall so much he wanted it to always be the tallest building on campus," he explained. "That's why Beering Hall has a separate ZIP code for its upper floors, so they're technically off-campus. Also, the Math Building isn't a building; it's a bridge."). He walked Beaumont past a statue of a lion some claimed roars when virgins pass by ("Damn, listen to that, Nugget!" Levar giggled. "It's like a coronation at Pride Rock when you come around!").

Despite his relentless teasing, Beaumont enjoyed Levar. He didn't rush the tour, and he asked Beaumont questions about his life. He was forthright and candid about his experiences on campus. "Bunch of white supremacist posters went up last November all over campus," he said, waving to a pair of girls exiting the music hall. "President Daniels said not to over-react. Most everybody played it real cool. Course, they don't put up posters where they don't expect to recruit."

They found their way back to Levar's room, and Beaumont shook his hand and thanked him for his time. "Where you going?" he asked. "Man, I gotta get you on my podcast!"

"You have a podcast?" Beaumont laughed.

"Beaumont, ev'eybody got a podcast 'round here. Shit, how else we gonna talk to one another?"

"I mean… what would we talk about?"

"Whatever you like. You my guest!"

Beaumont wasn't sure how he felt about his voice being frozen in digital amber. "I don't know," he said.

"Look, you seem like a real interesting kid," Levar replied. "Got your blue hair, your old-ass camera. Virgin. Seems like you'd have something to say." He grabbed his laptop off the couch and dug through a drawer, producing a USB microphone that he plugged into the side. "I'm an asexual panromantic mixed-race oboe player. I'm, like, a minority of a minority of a minority of a minority. Crazy-ass Venn diagram. And back in high school, I hated every single ring." He set the laptop on his coffee table and motioned for Beaumont to sit.

"The day's too long to wake up early and go to bed late hatin' yourself," he said. "A long silence seems more and more like the smart play. But if you don't start using your voice, you ain't never going to learn how to value it, take pride in it." He slapped the couch cushion. "So sit your ass down and be on my motherfucking podcast!"

An hour later, Beaumont's father picked him up outside Harrison. He was wielding a thick folder of handouts. "What'd you learn?" Beaumont asked.

"That I should' a made you keep taking those piano lessons," said his father. "What'd you learn?"

Beaumont smiled. "Dylan Thomas got a podcast."

19

ELSIE

Login
Administrator
Password
* * * *

The drawing of the Elbo Room was going well. She'd sketched the stage at the center, brilliantly lit with sharp, thick lines, surrounded on all sides by ethereal limbs, writhing and snaking around one another. It felt like it did that night. Mr. Lain nodded approvingly.

"Where is it?" he asked.

"Um… it's a club in Chicago," she said, before adding: "Have you ever been to any Chicago clubs?"

He looked at her without changing his expression for a long moment. "No," he said. "Can't say I have."

"So he's lying?" said Dale later at lunch.

Elsie shrugged. "Well, we know he's been outside the club. We don't know if he went inside."

"Yeah, but why would he lie?" Dale asked, dabbing a tator tot in ketchup.

———————————

"Because it's a sex club," said Cooper, handing Elsie a calculator. She rolled her eyes.

"It's not a sex club," Elsie said. "I looked it up online. But it is fairly new. We don't know when he was there."

"So when are we going?" Cooper asked.

———————————

"This weekend!" said Yael, nodding approvingly. "Can you get off?"

"Um…" Elsie said, pouring the batter into the baking pan. "I quit."

"What?" said Denver. "Why?"

"I don't want to talk about it."

"Well, I know a couple of older guys at UIC that I think could get us in," said Yael, swatting Denver's attempt to lick batter from the pan. "Lemme see if they'll meet us there."

And so, they left at 5:30 P.M. on Saturday evening, the sun already gone and more than three hours of driving up 65 ahead of them. Elsie drove this time, with Yael navigating, and Cooper and the boys in the back seat. They talked excitedly about the club; Yael told them that college boys always had the best drugs, and Cooper bragged about a random hookup she had at a Yung Fi'ty concert. Dale was obsessed with "the acoustics of these old buildings—the bricks are baked to absorb the sound, so the music lives in the bones!" Denver mostly complained about the lack of Chipotle available on 65.

But Elsie was thinking about Mr. Lain. Why on earth would he travel this far away from his hole when the rest of his movements were so tightly localized around Clearwater? What was he hiding? *And why am I so obsessed with seeing it for myself?*

They didn't reach the club until nearly 10:00 P.M., and it was another 45 minutes before they could park and hook up with Yael's friends, Serge and Aram. They were tall, muscly engineering students who talked Persian to Yael and hooked everyone up with molly. Elsie had never done it before, and she waved it off for fear that she wouldn't be able to drive home, but each of her friends swallowed their pill, taking a pull from a shared water bottle, and were soon eager to visit Cyprus.

They could hear it before they could see it, trudging through the remnants of a once-vibrant neighborhood, now boarded up bodegas and vacant lots picked clean of precious metals. There were people moving with them now, streams joining together flowing towards their source. The music was Spanish, fused with driving rhythm and an electric throb that moved restlessly like a wasp through the glass surfaces surrounding the epicenter. Cars rolled past them, boys in mesh tops hollering out the window at Cooper, and she threw her hands around Dale's neck and laughed triumphantly. He wrapped his arms around her slender waist to keep her from spilling into the gutter, and Elsie looked away to keep from breaking.

There was a silver Accord parked in a side alley; she could make it out thanks to the brake lights from a passing F150. A Clearwater parking pass was visibly dangling from the rearview mirror. "He's here!" Elsie shouted, seizing Denver by the sleeve, but he wrenched free with a great bear's indifference to tangled fur. No one was listening to her; they were marching on with a singular purpose, hypnotized by the laughter and lights waiting for them ten minutes in the future. As they talked excitedly, words coming almost too fast to process, Elsie could feel them receding into the distance, almost like they were bright and clownish floats in a parade, and she was the lone anchor dutifully marching below, tugging the rope to keep them from soaring away.

Cyprus was indeed an older building, and she checked her phone to verify the GPS coordinates. In the moment it took her to peer at her screen, my friends were gone, absorbed into the tangle of bodies and faces, the taut muscles and long legs, bared to the feathering of their panties, the sweat and fingers, the strobes and shot glasses, the missing purses and discarded jackets. It was the most people she'd ever seen moving with one purpose, a singular undulation, and for the first time in her concert-going life, Elsie felt herself on the outside, painfully alien to her own body and its ungainliness. The DJ was perched on a lattice stage at the front of the dance floor, a spider suspended by shafts of orange light and columns of hammering bass. The smells of spent gym clothes and wet flesh pressed down on her, and she couldn't imagine Mr. Lain surviving anywhere near this bedlam.

Think, Elsie! She told herself. *Where would I go if I were a lonely old man?* But of course, the answer was *out, out, out, away.* Like a blind beggar, she found her way to a wall and felt along the paneling until she hit a crash bar nestled in a metal door. She pushed through and escaped to an alleyway. There—under a fire escape and next to a grease trap—was a stairway leading into a cellar of some kind. It was better lit than the rest of the dim corridor, and what caught her eye was some sort of stenciled garland winding around the metal handrail bolted to the brick wall. As she approached, she realized that it was ivy, spray-painted in blue and dotted with green roses all down the passageway into the basement chamber. She used the light on her phone like a torch and descended into the earth.

The door at the base was open, and she pushed against it lightly; it swung on rusty hinges to reveal a small anteroom. The ivy winding into the room spread out along the wall to a lushly painted orchard—lilies and amaryllis and baby's breath and flowers she couldn't name and perhaps didn't even exist—twisting, bending along the floor, onto the ceiling. There were mythical creatures depicted—tiny winged fairies and one of those half-man/half-goat creatures reaching towards a second door in the corner. The sound of Cyprus fading behind her, Elsie turned the knob and pressed on.

Mr. Lain looked up from the far corner of a large, cavernous room with a high ceiling held up by four large concrete pillars equidistant from one another. He staggered to his feet when he saw her, and it was only when he backed against the wall that she recognized with astonishment what he had done. The entire room—every square inch of available concrete, from floor to ceiling, has been concealed by paint. It was like standing inside Guernica if the dominate theme of madness were replaced by celebration. Human figures with long, supple bodies and smiling purple faces danced on a cliff overlooking an emerald sea; birds flocked across the ceiling; the cement floor had been remade in the image of a multicolored poppy field. Horses galloped; elephants pushed against one another; a town in the distance ringed a watchtower. Two suns adorned the far wall behind Lain, who was holding a brush in his right hand.

"Elsie," he said after mouthing her name twice. "Elsie, wh-wha-whaat are you d-d-d-doing here?"

"Um..." she said, and she suddenly realized the horrible truth of her sin. *This is not for me*. This was never meant to be seen. "I'm sorry, Mr. Lain."

He set down his brush in a bucket and brushed his hands on the back of his pants before pulling a rag from his pocket to clean them properly. "Did you," he said slowly, mastering his stutter. "Did you follow me?"

She nodded once.

"W-w-why?"

What do I say? How do I hide what I've done? But of course, she couldn't. "I found this online," she admitted. "I was curious."

He nodded and looked at his feet. "Well," he said after an agonizing moment. "W-w-what do you think?"

"It's… it's amazing, Mr. Lain," she said. "It's the most beautiful thing I've ever seen."

He looked up at her, then at the ceiling. "Thank you," he said simply.

"But…" she said, ignoring the opportunity to excuse herself with grace. "But… why a basement? Why this basement? Here? Tonight?"

"Hmmm," he said. He was thinking; she couldn't tell what that meant for her. "This room… it used to be very different. Not just the paint. There used to be a toilet there," he pointed to the corner. "And a bed over there," he pointed at the far wall. "The door you came through, it locked from the outside. And there was a slot on the door, large enough to pass a tray of food to a small boy. Who slept in that bed. And u-u-used that toilet."

He was looking at the cliff where the dancers were painted, and as she followed his eyes she noted that amidst all the joyous revelry, there was a smaller figure that was standing still, its tiny arms dangling from its sides, its wide eyes upturned at the raucous celebrants crowding him. "I don't… I don't understand, Mr. Lain."

He spoke as though she was not even in the room. "I was taken from my yard quite suddenly, brought down here, kept for ten months. Almost a year without the sun, without other ch-ch-children to play with. Only the sound of her voice through the slot every day, reading me wonderful stories."

"Whose voice?"

"Mrs. Willos. You saw her when you came in—the s-s-satyr. Of course, she wasn't really a satyr. She was a frightened old woman who was convinced that 1978 was the end of the world, and she had brought me down here for safekeeping. I didn't know that at the time, Elsie. I simply always imagined she was a m-m-magical creature."

"She never touched me, never harmed me, brought me whatever I asked for to eat. It's funny—the landlord spotted her bringing ground beef down here and thought she might have a dog, which was against her lease. I im-m-magine that when the truth came out, he wished I had been a dog."

"So she… you were…"

"Yes," he says. "My mother wept when they brought me up. She thought I was dead. I couldn't open my eyes—hadn't used them properly in three seasons. I still prefer the dark, Elsie. I only really feel s-s-safe at night."

And slowly, it all made sense. "They brought you out," she said slowly. "But you never left this room."

He smiled. When he spoke, she could sense his stutter receding. "That's right. I was different after that. Kept to myself, preferred tight spaces. Pushed my bed up against the wall. At first, it felt good to keep everything simple, but as I became a m-m-man, I knew that I had to find some way to join the world. So I… I brought the world to this room."

For reasons grossly unfair and never to be understood, Mr. Lain had been bent while he was very young. He would never be right again; he would never feel comfortable in crowds or among others. Yet he had taken that trauma and painted over it. He had become a teacher, surrounded by animals incapable of recognizing the beautiful link between his imagination and his hands.

She felt a trembling awe for what he had done. "Mr. Lain, I—"

There was a light flash behind her, and she saw the color ebb from Lain's face. She whirled to find Denver behind her, snapping pictures with his phone. "Hey, El," he said as almost an afterthought. His hair was sweaty and clumped together, a thick black tangle hanging over his forehead. His eyes were glassy and vacant, and the look on his face was one of weary delight. Mr. Lain's face, however, was pure horror.

"Denver, give me the phone," she said, keeping her eyes on her art teacher, who was hastily gathering his supplies. "Denver!"

"Naw, naw, El," he said, snapping a few more shots before dropping it in his coat pocket. "S'up, Mr. Lain," he waved. "Cool place you got here." He turned and ambled out.

Elsie knew she had to get that phone from him. He would put those pictures on Instagram or Snapchat—he would turn Mr. Lain's sanctuary into a gallery for students to gawk at. It was not that Denver was malicious or cruel—he just couldn't possibly understand the value of the door, the lock, the barrier between the fury of the club and the stillness of the art. Denver never aimed; he just shot into the darkness. She broke eye contact with Mr. Lain and raced out the door to try and convince her friend to delete the footage.

But midway up the stairs the chirping of her phone told her that she was already too late, that he had sent them out. She shut her eyes, letting the cold air penetrate her, feeling the shame that she deserved. She had brought a great recklessness to a delicate man. It must have taken Mr. Lain years to make that room into a living storyboard. It took less than a second to flatten it, transmit it, and send it capering across five hundred student feeds.

She turned to look back; for a moment, she could see Mr. Lain framed by the light of the anteroom behind him, his face indistinguishable from the shadows. Then, without another word, he shut the door on her, leaving her to climb the rest of the stairs back to Cyprus, to the presence of bodies all too eager to mingle and share.

She walked the four blocks back to her car alone, thick, sticky snowflakes starting to drive against the purple sky. Though the night was alive with laughter and singing, she could only hear the words of her art teacher. *"This is the problem of being an artist, Elsie,"* he told her.

"Your head is a closed box." But she had forced his open, like a burglar smashing at a lock, like a raider profaning a tomb. *You're not allowed to look in any other box but your own.* They had all forgotten.

As she approached the car, she heard voices, and she could see two bodies sitting on the hood, talking softly as the snow melted against their skin. Cooper's head was on Dale's shoulder, her shirt misbuttoned, his arm around her waist. He was laughing, his nose in her hair. The windows of Elsie's car were fogged and smeared. She stayed in the shadows and watched them, the chemicals accelerating whatever simmering heat she had ignored for too long. The boy who taught her to listen for silence. The girl who always filled it. They, too, had hidden boxes. Once again, she would pay for trespassing.

With nowhere to go, she turned and walked down an adjacent street, away from all the things she could not see. Strangely, she thought of Gouth, the thief and reprobate, paranoid and dreaming of teenage degenerates. She thought of Dr. Partking, making runny eggs and trying to get through a story she could never escape and never fully understand. Elsie thought of Gods who make plans and boys who lack eyes. She thought of a small child snatched away without warning or explanation, thrust into a room that would come to define the rest of his life. It was happening to her—Elsie was being sealed in a room that locked from the outside. *So be it,* she thought, and in her head, she started sketching her beetle.

20
CONNOR AND COLLEEN

She was crying now, finally. It was the first time she'd allowed tears since this whole thing started. It was embarrassing. She was embarrassed. But she couldn't help herself.

"Why?" she asked him. "Why now?"

"It's just…" Kenny put his hands behind his neck; he had never been a fluent communicator, and this face-to-face confrontation was exacerbating his caginess. But Colleen had been so damn insistent. "I just don't think I should go to the prom…"

"At all?" she said, wiping her nose. "Or with me?"

"With you," he said.

She nodded. "Is it because of the memes?"

"What memes? What are you talking about?"

She laughed. "I am so… fucking… tired of everyone lying to me. All the time."

"Colleen," he said slowly. "We said we'd go together in November.

I never thought we were serious. And… things are changing between me and Melissa…" He held his hands up in a supplicating gesture when she glared at him. "It has nothing to do with… with memes."

She wiped the corners of her eyes; her mascara bled onto her sleeves. "You're a liar, Ken. That's the latest in a long line of personal failings, but it's the worst. Because you'll go to bed tonight a coward, a weakling, and a sexist pig, and before sleep takes you, you'll tell yourself that you're actually not a bad guy. Which is a lie."

He balled and unballed his fists, glaring at her. "I know you've been going through some shit, so I'll let that go. But I'm going to give you some free advice, and you need to hear it." He paused and bit his lips before continuing. "Not everything is about you and your little quest. Some things are about other people."

She nodded. "Okay," she said finally. "Have a great fucking time with other people."

She tried to walk out of the choir room with a measure of composure, but as soon as she felt herself slip out of his sightline, she burst into a sprint and didn't stop until she was in her car in the parking lot. She wanted to scream, to claw at the steering wheel. But instead she pushed it all down, dried her face, put on some Girlpool, and turned up the volume until it drowned out the yelling in her head.

She remembered Eileen's joint in the glove compartment. Colleen— the dutiful athlete—had never smoked before, but she had seen her sister do it and pretty quickly felt the mellowing effects of the THC. Kenny… was a liar. So was Megan, Peter, Aditya, Lettie. So was Paige, Principal Darten, that Connor kid. So was Alice. And Mr. Cespids? Who the fuck knew? Maybe he *was* a pedophile.

She was so tired. Colleen closed her eyes and breathed smoke. She began to fantasize about cutting up pictures and captions. She was writing them now in her head.

Evan kept breaking into peals of laughter, so Patrick had to tell the story. "Cespids dropped all his folders, right? So he's bent over on his hands and knees, right in the middle of the hallway. And people are just walking past him, like he's invisible or something."

"Crawling around like a bear," Evan laughed.

"Right, right," continued Patrick. "And here comes Colleen. Now, I didn't have a direct eye-line on her, so I can't say what was going on up top, right? But I heard it from Anna that she had full-on crazy eyes. Like, Winona Ryder in *Stranger Things* or some shit."

Connor shifted uncomfortably in his seat. They were drawing too much attention, these two clowns. People were watching them from across the LMC.

"Anyways, she rounds the corner, and she's funneling right towards him. He's hugging all these loose papers to his chest. And he does one of these—" he lunged right.

"And SHE does one of these—" said Evan, mirroring Patrick's movements.

"—So he goes back the other way—"

"—And she does, too—"

"—And then all of a sudden she's suddenly screaming at him. 'YOU'VE GOT TO GO! YOU'VE GOT TO FUCKING GET OUT OF HERE!'"

"Did she say 'fucking?'" laughed Evan.

"She did. I heard it. 'Course, I don't know who was listening to her after that. Her voice just hits this registry, like she's some shrieking, crying howler monkey. She starts hitting him—I shit you not, she's clawing at his face. Papers are flying everywhere—"

Evan was laughing again. He sounded to Connor like a lower species of water fowl.

"A full-on nervous breakdown, right there in the hallway. They had to pull her off of him, two football players on each arm. Another ten seconds, and she would have had both of his eyes."

They had done it. They had broken her. It had taken weeks longer than he expected. But Connor felt no pleasure in his victory. He could not so much as meet his friends with a smile.

"I mean, it was beautiful, man. Just breathtaking," said Evan. "He didn't even *say* anything to her, and she just *flipped out*."

"It's like that Napoleon quote, right?" said Patrick, showing off as always. "'If you wait by the river long enough, the body of your enemy will float by.'"

"That was Sun Tzu," said Connor. "Christ, you sound like a fucking idiot when you get it wrong."

He drove home in silence, parked the car, left his bookbag in the laundry room. His mother greeted him, but he walked right past her. He went to his room, locked the door, and scanned the chatrooms. They were filled with stories about Colleen's collapse. There were new memes, new Tweets. He found a video of the whole thing. He watched it again and again, freezing the image so that he could stare at her face. He wanted to see her eyes. But they were shut.

She really was a beautiful girl. He felt himself shaking. He bit his lip, closed his laptop, covered his face. Suddenly, he rose, crossed the room, and began punching the wall where the Paul George poster hung. Again. Again. He smashed through the plaster, tore up his knuckles, kept going until he could see the studs nestled in the insulation. Downstairs, his mother worked on the stuffed peppers, her earbuds tamped in, listening to Michael Bublé.

Two days later, his mother received a Google alert on her phone. She began whooping so loudly that it drew her husband out of his den.

"What's up?" he asked.

"He quit!" she said. "Resigned! Cespids resigned!"

"When?" he said, reading the phone screen over her shoulder.

"This afternoon!" she said, scrolling through the story. "Gave the board notice… felt he had become too much of a distraction… will receive the remainder of the year's salary…"

"That's too fucking generous," said Tanner Marder.

"Who cares? We won!" she said, throwing her arms around his neck. He kissed her forehead.

"What did I tell you? You just have to make sure you're heard," he said, smoothing back her hair. "Power to the people!"

21
VINCE

By late March, it was not unusual for Vince Darten to work so late into the evening that Elizabeth was asleep when he arrived home. At first, he would discover her curled up on the couch beneath the quilt his grandmother had left him, the television talking quietly to itself. But of late, he would find her in bed, her sleep apnea mask already affixed, so dead to the world that she wouldn't stir when he'd kiss her lightly on the brow. Something wordless had crept into their marriage, but such was her faith in her husband that she trusted him to independently repair it, just as he had eventually recemented the loose bricks in their patio.

Vince had asked for computer user logs from the past calendar year, and they had come to him, printed in ten-point font, single-spaced and filling four moving boxes the size of small engine blocks. He smiled grimly, pushing his reading glasses back up his nose, highlighter in hand. How he had bragged to the PTA about Clearwater's online learning initiatives.

A high school is somber place late at night. The lights switched off, the locker banks silent as sepulchers, a midnight vagrant would never know that the halls swelled with activity each morning with the hope, energy, and ambition of a 19th century border town. Schools are meant to inculcate life, and emptied of their vitality, they take on the sad poignancy of abandoned factories.

Vince filled the quiet with Al Green on his iPhone, but not so much that he could not hear a stirring outside the window to his office. He leaned forward and stared into the silhouette of the dogwood and birch backlit by a distant streetlamp. Had he heard voices? A shuffling? But there was nothing in the darkness save for the distant play of headlights bending a corner. He resumed his work, as Green dedicated a song to his cousin, Junior Parker.

Yet there was again a noise, and this time Vince thought he could see a body moving, ink-like and formless. He rose and rounded the corner, now staring out the Plexiglas panes of Clearwater's front doors. Who was there? A student? Once, he had pulled into the parking lot to find the stadium emblazoned with green spray-paint, an epithet telling of the sexual impropriety of one of his students. He had tried to cover the words with a beach towel, but they were too big and too many.

He pushed through the crash bar of the front door. "Who's there?" he called out. "Show yourself!"

The only sound, however, was the clicking of the lock behind him, an automatic feature of the doors after 8 PM, and it was too late that Vince remembered his keys, sitting in his work satchel by his desk, where his phone cycled through Soul hits of the 70s.

"Shit!" said Vince, tugging on the door handle. "Shit! Shit! Shit! Shit!" He peered through the window to his office, where he could clearly see his coat draped over the back of his desk. His breath fogged the window pane.

There were 48 doors that entered Clearwater, and Vince knew that every single one of them was locked. Still, he paced the perimeter of his school, checking each one, pulling at windows that he knew had been sealed since November, testing for some breach in the castle.

His car, too, was locked, and a light frost had begun to form on the windows. Elizabeth was already in bed; she would not miss his presence until morning. He thought of walking the mile down the hill to the CVS on the Guild Street, but he remembered two years ago when a police officer had stopped by his office, following up on a call from the neighborhood of a suspicious figure lurking in the streets. Trembling with indignation, Vince had explained to the officer—Peter McTaggert, badge #1450—that the menacing drifter had been him, the principal, walking to the library to return a book.

And so, at 11:43 P.M. on Thursday, March 21st, Vince Darten sat huddled on the loading dock outside door #23, waiting for the third shift janitor to arrive and let him in. It was the stillest Vince had been in two months, and in the day's last shivering winds, he gave himself over to all the thoughts he'd held at bay.

He thought of his teachers, asleep and haunted. He thought of Ryan Cespids. Vince hadn't seen him when he left, box in his arms. But he had seen the empty desk, and Betsy Rilke comforting a tearful Liza Gay. Ryan had not answered his phone, had not responded to texts. He was gone, and Vince was afraid to grieve.

He thought of Andy Waters and Carlton Wemish, young men of wasted privilege, of Kevin Lenk and Leila Bells, of Lana Collins and the enmity she bore, perhaps even into the tranquil fields of sleep. He thought of Katherine Sawyer, stripped of the dignity of her age and station, alone and cold, of Leonard Fisk, alone with his shame, standing sentinel by his sleeping wife. He thought of Jennifer Watson—the math teacher, the pornographer, the anonymous face buried in a pillow somewhere far away.

He thought of the students, with their faces trained on phone screens, magic glass manufactured on the other side of the world, bringing them together even as it partitioned them into anchorages. He thought of the student without a face, the one who had wrought such chaos. He thought of the serenity of his untroubled sleep—for it had to be a he, didn't it? —and Vince thought, as he often had, of awakening him with violence.

He thought of Elizabeth, his wife, and their daughter. He thought of the space that had grown between them. Once, when he was visiting an old classmate in the hospital, she had told them how the cancer was destroying her marriage. "He's a good man, and he's given me everything these past five months," she told him flatly. "But he can't understand. There's no bleach in his bloodstream. He's not here with me, not really. I know it doesn't make sense, Vince, but I think I hate him for it."

He thought of his blackness, as he often did, in the eyes of his white community. He thought of his father and grandfather, of the streets of Gary, of the shouts of panic and glee as the neighborhood boys tore through the alleyway while someone's elderly uncle listened to Jack Brickhouse on the radio, fanning himself on a fire escape. He thought of friends without fathers, of a handgun in a cousin's glove box, of watching Patty Hearst receive a pardon from President Carter.

Finally, at 12:17 P.M., the lights of a station wagon blinded him, and a trim figure in a wool-lined coat got out.

"Julio!" Vince waved. "Thank God."

"Mr. Darten," said the janitor. "What are you doing here?"

"Locked myself out," said Vince sheepishly, blowing into his hands. For an uncomfortable minute, Julio said nothing, simply staring at him, and Vince could smell cigarettes on his coat. Finally, Julio nodded and fiddled with his key ring. "Well, let's get you home," he said.

They walked through the halls to his office, and Vince felt a deepening embarrassment in their silence. "I'm sorry to interrupt your routine," he said.

"It's no trouble," said Julio. He unlocked the door to Vince's office and stood to the side. Vince realized that this was perhaps the longest conversation he'd ever had with Julio, and certainly the longest he'd been in his presence. "Come in. Sit," he said, gesturing to the chair by his desk. "It occurs to me that I don't know much about you."

Julio shifted uncomfortably. "Don't you want to get home?" he asked.

"No," said Vince in a voice that surprised him. "No, I don't."

Julio shrugged and sat. He was tall and thin, but his face was wide and weathered, hair graying at the temples, but a thick mustache hung over his mouth as black as obsidian. He crossed his legs, then thought better of it, put his hands in his lap before letting them dangle at his sides.

"Where are you from?" Vince asked, and then immediately regretted it. The janitors worked for a maintenance firm contracted to the district. One day at a barbecue, Gary, their foreman, had cautioned Vince not to ask them where they were from.

"Somewhere else," said Julio coolly. "Like everyone else."

"Right," said Vince. He looked down at the user logs in front of him. The phone was now playing Fontella Bass.

After a moment, Julio gestured to the pictures on Vince's desk. "You got kids?" he asked.

"One," smiled Vince. "She lives in New Mexico. I don't see her enough."

"Hmmph," said Julio. "You are lucky. I have boys. They live in my basement. I think they will never leave."

"How many?" Vince smiled.

"Three. Could have been more. When we were younger, it felt like we were fielding a soccer team."

Vince laughed. It seemed to put Julio at ease. He shook a cigarette box in his hand reflexively. Vince pushed an empty coffee cup across the desk to him. "Be my guest," he said. Julio nodded and lit a cigarette. "Just the three boys?"

"And two girls," said Julio, breathing smoke through his nose. "My wife, when she missed me, would pack me conchas. Just to let me know. It got to feel like all I had to do was think about conchas and she would be pregnant."

"One man's curse," Vince nodded. "We tried for a long time. Began to think it would never happen. And then, just when we'd given up..." he clapped his hands. "A miracle."
Julio nodded. "*Si*," he said. "A miracle."

"How long have you been married?"

"28 years. You?"

"33."
Julio shifted again, leaning back and studying Vince, his brown-black eyes shaded by thick eyebrows. "You don't make it to 33 sleeping in your office."

"No," Vince admitted.

Julio ashed in the cup and gestured to the user logs. "A lot of work, being principal?"

Vince shrugged. "The work, I can handle. But this year...." He dropped his arms to his sides, reclining in his chair. "If we don't catch this kid," he said, nodding at the papers, "I won't make 34."

Julio said nothing for a moment, smoking and staring at Vince pensively. "You think I'm lucky, don't you?" he said finally.

"I don't think anything of you," said Vince honestly. "I go home and come back in the time that you're at Clearwater. Our paths never cross. How long have you worked here?"

"Ten years."

"Ten years," said Vince. "I didn't know you had five kids, Julio."

"And two cats and a turtle."

"Maybe I am jealous," Vince admitted. "Right now, everybody's looking at me. Staring. It feels good to do my work at night, in the quiet. Where no one can see me."

Julio scratched his face lightly with the back of his hand. "You think I'm invisible?"

Vince waved gently in supplication. He felt tired. "No," he said. "That's not what I meant. I don't think you're invisible."

Julio nodded. "Yes, you do. And that's all right. When I came here, I worked very hard not to be noticed. There's nothing in those computers about me, is there?"

Vince shrugged. Julio continued.

"But I am not invisible. Want to know how I know that? It's like this," he said quietly, extinguishing his cigarette in the coffee cup. "Two years ago, I was driving here. It was late, raining. And I don't know why, but I got it in my head to take the long way. You know Garter Street?"

"Yes," Vince nodded. "The country road. Goes by Casey's."

"And two covered bridges," said Julio. "I love those bridges, like to see them in the rain, I guess. Anyway, I decide to drive by them this night, and as I do, I see a man standing on the rail, leaning forward over Marshall Creek. It was dark, this night, and there are no lights by that bridge. I still don't know how I saw him."

"What did you do?"

"I pulled over. I called to him. 'Hey! Hey you!' I said. 'What are you doing up there?' But he didn't answer. Didn't even look at me. Just kept staring at the water."

"So I went out there to him, first on the bridge, then by the rail. He just kept ignoring me. So I climbed up on the rail with him."

"What did he say?"

"He said nothing. Just kept staring. But I knew that he was yelling on the inside, and pretty soon he would be out of voice. So I said to him, 'Don't I know you?'"

"Did you?"

"I don't think so. Young kid, probably 19 or so. But he finally looks up at me. 'Huh?' he says. So I say it again: 'Don't I know you?' It's a shot in the dark. But then I say, 'Clearwater?' and he says, 'Yeah.' And I say 'When did you graduate?' and he says 'Two years ago.' So now I've got him talking. 'What was your locker number?' I ask, and he says '215.' That's when I know that this is fate. '215?' I say. 'Did you have a cactus?' And he nods. 'I cleaned out that locker!' I tell him. 'I still got your cactus on a desk. You gotta come pick it up!'"

Vince shook his head. "You're kidding."

"Swear to God. And he did."

"A miracle," said Vince.

"A miracle," Julio nodded. He looked down at his boots. "My home is not my home. My name is not my name. I don't think that I will see my brother again or hear my aunt play her guitar." He looked up and met Vince's gaze. Neither man blinked. "But I am not invisible."

Julio started to leave. Vince unplugged his phone and let the office fall silent. "Julio," he called after him. The janitor stopped and faced him. Vince paused before speaking. "Where are you from?"

Julio shrugged. "Clearwater. Indiana. You?"

On the drive home, Vince thought of what he might have said, how he could have spoken of the smell of the trainyards, the laughter of kitchens, of the sad silence that had fallen between him and his father when Vince told him that he was leaving to work in a white suburb with his white wife and their infant. But more than anything, he thought about how quickly he had answered Julio, and the thoughtlessness of his response.

"Same," he had said.

22

THE ONCE AND FUTURE KING

As Marshall Heitz aged, he developed a painful case of arthritis. It kept him from pursuing his hobbies—Spanish guitar, woodworking. It also significantly impacted his work as the school automotive instructor. Unlike other departments that enjoyed compulsory enrollment, the Department of Technology and Engineering relied on recruiting students to take their courses in construction, welding, and computer programming. Each year's budget constraints brought with it fresh whispers that the department's low numbers had marked it for shuttering, that they could no longer justify the expense of vocational training when the community looked down upon vocational training. Some nights the old bachelor would sit at his table and stare at his hands in despair. An automotive teacher who couldn't loosen a lugnut was not good to anyone.

To manage his stress, Marshall was forced to seek out other hobbies. He tried painting but found he had no aesthetic; he tried running, but found it too painful on his knees. Visiting his brother's for Thanksgiving two years ago, his nephew introduced him to a computer game called Eldritchquest. "It's an immersive MMORPG," Justin explained. "That's 'Massive-Multiplayer-Online-Role-Playing-Game,'" he added.

"What do you do?" asked Marshall.

"Anything you want. It's sort of a combination of Minecraft and Elder Scrolls. You can quest on your own, or with a guild. You can build up a keep and guard a village, or you can raid and sack. You can build a nation, or you can just sort of walk around and kill goblins." Justin showed him the controls—it was mostly just point and click with the mouse, with a few keyboard options. He wore a headset to talk to other players.

"What do you like to do?" asked Marshall.

"I dunno. Mess around. Go after other guilds. You know," said Justin. Marshall did not know.

But he learned. Over the next twenty months, he looked forward to the hours of 8 and 10 PM, when he would log on with the rest of his guild and quest. Marshall had quickly grown in skill and power as a character, but his real gift was a sense of honor and conduct that was often absent from the fields of Gharnos. He believed in fair conduct, in the honoring of treaties and boundaries, in upholding justice, in showing mercy to the vanquished and cold steel to the rapacious. He protected a vast territory from reavers and hoards, and in time his people grew plentiful and prosperous. His men were loyal to his banner, particularly when he ordered them to bring his nephew to justice for the slaying of an ambassador. The Wyvern Guild, as they were called, swelled in number and good esteem under the command of Lord Ernst Proudlion of the Highlands.

The second data dump ruined everything. Included in the files were the old man's gamer tag and logon information. When it was revealed that the old shop teacher Marshall Heitz was Lord Proudlion, his students flocked to the Highlands, looking to taunt the proud warrior. Marshall had enjoyed the anonymity of the game, but all of that was over. He did not log on for all of February.

He was checking inventory one afternoon in early April when Alden Marst stuck his head in the door.

"You busy, Mr. Heitz?" the sophomore asked.

"I am, Alden," said Marshall. "Make it quick."

"Oh," said Alden. "Okay." He took a deep breath. "When are you coming back to Eldritchquest?"

The old man flushed; he set down his binder. "Excuse me?"

"I'm… I'm Hansie. I'm in your guild," said Alden. He crossed his arms and stared at Marshall's feet.

"Hansie?" said Marshall. "You've been Hansie all this time?"

Alden nodded. "I didn't know," he said. "I mean, I knew your voice, but…"

"…But you couldn't be sure," Marshall said. Hansie had been an invaluable warrior. He was brave, clever—always willing to scout an enemy camp. Over the past few months, he had developed some rudimentary spellcasting. More critically, he played the game the *right way*. For justice. For honor.

"Alden," said Marshall. "I didn't know it was you."

"We sacked the Tower of Blight! Side by side, back to back!"

Marshall laughed. "We did; we did. You are quite good with that axe of yours."

"You taught me to cast Light Pillar," said Alden.

"A dangerous spell," nodded Marshall. "Brings friends and foe alike."

"So when are you coming back?"

Marshall shifted uncomfortably. "I'm not," he said quietly. "I can't."

"I won't tell!" said Alden. "No one will know it's you!"

"I'm sorry, son," said Marshall. "I can't quest with students. It's not appropriate."

Alden hung his head and slung his backpack over his shoulder.

"Okay, Mr. Heitz," he said. "Good talking to you." He slouched away, before suddenly rousing himself and turning back. "What about when I graduate?" he asked. "Could we quest then?"

"Alden," said Marshall. "It's done."

But Marshall couldn't quite stay away. Though he deleted his account and foreswore his guild, he still logged on from time to time under a new name. He wandered the fields, fought smaller game and monsters. But he was purposeless now. There was nothing to build, nothing to defend.

One night he saw a column of light shoot into the sky, a tower of flame spinning clockwise against the horizon. *The Light Pillar*, he thought. He mounted his steed, spurred the sides, rode towards the beam, sword drawn.

He arrived at a keep, emptied of people. There were no raiders, no orcs, no battle. At first, he saw no trace of the powerful caster who had signaled him from the distance. But examining a wooden table in the hold, he found a parchment that had writing. He read:

We are the Wyvern Guild. We serve this keep's rightful lord, Ernst Proudlion. Though the ride be long and battle fierce, we stand at ready to defend the helpless, afflict the greedy, to hold fast for all that is right and good in the lands of men and gods.

23

JENN

It was early April when it all came undone. She arrived for her shift early, but Ruth was already waiting. "Sit down, Employee. We need to talk."

"Sure, I'll be right there," said Jenn. "Let me just get some coffee—"

"Sit down, Jennifer."

Her blood stopped pumping; she could instantly taste bile. *Oh God, please no,* she thought. Wordlessly, she slid into the booth across from Ruth.

The old woman coughed. She was perusing an invoice from a supplier and didn't look up. "I come home early yesterday. Maybe I called; I can't remember. Anyway, I wasn't expected. Reuben always tells me I need to announce myself, but I'm so noisy, I think 'Why bother?' I'm like an elephant over bubble wrap."

She looked up. "He doesn't hear me come in. And do you know why?"

Jenn shook her head. Words were too hard to form.

"He's watching a video on his computer. Pants around his ankles. Hand on his *schmuck*. A mother's worst nightmare. But I barely notice; instead, I'm looking at this video. And I think to myself, 'Hey, I *know* that girl.' And I..."

But before she could finish, Jenn vomited all over the table, the invoice, and Ruth. "I'm sorry! I'm sorry!" she said, mopping up the chunks with paper napkins from the table's dispenser. "Gah, what a mess..."

"Finally, some honesty," sighed Ruth, grabbing a rag from under the counter. "Good gravy, what are you eating? It smells like valve oil."

Despite her humiliation, Jenn began to laugh at this woman and her stained shirt, which quickly led to tears and uneven sobbing. Ruth patted her awkwardly.

"All right, enough of this. What you do with your body is none of my business, young lady, and I'm not so sheltered that I don't understand the mischief people get into on those idiot boxes. You've done good work with my son, but I'm here to tell you that it's done between you now."

Jenn couldn't look at her. "Because of my video," she said.

Ruth shook her head. "No. I told you, that's your business. It's because of your kids."

"I'm... wait, what?"

Ruth pointed a swollen finger at Jenn. "You—you were a teacher. I read up on you. Hundreds of kids you're charged with. And you abandoned them all in the middle of the night."

"It's not like that—"

Ruth cut her off with a sharp strike to the table. "It's *exactly* like that. Exactly. What, you're going to tell a divorced woman something she doesn't know about abandonment? I can have *chatta* in my house, and all this pornography. But I will not have cowards around my son."

Now Jenn felt rage shake her frame. "You're… judging me? You have no idea—*none*—what it's like to have *that* video on the phones of every fifteen-year-old in my classroom."

Ruth snorted. "Oh, poor you. The video isn't so bad—at least people can see it and know what you are. What's worse—so *much* worse—is what they can't see. What they imagine." She paused, massaging her fingers, before fixing Jenn with a look that could cut glass. "My mother was pregnant with me at fifteen, taken for a fool by a soldier boy who went off to fight his war. Oh, the things people must have imagined when they saw her and that swollen belly at the market. In the synagogue. But she met their eyes, stood in her place. She told her story. A fool yes, God rest her. But a coward? Never."

"That's what you think of me?" Jenn asked. "You *know* me! I've been here every day for three months!"

"That's right. Three months out of your classroom. Three months away from your kids. A quarter year playing house in that urine trench with that pill pusher and your trailer junkie. A coward. Worse, now. I'd spit on the floor if it weren't me that had to clean it."

Jenn nodded and dried her face with more napkins. "Thank you for the job. You saved my life."

Ruth shrugged. "Don't thank me for that until you do something good with it. You can go another way. Or you can keep going the way you're headed."

Jenn stood and absently scrubbed at the drips of phlegm staining her blouse, then thought better of it. She went to the kitchen to say goodbye to Juan and Estevan, wiped her hands with sanitizer. She looked at Ruth, hoping to say something to her, to win back a small measure of her good esteem, to tell her how deeply she admired her, how much she liked Rueben and the diner. But the older woman never looked up. So Jenn left without saying anything and walked back to her trailer, where she drank until her legs gave out.

⸻

"Mary Anne, get up."

She swatted at him absently.

"Get up, Mary Anne," said Hobby. "There's something I need you to do."

He helped her to her feet and walked her to his truck, which she climbed into with some trouble. "Fuck you, I'm a good person," she told him. "I'm Mary Anne."

"I know," he said, climbing into the driver's seat.

"Where have you been?" she asked. "Where did you go?"

"I've been out, Mary Anne," he said. Something was wrong; even through the haze of her drunkenness, she could sense it. There was an edge to his voice; he gripped the steering wheel too tightly. He kept glancing at her, reaching over, moving her hair out of her face. "Sit up, Mary Anne. Don't fall asleep."

She nodded. "I'm awake, I'm awake," she said, wiping her face. He handed her a stick of gum. "Aw, thanks, Hobson. You're a pal."

"That's right, Mary Anne. And pals help each other out."

"You don't think I'm a bad person, do you? A coward?"

He scoffed. "You walked into the den of my ex, Mary Anne, with a smile on your face like you had balls the size of basketballs."

"Well, I'm not sure I'd be smiling about that…"

"Point being that you're fucking fearless."

"That's right, Hobby, that's right. I am fucking fearless. I left my home without a phone or money or anywhere to go. And you know what? I didn't die! I'm fucking thriving right now!"

He pulled into a driveway. "Damn right," he said.

Jenn squinted through the windshield. In the distance was a cabin; she could make out a light in the window. As she got out of the cab, she could hear male laughter. "Where are we?" she asked.

Hobby came up beside her and draped an arm around her. "Like I said, I need you to do something for me, Mary Anne."

"What's that?"

"In that cabin, there's this guy. Named Arnie."

"Okay."

"I just want… I just need you to hang out with Arnie. Have a good time."

"Okay," she said. "Okay. I could use a good time. Are you coming?"

Hobby pulled his arm away. "I'd love to, Mary Anne. I'd love to. But I gotta get back to the trailer…"

"Wait… wait, what?"

She shoved at him and caught him in the shoulder. He reeled back and looked at her, panicked. Jenn focused. She looked into his eyes. They were glassy, distant. Hobby was sweating again.

"Jesus Christ," she said. "Hobby, what did you do?"

"It's cool, Mary Anne. Calm down."

"I am… calm. I'm just asking you… what did you do?"

He ran his hands over his hair. "I just need you to go into that cabin and have a good time with those guys."

"Or what?"

"Or… or something bad is going to happen to me."

She closed her eyes and shook her head. "Fuck you," she said. "Fuck you so much. Take me back."

"Mary Anne—" he reached for her.

"Don't TOUCH me," she swatted his hand away. "What is wrong with you?" Suddenly, she couldn't speak; it hurt too much for language. Finally, she found herself. "Why would you think I would do this?"

"Because," he said sheepishly. "I mean, you made that video, right? That was you… wasn't it?"

He knew. How long? But of course he knew; everyone knew, would always know. Online is forever. She could move states, cut her hair, buy new clothes, take a different name. It didn't matter. The past was in her scent, written into her DNA. It had become her skin. There was no where she could run.

"Mary Anne—" he started.

She wheeled on him, clocking him with her keyring. He staggered; she drove her knee up between his legs, and he collapsed with a whimper. She fished his keys from his pocket and ran to his truck.

"Mary Anne!" he shouted. "MARY ANNE!"

She watched him stagger in the rear-view mirror as she sped away. There was blood on her knuckles. "That's not my fucking name."

— — — — — — — — —

They would come for her now. Arnie and Hobby and whomever else was in that cabin. She had seen it. It was the way of weaker men.

How much time did she have? Maybe five minutes? She had to ditch the truck, to find another route. She pulled into the trailer park, swept through her trailer. She grabbed her toiletries, a few articles of clothing, the coffee can of cash, her toaster, the stack of student worksheets. She ran to Cy's house and banged on his door, shouting until the old man appeared, a CPAP apnea mask strapped to his face.

"I need my car back," she said.

"Come again?"

"I don't have time, Cy. My Nissan. I need it back."

He pulled his mask up onto his hairline, showing off that mouth full of rounded teeth. "You mean *my* Nissan."

"You can have your trailer back. I'm leaving."

He smiled. "What's your hurry? Stay for breakfast."

"Look," she pushed past him, pacing amidst his pile of bartered treasures. "I don't know what you're into here. Pills. Meth. I know it's bad. Help me out, or I'll call the cops."

He nodded. "Give 'em a call if you think it's a matter of public safety. I'm sure they'll be by in the morning."

Goddamn this little goblin, she thought. A pair of headlights swelled in the darkness and drove by. There wasn't time.

She fished a key from her pocket and handed it to him. "Ruth's diner," she told him.

"What good is this to me?"

"Give me my car, and I'll tell you."

He shrugged and moved with maddening leisure to his rack of keys. Selecting the Nissan's, he tossed it to her.

"There's a safe in the back," she said. "The combination is 3-34-60."

"3-34-60," he repeated. "I hope you're not inventing those numbers, Ms. Spier. For Hobby's sake."

"Fuck you both," she said fiercely, shoving him on her way out. She stopped and grabbed Hobby's keyboard. "And I'm taking this, too!"

— — — — — — — —

And so for the fourth time in her life, Jennifer ran. She had done it again, ruined something good out of selfishness and cowardice. She thought of Hobby, of his betrayal, of his tap-water blood on her knuckles. But as she turned the episode over in her thoughts, she felt no anger, only a sad recognition. He had sold her just as she had sold Ruth. He had lost himself to addiction and despair just as she would no doubt do in the years to come. Like her, he was a waif who foreswore his past and undermined the levees that held his worst features at bay. To a man without commitment, anything was possible, and the worst was more than likely.

For the first time running, Jenn knew where she was going. She drove through the night, keeping an eye on the fuel gauge. She stopped at a truck stop to leave a message for Ruth, to wash herself in the bathroom. *This is what I am,* she thought, scrubbing her face in a mirror. *I am not clean.* But perhaps there was still time.

She caught him in the parking lot before he entered the school. "Mr. Darten!" she called. "Vince!"

If the principal was surprised to see her, he didn't betray it. "Jennifer," he said. "You're alive."

"I... yes," she said clumsily. The speech she had rehearsed was already floundering. "Can we go someplace to talk?"

They found an empty classroom; Vince leaned against the teacher's desk while Jenn slid into a student's. "I'm sure there's quite a story," he said.

She nodded. "You too, probably. How have the last few months been?"

"Difficult."

"I'm sure."

"You're okay?"

She nodded. "Yes. No. The truth is, I'm not doing well."

"I'm sorry to hear that."

"Mr. Darten. Vince. I... I want to come home."

He shook his head. "No."

"Vince, please..."

"There's no way, Jennifer. I'm sorry, but there's just no way."

She nodded, tears coming hot and steady. But she didn't make a sound. He came over and sat next to her.

"I understand, or think I do, why you left. It was humiliating. Unprecedented. I wanted to leave, too."

She couldn't look at him, so she shut her eyes.

"The board right now is crumbling, but swamped as they are, if I handed them paperwork with your name on it, they'd send it right back. Even if they didn't, I don't know how I could sell it to the staff, the kids. The community. You left us, Jennifer. When you were most needed, you ran."

"I know," she whispered. "I know, I know. Vince, you have to believe me. I am so sorry."

He folded his hands, tapping his index fingers together. "I believe you."

She looked up. He was looking at her intently, his reading glasses dangling around his neck. She let out a shivering sob. "I ran," she started. "I run. All my life, when things got difficult, I run. And… and I fuck. Usually one follows the other. I don't know why, but when I'm with someone… when I'm *fucking* them… it's like all the truth of me is blotted out for just a minute. Like an eclipse."

She sighed. "And then it wears off, and I'm standing still, looking at him looking at me. And I just want to run again." She reached into her bag and produced the student worksheets, handing them to Vince. "I'm not asking for my old job back. I'll take anything. Janitor, lunch lady, crossing guard… Vince, without this school, I am lost. I see that now. People think it's the teacher holding the classroom together. They don't get that it's the other way around."

He flipped through the papers, reading her comments. She was in agony, waiting for him to speak. Finally, he shook his head again. "I'm sorry, Jenn, but I just can't do it. I feel for you. I really do. But this district will never put you in front of children again."

She flinched and reached out to him, grabbing his forearm. "Please. I'm begging."

He stared at her for a long time. Then he slipped his arm out of her grip, stood, and walked to the door. "I was a dean when I was at Theodore Roosevelt in Gary. Did you know that?" She shook her head. "Six years," he nodded. "I had a joke I would tell our problem cases. A cop is walking his beat when he comes across this guy banging his head against a wall. He's tearing himself up something awful. The cop says to the guy, 'Buddy, what are you doing?' The man responds, 'I'm tunneling through this here wall.' The cop pulls him back and says, 'Man, if you keep this up, it'll kill you.' And the man responds, 'Yeah, you're probably right. The last six didn't, but this one feels different.'"

He laughed at that; Jen looked down at her own hands. Her knuckle.

"This job won't save you, Jennifer. We can't help you. But maybe you're done with walls just in time."

She forced a weak smile. "Thank you, Vince."

"Take care of yourself, Jennifer. Let me know where you end up."

She nodded. He left her alone. She wept for all that was lost at Clearwater High.

———————

She slipped out of the classroom during a passing period, the halls swollen with teens. It felt strange to be around so many people again, and she kept her head down to avoid recognition. But on her way out, she spotted Betsy Rilke at her door, slapping high fives with her students as they entered her classroom. Jennifer was frozen for a moment. It felt like the most beautiful thing she'd ever seen.

Later that day, she went to the post office to mail three items. One was a keyboard addressed to 246 Kickapoo Ln, Vincennes, IN. Another was a long, penitent letter to Ruth Cohen, thanking her and apologizing in equal measure. *I'm not good. I know that,* she wrote. *But I have an opportunity now to make things right. To be brave. I'm taking it.* She took the money from the coffee can and put it in the envelope.

Finally, a letter to Reuben Cohen. She put his corrected worksheet in the envelope. *Sloppy, lazy work,* she wrote. *You cannot divide by zero. Do better. Sincerely, Jennifer Watson.*

24
BEAUMONT

Mrs. Moresoe looked at Beaumont, panicked. "I don't want to do this," she said.

Four months ago, when he began working with Mrs. Moresoe, the Talon Editor-In-Chief Joyce Hui had approached him with a fundraising idea. "What if," she said, spreading her palms dramatically, "the school sold tickets to see our very own rock-n-roll legend play some covers? You know, for charity?"

"I don't think the school's resident legend would be interested in that," Beaumont said.

But Joyce had the tenacity of athlete's foot. And gradually over the weeks, she wore him down. Moresoe, on the other hand, was a tougher sell. She cited every excuse within arm's reach—Cub Scouts, dental appointments, a weird case of food poisoning—and then reached for the truly exotic. Finally, he put her on the spot.

"Why don't you want to play for people?" Beaumont asked. "Why weren't you at that barn with the Mudskipperz?"

She took her time working up to an answer, piecing out some Blue Oyster Cult chords. "Because I don't want that attention anymore," she said softly. "I want to be left alone. I just want to be a teacher." She stopped playing and let out a little laugh, like a kink in a garden hose. "Actually, that's not even true. I just want to be a mom."

"I thought you were teaching me to be a punk," he said.

"I told you," she said. "That's all done."

"You also told me you're still angry. Where's your rage?" She scowled at me, so he let slip some charm. "You know—for charity."

But now that they were backstage, now that 405 tickets have been sold at $10 a pop, now that Joyce Hui had relentlessly hyped the evening so that the student media class has set up some cameras to broadcast the event on Facebook Live, Mrs. Moresoe was having second thoughts.

"This'll be easy," I said. "Just… you know, go out there and play a few generic covers. Five songs, max. Maybe some Fleetwood Mac. White people love Fleetwood Mac."

"We do," she said grudgingly.

"Just five songs."

"Five songs," she repeated, and she walked out to a raucous applause.

There was a chair and a microphone; Mrs. Moresoe had elected to play an unplugged acoustic and had brought out her Seagull S6. She was dressed in jeans and a gray flannel; her hair was pulled up hastily in a bun. She looked like she was spending a Sunday at a laundromat. The applause emboldened her, but Beaumont could see the nerves working on her as she sat down—a line of sweat was visible on her lip and her leg thumped spastically as she adjusted her strap.

"Hi, I'm, uh, Linda Moresoe," she said into the microphone. Too loud—she jerked back, blinking at the reverberations of her voice.

"WE LOVE YOU MRS. MORESOE!" yelled an unseen student in the audience, and the accompanying laughter seemed to calm the English teacher. She began to play, then to sing.

They paved paradise
And put up a parking lot
With a pink hotel, a boutique
And a swinging hot spot
Don't it always seem to go
That you don't know what you've got
'Till it's gone

And then, she stopped. For a moment longer, she kept playing, but then her fingers ceased to move. She looked up, blinded by the auditorium lights, then restarted, her voice now thinner and unsteady.

They paved paradise
And put up a parking lot

She stopped again. She looked to the side of the stage just behind the curtain. Beaumont could feel her eyes searching for him. But he was too afraid. Before his eyes, she was having a breakdown on stage.

"I'm… ah, I'm sorry," she said. She was mumbling, brushing stray hairs off her forehead, which was now beading with sweat. "It's just been a long time since I've played for… um…"

"YOU CAN DO IT!" yelled a voice in the auditorium. It was immediately followed by clapping, hooting, shouts of encouragement. Somewhere in the audience was her husband, her children. Beaumont hoped that she found their faces and relaxed. She gripped the mic again and tried to restart, but then almost immediately abandoned the effort.

"No, I'm… I can't do this," she said, blinking. "I'm sorry. I know this is for charity. I told myself I could do this, but… but I find the whole thing disgusting. Fuck."

The last word silenced the audience. 400 bodies sat absolutely motionless. The lights on their phones awakened. Everyone was recording.

"I know you invited me here because you all think I'm some sort of rock musician," she said, and her voice had taken on a tremulous edge. "And I used to be, a long time ago. But lately, all I've wanted to be is Mrs. Moresoe. Talk about Shylock and Tom Robinson. Teach a lesson on subject-verb agreement. That was a simple life. I needed simple."

"And then, four months ago, somebody ripped open the lives of the teachers of this school. It was a horrible crime. A violation. I didn't even have it that bad—just a few videos, a tax return. Many had it worse. But that act was compounded, over and over again, by all of you. You clicked on it. By choice. You picked over the… the open wounds. And you never called it a crime. And you never shared our grievance. You just… scrolled through all of it like our lives were something to binge on Netflix."

"And now I'm… playing for you. Like it never happened. Are you ever going to acknowledge it? What happened to us? What you did? You made us feel like we deserved our shame, for having secrets. For keeping things to ourselves… God, you must hate us…"

He expected someone to do something, to say something. But the entire auditorium was silent. Mrs. Moresoe had put her head down, hair curtaining her face, the guitar hanging off her by the strap like a lifeless child. He thought of all the messages not being sent right now, the voices hushed for lack of consolation.

And suddenly Beaumont was on the move. He strode out on stage, a folding chair in one hand, his guitar in the other. He set up the chair, sat next to Mrs. Moresoe, squeezed his mic, and began to play. He sang.

Reconcile to the relief
Consumed in sacred ground for me
There wasn't always a place to go
But there was always an urgent need to belong

It was Rancid. "Journey to the end of East Bay." He learned it to play for her. And now he was. He was singing to Mrs. Moresoe.

All these bands and
All these people
All these friends and
We were equals but
What you gonna do
When everybody goes on without you?

Somehow, she found her grip. She strummed. They harmonized. She added her voice.

To the end, to the end, I'll journey to the end
To the end, to the end, I'll journey to the end

When they finished, she smiled at him, then began another acoustic punk song, daring him to keep up. It was "Kill the President" by the Offspring. He couldn't move as fast as she could, but he could play a few chords. She let him sing. He was really bad, but it didn't matter. Punk is supposed to be ugly.

It wasn't a late night for Beaumont, but he was still surprised to see a strange car in his driveway as Jono dropped him off. He let himself in and strolled into the kitchen, where he found his father sharing a glass of wine with a coworker.

"Hey, Ms. Evans," said Beaumont.

"Hello, Beaumont," she said. She made excellent eye contact. His father did not. For a moment, none of them said anything. Finally, she turned to his father and set down her glass.

"Well, we can finish going over this tomorrow," she said, getting up.

"Right, right," said his father, standing hastily. He helped her with her coat and walked her to the door.

Beaumont was upstairs lying on his bed when his father knocked fifteen minutes later. "May I come in?" he asked.

"Of course," said Beaumont.

He sat on the edge of the bed, facing the wall. Beaumont had pinned a dozen or so black and whites; they still smelled faintly of developing fluid. There was Jono pulling an ollie, Jhanelle dancing. The bar, lit from the inside like a jack-o-lantern. A claw machine at Denny's. Levar's cat. Mrs. Moresoe on the phone, helping her son with his math homework.

"These new?" he asked.

"Yeah," said Beaumont. "Finally got around to developing a few rolls." *I've got Mom's picture by my bed*, he thought. *I wonder if he'll look at us.*

"Son, I, uh…" he started. He smoothed the comforter, then the crease in his trousers. "I just wanted to explain what Ms. Evans—Brianna—was doing here tonight."

"Dad, it's cool," said Beaumont.

"No, no. You deserve an explanation," he said stiffly. "She had a… a question about a file. And she came by to ask it."

"It's okay, Dad."

"It's just work, Son. I would never…"

"Dad," Beaumont interrupted. "Dad, it's fine. She wouldn't want us to be alone."

He didn't say anything to that. For a long time, his father was silent. Then Beaumont realized that the old man was shaking. His father was crying.

Beaumont sat up and slid next to him. His father's eyes were squeezed shut. He was trying not to sob, but they were coming out in sharp gasps. Beaumont put an arm around him awkwardly. For the first time, he leaned into his son.

"It's just…" he said, his voice wet. "You're leaving. It's over. God, it went fast."

"I'm an hour away, Dad. I'll be home every weekend with laundry."

His father straightened up, took off his glasses and cleaned them. "No, I know, I know. I just… you always think when you get to a certain point, you'll know what you're doing. But all I got was old, Son. When did I get so old?"

He turned to look at his son. "I'm 51," he said. "Can I still do this? Can I start again?"

"Dad," said Beaumont. "I know I'm biased. But you are the sexiest accountant in that office. It's not even close."

He laughed. "Damn straight," he said. And once more they descended into silence.

Beaumont didn't know what was happening to them. They had always struggled to talk to one another, and he understood that it was symptomatic of an eternal blockage. But tonight, they had both engaged in quiet rebellion—him against a suburban audience, his father with the ghost of his great love. Right now, Beaumont didn't feel like a bird about to plunge into an Indian firepit; he sensed a great wind beneath him, behind him, a powerful voice ready to rage.

The father was a widowed accountant, his face streaked with tears. The son was an engineering student who took pictures of geese. *But we're not going gentle,* thought Beaumont. *Both of us are punk as fuck.*

The Third Doxxing

MAY 1ST

23

THE BOXCAR

On Saturday, April 14, at 2:32 P.M., Vince Darten received a call from Detective Vance Matinelli, the county officer who had been assigned the case back in December. "Vince," he said. "They got him."

"Him" was Adam Wramuder, a 16-year-old junior at Clearwater High. Vince had never heard of him before. Matinelli said that federal agents had picked him up at his home just after noon and had brought him down to a regional office for questioning.

"Where is he?" Vince asked. "May I see him?"

"No, Vince," said Detective Matinelli. "No one's allowed in right now. Not even the kid's mother."

Vince had secretly fantasized about this moment for months, but now that it had arrived he found himself at a loss for words. "How did they catch him?" he asked.

"I don't have all the details," said Detective Matinelli. "There are a lot of agents down here. A lot. And they're treating information like it's goddamned Mother Superior's virginity."

"Where will they take him?"

"Depends on what the lawyer says. My guess is Terra Haute."

Vince nodded. He felt tired, and this thing was just getting started. "When will they release a statement?"

"Probably tomorrow," said Matinelli. "This is a big deal for a lot of people." For a moment, both men were silent, and Vince could hear the detective breathing through his hooked nose. There were voices somewhere in the background, the ambient noises of an office. "Anyway, I thought somebody should call you," said Matinelli finally. "Feels like we owed you that."

Vince was suddenly aware of how tightly he was gripping the phone. "Thank you, Detective," he said. "That means a lot to me."

They agreed to speak again when Vance had more information, and then they hung up. Seven minutes later, Elizabeth came in caked in mud and grass stains. "This may be the spring I give up on tomato gardens," she said. "I'm just warning you ahead of time. I'm tomato disillusioned."

She found her husband sitting at the kitchen table, weeping.

———————————

The next day, Vince attended a press conference held in an FBI field office in Indianapolis. A row of chairs had been arranged behind a podium; Vince sat on the far edge, beside his superintendent. "Mad times, eh Vince?" smiled Darren Broach, shaking his hand.

"They are indeed," said Vince.

"Did you know this kid?"

Vince shook his head. "Darren, I couldn't pick him out a lineup of two, even if the other kid was a girl."

The press conference was led by an acting field director with a bald head and husky voice; a pair of investigators—Elsburth and Davis—took a few questions that revealed little about the investigation and less about Adam's fate. "We became aware of the suspect's activities through information acquired through another ongoing investigation," said Elsburth, the taller investigator. "That's all I'm at liberty to say."

Darren Broach made a short statement about the district response and the role they played in cooperating with the investigation. Vince was mentioned twice; after the press conference, two reporters asked him for an interview, but Vince declined to comment at this time.

"Nothing?" asked the second reporter. "There's nothing you want to say? Off the record?"

"Not today," said Vince, smiling. *Not to you,* he thought. This was the same reporter who took an hour-long interview four months ago and edited it down into 450 words about Jennifer Watson's sex video. It was all click-bait. All of it. Vince watched the evening news later that night and saw the entire afternoon compiled in a 75-second package, followed by a story about the governor's Easter party and a review of a new restaurant in Noblesville. "You look handsome," Elizabeth said, swishing her Pinot Noir. "Of all the principals at the FBI press conference, you are the handsomest."

"That would have made a good chyron," he said.

"Did you get to talk to the investigators?" she asked.

"A little," said Vince. "The shorter one—Agent Davis—interviewed me back in December. He was in and out of the office a lot for a while. Then nothing."

She put her feet across his lap; he wordlessly began to massage them. "What happens now?" she asked.

He had been wondering that himself. "Now," he said, changing the channel, "we learn about Adam Wramuder."

Clarence pushed the iPad across his desk. Matt Reynolds, the school resource officer, picked it up. He stared at the schedule.

PERIOD	SUBJECT	TEACHER/ CLASSROOM	CURRENT GRADE
1	AP Euro	Welk (D120)	B+
2	English III	Carmichael (C215)	B-
3	AP Environ. Science	Hapsten (E105)	A-
4	Lunch	N/A	N/A
5	Journal. Lab	Gouch (C110)	A
6	AP Macro	Kooner (D202)	A
7	AP Calc AB	Cespids (B122)	A
8	P.E.	Lenk (Gym)	B

"Anything jump out at you?" he asked the three men sitting across from him.

Harry Buchanan shrugged. "Good kid," he said. "Four AP classes, J Lab. Seems to be pretty decent at STEM."

Vince scowled. Leave it to Harry to dispense with the obvious. "Bryan? Matt? This kid ever come across your desk?"

Bryan Yulders shook his head. "A couple of tardies. Katie stickered his car last fall when he parked in the senior lot," he said, referring to one of his Dean's Assistants.

Matt Reynolds was a police officer assigned to Clearwater; he had an office and coordinated police initiatives with school personnel. Although he was the only person in the building licensed to carry a gun on school grounds, accepting the role as school liaison largely signaled to other cops that Reynolds had opted for a softer beat. Still, Vince had always found him to be perceptive about teenagers, and, as one of the few adults of color in the building, invaluable when it came to reaching out to certain at-risk populations.

"We profiled him in January when we were going through current and former Computer Science students," said Matt. "I think I spoke to him with three other students. I dismissed him at the time." He shrugged. "Didn't fit the profile."

Vince laced his fingers, tapping his pointers together. "Remind me of the profile."

Matt flipped through his notes, sketched out on a yellow legal pad. "He just… he just didn't set off any alarms. Made eye contact. Couldn't answer some fairly routine questions about coding."

"The FBI thinks he may be the most gifted hacker in a decade."

Matt shifted in his seat. "I dunno, Vince," he said. "I just didn't get a vibe off him."

Vince nodded. "Well, let's start talking to people," he said, picking up his phone to ask for Yasmine to clear his schedule. "Find out if anyone else did."

That day, they spoke with Clarence Welk, Steve Carmichael, James Hapsten, Laura Gouch, Erin Kooner, and Kevin Lenk. They put a call into Ryan Cespids, but he had not been answering his phone. One by one, the teachers expressed surprise, frustration, and confusion at Adam's arrest. "I'm sorry, I just don't see it," said Laura, the newspaper advisor. "He's such a goofball in class. Has a lot of friends."

"You were expecting a loner?" asked Vince.

"I was expecting a cackling Bond villain," she said. "For Christ's sake, Vince—the kid likes K-Pop."

Though there seemed to be universal astonishment, there was little consensus on Adam's character. James Hapsten described him as a crusader for the environment ("He spent an hour at the park, picking up litter for extra credit," James explained. "You should see his Fitbit data—the kid was *motivated*."). Kevin Lenk thought that he was moody and secretive ("I want to say I caught him hiding next to the tennis courts when he was supposed to be running laps," Kevin said.). Erin Kooner told a long, rambling story about how Adam had tutored a classmate in the relationship between unemployment and inflation; Steve Carmichael saw him as lazy and unmotivated and suspected he'd plagiarized sections of his *Great Gatsby* essay. When they finally got ahold of Ryan Cespids, the former Math teacher didn't have much to say. "I don't remember him very well," said Ryan, before adding, "I find I don't remember any of them very well."

Vince deepened the investigation. He interviewed every teacher who had taught Adam as a sophomore and freshman. He talked to classmates, peers, and friends. The students tended to be less forthcoming—two of his friends from Tech Club claimed to know very little about Adam. "They're lying," said Matt. "The FBI was talking to them for two hours yesterday." But Vince had no leverage to compel testimony, and only a vague sense of what to even ask.

"What are you hoping they'll tell you?" Elizabeth asked one night as he summarized the interviews.

"I don't know," he confessed. "I just find it incredulous that we had this savant, this reptile, this… this psychopath who sat in my classrooms for years. Ate in the cafeteria. Attended football games. And no one suspected a thing."

Elizabeth took a bite of lasagna, made a face, and chewed it silently. "You know, I read that book about the Rosenburg's last summer, the Soviet spies," she said finally. "There's a whole section in there taken from an interview with a neighbor who grew up around Ethel in the 1930s, went to high school with her. Here she was, 55 years later, and she still believed that Ethel was innocent. 'I don't care what Truman says, what Eisenhower says,' she told the author. 'Ethel was a good girl. She acted in *Saint Joan*. She was in the Baking Club. And Communists don't bake pies!' That's what she said."

Vince chuckled. His wife jabbed her fork at him. "Wherever this investigation takes you, Vince, I want you to remember that—even Communists bake pies."

He made an appointment with Special Agent Davis and drove to the Indianapolis field office to meet with him. The agent greeted him with a crushing handshake. "Vince," he said, his teeth a gleaming white. "Good to see you again."

He invited him into a Spartan office— "It's temporary," he said sheepishly—and motioned for Vince to have a seat. "How are the good people of Clearwater?" he asked.

"Gathering their pitchforks and torches," said Vince. "There's a sea of discontent amongst my teachers and students. The kid's locker has been vandalized, and I hear talk of retaliation. People want to know how certain you are about the arrest."

Davis sat and gripped his armrests, leaning back in his seat. He was in his early 40s, clean-shaven, gray hair creeping out from his temples. "I don't really get to deal in certainties," he said. "But let's just say it would be safe to move your chips to this particular square."

"How much are you allowed to tell me?" asked Vince.

"That depends," smiled the agent. "What do you want to know?"

"How did you catch him?"

Davis's cell phone rang; he checked the caller ID, then set it aside. "There was a separate investigation in Spokane that was monitoring a chatroom Adam frequented. One of the users posted some—how do I put this?—information about the firewalls that are used by districts like yours. Adam noticed that the code was incorrect, and he posted a correction. The tell there was that only someone who had been inside the server would recognize this other user's error. Another agent logged this exchange, knew I was working the Clearwater case, and passed it along to me. A few weeks later, we felt we had enough PC to hook him."

"How did he react?"

"Calm. Collected. He answered a few cursory questions, then asked for a lawyer." Vince smiled, which drew a grin from Davis. "What?"

"I can't tell you how many interrogations I've sat in on as a teacher, dean, and principal," said Vince. "There are career criminals with less savvy and composure than the average trapped teenager. I could have a plagiarized essay and the original right in front of them, and they'd profess their innocence with the conviction of Atticus Finch."

Davis laughed. "Well, maybe I should have had you in that room with me."

"Did he confess?"

"He did not."

"And the evidence?"

"I'm not allowed to say," said Davis. "But we like our case."

This was not what Vince had hoped to hear. In March, he had resigned himself to the likelihood that the perpetrator of the Cloudburst would never be caught. Davis himself had said so earlier; that it was too easy for Anons to cover their tracks, that after a while, cops could only hope that one would make a mistake. But now that there was a name, a face, a body on which to hang the humiliation and frustration of so many victims, anything less than a kill shot seemed unacceptable.

"What happens to him at trial?"

Davis shrugged. "Well, it's tricky, isn't it? First of all, he's a minor. Second, technology moves faster than the law. We're still talking about what's the best strategy—you have to be careful. We botched one of like this two years ago, and the kid is now working for Facebook. I won't quote his salary to you, but it gives me pause about my career choices."

"What can I do to help?"

The agent nodded. "I expect you'll be called as a witness, as well as several of the teachers. There will be an opportunity to file for compensation funds, and I would start educating your people on how to document their losses. This is what we call a Martian trial—it'll feel like trying a case on Earth, but the gravity will be all different. We've got dozens of federal instances of doxxing, and we learned a lot working with Sony over that whole North Korea thing. But 82 teachers?" He whistled. "Un-fucking-precedented."

He picked up his phone and pecked at it for a few seconds, then slipped it across the desk to Vince. There was a story from the New York Times for him to scan. "That kid's name is Jerry Gondos. From Connecticut. A few years ago, Acer released this new laptop and mentioned in the press release that it was un-hackable. New encryption technology. The most secure system in the world. So this Jerry Gondos, he takes that as a personal challenge. Hacking is sort of a macho sport—it's all about hypnotizing a system, making it do something it doesn't want to."

"You make it sound like a frat party," said Vince.

"Maybe the same energy," said Davis. "But a different kind of kid. Anyway, Jerry buys a laptop, pulls it apart, fiddles with the hard drive. And a couple of months later, he's posting this YouTube video about how he hacked the toughest vault on the web."

"I remember this," said Vince, reading. "Acer pressed charges."

Davis shook his head. "Hacking the system was legal. Posting it was his mistake. They filed a lawsuit, requested a restraining order for violating the Computer Fraud and Abuse Act and facilitating copyright infringement. They thought that would scare the hacker community. Instead, it pissed off the hornet's nest. A group I was investigating organized a hack on Acer, then Dell, then Microsoft, then Nintendo. I didn't sleep for weeks. That was the summer of Lulz."

Vince handed the phone back to him; Davis tucked it into his desk.

"These kids are smart, bored, and angry. They play hours of video games where they rule universes like gods, and then they're told the best job they can expect is at Target. A lot are rejected by women, so they grow hostile to women; others are rejected by society, so they grow hostile to society. For the most part, they're not bad people or assholes one-on-one, but they don't like being told what they can and cannot do."

"Who does?" asked Vince.

"Yeah, but when the average mid-level employee is yelled at by the boss, he doesn't use that as an excuse to release the boss's credit card information. For a long time, we had peace because all the hackers wanted was to be left alone to say and do whatever they wanted online. 'Free speech' and all that. It wasn't a problem because the majority of us weren't online, poking around their space. But that's all changing."

Davis began counting off on his fingers. "I've got a friend who's in Lincoln right now, investigating a hack on the phones of 32 bank employees. There's another agent in Brentwood looking into a Smart House that was turned into a 5,000-square foot listening device. And another agent in Tucson who swears that a new fleet of self-driving cars are being weaponized by a pair of nerds who work at a carwash. Twenty years from now, I have a feeling your little school is going to be the first chapter in a book about the Dawn of the Hacker Wars."

Vince smiled, but he couldn't match Agent Davis's jocularity. He felt his acid reflux burning in his chest, and a pang of arthritis in his knuckles. He looked out the window at the FBI courtyard; a dogwood was flowering in the April rain. "What happened to Jerry Gondos?" he asked.

"He works for the good guys now," said Davis. "Somewhere in Langley there's a room where six or seven dozen Jerry Gondoses sit around, preventing World War III with their laptops."

"Are we sure they're not starting World War III?" said Vince, rising to leave. He shook Davis's hand and thanked him for his time, fastening his coat as he walked out. Davis called out to him.

"Don't you want to know how he pulled it off?" he asked. "How he hacked your teachers?"

Vince turned and looked at the agent through his doorway. "I figured that out months ago," he said. "Vault 7. The stolen CIA cookbook that was published by Wikileaks. He got ahold of that and set to work hacking his teachers. Everything was right there, courtesy of the Good Guys. Am I right?"

Davis nodded. "Yes," he said softly. "That's how he did it."

"The 'how' is never the story," said Vince. "It's always the 'why.'"

____

It was already growing dark when Vince left the field office. Traveling northwest on I-65, he called ahead to his last appointment to warn them of his late arrival. By the time he began winding his way through uncurbed roads towards Clearwater, the purple evening was upon him. It was time to meet the Wramuder's.

He had, of course, seen them on television, and he had waited until the last reporter had decamped before making his approach. Beforehand, he had consulted his teachers for anecdotal background. Dillon McMurth had their daughter in his freshman Bio class and said they seemed informed, conscientious, and supportive. He shared an email exchange where they thanked him for giving Trudy an extension on her organelle assignment. "They didn't have to send that," he said. "I dunno. It just shows they're engaged with their kids' day-to-day."

But surely, they had missed Adam's extracurriculars. Vince wanted to know how, why. He passed over the tracks that divided the high school district from the unincorporated portion of Clearwater where he and the rest of his teachers lived. Now the canopied country roads, snaked by woodbine and wild oxlips, gave way to the emerald yards and solar-powered streetlamps. The developers, with an eye towards market fluctuations, had only used three different home designs here, the million-dollar palatial single-families repeating one another—brick/siding/cut-stone, brick/siding/cut-stone —like dots and dashes in an endless telegraph.

He had traveled these cul-de-sacs for years, wondering at the money it must take to maintain such compounds, with their SUVs hitched to trailers carrying weekend Wake Jumpers. Could there be this many good-paying jobs left? He knew that many of these families were over-leveraged, the slow-wick of credit card interest burning towards the dynamite. That he could understand. But the values of these homeowners were fundamentally different from the ecosystem of teachers, police, mechanics, and vendors who supported them. "Tell you something about Christians," his uncle had once explained to him. "White, Black, Asian—it don't matter. They always resent when the pastor has a nicer car than them." His uncle was right. They could only speak to one another for so long before the conversation revealed how little one side cared for abolishing the estate tax and how much it mattered to the other.

The Wramuder's lived on Warm Spring Drive in a charming two-story with a basketball hoop mounted over the three-car garage. Vince admired their covered porch with its swing decorated with scalloped patterns before ringing their doorbell. Mr. Wramuder—"Benson. Like the television show."—answered the door. He was a solid man with large hands in his mid-40s, his once imposing physique now sagging around the chest and mid-section. He was soon flanked by his wife, Karen, who greeted Vince warmly with a two-handed handshake.

They invited him in and, to Vince's relief, avoided much of the Caucasian apologies and explanations for their Pottery Barn décor. It was a house without much distinction from the dozens he'd called on over the years—pictures of family camping trips, of Disney

World, of Benson and Adam holding up bass caught in some indistinct midwestern lake. The carpet was beige, the trim was white, the walls were dotted with prints of starfish, clocks, and inspirational messages, the sort of art that one might purchase for $30 at TJ Maxx. Vince paused by one to read it—"Nothing Haunts Us Like the Things We Don't Say."

"It's from *Tuesdays with Morrie*," said Karen. "I just love that book."

"I've never read it," said Vince.

"Oh! You have to!" she smiled. "I'll lend you my copy on the way out!"

They found their way to the kitchen, an opulent gallery with a gray tile backsplash and sandstone-colored granite surfaces. All of the fixtures were brushed copper. Trudy was at the sink, cleaning a crockpot; when she recognized Vince, she sighed heavily and walked out mid-task, slamming the door behind her.

"You have to forgive her," said Benson, pulling out the sink sprayer and assuming Trudy's dish duties. "This thing with Adam has been hard on her."

"I can imagine," said Vince. "It came as quite a surprise."

"For all of us," said Karen, sitting at the table and tapping an iPad. "You must think we're terrible parents."

"I have a grown daughter," said Vince, sitting across from her. "I learned long ago not to judge."

"Well," said Benson. "I'm sure your daughter never hacked an entire school."

Vince smiled. "Once she backed my Nissan into a mail truck. I was mad at her for a week."

"That's nice," said Benson, setting aside the dishes and toweling off his hands. "We're glad you came by. We've been wanting to talk to you."

"You know, our lawyer said not to," said Karen, as Benson sat down beside her. "But I just… I just want to tell you how sorry we are."

"We can't imagine what you've gone through," said Benson.

They think he's guilty Vince thought to himself. *They believe he did this.* He was moved by their sincerity, by the mortification that seemed to leak from Karen through her shaking hands and glassy eyes. "Thank you," he said simply. "You'd be surprised how few people have thought to say that to us these past few months."

Karen slid the iPad across to him. "This is Adam," she said. "This is a slideshow I made last summer for his 16th birthday. I thought you'd want to see this."

He did. He wanted to know how this mother saw her son, what images she selected to tell his story. A trip to the Indianapolis Zoo. A pinewood derby competition. A 13-year-old boy smiling in a Confirmation suit. But there was no monster here. She had sleeked over the darkness. Or else it dwelt within.

"You know, it's been a long time since Columbine," he said, peering over his reading glasses. "Almost an entire generation. And we've worked to prepare ourselves for the day when our own Dylan Klebold or Eric Harris would appear. We practice lockdowns, Code Red drills. We learn about the psychology of outsiders. We think we're ready. We *are* ready." He slid the iPad back to her. "Until we're not."

Karen was crying inaudibly, nodding to her husband. "We never saw it," he said quietly. "We never knew what he..." but he cut himself off when he caught a warning glance from his wife. "He's a good kid," he said. "He likes his teachers."

"Mrs. Gouch," said Karen, dabbing her eyes. "He'd do anything for her."

Vince smiled and stared at his hands. Adam had released Laura Gouch's credit card statements. *They're rewriting him right in front of me,* he thought. "I'm just trying to know Adam," he said. "Your son is a Rorschach test. Every single person I talk to sees something different."

"He… he's always been bright," said Karen. "I remember when he was six, we found him disassembling the DVD player. Had the whole thing apart."

"But we told him to stop, and he did," Benson added.

"And… and when I got an iPhone and wanted to keep T-Mobile, he figured out how to rig it up so that I didn't have to get AT&T," she said.

"I mean, we did get AT&T," said Benson. "You know, just to make sure we were compliant."

"We'd show you his room, but the FBI took most of his equipment…"

"I'd like to see it nonetheless," said Vince. "If you don't mind."

It revealed nothing. A made bed, a nightstand, some comic books, a lamp. *This is where he must have done it,* he thought. Night after night, he whispered his incantations into the hard drives of his teachers and poured over the contents of their vaults. Vince found himself growing jealous at such access. There was no way for him to hypnotize the boy's denim duvet.

They will give me nothing, he thought, glancing at the parents. *Their instinct to sanitize is too strong.* This trauma had caught them unprepared; already, they were scrambling to tell a story about Adam that contained the shell of the boy but lacked the soft tissue. In a week, there would only be Adam Wramuder, the nice kid who liked his classes and tinkered with appliances.

He thanked the Wramuder's for their time and promised to stay in touch. Karen lent him her book. Outside, Trudy was standing in the driveway, shooting free throws with crisp form and perfect arc. Vince rebounded a miss and tossed it to her.

"I'm sorry if I made you uncomfortable," he said. "I just wanted to learn more about your brother."

"Did you?" she said, shooting again. Swish.

Vince shook his head. "No."

She glared at him as the ball bounced back to her. She dribbled a few times. "He caught mice, you know. In the basement."

"Did he?"

"Oh yeah," she said, shooting again. *Swish*. "He must've had two dozen. He ran these experiments with 'em. How little can you feed a mouse before it starves. How much before it explodes. Kept a journal filled with data on his dead mice."

He stared at her. The ball bounced back to her. "Is that true?" he asked finally.

She shot again. Miss., He rebounded it and tossed it back to her. She smirked. "No," she said. "Maybe. Either he did, and he's messed up, or I made up the story, and I'm messed up. What d'you think?"

"You're angry at him."

"Everybody's angry," she said, dribbling, left hand/right hand/ left hand/right hand. "All the time. Do you know what Mom said about him? She wishes he'd never been born." She shot again. *Swish*. "Me too. I wish that, too."

Vince crossed his arms. "I can't tell if you're telling me the truth or not. It feels like I've done something to offend you."

She turned to face him and dribbled in his direction, approaching him like a prizefighter. "Not to me. I can't say I ever once think of you, any of you. But to Adam… he'd be pissed to know you came over here tonight."

Vince narrowed his gaze. "How would he feel if his entire life was stolen and published without consent?"

"That why you're here?" asked Trudy. "To doxx us? Fuck that." She tossed the ball at him roughly; Vince caught it in the chest. "You deserved it." She turned and ran into the night. For a moment, Vince thought about going after her, demanding she tell him the truth, to account for this mysterious anger, hatred, and violence. But as he watched her disappear beyond the cones of light cast by the streetlamps, he saw her as just another smoky promise, swallowed by night. Vince was too tired to run her down.

He drove the eight miles in silence. As he approached the outlands of Clearwater, a passing freight train forced him to stop. It summoned a memory of Gary, of his youth, when the older boys would chase after the slow-moving boxcars, hoist themselves into their empty holds, and catch a day-ride to Chicago. Vince had stayed away from those nicotine boys and their profanities, but he wondered endlessly about those canisters, adorned with inscrutable graffiti. Where had they come from? What did they carry? To whom did they bring their shipment, and what vandals had tagged them in transit? He watched the freight line zipping past, dozens of cars orange and red in the light of the warning beacon. Even if he wanted to track them, to know their story, he couldn't. He thought of one such car breaking loose, careening through the adjacency. It could cause unfathomable damage.

Elizabeth was asleep when he found her in the bedroom. She had fallen asleep with her light on, a book by Colson Whitehead still propped open in her hands. He plucked the book, marked the page, and kissed her lightly on the head. She stirred and groggily spoke to him. "Did you find Adam?" she mumbled.

"Yes," he lied. "It's over now."

— — — — — — — — —

Following the arrest of Adam Wramuder and the public meltdown of Linda Moresoe, a subtle change had come to the school's atmosphere. Students who had been ignorant or apathetic to their teachers' plight began discussing how to acknowledge their trauma. There were anonymous notes of apology tucked under the windshield wipers in the faculty lot, a significant donation on Trivia Night from the PTA, and a noticeable drop in behavioral referrals. Chloe Fichte told him that a few former students had emailed her out of the blue, asking if she was okay. Suzanne Friedan said she'd been hugged by a stranger in the hall.

A group of students approached him about forming a committee with some teachers. "We want to find some positive way to talk about everything we've been through," said Preshit Garg, a junior. "We think we can put on some kind of… of forum to help us heal."

"We need this, Vince," said Leonard Fisk, who had signed on as sponsor. "These are good kids. They'll do it right." And so the principal, too, had signed on.

The Clearwater Climate Committee met three times before settling on an evening held in the courtyard. "It's sort of a night of storytelling," said Rudy King, a senior.

"The kids felt it was unfair that they know all about their teachers, but we don't know anything about them," explained Sheila Roth. "It was their idea."

"So… we'll just have a stage, and some lights… and people will sort of stand there and open up," said Emily Falsoft, a sophomore. "Like a chat room. But with faces, voices."

"What do you think?" asked Preshit.

Vince was concerned. Open forums were an attractive novelty exactly as long as people were comfortable with other peoples' degree of openness. Once someone went too far, confessed too much, it could collapse into controversy. He was not in the mood to take unnecessary public risks. "I'm not sure we need to be opening any more locked doors," he said. "It's been a semester of painful revelations."

"But that's exactly the point," said Rudy. "All of our teachers were exposed. We want to stand with them."

"Look at it this way, Vince," said Leonard. "After everything we've been through, what's three or four more secrets?" Vince did not find that particularly reassuring, but he decided to trust his committee.

On May 1st, 525 students, teachers, and parents gathered in the courtyard. A makeshift stage had been erected, beneath a left-over trellis from the school's production of *Carousel*. Several floodlamps were donated by the Boosters, and people had spread towels and folding chairs under the cool, clear night. Vince had to admit he was impressed by the speed and competency with which the committee had put this together, and he smiled as a group of freshmen had their frisbee intercepted by an athletic-looking parent.

At 7:05, Rudy and Andy Waters took the stage and introduced themselves. "We want to thank you for coming tonight," said Rudy. "It's been a hard year for this school. For Clearwater. Everyone has sort of been divided between the teachers, who had this… this thing happen to them," he gestured to a group of 20 or so faculty members encamped near the stage, "and, you know, us. The students. We wanted to do something to bring us all together."

"WHOOO! THAT'S MY BOYFRIEND!" shouted someone in the crowd, and a wave of laughter swept through the courtyard. Andy smiled and took the microphone. "Y'all know me," he laughed, and a loud cheer swelled from the crowd. "Seriously, though. It's been a rough couple of months. Had my life split open. Lost some friends. A few relationships. My mom's still mad at me."

The crowd thought this was very funny. Vince couldn't tell if his charismatic young English teacher was performing or not. *Has he learned anything?* he wondered. As if he could sense his principal's attentions, Andy dropped his gaze and lowered the microphone for an uncomfortable moment.

"I… I know I let a lot of you down. I'm sorry. Truly. But the funny thing about being naked in front of everyone is that you gradually stop worrying about covering your ugly parts. I mean, there's really no point. And I gotta tell you—I don't think I really understood what it meant to be a teacher until I accepted that."

They were silent now. They were listening to Andy open up by choice. The young teacher seemed at a loss for words for a moment before he rediscovered his lopsided grin. "So," he said. "We've got a group of students who want to share with you tonight. It'd be a personal favor to me if you listened to them. Can we do that?"

The audience roared an assent, and they began. A small Asian girl told a story about how she set up her best friend with a sophomore because she couldn't stop thinking about her. A parent explained how he had lost his marriage and found adulthood in a Winnebago in the New Mexico desert. Juliet Brocius, an English teacher, explained that her OCD used to be so bad that she rewrote her grocery lists so that they looked neater.

This is ridiculous, Vince thought to himself. *Safe secrets… a cultivated candor. There's no risk here, no pain or sense of violation of being privy to another person's disgrace.* But one by one, they took the stage, and gradually seemed to alter the audience. He could see tears in the faces of students, reclining in the arms of their parents. There was Katherine Sawyer, the indomitable *bête noire* of the Social Studies department, taking in the spectacle at the edge of the gathering. He had never seen her shoulders so slack.

"Hi, my name is Priya Pandacherry. Ten days ago, I swallowed all the pills that came out of an unmarked orange bottle. I don't even know why."

Vince could see their phones out, dozens of them. They were recording, cropping, transmitting. Those images would be sent and resent, favorited and liked. There would be captions and comments, some inscribed on a timeline that would resurface years from now. Others would feed their stories, where the words would live for a day and then be lost. Like memory. *And if it doesn't stay, did it even happen?*

"Hello. I'm, uh, Yael Abbas. My dad and I… we had a fight two weeks ago. I haven't been home since then. Dad…. I'm so sorry."

When he had been ten, his brother and he had spent hours at the Venture department store, wandering the toy aisle, talking about what they would do with $20. Leroy liked to open the board games and puzzles, to mix up pieces so that the rich kids who bought them wouldn't be able to enjoy them. That had always bothered Vince. There was nothing worse than a puzzle that couldn't be solved, a piece that didn't fit, an image that misled. And how would any of them know?

"My name is Evan Zurich. I made memes of Mr. Cespids. It was wrong. I was wrong. I don't think I'll ever forgive myself."

He had lost Cespids. And Carlton Wemish. And Jennifer Watson. A fifth of his Math Department. Good teachers, all of them. He had lost Katie Caspers and Allen Richardson, two Dean's assistants. Howard List, the Water Polo coach, a very hard position to fill. Liz Fulton would not return in the Fall. He knew Harry had had a third interview for the Athletic Director position in Beverly. A school is a living organism that changes, teacher by teacher, cell by cell. But there had been a radical disruption to the school's ordinary respiration. He felt like Clearwater had been in some horrible car accident and received new blood, new organs. A new face in the Fall.

"My name is Winn Huang. Some of you know me as Winnie. But that's not my name anymore. I don't think it was ever my name."

Who was this child? How did he get to this stage? What was his background, his parents, his home life, his precipitating incident? What was the genetic secret that put a male spirit in a female body? There was so much that was missing, so much context that was simply inaccessible. He felt the frustration that must have enraged Adam as he poured over those stolen files. He held their dating profiles, their bank statements, their correspondences. But none of their private causes. That was the greatest failing of all their vaunted technology— it promised more knowing than it could ever deliver.

And suddenly, Vince was struck by an insane vision. He imagined himself striding through the crowd, ascending the stepstool, approaching the microphone, and introducing himself.

"My name is Vincent Darten. I am the principal of Clearwater High," he imagined himself saying. "Over the past four months, I have done my best to hold this school together. I have counseled my colleagues with what little advice I could offer. I have tried to shield the students, to restore the sense of professionalism that fell apart when all our confidences came undone. I have conducted myself with a heavy heart, a sense of guilt that my secrets—my secret, really—went undivulged. I've spent hours trying to understand why it never came out, afraid of what it would mean or what you would think. So now I think it's time for me to unburden myself. So that you can understand who I really am."

"I have been an educator for 35 years. When I started, teaching was much different. There were fewer eyes on us. And I was teaching in a building where no one seemed to be paying attention."

"I had 112 kids on my roster. Rough customers. Some were from group homes, some orphans by choice. One drowned himself on Miller Beach in the Great Calumet River. Another got jumped by some bangers in the vacants of Black Oak. In the 70s there were still a few steel mills running day and night. They made a horrible stench, the smelters. You couldn't escape it. Sank into the upholstery of your car, between the threads of your clothes. When you cried, your face stank like melting steel. It was a part of us."

"I grew up in Gary, and the schools saved me. Made me love History, believe in the mission and all that. I wanted to save my kids, too. But there were too many, and their needs were too severe. *'You can't take them all home with you,'* one of the older teachers said to me. *'And you can't bring them each a piece of you. There won't be anything left.'* He was right. I was only 23, and I was already bone tired."

"So I made up my mind to pick one. Just one kid. Save that one kid. I found her in my American Government class. She was a senior, taking it all over again because she'd had to leave for four months her sophomore year. To this day, I have not met a smarter, harder working student. She was always prepared, always serious. She read voraciously, drank ink by the gallon. Every teacher knows the thrill and terror of meeting a pupil who is smarter than him. I found myself staying up later, trying futilely to read something that she hadn't, to have something to offer her hungry mind."

"She was the eldest of nine children. She woke every morning at 4:30, mended clothes, cooked the oatmeal, laid out their shoes, their coats, their backpacks. She dressed her autistic brother, combed their tangled hair, reminded her mother to pay the bills, knowing full well that she would have to pay them after school, after work. She slept on a cot under a beach towel. One day I saw her walking to school in the rain without an umbrella. She was crying. I asked her why she had no umbrella. She said, 'I thought the rain would wash the smell away.' But it didn't."

"It was then that I kissed her. I didn't know in the minute that I was in love with her, that I treasured her voice above all others. And I didn't truly understand her, not really. But in that moment, I was reacting to the wound in her that would not close."

"At first, I said nothing about the kiss, and she didn't so much as make eye contact for a week. I later learned about the psychology of abuse victims, and to this day I am ashamed of what my silence must have put her through. But I could not hold back what was growing in me, what had developed in the quiet between us. I began seeing her after class. We were lovers the day she graduated."

"We kept it to ourselves. She moved in with me, took classes at Ivy Tech. We never went out. We made sure not to appear together in public. I didn't socialize. No one paid attention to the quiet history teacher who ate lunch in his room. After a few years, everyone forgot about the girl who gave away her umbrella. I got another job, and we could finally introduce ourselves together."

"Her name was Elizabeth Jansen. We've been married for 33 years. We've raised a daughter together. Rescued a few dogs. I love her beyond music, beyond History, beyond feeling or expression. She is the great truth of my life."

That was his secret, the core of his being. Every good thing that he had ever done, every student he'd helped or teacher he'd coached, had been patterned off of the love he felt for her, his Elizabeth. No other context was necessary.

But Vince Darten said none of those things to those students, to that audience. He didn't so much as appear on stage. Instead, he watched fifteen kids, three parents, and another teacher chronicle loneliness and shame, hope and ardor. Because even in his public decency, Vince Darten was also a coward, a criminal. Because they would plainly see the taboo, but never feel the gravity that demanded its transgression. Because some stories cannot be understood, no matter how complete their telling. Because sometimes a life depends on the dignity of its privacy, on the integrity of its silence.

As the evening ended, the crowd thinned and the spectators disappeared into the night. Vince lingered a long time, watching the committee disassemble the stage and shut down the floodlamps. In an hour, the courtyard would be empty again, not so much as a plank left to memorialize what had just happened. In three months, Vince would welcome a new freshman class, a cluster of strangers completely ignorant of the stories and voices that shared this space.

Fifty feet away, he could make out a slight figure, hands stuffed in the pockets of a gray-green hoodie. It was Trudy Wramuder, Adam's sister. She realized he was staring at her, and she raised an arm to wave to him vaguely. Vince waved back. For a minute, he thought he might go to her, ask how she was doing, what she thought of the evening. But the moment passed, and she turned and walked away. *Another boxcar*, he thought, *going someplace else. Carrying unknown cargo. Marked by hands I'll never see.*

ACKNOWLEDGEMENTS

Thanks to the good people of Neuqua Valley High School for the forgiving home, Gary Anderson for the sage advice, Dani Segalbaum for the eagle-eye proofing, and Jordan Wannemacher for the gorgeous design. Thank you to Raja for her determination, Ereni for her inspiration, and Paula for making a story with me.

ABOUT THE AUTHOR

 **MICHAEL ROSSI** is a high school English teacher and Cross Country coach. This is his first book, and he thanks you for reading the author bio, where he's mostly telling the truth, and he'd like to apologize to his mother for licking all the frosting off the cinnamon buns and then blaming the dog. He lives in Aurora, Illinois, with his wife and two daughters.

www.ingramcontent.com/pod-product-compliance
Lightning Source LLC
Chambersburg PA
CBHW070616300726
48975CB00006B/1834